FALLEN PAST

STUART G. YATES

Copyright © 2024 by Stuart G. Yates

Layout design and Copyright © 2024 by Next Chapter

Published 2024 by Next Chapter

Edited by Gemma Clarke

Cover art by Jaylord Bonnit

Large Print Edition

This book is a work of fiction. Names, characters, places, and incidents are the product of the author's imagination or are used fictitiously. Any resemblance to actual events, locales, or persons, living or dead, is purely coincidental.

All rights reserved. No part of this book may be reproduced or transmitted in any form or by any means, electronic or mechanical, including photocopying, recording, or by any information storage and retrieval system, without the author's permission.

*For those who never stop believing ...
and for Ray because you were my friend then,
and you're still my friend today.*

POINTERS TO THE PAST ...

THE DAY he dreaded for so long finally arrived. *This* day. The trill of the telephone, the voice he knew so well, its tone, the chilling words, "I told you what will happen so I'm going to tell you *again* – you say anything to anyone and you're dead." Those words brought it all back. The memories, the horror. The guilt.

From his conservatory window, Billy Baxter gazed out to the jungle that was his garden and thought back to the telephone call, the ice-cold reaction it brought to his guts. It was because of the girl, of course. She had called at the house earlier. A pretty girl, her features so smooth, hair pulled back in a ponytail and a smile that would win over even the hardest of hearts. She easily won over his. He invited her in without hesitation, listened to her probing questions, which confirmed his suspicions: the past had caught up with him at last.

"I found a diary," she said, sitting across from him in the large, tired sitting room, one slim leg crossed over the other. He did his best not to stare but it proved difficult. She didn't seem to notice or, if she did, she took no offence. "Can I tell you how I found it?"

He lifted his gaze, nodded, and waited, expectant, heart drumming.

"I wasn't prying, you understand."

He melted under her smile. "Of course you weren't."

"It was there, you see, in the bedside cabinet. I was in his bed. I am always in his bed." An impish smile, almost as if she were enjoying toying with him. "Does that shock you?"

"Not sure ... No! No, not shock."

"Curiosity then? How someone, young like me, could be attracted to him?"

"I suppose, yes. Curious. He always was one for the ladies but I thought that perhaps he was, you know, past all that by now."

"He's not. He has a power about him, a strength. It's difficult to explain but his hold over me is total. I can't get enough."

He felt his jawline heat up. He looked away.

Unfazed, she continued, "We'd spent the afternoon in bed, his wife was at the cinema. So he said. When he went out to make us something to eat, I rolled over, searching for a cigarette. He kept them in the bedside cabinet drawer and it was in there that I found it. A thin notebook, the cover battered, well used. I opened it, out of idle curiosity nothing more. I'm a journalist, so it's hard not to … You know, *snoop*." A little laugh, to reassure them both perhaps. "Anyway, the title drew me in. Simple. Nineteen Forty-Four. I thought at first it was a play on Orwell's work. You know the one? Well, it wasn't, it was something different entirely. As I started reading I couldn't put it down."

"A diary? Of what happened over there?"

"Not a diary, with dates and such, more a collection of random notes, lots of them, covering his thoughts and feelings. Did you keep such a thing?"

"When I was over in France you mean?" She nodded. "No. I never seemed to have the time, but I do remember him scribbling things down every time we had a moment. Which wasn't often. Not often at all."

"It must have been terribly scary."

He flinched, her words like tiny projectiles, stinging his face. He stood and went to the mantelpiece to pick up the model of a Bren carrier. For a few seconds, he disappeared into his past. "Yes," he replied simply. "It was. I was always scared. Sick with it I was. We all were."

"His writing was wistful in places, hastily scribbled notes rather than proper sentences. Until he came to the part about the killing."

Carefully, Billy replaced the model and turned to her. "Detailed was it?"

"Yes." She snapped open her small clutch bag and brought out her cigarettes. "Do you mind?" He shook his head and she lit up her smoke with a small, metal lighter. "He made it all sound so awful. Did it happen the way he told it?"

"I'm not sure. I haven't read it."

She set out the story she'd read and the more he listened the more he withdrew into himself. By the time she'd finished, he was breathing erratically as he stared into space. "That's just about how it was."

"But," shaking her head, she leaned forward, her face hard, her tone accusing, "why didn't you ever report it? I know it was wartime and there must have been lots on your mind, other things, but even so … What he did. Murder."

"I suppose. I wouldn't know. As you said, it was wartime."

"It's still on the statute books. You could report it if you—"

"I'm not going to do that."

"But why not? It's a war crime if nothing else."

"Because I'm a bloody coward if you must know."

He spat it out and she sat looking stunned, incredulous, the fingers holding her cigarette shaking. "Coward or not, you have a duty—"

"The only *duty* I have is to myself. Besides, it wouldn't stand up in any court of law. There are no witnesses and it's my word against his."

"There's his wife. She knows. It says so in the journal. He confessed."

"Perhaps. I don't know. Even so, she couldn't testify. It would be inadmissible."

She looked at him, dissecting him with those eyes of hers. For a few moments, she quietly smoked. "There's the journal, of course. It's all there, like a form of confession."

"Anyone could have written it."

"Yes, I can see his defence lawyers making the most of that. There is no proof as such, except you. You are the only one who knows the truth."

He nodded and collapsed into the other armchair. The sunlight pouring through the window made him feel unnaturally hot. "Yes," he lied.

"And it's a truth which you've had to bear all these years." Her hand snaked out and settled on his knee. He stared at it in amazement. "You owe it to yourself to come forward."

"I can't."

"I can help you."

"You can? How? How can you help?"

"I'd write a piece in the local newspaper, not with any great details, just hints. It might draw him out."

"It would do more than that. He's dangerous, capable of anything."

"I can't believe … No, he wouldn't do anything."

"You don't know him."

A self-conscious smile. "Oh, I think I do."

"I don't mean in that way." He grew impatient, pulled away from her, and stood up. "You write such a story, he'll come after me because he'll know where the story came from."

"Come after you? What do you mean by that? Has he threatened you?" He shrugged, not wanting to be drawn into the details. "I won't mention you by name, so don't worry about that. All I need is your story, how you saw it happening."

Those words, so simply spoken, so full of dread, how could he make her understand, make her realize the danger? He'd lived with the horror of what had happened for over two and a half decades. Sleepless nights, sometimes sitting up, drenched in sweat, his wife forcing him to tell, and then, after he had, her leaving. Consumed with indecision, he looked out into his conservatory, the conservatory his wife had wanted so much, and the garden beyond, memories swirling around inside his head, confusing him. "If I tell you," he said, voice little more than a croak, "and it's made public, he'll kill us both."

"*Kill us?*" Laughing, she jumped up and placed her hands on his shoulders. "No. Nothing like that's going to happen. Look, tell me and I'll only use those parts that are relevant."

"It's all relevant."

"All right, I'll only use the parts that confirm what I read in his journal. No one will be able to link any of it to you. I give you my word." She turned him around and gasped when she saw the tears. "Oh my God. Are you all right?"

He shrugged her off. "I'm fine. But why? Why are you doing this? I thought you and he had a relationship?"

She shrugged. "He has grown bored with me. Or so he says. I'm not what he wants. Not in that sense. He finds me too much of a challenge. He's said more than once that he won't share me, not with anyone."

"I don't understand."

"It doesn't matter." She took a final pull on her cigarette and stubbed it out in the little glass ashtray on the table. "I have a girlfriend."

"Oh." His turn to draw in a deep breath. He was confused. A girlfriend? But, she was sleeping with him? Weird. He didn't understand the world anymore, its ambiguities, its openness. "All right. Have you got your notebook?"

She immediately tugged out a device from her bag. "This is the latest Philips portable cassette tape recorder," she explained with a proud grin. "It's good, isn't it."

"The wonders of modern science."

"Yes, exactly. Now, just talk normally, as clearly as you can. I'll type it up later."

She switched the little machine on and indicated he should start.

Billy cleared his throat, sat down, and slowly relayed it all.

By the time he'd finished both of them were feeling as if they'd just completed ten rounds of boxing. With no winner.

A KILLING

NINETEEN SIXTY-EIGHT AND, for Tony and Arthur, although the sun shone brightly, neither of them felt like smiling the day they discovered the body.

They pulled it out of the river after Tony's fishing line snagged on the material of the stinking, oily sheet in which the corpse was wrapped. A piece of thin, green garden twine kept it together, but only just. The material gaped open as the two anglers hauled the body up onto the bank, a limp, putrid white arm flopped onto the grass, naked, the veins like lines of piss along the flesh, and Tony swung away and threw up in the grass.

It took some time for Arthur to reach a public phone. He didn't need any coins to call the emergency services, but that was not his main concern as he gained the top of the steep path and crossed the main road to the telephone box standing a little way beyond the small gathering of shops. The run from the river to the main road caused him to falter, his voice cracking, frayed emotions mingling with his gasping for breath. "Take your time, sir," the operator said, but Arthur had no time. There was a dead body lying on the river bank, and children were down there, out with dad for a Saturday afternoon's fishing, so he battled with his pounding heart, his screaming lungs, the rising nausea, and managed to get the dreadful news out of his mouth.

A short time later, various police and ambulance people milled amongst the overgrown riverbank like flies around a juicy titbit, none of them appearing ill at ease with the dead body in their midst. Maybe they were used to it. Maybe they just didn't care. As Arthur stood and stared into the surface of the river ambling by, Tony sat in a heap, knees pressed up against his chest, weeping softly. He *did* care. It was his hook that had pierced the material holding the body. His hands had brought it in, his eyes which gazed in disbelief at what he saw. Arthur studied his friend for a moment and didn't like what he saw. Tony was suffering.

"How long?"

Blinking, Arthur snapped himself out of his reverie and turned towards the owner of the voice, a rumpled man of indeterminate age, hair tussled, chin sporting a grey rind, the stub of a pencil clamped in his thin mouth. He wore a leaf green raincoat which had seen better days. Hell, *he* had seen better days. Tired eyes didn't hold Arthur's for long.

"Eh?"

The man in the raincoat nodded his encouragement. "I'm Detective Fallon, and I'm the investigating officer. Can you think as clearly as you can, please? How long ago did you find her?"

Turning to Tony for some confirmation, Arthur shrugged his shoulder. "Half an hour."

"Thirty minutes? Are you sure?"

"Maybe. Maybe twenty. Why, does it matter?"

"It might. Did you see anyone else?"

"No. No one."

"There was a dog," said Tony in a small, distant voice. He sniffed and dragged a shaking hand across his nose. "There was a dog here when we came down earlier. It ran off."

"What sort of dog."

"Alsatian." He looked up hopefully towards Arthur, who nodded. "They call them German Shepherds now."

"Where did it go?"

Tony waved his hand in a vague sort of way to his left. "Along the bank. He wasn't with anyone, although the owner might have been farther down."

"Twenty to thirty minutes you said? That's when you found her?"

Tony nodded and Fallon lifted his voice and shouted across to a bunch of uniformed officers sharing a joke with one another. "Taylor. Get yourself and Emery down along the bank and try and pick up any signs of a dog. Big dog…" he shot a questioning look at Tony, who nodded. "Big German Shepherd. His owner might be still around. Hurry up."

The two officers jogged off without a word. Fallon flipped open the notebook he'd taken from his pocket and wrote something down using the stubby pencil. "Do you come here often, gentlemen?"

"Every weekend," said Arthur. "Whatever the weather."

"Fishing." Fallon peered towards the body, with the sheet pulled back to reveal the ghastly white corpse of a young woman. "We can't be sure, but the medical examiner says she couldn't have been in the water for more than thirty minutes."

"How the hell does he know that?"

"Puckering."

"Puckering? You mean—"

"I mean the way the skin is. It's puckered."

"Jesus."

"You arrived here how long ago?"

Arthur sighed. "About twenty minutes or so before we made the first cast."

"Cast? That's throwing out the line, yes?" Arthur grunted. "So, you discovering her only thirty minutes ago means…"

The two anglers exchanged a look. Tony's face drained of colour and he put his face in his hand, whilst Arthur dragged in a huge breath. "Jesus, whoever did this put her into the water at almost the same time we arrived?" Detective Fallon stared. Clamping a hand over his mouth, Arthur groaned, "Oh God, we must have just missed him!"

Fallon said nothing. He did not have to. The news was devastating.

A man was sitting on a bench near the small bridge, which spanned the river. He was a big man across the shoulders, heavy set, and he had a greyness about him, forehead covered with a sheen of sweat. Perhaps he was sick. Constable Taylor, breathing hard, stepped up close, frowning. There was an unsettling air about this man, as well as there being something vaguely familiar about him. Taylor coughed. The man did not stir.

"Do you own a dog, sir?"

Emery arrived, dragging off his cap and running a handkerchief over his face. "Christ, it's hot. Who's this?"

Eyes narrowing, Taylor did not respond to his colleague. Instead, he prodded the man with a stiff forefinger. "I asked you a question, sir."

"I did have a dog," the man said without raising his head. "He ran off."

"He ran off? What, just now you mean?"

"No. Months ago. Why?"

Emery stepped closer, his voice quaking slightly when he spoke. "Can we see your hands, sir?"

The man's head came up slowly, the eyes piercing blue, the jawline hard. Without a word, he raised both hands, hands as big as plates, gnarled and rough. He spread them so the two officers could examine the fingers. Taylor sighed and Emery rocked back on his heels. "Sorry to have disturbed you, sir."

"What's happened?"

"Nothing to worry about sir, just an incident down at the river. Have you seen a man with a dog anywhere nearby?"

"Middle-aged fella, with red hair and a deep scar running down the side of his face, dressed in a blue denim jacket and corduroy trousers. Brown coloured. Workman's boots."

The two officers exchanged incredulous looks.

Clearing his throat, Emery forced a smile, "That's extremely detailed sir ..."

"I was an MP in the War."

"An MP?" Emery sniggered. "Tory or Labour, sir?"

Pulling in a breath, the man sat back on the bench and stared blankly ahead, clearly not amused. "Military Police," he said in a dull, flat voice. "He had a dog. Big one. German Shepherd."

Gasping, Taylor gripped his colleague's arm. "How long ago did you see him, sir?"

"No more than ten minutes. But I think he had a car. At least, I *heard* a car starting up as he turned the bend over there." He pointed to where the road crossed the canal via a short bridge and curled off to the right.

A few moments to allow this news to settle followed, the only sound the laboured breathing of the two police officers.

"Would you be willing to come to the station, sir, and help an artist do a likeness?"

Shrugging, the man nodded towards Emery. "Why not."

The dog was big, its fur thick, especially around the neck, but not so thick it protected the animal from the knife blade, which had sawed through its throat. Well covered with bracken, leaves, and soil, anyone would have to be purposely looking to see it partly buried there. And if anybody was looking, they would also see the gloves and the knife lying next to the dead animal.

But nobody did look.

At least, not for quite a long time.

MEMORIES

CRAIG KEPT A SECRET, one which refused to leave him no matter what went on around him. For everyone else, life appeared so much simpler, normal. The burden of what he did, what he allowed to happen, branded him as a person apart from the rest. There were times when he did not believe he could find the strength to carry on, live with the shame, the guilt. Now, with the memories flooding back, he wondered how he ever got through it all, how he didn't break down, or, perhaps more chillingly, how he survived. Nevertheless, he somehow did. Thanks to someone, the unlikeliest person of them all, who helped him see the sense in talking, of sharing, and guided him on the path to forgiveness.

As he lay in his bed, staring at the ceiling, he drifted back to how it had begun, at how different everything was then, mere weeks ago.

THE MEETING

THE DAY he'd woken late, with the dream still vivid in his mind, was the day Craig met old man Baxter. The dream rarely changed. Dad's face, dominating every moment, but not the face he remembered. In life, deep creases cut into Dad's cheeks, and flat forehead, grizzled chin, and a steely glint in his eyes made him, what Mum described as 'rough and ready'. Whenever she said that her words were accompanied by a dreamy look. Instead, in the dream, every feature seemed ... Craig sucked in his bottom lip as he groped around inside his head for the right word to describe how his Dad's face transformed into a softer, kinder face, one so much more ... *forgiving*. Yes, that was it. Forgiving. He didn't know why he dreamed about him like that. Dad had never ever been *forgiving*, quite the opposite. A hard man, chiselled from the granite of life, meeting every problem head-on. In the dream, he appeared as a different person altogether, but still his dad.

There were never any sounds in this dream, no voices, nothing at all in the way of explanation. Just Dad, standing there with an altered face, staring, waiting, almost as if he were expecting something to be said to him. What that might be, Craig couldn't work out.

Putting the heels of his palms into his eyes, in an attempt to squeeze away the images, Craig sat up. Would the dreams ever stop? Might a time come when he wouldn't feel so guilty, so responsible? But how was that ever going to be, because he *was* responsible, and that was the simple truth of the matter. He knew it and it ate away at him, making him empty and sick inside. Pushing his palms harder into his eyes, he fought against the tears threatening to break out and managed to win a tiny battle, for the time being at least. He often cried nowadays, and the tears came at the most unexpected of moments. It happened in school once, as he sat gazing out of the classroom window. No one said anything, but their faces spoke volumes. One or two were grinning, others prodding one another, a few sniggers but whatever the reaction, he knew what they were thinking. He was a weakling, a *weed*. Nobody understood the torment he experienced every day because nobody knew. They probably wouldn't care even if he did try to explain. However, he never attempted, not once, to tell them. Not even his English teacher, Miss Rose, such a kind lady, so patient, even her caring attitude, those huge eyes, so soft, telling him, begging him, to let her into the secret didn't compel him to open up. To trust her. No. Better to keep it all hidden deep inside from view. And yet, this very act, this deliberate desire to keep everything locked away, was the very reason for his tears. For how much longer would he suffer from the grieving?

He tried to convince himself that what happened was an accident. His dreams, however, did not allow him to think that way. On that morning, the latest, haunting nightmare still vivid, he decided not to try to find an explanation, swung his legs out of the bed, sat on the edge, and stared down at the carpet. Green carpet, speckled with splashes of red. He smiled, another memory forcing away the images of Dad, easing his soul. Dad used to act, years and years ago in what he called a 'repertory company'. The blood was 'stage blood'. Now it was on the carpet and Mum would hit the roof when she found out, so Craig strategically moved his rug to conceal the blotches. He had daubed his 'Action Man' soldier in the stuff, bore a hole in the doll's chest, forcing the blood inside. When another soldier shot this one, the blood spewed out in every direction. Craig loved it.

Nothing like real blood of course. Nothing like how a body undertook a strange, alien-type change as soon as death cast its shadow. How the pallor grew waxen, tinged with green. Green, not red. There was blood – real blood – the day Dad lost his battle for life. One moment there, the next …

The memory returning of blood-drenched Action Men did little to lighten his mood. Death, actual death, was nothing like those games. He no longer had a yearning to revisit the theatrics with his toys. Not now that life was so bleak.

Sighing, he stood and went over to his window to look out.

Running along the back of his house a world of alleyways waited, where Craig and his friends would often play. Sometimes, if money was available, they would go up to the park and hire a tennis court for an afternoon.

It was on one such day, he recalled, that he saw her for the first time.

She stood on the other side of the high fence surrounding the tennis courts. It was a glorious day, the sky clear and blue and bright. Perhaps that's what made her look so beautiful, the sunlight bathing her in a strange, otherworldly aura, lending a glow of pure gold to her skin, a radiance others did not seem to possess.

His heart sang for one, brief and intoxicating moment. She was dark-skinned, wonderfully slim, with long raven hair tumbling to her shoulders. Her eyes, huge in her perfect face, smouldered with a curious intensity, her stare, never faltering, possessed with self-confidence. She wore a figure-hugging light blue top and black skirt, attracting every boy's eye.

He noticed her approach halfway through delivering a serve, his attention instantly grabbed by her. How could he resist – she was stunning. She paused by the fence, a tiny smile playing around her mouth. Not daring to believe she might be watching him play, when he realised she was his game went to pieces. He managed to serve but missed the simple return with a desperate swipe. His heart lurched and he snapped his head towards her, to check if she had noticed. To make it clear she had, she giggled and he felt his face burn. When she smiled directly at him, his stomach turned over, as if blended in a liquidiser. A tiny nod of encouragement. Was that really what she did? Dare he convince himself of her interest? Drawing in a huge breath, he steadied himself, strode back to the baseline, and put in a devastating serve. He glanced in her direction and almost yelped when her hands came together in silent applause.

From then on, thoughts of her consumed every passing moment. He barely touched his evening meal and, playing with the food with his fork, he mustered up the courage to ask, "Mum, I want you to answer me honestly. Honestly."

She stopped, looked at him with a frown. "All right. What's wrong?"

"There's nothing *wrong*, I just ... Do you think I'm good-looking? I mean, I'm fourteen and—"

She didn't laugh, didn't mock. She carefully put her fork down and considered him for what seemed an age. "I might be biased, Craig, but you are *very* good-looking. Why do you ask?"

She said it as if she knew, but that couldn't be. Could it? After he went to bed, he lay outstretched, images of the girl's face dancing before him. Every fibre of his body sang when he rose early the next day, expectant and alive with the thrill of seeing her again. After throwing down his breakfast, he ran to the park, heart thumping in his throat.

Reaching the tennis court, his stomach yawned wide with disappointment. Emptiness. There was no sign of her. Kicking his heels, he hung around, hoping she might turn up. She didn't and he chastised himself for being so stupid, for allowing himself to believe such a girl might be interested enough to make a return visit and flash him that beautiful smile once more.

A vestige of positive attitude remained. She wasn't a dream. Something passed between them; a connection. So, over the next few days, Craig returned to the park in the off-chance she might be there, but each visit ended in gut-wrenching disappointment. He cursed the unfairness of an existence that forever left him barren, unfulfilled. He should have returned her smile when he had the chance, gone over to her, spoken at least one, simple word. His courage failed him like it always did and regret returned as his constant, clinging companion.

So, Craig returned to the comfort and safety of dreams. Sometimes, they overrode everything. The morning he presented the deputy head teacher with a science fiction story he'd written, Mr Forester could barely contain his rage.

Clicking his tongue, circling sentences and sometimes whole paragraphs with exaggerated flourishes of his red pen, relishing his power to reduce students' self-esteem to nothing more than a vague shadow, Forester slapped the finished story onto his desk. Blowing out a sharp sigh, he stabbed the cover of the exercise book with a rigid index finger. "Where does all this rubbish come from, Archer?"

"Just pops into my head, sir."

Forrester pulled a face. "What nonsense you talk. Blasted television more like!" He sat back, flicking through Craig's story again, scanning the closely written script, pausing to study a passage here and there, mouth noiselessly reading the words. "This is all just garbled junk, Archer. You need to write with more...conviction. Why don't you read more books, pick up some tips on how to construct your sentences?"

"I do, sir. I finished reading 'The Lord of the Rings' only last week."

Forrester looked up, astonished. "The Lord of the ...? *Don't be ridiculous*! How old are you?"

"Fourteen, sir...fifteen in a few months, sir."

"Exactly. Reading 'The Hobbit' is more suitable for your age – ridiculous nonsense you talk, Archer!" Forrester shook his head, and Craig noted the sad look clouding the teacher's face. "One sentence paragraphs, Archer, what is all that about? You need connectives, subjunctive clauses, lad. You can't write like this ... you need explanation and structure. Plot. Too much dialogue. I mean, look at it," he flicked through the pages, "line after line of talking. It's not a play. You can't do that in stories. No one does that."

"I think Hemingway might have done, sir."

The teacher almost fell off his chair, his face

turned ashen, his brows furrowing. "*Hemingway?* What the devil do you know about him?"

"I read 'The Old Man and The Sea', sir. 'For Whom the Bell Tolls'. Hemingway said he wanted to see lots of white on the page, sir."

"Rubbish. You'll be telling me you polished off some Steinbeck next."

"Actually, sir ..." Craig bit his bottom lip as Forester's face turned purple.

"Don't push your luck, Archer. Someone must have told you all about this, your father probably." Forrester blew out his breath and shook his head. "Ah, yes, you haven't ..." Craig felt the bile rise in his throat. Forrester was an arrogant old git, with no imagination and very little appreciation of literature, certainly nothing 'modern'. If it wasn't a classic, written by someone nobody had heard of for a thousand years, then it wasn't worth the paper it was printed on. Craig held his breath, allowed the anger, and the urge to shout out, to slowly trickle back down into the core of his being. Forrester, as usual, didn't notice any of it. "You've got this from the television, not from any book or supposed imagination. Scribbled this whilst you watched some puerile nonsense on the box, no doubt. What was it, something on Blue Peter? Beep and Booster I shouldn't wonder."

"That's '*Bleep* and Booster'. And no, I didn't get

the idea from that *'puerile nonsense'*." Forrester raised an accusing eyebrow. Craig struggled with his emotions again. This man certainly pushed him to the limit. He felt himself redden before he added quickly, "Sorry...*Sir*."

Forrester grunted, obviously not believing a single word Craig said. He threw the exercise book down, jabbing at it again with his finger. "If you continue to churn out this sort of abusive, reprehensible junk, Archer, and insist on telling me lies," he paused for significance and raised both eyebrows, giving more weight to his final blast, "I shall be inviting your mother into school so I can talk to her about it."

Craig took a breath. "What exactly is wrong with it, sir?" Forrester blinked and Craig closed his eyes. It was time to make a stand. "Have you never read anything by Heinlein, Pohl, or Vance, sir? What about Ray Bradbury?"

Forrester levelled a glare at him that would crack glass. "Who are they, American pulp-fiction writers, Archer?" He shook his head again. "This sort of trash has no place in my classroom."

With that, he took up Craig's exercise book and went to rip it in half. Craig's stomach tightened, but he immediately smiled when Forester's face contorted, the veins pulsing as he tried but failed to destroy Craig's work forever more. Dropping the book, he ran a hand over his face and let out a blast of air, to disguise the embarrassment of his failure.

This brief, delicious taste of seeing the deputy head flounder disappeared as he watched Forrester grit his teeth and slip the book under his desk to surreptitiously snip through the cover with a pair of scissors. A realisation hit Craig with the power of a punch right then.

He hated Mr Forrester.

This hatred soared as Forester used the cut pages to aid him in the final ignominy. "There," Forrester cried in triumph, tearing the book in two with relish. Beaming, he threw the two halves into the waste-paper basket, "that's where that belongs. Now sit down, Archer, and get on with your 'Beta Maths'.

"I'm on 'Alpha Maths', sir."

Forrester bristled, and snapped, "Since when?" Craig stared and Forrester turned away, not willing to waste any more of his time. "Just get on with it."

Forrester personified everything about adults that Craig despised. Dismissive, uncaring, totally self-centred. In his experience, they were all the same. He had little idea that soon these perceptions would be almost completely undone.

Two weeks into his summer holiday and the memory of Forrester's actions continued to gall him.

The thought of September hung like a cloud, threatening everything, dimming even the sunniest of days. Forrester would be there, pacing up and down the corridors, shuttling pupils out into the cold and the wet of the playground. *"Come on, Archer, go and chase some rabbits!"* Chase some rabbits? Always the same, tired joke. The tarmac-covered school playground offered nothing any sensible rabbit would ever want.

Muttering a curse, he pulled out his bottom drawer where he kept his soldiers. He was determined to try to forget about school and Forrester in particular. Better to enjoy his freedom, whilst it was still here, and his soldiers, his pride and joy, would help.

He picked out a small shoebox and peeled back the top layer of cotton wool to reveal what lay beneath. This was his treasure, the heart of his world. Metal miniatures, painted with loving care, bought with his savings.

Craig's uncle had put in an order to a hobby shop down south for them and, recently, he'd sent off another order for twenty Greek spearmen. Uncle Eric had pointed at the advertisements populating his favourite modelling magazine. "These companies, they make metal miniatures – soldiers, you see? Just like in the TV show. Callan? You seen it? He plays with model soldiers like these. You have to paint them, but that's half the fun. Getting a hobby, Craig, your dad would have liked that."

"He would?"

"Of course he would. Now, have a look..."

Craig read one and whistled. "This one, they have a catalogue, Uncle Eric. But..." He made a face, "It costs two-and-six."

Eric shrugged, "I'll send off a postal order for you."

Craig felt his eyes filling up. "Thanks," he managed to say.

The days crawled by, but the catalogue failed to arrive. Craig tried his best to put any thoughts of models to one side, but when it finally did come, it was as if all his birthdays had come at once! He ripped open the brown paper wrapper and spent hours drooling over what was available. Changing his mind many times, he finally settled on Ancient Greek hoplite spearmen.

He ran a finger over the few models he already had. He'd found a tiny shop in Chester that stocked a few models, bought a small selection and painted them. The Greek hoplites would soon be here and his collection would grow. He simply needed patience.

It was usual for him and Ray to fight long drawn-out battles during the weekends, but when one day, Ray suggested going to the old disused quarry known as 'The Pit', Craig jumped at the chance of putting the hoplites to the back of his mind. An afternoon of fun would do the trick.

That was the plan, as far as it went.

Because it was during that afternoon when they first came across old man Baxter. And fun wasn't a word that seemed to figure very much in that man's vocabulary.

BAXTER

PAUSING for breath at the top of the steps, Craig wiped the sweat from his brow. The sun beat down relentlessly and he'd run all the way, doing his best to get there before his friend. Nevertheless, as he staggered onto the trackway, sucking in great gulps of air, there stood Ray, imperious, waving to him in triumph from the middle of the old quarry. Suppressing his disappointment he would not allow himself to become downhearted. Averting his eyes, Craig scanned the great gash in the yellow sandstone. Abandoned over a century before, nature had reclaimed the old, deserted working, gorse growing thick, a profusion of thistle and cow-slips, overgrown tracks created by the tramping of numerous feet. 'The Pit' was one of those wonderful, almost mystical places where new discoveries awaited every time it was visited. A small untouched copse, a hidden tangle of bushes, an abandoned cave. All perfect for adventure games and den building. At its centre, a large, imposing rock of granite sprouted, a great jagged tooth known locally as 'Grannie's Rock'. Every boy from the local area dreamed of climbing it. Craig had already done so, Ray too, now the competition was who could scale it the quickest. Ray, always a good climber with bags of self-confidence meant he tackled problems head-on, hardly ever worrying about the outcome, always assured of his own abilities. Craig was the complete opposite, often reluctant to 'have a go', struggling to get there in the end.

Ray grinned down from his perch. "Come on," he urged, eyes glued on Craig.

Inside, Craig groaned. Another test, with the inevitable result. Ray was a good friend, but the silent criticisms, the mocking half-smile, all brought increased stress and yes, it had to be said, shame. He did not want to appear weak or nervous so pushing any negativity aside, he looked for the first foothold.

He knew not to look down, or indeed up. Sensing Ray judging him, Craig pressed his face against the granite wall, whilst his fingers searched out whatever purchase he could find. With painful slowness, he hauled himself upwards, stress increasing the higher he climbed. Failure was not an option. Better to slip and fall than suffer the jeers. Gritting his teeth, he pressed on.

Then, at last, he made the top. A surge of pride jumped into his throat and, with a final lunge, he rolled over onto his back to stare up at the clear, blue sky. Safe. Success. Victory. He gulped in air, allowing the happiness and relief to overwhelm him.

Like a Buddha, Ray sat cross-legged, checked his watch, mouth moving soundlessly, counting. "You made a meal of that," he said. "You only just broke twenty seconds."

"*Twenty seconds!*" Craig sat up, shaking his head sadly as the disappointment hit home. He couldn't believe it, sure that this had been his best climb yet. His sweat-soaked shirt, sticking uncomfortably on his back, was testament to his efforts. Efforts that proved simply not good enough.

He tugged off the small canvas bag slung over his shoulder. It was hot up there on the flat, dusty top of the rock and he took a moment to use his shirtsleeve to wipe his face dry. Sighing, he delved into the bag and pulled out a sandwich. "I could easily do it quicker next time."

"Yeah. I'm sure." Not looking, or sounding convinced, Ray studied his own sandwich and smiled in expectation. "Golden Toms," he said musingly.

"Golden what?"

"*Toms*. Me Da' grows 'em in his greenhouse down his allotment. Me mam has put lots of mayo on 'em. Lovely," and he sank his teeth into the soft, white bread and munched away ravenously.

"What does your dad do again?" asked Craig. He had never met Ray's dad, never even seen him. Ray was always secretive about where his dad was anytime Craig went to his house. Still, it didn't matter, Ray seemed happy enough. Looking at his own, miserable offering in his sandwich, Craig sighed. He'd made it himself, not wanting to disturb Mum who seemed more distant than usual that morning.

"Electrician," replied Ray with obvious pride. "Has his own business. He works hard. Hardly ever coming home until really late, even so, he says it's the best job in the world. Think I'll be one when I grow up."

"Really? Don't you have to be clever for that?"

For a moment, Ray's icy blue eyes sparkled with something like menace. Then he caught the joke and laughed. "Yeah, well I am clever, aren't I?"

It was Craig's turn to smile. "I've no idea what I want to do when I grow up. Tank driver maybe."

"Tank driver? What's that?"

Craig looked at his friend for a long time. "Er – someone who drives a tank."

"Like in the army?"

"No, in the Air Force, you divvy!"

Ray laughed again. "Okay, yeah, I get it." Sandwich finished, he wiped his mouth and lay back on the rock.

The day was warming up beautifully, the kind of day everyone wished would never end.

"I used to think I'd like to join the army. But me Da' says it's not such a good idea. He served in the army in the War see. I think he had something to do with tanks."

"Oh?" Craig sat forward unable to keep the eagerness from his voice. "What did he do exactly?"

"Dunno. He never talks about it. I remember there was one of those documentary things on TV, 'All our Yesterdays', that one, and me Da, he got up and walked out, muttering something about officers and cowards. He told me it'll be stupid being a soldier if a war was to come. We'd all be killed in just a few minutes, he said."

"Another war?" Craig peered intensely at his friend. He needed some explanation because the idea of fighting didn't fit in with his plans at all. "What sort of war?"

"Dunno. Any sort of war, I suppose."

"Against the Germans?"

"Nah, shouldn't think so. Me Da' says we're friends with them now. On the same team, he said. Nah, he said it would be against the Ruskies. Said they had thousands and thousands of tanks, all lined up."

"Lined up where?"

"In East Germany. Me Da' says we couldn't stop 'em and that the only way we could ever manage that would be to drop atomic bombs on 'em."

"*Atomic bombs!*" Craig's stomach turned inside out, frightened. He wished he had a dad, like Ray, who would explain such things. He swallowed hard. "They can kill thousands, those bombs can."

"Millions, more like. And they blow up houses and stuff. No one could survive."

"We might be able to. We could go up to Scotland or somewhere like that."

"Scotland? How would that help?"

"I dunno. Lots of mountains and caves and... We could hide in one of them, or something."

"A *cave*? What would you do in a cave?"

"Dunno. Survive."

"On what?"

"I... I dunno. I'd find something. Make myself a bow and arrow, hunt rabbits."

Ray gaped at him. "How would you get all the way up there, to Scotland? You haven't got a car." Sniggering, he shook his head. "You can't even drive if you had one."

Craig looked out across the old quarry. On a day such as this, with the air thick with warmth, insects playing around the wildflowers, birds singing so beautifully, it was difficult to believe it could all come to an end. He wished he'd never mentioned anything about the army now.

"Still," said Ray, closed his eyes and breathed out a contented sigh, "they'll be needing lots of tank drivers when the war comes."

Craig shot him a glance, then dug his friend in the ribs playfully, "Shut up, you!"

They both laughed and when Craig finished his sandwich, he threw away the crust and settled down next to his friend to enjoy a few golden moments of peace.

Raised voices stirred them from their slumber. They sat up and looked down to see two figures waving madly at them. Ray groaned and Craig felt a tiny tremor of fear ripple through him.

Adam Crossland caused every school day to be like hell. An arrogant bully, he took great delight in causing Craig pain and humiliation. For reasons, which Craig didn't fully understand, Crossland hated him. Ray had stood up to him once and received a punch in the face for his troubles, but Crossland had never again bothered him. Craig, on the other hand, knowing he could never be so brave, suffered every humiliation, always hoping one day it would end.

This time, Crossland was with another school bully, Samantha Lloyd. Taller, older and infinitely crueller, as well as being the prettiest girl Craig had ever seen. He saw her and his stomach lurched, but not with fear this time.

The pair stopped at the foot of the rock. Shielding his eyes from the sun's glare, Crossland peered upwards. "Is that you there, Craig? What yer doin'?"

"With his boyfriend," said Samantha, sneering. "That's right, isn't it Ray*mond*?" Samantha enjoyed emphasising the last syllable of Ray's full name, thinking it hilarious.

Craig could feel Ray bristling next to him. "Go away," said Ray, his voice sounding surprisingly confident.

"Don't be like that, Ray*mond*," laughed Samantha. She tested the rock face with her foot but thought better of it. "Why don't you come down?"

"Why don't you come up?" Ray shouted back, knowing full well that neither of them could. It was a small victory, but a sweet one nevertheless.

Crossland chewed his lip, face growing red. "We said, come down!"

Craig looked at Ray, who shook his head slightly. "No."

The two bullies exchanged an infuriated look. "There'll be another time," spat Crossland and reached down to pick up a stone. He hurled it upwards but it sailed harmlessly past the two boys' heads.

Ray giggled, "Not much good, are you, Crossland?"

"I'll fix you," said Crossland.

"And me," chimed in Samantha. She waggled her finger towards the boys. "I'm going to hurt you, Craig. Get you down in the dirt, and make you beg for mercy."

Unconsciously, Craig scrambled backwards, putting more distance between him and the tormentors. The thought of her over-powering him caused a curious mix of emotions to swirl around inside. He at once feared Samantha and found her irresistible. He'd often watch her moving across the school playground, his attention focused on her legs, the way her calf muscles flexed as she walked. Against every school rule, she wore high-heeled shoes, which accentuated the shapeliness of her long, smooth limbs. And then there was her face...

"What you looking at little Craig?" came her voice, snapping him back to reality. "See something you like?"

Face burning, he quickly looked away from her penetrating blue eyes and forced a cough. Perhaps the girl at the tennis courts had stirred up some alien feelings, made him aware of how lovely a girl could be.

Samantha said something to Crossland. As they turned to go, an elderly man appeared, breathing hard as he came over the top of the steps that rose from Breck Road. Stooping forward, leaning on his walking stick, mouth open and face strained, he struggled to gain a breath. Around his feet scurried a small, wiry Border terrier, which proved a much better sport for the bullies. With the two boys forgotten, they danced around in exaggerated, weirdly grotesque movements, calling the dog names. Straining at its leash, the dog barked furiously, which only served to make the bullies dance with more passion. The old man cursed and hissed, waving his stick at them, causing nothing but uproarious laughter from the bullies as they finally loped away, firing off rude words as they went.

Craig breathed a sigh of relief. "I'd forgotten how horrible those two can be. Especially her."

After a brief silence, Ray's voice came drifting wistfully through the air. "I think she's quite nice."

Craig, incredulous, gaped at his friend. Ray had voiced exactly what was in his own mind. However, to keep his feelings well hidden, he feigned surprise and said, "*Nice?* Are you serious?"

"She's the prettiest girl in school, Craig. There's no argument about that."

Forced to admit this was true, Craig's thoughts again turned to the girl from the tennis court. For a brief, glorious moment, he imagined seeking her out, greeting her with a smile and seeing her return it. He sighed. "Do you think all girls are like Samantha?"

"Eh?"

"You know, the way she is. Like she has to prove she's tougher than us boys? I thought girls were supposed to be softer." He caught Ray's look and again he felt the heat rise to his cheeks. He rushed on, "I think it's all a big act, that she's not tough at all. I think she puts it on, for Crossland. She must fancy him like crazy."

"Yeah...well..." Ray looked troubled. "Big act or not, we'll have to take care going home. We'll wait here for a while longer, just in case. They may not have gone."

Craig nodded. He noticed the old man bending down to rub his dog's flanks. Had the bullies hurt the little dog, he wondered? Clearing his throat, Craig called down to the man. "Is he all right, mister?"

The old man turned a perfect mask of fury towards him. "You mind your own damned business!

I've a good mind to call the police, you snivelling little runt."

Gawping, Craig couldn't believe what he'd heard. "It wasn't *us*, mister. We didn't do anything."

"You're all the same you young people – causing trouble. You've got nothing better to do with your time, that's what it is. Why aren't you at school?"

"It's the holidays."

"Bah!" The old man turned away. "If I see you around here again, I'll give you what-for."

"*It wasn't us!*"

But the old man was no longer listening. Shuffling away, dragging the little dog with him, he muttered something under his breath. The little dog strained on the leash, forcing the man to stoop down and release him. Instantly, the terrier scampered ahead to explore the nearby undergrowth with great enthusiasm and no apparent injuries.

"Caw," said Craig and shook his head, "he's a bit of a nark, isn't he?"

"Old and bitter," said Ray. "That's what my Da' says. Old people get like that, he says. It's not their fault, just the way it is."

"He looked old," said Craig softly, "but I don't think he really was."

"Eh? What d'you mean?"

"Dunno. Something about him. Maybe, using

that stick, he's ill or something. He didn't have grey hair. And that scar. Wonder where he got that."

"I didn't see no scar."

Unconsciously, Craig traced a line down his cheek with his index finger.

"My Da'," continued Ray, "says that people can be old before their time – smoking and drinking he says, they're the worst."

"Your dad knows a lot, doesn't he?"

"Yeah." Ray smiled.

"I've never met him."

Something changed in Ray's mood and he looked away, chewing on his bottom lip. "Yeah well, he's not in much, like I said. But he tells me about a lot of things. He's great."

Craig wondered why Ray's words didn't match his voice, which sounded low, sad almost. It made Craig miss his own dad. The pain bit deep and he had to struggle to keep the tears at bay as he always did, every single day since it happened. If only he could make amends, undo it all, turn back the clock and make life good again. If only Dad were still here...

DRAWING BLANKS

FALLON SLUMPED down behind his desk and lit himself a cigarette before sifting through the numerous pieces of paper spilling out from a thin, manila-coloured file. Around him, the room buzzed with activity. Someone in the press had managed to get hold of Arthur Phelps' address. His story appeared on the front page of the local press. Now, the Fleet Street boys had it. The pressure mounted. People were scared and Fallon cringed at what the response might be if the details of the attack came out. It was all here in front of him but more than that were the chilling words he'd listened to less than an hour before.

"He'd smashed her around the face, almost certainly with his fists, then strangled her before bashing the back of her skull in with a flat-headed instrument," Crenshaw, the on-duty pathologist, had informed him. Summoned to the lab, Fallon had stood, hands in raincoat pockets, staring at the floor, not wanting to look but knowing he had to. When Crenshaw drew back the sheet covering the body, the detective flinched.

"I'll never get used to this," said Fallon, pressing a hand to his mouth. Out in the field, seeing a body, that was something which never bothered him, but here, in the cold, clinical glare of the laboratory lights, everything so sterile, so *final*, his stomach twisted into knots.

"So," he said, shuffling his feet, "a mallet, or a hammer?"

"A hammer. Almost certainly, due to the size of the wound and the penetration. Struck with great power."

"Angry?"

"Or demented. He beat her to a pulp before killing her."

He'd listened to Crenshaw drone on, inwardly digesting the information, ticking off the attack's sequence. Punched repeatedly by someone who knew what they were doing. Then strangled. The pressure on the throat so massive it crushed the larynx. Finally, the hammer. A single blow, delivered almost certainly after she was dead. This was a vicious assault, but the use of the hammer almost certainly meant it was premeditated. But why. Who was she, and why put her in the canal?

Now, sitting at his desk, Fallon's job was to try and make some sense of who this girl was. Fingerprints had so far drawn a blank. There were no reports of anyone missing, but then it had been only two days since the discovery of the body. The newspapers, however, made it seem this could be the beginning of a murder spree. The Assistant Chief Constable wanted a result. Quickly.

"We've managed to cobble together an identikit picture of her," said Emery from the door, voice raised above the hubbub. He strode over to Fallon and laid the picture down on the desk. "It was difficult, her face so bloated, the eyes bruised, the mouth all—"

"Yeah, all right constable," said Fallon, studying the face. "Pretty."

"Very." Emery sat down. "It's our one advantage over the press, boss. They seem to have everything else. The cause of death, where they found her, *how* she was found. That Phelps bloke told them and I'm betting they paid him a few bob."

"Almost certainly."

"Wonder why they haven't spoken to the other one …" He fished inside his jacket and brought out his notebook, flicking through the pages. "Anthony Franks."

"He seemed affected quite badly. Maybe he doesn't want to talk about it."

"Maybe it was him that did it, boss."

Looking up, Fallon fixed the young constable with a glare. "First time on a murder case, is it?" Emery nodded, frowning. "They teach you at college, don't they, to *suspect everyone*."

"That's what I'm doing boss."

"They also teach you to stick to the facts." He pointed to the mock-up picture. "If he'd done it, Phelps must have been in on it too. Mutual alibis. No one else saw anything, they were the only two at the scene."

"So, they could both have murdered her."

"Possibly. Killed her, tied her up, rolled her into the water."

"But why inform us, boss? So soon after, I mean. Why not wait an hour or two?"

"What, and risk someone else finding her?"

"It doesn't seem likely, does it, boss."

"No. It doesn't." He slid the picture closer. "So, there we are. The facts. Not speculation. We know next to nothing about this girl. Crenshaw guessed at her being around twenty-five. Tall, slim, manicured nails, hair recently cut. She was a girl who cared about her appearance, not that you'd know it from the state of her face." He shook his head. "Poor kid, to end up like this."

"We're continuing to scour the immediate area, but so far nothing."

"And what do you make of that?"

"That she was not attacked at the canal."

"So, murdered elsewhere, then brought to that spot and placed in the water. That would mean the killer most probably brought her there in a car and carried her from the road to the toe-path. And nobody saw anything."

"Except for the big bloke we spoke to. His statement doesn't mention anything about seeing the person he witnessed driving away or arriving."

"We don't even know if it was the same person."

"To be honest, boss, we don't know very much at all."

"Not yet." Placing his hands behind his head, Fallon leaned back, cigarette dangling from his lips, "Anything in the road? Car tracks?"

"Hundreds, boss."

"What we need is a witness, someone who saw that car driving away."

"Or a concerned parent, or boyfriend maybe, anxious about her not coming home."

"Put out an appeal. Get in touch with the same newspaper that ran Phelps' piece. They're our allies in this, so we use them. Get onto 'Look North' too, get them to air an appeal for witnesses." He narrowed his eyes. "You can do all that, can't you?"

Emery stood up, back straight, jaw tight. "Absolutely, boss."

Grinning, Fallon rolled forward and stubbed out his cigarette. "If we're lucky, it might prompt somebody to come forward."

"And if we're not lucky?"

"Then we just keep looking. There's not a lot else we can do, is there."

"I suppose not."

He turned to go just as the telephone at Fallon's elbow trilled, who lifted the receiver, listened for a few moments, then replaced it on the cradle. Pursing his lips, he released a silent whistle.

"Something up, boss?"

"A woman walked into Ellesmere Port headquarters five minutes ago to tell them about the disappearance of her flatmate."

A short silence followed. Emery didn't move, waiting.

"We have a name, constable." He winked and, by way of celebration, lit himself another cigarette.

THE DISAPPOINTMENT OF FRIENDS

THE TWO FRIENDS decided not to play at the Pit for the next few days, just in case the 'bullies' made another appearance. Instead, they met up with some other boys they knew, one of whom lived in a small cul-de-sac where the houses provided them with a perfect target for playing SLAM.

Where the gang played was a part of Station Road that Craig had not been to before. Here the houses were grander, semi-detached, with large walled gardens to the rear and much smaller, ornamental ones at the front. Everything about them was so very different to Craig's own, compact little terraced house. His dad used to call their own backyard a 'postage stamp' and Craig smiled at the memory.

Ray introduced him to a gaggle of boys spewing

over the pavement. A good bunch, happy to be off school, enjoying the fine weather, all of them to get the game going.

The game was simple enough. Each took turns, kicking a ball against a wall without missing or letting it bounce twice, to spell out the word SLAM. If you succeeded, you next had to try to spell out your name.

A good game, Craig's turn came after Davey, the owner of the ball, had missed the third letter of his own name. Taking his time and concentrating hard, Craig steadied himself, feeling like he was preparing to take a penalty in the FA Cup Final. At last, when he finally swung his foot, he kicked the ball with such exaggerated force that he managed to hoik it high into the air and straight over the back garden wall. Everyone exploded into laughter.

"You'll have to go fetch it," said Davey between guffaws. "But watch out – that's old man Baxter's house, and we all know what he's like." The group exchanged looks, accompanied by more giggling.

Nobody explained this. Craig turned to Ray, but his friend offered no words. The rest of the gang seemed to Possess some dark secret about this man Baxter. "Who is he?" Craig asked his friend.

"Remember the guy from the Pit, with the little dog? Him."

A dark cloud came down as Craig recalled the old man's scathing words. "Oh."

"Yeah, *oh*. So be quiet, but be quick!"

Craig scanned the faces fixing him with hard stares. The pressure mounted. He knew there was no getting out of this. He'd kicked the ball and it was his responsibility to fetch it back. Turning to the garden wall, he groaned. Hopelessly high and nothing like Grannie's Rock; not a single foothold to be had.

Stepping forward, he decided to try the back door first and eased down the latch.

Locked, he should have known.

With no other options available, he would use the handle as a scaling aid. He glanced over to the assembled group, "Can one of you give me a leg-up?"

The boys shuffled around, heads down, some of them giggling. Not one seemed eager to commit to helping, enjoying Craig's discomfort. Finally, with obvious reluctance, Ray sauntered over.

Ray bent down and cupped his hands together, waiting for Craig's foot. With it in place, Ray assisted by heaving Craig upwards. Taking a good grip on the brickwork, Craig hauled himself to the top of the wall and sat there, gazing down into the back garden. A large, tired-looking lawn surrounded by ill-kept bushes and masses of confused, straggling flowers spread out beneath him. The ball was nowhere in sight and he turned to the others to explain but was greeted by a hail of jeers. "Hurry up," said Ray, "we want to carry on with the game."

Craig surveyed the garden again, the silence unsettling. Turning to the house, he took in the shuttered windows, the empty conservatory, and it was clear nobody was home. He still had the uncomfortable feeling that lurking inside, hidden by the darkness, someone was watching.

Another shout from his friends jerked him into action. Twisting himself around, he pushed his worries aside and dropped down to the garden.

Holding his breath, Craig waited, straining to pick out any signs of someone coming to investigate, or a dog warning the owner of the intrusion. But the only sound was the gentle chirping of birds amongst the trees.

Keeping one eye on the house, he followed a small winding path, which led from the backdoor to the centre of the lawn where a sad and lonely ornamental fountain stood. Slimy, black trails ran down the arms and face of the statue of a naked woman holding an urn on her shoulder. But no water trickled from it to splash over its coarse surface. Its lack of care told him both statue and garden had known better, happier times. There was no love here, no sign of anyone ever enjoying the space. No deckchairs or other furniture, everything cleared away, antiseptic, sterile. More a painting than a garden.

His gaze wandered to the silent house, its crafted stonework and clinging wisteria lending it a melancholic beauty. It spoke of past wealth, comfort, an ordered haven from which to escape the mad, hectic world. Large French windows opened out onto a patio, where an iron table and two matching chairs sat, the only clue that someone lived there. As with the garden, not abandoned but too quiet. Baxter was out. Yet, that awful sense of somebody observing him remained.

Easing himself along the path to the fountain, Craig crouched to search the nearest bushes and flowerbeds before moving around the perimeter on his hands and knees. His search proved fruitless. The ball could be anywhere but he knew failure was not an option. Careless now, he pulled aside portions of shrubbery, groped between overhanging branches, every effort resulting in more and more frustration. His stomach knotted as panic mounted. How long was this going to take? Conscious of the gang waiting beyond the wall, he could almost hear their impatience, and more careless still, he frantically pulled at the undergrowth, desperate to find the ball. He cursed aloud, his voice, shattering the silence. At any moment, Baxter might appear, screaming his outrage and that would be the end of everything. Soon there'd be police, then Mum. A nightmare.

Breathing hard, more through exasperation than fatigue, he sat down in the grass and wondered what he could do. Why had he been so damned stupid, trying to impress the others? All he'd succeeded in doing was to make a fool of himself like he always did. He'd be ostracised for losing the ball and ruining the game. An idiot. A wimp. He sniffed loudly, ran the back of his hand under his nose, and succeeded in smearing wet soil across his face. He didn't care. His 'new' friends had invited him into their gang and he'd let them down. They'd never invite him again, for sure.

Towards the far side of the lawn, close to the raised patio, stood an old wheelbarrow heaped up with grass cuttings. Alongside a rusted bucket lay on its side. A tiny tingling sensation rippled across his neck. Frowning, he craned forward, realising that something may have knocked the bucket over. Straining to focus, his heart gave a little leap when he saw what it was.

Wedged beneath the barrow sat the ball.

Stifling a cry of triumph, he sprang to his feet, ran over to the barrow, and set about trying to kick the ball free, but only succeeded in wedging it ever more tightly underneath. Struggling to keep his rising panic from overwhelming him, Craig grabbed the handles, took the strain, and put all his strength into pushing the barrow forward. It didn't budge an inch and he collapsed with a loud grunt onto his hands and knees. Head down, he tried to summon up some reserve of hope. The old thing had proved too heavy and awkward, its ancient frame groaning as if it might fall apart at any moment. Clearly forgotten amongst the tangle of weeds it had remained this way for years, decaying into uselessness. But there were no alternatives left. If it collapsed, then so be it. He had to get the ball. Gritting his teeth, he put his shoulder against the end rather than using the handles this time and heaved with everything he had, determined not to give in, not now. A tiny movement, a fraction at first, provided him with a new surge of energy. Gritting his teeth, he pushed again. The wheels slid rather than ran over the damp grass, but it did budge, inspiring him to continue. One last grunt and the ball drew closer to the rear end of the barrow. He could see it, still lodged underneath, but not as tightly and so tantalisingly close. A well-aimed kick and it shot out towards the far wall. Without a pause, he scooted across the grass, relief flooding over him, and lifted his new trophy, grinning so wide his jaw ached. He drew back both hands, ready to throw it over the wall to his eager friends waiting on the other side. With a loud, guttural yelp, he launched his projectile high and wide into the air.

Craig was not a great one for football. He could kick, but only in a sporadic, un-schooled fashion, as proven by his ludicrous attempts to play the game of SLAM. Throw-ins were an even worse failing. The ball went up all right, high up, far too high up. He had totally misjudged the trajectory and he watched in wide-eyed horror as the ball hung in the air for a moment before beginning its rapid journey back to earth. Before it did so, however, it struck the near edge of Craig's side of the garden wall and ricocheted back at an impossible angle towards the French windows.

With eyes closed, he waited for the inevitable sound of breaking glass. A fearful thud, but nothing more. The weight lifting from his shoulders, he grinned at the sight of the untouched, unbroken glass. But his relief proved short-lived, as everything spiralled into chaos from that point on.

A small, sandy-coloured, wire-haired dog appeared from the depths of the house. It charged into the conservatory, teeth barred, and leaped high into the air, desperate to break out, yapping like it had lost its mind. Hurling itself repeatedly against the glass, out of control, saliva drooling, eyes mad with rage, the dog's barking grew ever louder. Craig didn't wait to see what would happen next. In a desperate lunge, he swept up the ball and, without any football antics this time, raced to the backdoor. He was almost there when he heard the French windows behind him crashing open and a voice shouting, "Oi, you! What the hell are you doing?"

With no time left to stop or think, Craig threw back the bolt, ripped open the door, and bounded out, the terrier snarling and snapping at his heels. In his rush to escape, Craig didn't pause to close the door firmly. The latch hadn't engaged and the little dog nosed open the door and sprang out into the street.

For one awful moment, Craig didn't know what to do, thinking he should turn and face his attacker, perhaps scare it off. The thought of those vicious-looking teeth decided it for him. His friends must have believed the same and when John screamed the only practical, sensible word, *"Run!"* they all did just that.

Barking maniacally, the dog rushed forward in a mad, chaotic dance, first one way, then another as each of the boys zigzagged in different directions. Lost in the confusion, it could not decide who to follow and turned upon itself, spinning frantically in its frustration, trying to catch its own tail.

Craig proved the fastest of the boys that day. Head down, football under his arms, he made good his escape, pounding along Station Road towards the safety of his own, wonderful alleyway. He dared not look back. A simple, but dreadful thought, consumed him: 'I've done it again – I've let everyone down.'

Later on, Ray came round to Craig's house. He appeared sullen, shuffling his feet, speaking in a low, grumpy voice. He explained he had only called to fetch Davey's football. Craig handed it over, the misery making his movements heavy, slow.

"I'm sorry, Ray," he said in a small voice.

"Yeah...well..." Ray took the ball without another word and disappeared into the warm, summer night, bouncing the ball as he went.

Craig knew he had probably lost the only real friend he had left.

SEVERAL DISCLOSURES

"THE WOMAN WHO'S COME FORWARD," said Fallon, sitting in the passenger seat with Emery driving beside. He studied the hastily written notes he'd made during the telephone call from Ellesmere Port, "She's twenty-seven, an Art student studying graphic design at Chester Uni. She's known this Janet Stowe for only six months. They share a flat together."

"Anything else about Janet's social life, friends …?"

"We'll get all of that when we have a chat with her. Emery, do you have to drive so bloody fast?"

"Just my way, boss."

"Well calm it down will you, this isn't Le Mans."

They were in the fast lane of the A41 heading across the Wirral Peninsula towards Ellesmere Port.

Rush hour was over, the traffic scarce. None of this seemed to temper Emery's love of speed and the little Viva HB responded gallantly.

Her name was Millie, so the desk sergeant informed them on their arrival, and she sat in the tiny, airless interview room wearing a short skirt over black, fishnet stockings. Fallon did his best not to stare but failed. He caught her hard eyes boring into him. He smiled. She didn´t return it.

"So, Miss…"

"Everyone calls me Millie," she said and watched him as he carefully pulled up a chair and sat down opposite.

Exchanging a glance with Emery, Fallon shrugged. "So … *Millie*. How long have you known Janet Stowe?"

"Since the start of term, when we moved in together."

"Not before?"

Her eyes stared, expressionless. "No."

"And you were close." She nodded. A tiny tic played at the corner of one eye and it looked as if she would break down at any moment. "I'm very sorry for all of this," Fallon said. He took a deep breath. "We're trying to ascertain some details. Personal details about Janet. We don't seem to be able to find very much, not until now, so thank you for coming forward. Perhaps you could tell us some things. What was she studying?"

"Why don't you ask the college?"

"Because I'm asking you."

The silence didn't improve anybody's mood, certainly not Millie's defensive attitude. "Journalism."

"Thank you. How come you got to know one another if you were on different courses?"

"I put an ad up, asking for a flatmate."

"Okay ... and the flat? It's nice?" She shrugged. "Central?" A nod. "Did she have any special visitors? Friends. *Boy*friends."

"No."

Emery cleared his throat and pulled up another chair. Fallon waited. Her attitude troubled him. Not openly aggressive, but something didn't sit right. Resistance? Dislike? Maybe she had a problem with authority. Maybe ... "Girlfriends?"

Shifting her gaze from Fallon to Emery, her face seemed to thaw a little. "One or two."

"Ah," breathed Emery.

"What does that mean?"

"Nothing," said Fallon quickly. "We´re just trying to build up a picture, that´s all."

"Then why not just ask me straight out?"

"Ask you what?"

"If she was a Lesbian?"

"Was she?"

"Yes. We were lovers."

For the first time, not only the iciness of Millie's expression changed, but her eyes grew soft, her mouth fluttered, and she looked away, pulling out a tissue. She pressed it into the corner of one eye.

The two policemen sat in silence. Gathering herself, Millie stuffed the tissue into her sleeve and repositioned herself on the seat. "So, there you have it. Happy?" Fallon sighed. "Anything else?"

"When did you last see her?"

"Friday night."

"Four days ago?"

Emery leaned forward. "Why didn't you report her missing before now?"

A shrug. "She sometimes goes on walkabout. Neither of us were exclusive, if you know what I mean. It was only when I saw her on the tele, I got in touch. We often had fights and she often ran out. She always came back, tail between her legs."

"But not this time."

"No. Not this time."

Another sniff, another dab of the tissue.

"The other times," said Fallon, "the times she ran off, do you know where she went?"

"Usually to some bar or club. She'd pick up someone, go back to their place. She always told me."

"'Pick up someone'? Girls, you mean?"

"Sometimes. Sometimes it was men."

"But you said she was a—"

"Yes. But she liked men too. Sometimes." A loud sniff. "To be totally accurate, she was bi-sexual. It all depended on her mood."

"She went with men as a way of getting back at you?" suggested Emery. "After the fights, I mean. Like a sort of retaliation."

"Yes, I guess, but she didn't enjoy the sex with them. She did it to hurt me."

"But these men, they—"

"They got upset when she told them enough was enough. All she wanted was a quick snog, maybe a grope. Rarely a bonk."

"So, no real intimacy?" It was Fallon and he received the full weight of her glare. "Sorry, I was only—"

"You're just so typical – all you think about is the pleasure you get from your cock."

"I don't think that at all, I was merely—"

"There are other ways to be intimate, but because she wouldn't do what they wanted one or two got angry. One of them became more than angry, slapped her around a bit. I had to clean up the bruises."

"Did she ever tell you anything more about this man, the one who attacked her?"

"Oh yes, she told me everything."

The silence seemed to loom large in that tiny room, charged with expectation, the two men holding their breath, waiting. At last, unable to bear the tension any longer, Fallon blurted, "Why don't you just tell us what happened?"

This time her sniff was followed by a loud blow of her nose. Head down, she recounted what Janet had told her.

"She was doing a piece about something that happened during the War. She was so excited, full of it. Apparently, she met this guy. Older, *very* experienced. She was honest with me, saying she was having doubts about us, that this guy was reawakening feelings she'd kept hidden for ages. I got upset and it was then she told me about the beating he'd given her."

"And what had caused it?"

"She'd found a notebook, a journal. It told of something that happened over in France back in forty-four. She didn't say what it was but it led her to an interview she had with another man who was over there. A tank driver. When her lover found out, he went ballistic, started hitting her. A real, full-on beating."

"Why did he have such a reaction?" asked Emery.

She shrugged. "Jan didn't say but there was something in that notebook that this guy didn't want anyone to know about. All Jan said to me was that it was explosive."

"Explosive?" Fallon exchanged a look with Emery. "That sounds serious. Can you tell us who this man is?"

Emery agreed, "Serious enough to murder her."

Shifting in her seat, the girl cleared her throat. "I wouldn't know about that." She broke down, floodgates well and truly opened. Bending forward, consumed in her grief, she sobbed into the remnants of her tissue. Emery was on his feet, rushing out of the tiny interview room to return moments later with a plastic beaker of water and a handful of clean tissues. She took them without a word, slurped down the water, wiped her eyes, blew her nose. "I'm sorry," she muttered.

"You take your time," said Fallon.

After a few moments, pulling in a shuddering breath, she sat back downcast. "I don´t know his name," she said.

"All right," said Fallon. "Perhaps if you can remember a description, anything that would lead us to—"

"I may not know his name" she put in quickly, "but I do know his address."

In a blur, both men flipped open their notebooks and scrambled around for a pencil.

THE WINDOW CLEANER'S TALE

A FEW DAYS after the run-in with Baxter and his dog, no one had called. Not that he expected anyone to but he hoped Ray might get in touch. Staring at the telephone nothing came back but the shrill of silence. Head down, he wandered into the backyard to take his bike from the shed. If anything else, he could still go on a bike ride. He looked up at the window cleaner descending the ladder. He had the look of a rocker about him, long hair, a goatee beard, even a single earring. Craig had always been fascinated by him and, the way things were panning out, he took the risk, cleared his throat, and spoke up. "Can I ask you something?"

The window cleaner frowned. He was tall and wiry, the muscles in his forearms bulging. Not someone to mess with, Craig reminded himself. The man's dark eyes narrowed. "What sort of question?"

"Advice really."

"Advice? Not sure I'm the one to give advice but fire away."

"Okay ... When you were younger – my age I mean – did you fit in? With your mates and stuff?"

The man's frown deepened, and Craig began to think that somehow, he'd over-stepped the mark by being too over-familiar, but then the man's expression cleared and he gave a quick shrug. "Yeah, suppose so. The ones that mattered."

"I don't understand – which ones mattered?"

"The *real* ones, the ones who were there when things went wrong. The ones you didn't have to try too hard with. True friends."

"Yes, yes I understand, so... Can I ask ... I'm not being nosey or anything ..."

"It's all right. Carry on."

"Did things ever go wrong? I mean, with your friends ... Did you ever get into trouble, with them, have a falling out or anything?"

The window cleaner studied him, then smiled. "Lots of times. Mainly in the early days." He settled the bucket on the ground. "I didn't do anything at school, except bunking off. Spent time in lots of different foster homes, got into loads of trouble. I didn't have anyone, you see. No mum *or* dad. I felt cheated, cheated by life. So, I was always angry, and I couldn't control it, and school...Well..." His eyes glazed over. "Wasted my life really. But," he paused and sighed. "I always had good mates, mates who stood by me. Who *still* stand by me. With no parents, it was they that got me through it, every time. The thing is, mates, *real* mates, when you have no family, they are what really matters in life. The others, well, I couldn't care less if I never saw them. True friends, they're as good as family – especially if you haven't got one."

"So, you haven't got a wife or a girlfriend?"

He grinned. "Well, a girl can be a mate too, you know."

Craig nodded. An uncalled picture of Samantha Lloyd came into his head. He coughed, pretended to scrape something off the saddle of his bike. "So, things worked out for you, in the end?"

"Well, all depends on what you mean by 'worked out'. I don't own my own place, I don't drive a car, I have to scrimp and save every penny I make out of this," he kicked the bucket gently with the toe of his boot. Another brief moment of reflection. "Listen, if you're looking for advice, then stay at school and do the best you can. It's tough, but getting educated is the only way. Trust me," he picked up the bucket, "it's the only way." He turned and began to saunter down the alleyway.

Craig grabbed his bike and quickly caught up with the cleaner. "Wait." The man raised an eyebrow. "You said friends are the *most* important thing of all. More important than school, is that right? Is that what you meant?"

"Friends are important, for sure. In a personal way. They help you get through the bad times, but they won't put money in your pocket. Only a good job will do that. I came out of school with nothing and I've still got nothing. Never likely to, either. Probably the only thing I've got to look forward to is Saturday night when we all go down to the pub and get drunk. Still, I suppose that's more than a lot of people have got." He patted his pockets and found a crumpled pack of cigarettes. "You having trouble with your mates are you?"

Craig told him of the incident with the ball, how he'd let everyone down, ruined their game, made himself look like an idiot.

The cleaner lit his cigarette. "Well, that wasn't *that* bad. They'll get over it. No one ever lost their lives playing a game of football. Where did you say you were playing?"

"Down Station Road, far end. In one of my mate's streets. The old guy in the house was really... *mean*. Some bloke called Baxter."

The man's face grew hard. "*Billy* Baxter?" He blew out a stream of smoke. "Did he have a dog?"

"Yeah. Little brown thing, dead vicious."

The man nodded. "Yeah, that's him. Billy Baxter."

"D'you know him?"

"I know *of* him. Grumpy old fart he is."

Craig laughed. He liked the window cleaner. He wasn't a bit like he'd imagined him to be. Not mean or nasty at all, quite open and friendly. "Well, I didn't see him, just heard him. That was enough."

"Well, he's well known around here. Always in a nark. He's lived here for years and years, ever since I can remember. You're lucky to have got that ball back, he normally keeps 'em. You be careful next time you're round there."

They stood at the end of the alleyway. Craig prepared to ride off. "Thanks for the advice."

"Ah, you're welcome. Just try and follow it, yeah?"

"Yeah, I will."

He winked and walked away.

Craig suppressed a sudden urge to call after him, realising he hadn't asked the man his name. But already the cleaner's loping stride had taken him to the corner shop and then, in a flash, he was out of sight, the chance lost, leaving Craig to mull over what he'd said about. Baxter, *old man Billy*

Baxter, with his nasty temper and little dog. A *right nark* the window-cleaner had called him. What had happened to make the old man so bitter towards everyone? There could be so many reasons, reasons which Craig would never find out.

How wrong that assumption soon proved to be.

SUSPECT

WITH BOTH ENDS of the street blocked and four heavy-set officers waiting at the rear entrance. A set of well-worn stone steps led to the front door. Fallon gave a nod to Emery who, now dressed in plain clothes, somewhat reluctantly walked down the path. He scanned the names of the occupants. He looked over his shoulder and sighed. "There's six apartments and Fender's is naturally at the top."

"Isn't that always the way," said Fallon with a groan.

Emey pressed the bell, then almost immediately gave the knocker a good pounding in best rent-collector style. Meanwhile, Fallon gazed towards the upper-storey windows. All the curtains were drawn. It was seven-thirty in the morning. Nobody was about.

"Try it again," said Fallon and Emery did so, pressing buzzers and pounding at the knocker, much louder this time. He shouted, "Mr Fender? Mr Fender, this is the police. Open your door." A moment later the curtains twitched and a face poked itself out. A grimacing face. The face of a man angry at being woken up so abruptly.

"Someone coming down the stairs, boss," said Emery.

"Good." Fallon moved up to his younger colleague and fished out his warrant card.

The sound of a bolt drawing back before the door inched open. The same, scowling face peered out through the crack. "What the bloody hell—"

"We'd like a word," said Fallon, thrusting out his warrant card.

They sat in the kitchen, the man in his dressing gown making tea. "I did know her, yes," he said, with his back towards the policemen. The photograph Fallon had produced was at his elbow. Black and white, but a good image. The face of an attractive girl, with no signs of her ever being beaten up.

"Did you not know she was missing?"

The man turned and looked at them both. "No. I don't watch the news, nor take a paper. I prefer to live in blissful ignorance."

"Really?"

"Yes, *really*. What is it you want with me anyway?"

"That depends," said Fallon.

"On what?"

"On what you can tell us about the last time you saw Miss Stowe."

"Oh, was that her name?"

"Yes, it was. Janet Stowe. Didn't you know that?"

"We didn't make any formal introductions. I saw her at the bar, went up to her, and started talking. She seemed pleasant enough, easy on the eye, if you know what I mean."

Twisting himself in the chair, Fallon swallowed down his anger. "Mr Fender, this young lady has been found brutally murdered, trussed up in an old, stinking sheet, and thrown in the Shropshire Union canal. She's not *easy on the eye* anymore, I can assure you of that."

The kettle came to the boil, breaking the tension and Fender took the chance, turned down the gas, and filled up the mugs. "Yeah well, I'm sorry about all that," he said, spooning in sugar. "But, like I say, I didn't know her all that well." He brought the mugs to the table and set them down. "We just had some fun, that's all."

"Fun?" Emery picked up his mug, studied it, and

put it down again. "Would you care to tell us what happened, Mr Fender?"

Shrugging, Fender sat and took a sip of his tea. "Well, it was some time ago. Two weeks."

"Even so," said Fallon.

"Yeah. We, er, we had some drinks, got more friendly and I invited her back here. I didn't think she'd come to be honest."

"Why not?"

"Well, me being a stranger and all. Girls get nervous about that sort of thing, don't they? Going back to a stranger's place."

"Is that your usual chat-up line is it? Come back to my place?"

"No, I haven't got a … Look, we were two consenting adults, okay? She was old enough to say 'no' and walk away, but she didn't – she came back here."

"And the fun continued?"

Fender glared at Emery. "I didn't rape her, if that is what you are insinuating."

"I'm not," said Emery, his unblinking stare hard as flint, "but your idea of 'fun' wasn't the same as hers, was it? What happened when she got here?"

Fender's gaze dropped to his mug and he took another sip. "It got nasty. She started calling me names and stuff."

"Why would she do that?"

"I dunno."

"Take a wild guess, Mr Fender," snapped Fallon.

His face came up, the colour draining from his flesh. He seemed old all of a sudden. Perhaps he was old. He was a big man, balding, worker's hands clamped around the mug. "Just stuff."

"Stuff? You like that word, Mr Fender," continued Fallon, noting how Fender was growing increasingly more uncomfortable. "What sort of 'stuff' are we talking about? Didn't she take too kindly to your advances? Did you try to touch her up and she said 'no', gave you a bit of a tongue-lashing, is that it?"

"No, no, nothing like that! I didn't try to do anything, I swear. Look, we were just in here – well, in the front room and we were talking and we kissed. She didn't push me away or nothing. I touched her, not too much, but we both knew what was going to happen, so I touched her again. On her titties."

Fallon sat back, arms folded, glaring. "Titties?"

"Breasts! Jesus, I'd picked her up in a bar that is well-known to be a singles place, okay. People go there because they want company. There's no law against it."

"So what happened when you touched her?"

"Nothing. She seemed okay with it, so I ... Look, do you need to know everything?"

"This is a murder investigation, Mr Fender so yes, we need to know."

"All right. I undid her bra and kissed her. Not on the lips."

"What did she do?"

"Jesus," Fender put his face in his hand. He was red, lips trembling slightly. "It was nothing, okay. Nothing at all. She just said something and I lost my temper."

"You lost your temper enough to strike her, didn't you, Mr Fender."

Fender didn't take his hand away. "Yes. I was … I was *shocked* see, offended. I lashed out. I didn't mean to hit her the way I did and when she got up and stormed out, I didn't try to stop her. And that's the God's truth, I swear it."

"Offended by what she said?"

With his breath coming in short jerks, Fender stood up, taking the unfinished tea to the sink where he threw it away. He clung onto the edge of the sink, head down. "She was loving what I was doing, moaning, all of that. I went to … I moved down to her legs. Her crotch. She was wearing a little mini-skirt and I took it off, slipped my hand beneath her panties, touched her. She was soaking wet and she was telling me to fuck her. 'Fuck me' is what she said. And I moved away, and she went to my trouser belt and … Ah shit, that's when she said it, all right. She said, 'Where is it?' And when she groped inside my pants, she stopped and then ... Then she giggled, all right. She giggled." He swung around, and there were tears in his eyes. "I'm fifty-five years of age next month. I'm not a young man anymore, and I wasn't ... I wasn't *hard*. I have problems now and then. My ex, she knocked all the confidence out of me, so I have problems. Understand?"

"And yet you went to a singles bar?"

"Not often. Only when I've had a few to drink, a bit of Dutch courage."

"We'll check, Mr Fender. If you're a regular there, we can—"

"All right, all-bloody-right, you bastards! I go there every week, okay? Happy now? Every week, same time, and I hope and pray some girl comes in that I can talk to, who is understanding and patient. And she was. This Janet girl. She was friendly, chatty, we got on and so when we came back here and she said ... She said, 'God, not very big, are you,' then she giggled again, and the giggle became more of a laugh. She was laughing at *me* and I lost it and I hit her."

"More than once."

"Yes! I punched her, three times in the face, okay. I did, I did that. And she ran out and there was blood and she was crying and I felt bloody good about it."

Fallon's hands came down hard on the table, causing Emery to jump. "I'm nicking you, Fender, for grievous bodily harm." Fallon stood up. Fender was breathing hard, face contorting into a wild, mad look. "You don't have to say anything, but anything you do say may be used in evidence—"

"No!" roared Fender, "You can't do that! I've told you everything that happened. I didn't kill her, for god's sake! I gave her a slap and that was all."

"You can either come quietly," said Emery, standing up and producing a pair of handcuffs, "or not. It's up to you."

"Please. Listen, I've only just started a new job. If you arrest me, what am I supposed to do, eh?" Wringing his hands, the tears tumbled down his face. "Please. I never ... I never meant to hurt her, okay? It was just that she pushed the wrong buttons. I've got issues with my, you know, and her making those quips, well, they hurt. *Really* hurt. I'm not a violent man, not usually. I'm not."

"I want you to accompany us to the station, Mr Fender," said Fallon. "You can make a full statement there and then we'll decide what to do next. You can give Constable Emery here the telephone number of your employer and we'll explain the situation to them. Now, go and get dressed Mr Fender. And nothing stupid, mind. We have officers all around the building."

"Oh God."

"Exactly. Now, be a good lad, and get some clothes on."

"Listen, she said something, something else before she flew out of here."

"Another jibe?" asked Emery.

"No, a threat."

The two policemen folded their arms and stared. "A threat?"

"Yeah. She said she'd tell her boyfriend and he'd fucking kill me."

"Are you sure she said 'boyfriend'?"

"Of course I am. Why, what do you mean?"

"Never mind," said Fallon. He pointed to the untouched mugs of tea, "I'll get rid of those, you get your pants on."

A GIRL CALLED MELANIE

HE SAT ON AN OLD, worn-out bench, which sagged under his weight, gazing at the ripples moving over the surface of the lake. The bike stood propped up against a nearby wall, forgotten for the moment. Time had become meaningless. Craig didn't care. A slight disturbance at the back of his mind; concerns over Mum, what she might say if he rolled up late. Crossland and Samantha and their empty threats. He mulled over the window cleaner's words but all of these were only sporadic, fleeting thoughts, and he gave none of them any heed. Instead, the lake took his attention and he allowed himself to drift, not unlike the fallen leaves on the water. As he sank ever deeper into this state of near thoughtless meditation he failed to notice the figure looming up beside him until it spoke.

"Not playing tennis today?"

Craig jumped, turned, and looked up. For a second or two he thought he might have slipped into another dream, but this one so much better in every way. His heart juddered as if jolted by a surge of electricity. It was her, the girl from the tennis courts, and she was smiling at him. This close and so *real*, for a moment his tongue stuck to the roof of his mouth and the best he could do was gape.

She giggled and sat down next to him. "I've been watching you for a while," she said, eyes like lasers, penetrating, seeking out inner secrets. "If I could guess, I'd say you are worried about something." She stooped forward, picked up a pebble, and tossed it into the water. "Are you okay?"

Craig swallowed hard, not knowing what to say. Girls were an alien species, so how do you communicate with them? He longed to reach out, take hold of her hand, tell her everything, instead, he sat trembling, breathing in her perfume. The fresh, clean aroma of cucumber mingled with something else. Flowers or spices, he couldn't tell, he didn't care. Delicious, whatever it was. He shook his head, battling to find some words. Anything. "I'm Craig," he said at last.

She laughed, hand against her mouth. He gazed at the way her hair bounced around her shoulders, shining, reflecting the sunlight. And her face, smooth, skin like alabaster, perfect, no hint of a blemish, brimming with health. How old could she be? Fourteen, maybe fifteen?

"I'm sorry," she said through her laughter, "you must think I'm an awful cow." Another guffaw. She rocked forward, looked at him, spluttered, "You look so *shocked*." She took a few breaths and brought herself under control. "It's just that...well, you know. Craig? Is that all you have to say" She pulled out a tissue from her jeans pocket and wiped her eyes. "Sorry, but the way you said it, blurting it out like that." She shook her head, gave her eyes one more wipe, and put the tissue away. "Sorry."

Mesmerised, Craig took no notice of her words. For all he cared, she might have been reciting the English dictionary. Nothing else mattered except that delectable, lovely face of hers. He closed his eyes and breathed her in, tiny explosions going off across his body. Not in pain, but exhilaration, unlike anything he'd known. He wanted it to last forever, this feeling. Her. Time stretched out, a soft comforting blanket enfolding him, bringing him warmth, security.

"Look, I'm bothering you." She slapped her hand down onto his knee and stood up. "Sorry."

Craig's eyes sprang open, drinking her in. Those dark blue jeans, so tight. Probably *Wranglers*. She fitted them well, rounded hips straining against the material, legs long and slim. He felt the heat rising from under his collar. He swallowed.

"I'll, er..." She gave what looked like a forced smile and turned to go.

Craig's world snapped into focus at that point, and panic gripped him. She'd arrived without warning and he'd crumbled, not knowing what to say. A simple 'hello, lovely to see you again,' would have been enough. Instead, he'd made a total mess of it.

He watched her walking away and knew he must react. Gritting his teeth, he leapt up, a new determination giving him enough strength to call out, shocking himself, "Wait, don't go!"

He caught up to her, clutched her arm, turned her around, saw those big, baleful eyes, and melted. She held his gaze, waited. The seconds crawled by and he could feel his fledgling courage slipping away.

She came to his rescue then, those big eyes holding his, "You want to say something?"

He gulped. "I'm the sorry one," he said, voice tight, dry. "Not you. Me." He grinned, breath coming fast. "I'm really sorry."

A yawning chasm of silence followed. The evening sun played around with her hair, a golden haze backlighting her face. Birds sang, people walked by, but Craig cared for none of it, only the desire to be with her. "I'm an idiot," he managed at long last. "I meant to say 'hello', that was all."

"I didn't mean to laugh."

"I know, but...you surprised me."

"I guess so, yes. Sorry."

"You say that a lot." He smiled. So did she, and her entire face lit up. Craig's heart sang, then skipped a beat when he realised he still held her arm. He quickly let his hand fall away. She giggled. He liked the way she did that. "Can we, er, start again?"

She bit her lip. "You're not angry?"

"*Angry*? Why should I be angry?" He nodded back to the old bench. "Let's go and sit. Give it another try."

"Okay," she said, and they did.

Over an hour later, they were still there, talking and laughing. Her name was Melanie, she said and, after a little coaxing, revealed her age as fourteen. She seemed so grown-up, so wise and knowing, and yet so easy to talk to. Craig held nothing back, the floodgates opened. He told her about his life, his friends, what he liked doing, what he wanted to do after he left school. She listened, she commented. Not once did she seem bored, or irritated. When her own story came, her words sounded so sweet, lyrical even, as if she recited poetry or sang a song. Time disappeared, dusk giving way to night. Craig offered to walk her home, and she accepted.

He wheeled his bike beside her. They talked about the cinema and her favourite pop groups. He listened, logging it all away for future reference. He didn't so much walk as float.

At her front door, he waved to her in answer to her smile as she stepped into the hallway. After she had gone inside, he wanted to cartwheel all the way down the street. Instead, he rode home, twisting through the streets, veering left and right, his laughter ringing out across the night.

As he turned into his own road, grin as wide as the Mersey tunnel, he pulled the bike up short as a sudden thought smacked into him, almost causing him to lose his balance and fall over. He shook his head, ran a hand over his face. Of all the stupid, pathetic things to have done. "I really am an idiot," he groaned.

He'd forgotten to ask her when they could see one another again.

BUILDING THE PICTURE

"SHE'S DOING WELL, according to her tutors," said Emery, brandishing a slip of paper as if it were a trophy. "I've interviewed all of them, lecturers or whatever they're called. I've even interviewed receptionists."

"Was," said Fallon, pen poised above a piece of paper. Around them, the room buzzed with activity, people half-running, telephones blaring, and the thick pall of cigarette smoke everywhere.

"Eh?" Emery sat down, carefully pushing away a pile of tightly typed pages."

"You said she's doing well. She's not. Not anymore."

"Ah, yes. Sorry."

"She has no living relatives. Her mother and father died in a car crash over seven years ago. She had a brother, but he moved to New Zealand apparently. There's nobody else. Millie is the closest she had for family. Sad."

"So, who would kill her? And the way they did, with such violence?"

"Could be Fender. He's the obvious one. But there are no fingerprints connecting him to the scene. And there are plenty of fingerprints. She was wrapped up quickly and carelessly. The perpetrator wanted the body gone, out of sight, so he rushed it."

"So not Fender?"

"I doubt it. The bastard was crying like a little babe when I let him go. Millie came in, she didn't want to press charges about the assault. She's the only one who can."

"The only thing we know is that the killer may have had a dog. Seems strange though, doesn't it, to bring your dog to the scene."

"How do we know he had a dog?"

"Well, we've got witnesses, haven't we? The guys who discovered the body and the other one ..." Emery took out his notebook and leafed through the dog-eared pages. "The one me and Taylor interviewed ..." He ran his finger down the page he'd stopped at. "Howarth. David Howarth. He lives in Pelham Road. Ex-Military Police. His account of what he saw – and heard – was incredibly well detailed."

"Not unusual if he's an ex-copper."

"No, I suppose not."

"What do we know about him?"

"Who? Howarth? Not a lot. Basically what I've told you. Why, what are you thinking, boss?"

"I'm thinking we should go and talk to him."

"But he told us everything he knew. Boss, I checked his hands. They were clean. He hadn't just taken a dead body out of the boot of his car and rolled her into the canal."

"Maybe there were two of them. Think about it. She was tall and although she was slim, I'd say she was probably around one hundred and twenty pounds. A fair weight to lift on your own." Fallon reached behind him and tugged his raincoat from the back of his chair, "Let's go and have a little word shall we."

"He's not home," came a voice from behind them. Fallon and Emery turned to find a short, stout woman standing at the end of the path. Her enormous bosom strained against a white blouse, whilst a brightly patterned pinafore obscured the front of her skirt. Hair tied back in a bun, stockings around her ankles. Cigarette in her fist. She did not look happy.

Taking out his warrant card, Fallon approached

her. She didn't flicker. "Do you have any idea where he might be?"

"I haven't seen him for days."

"Is that unusual?" asked Emery.

"He keeps himself pretty much to himself, except when he's out on business or his lady friend calls. He's all bright and cheerful then, shouting across to my husband coming in from work, 'Evening mister Noble.' That's our name, you see. Noble."

Nodding, Fallon took a glance towards the bedroom window, hoping to see a face not unlike Howarth's peering down at them, but of course there was no one. "Where's the rear entrance?"

"Down there, to your left. There's an entry. Most of the back doors have the numbers on them. I'll show you if you like."

"That would be very kind," said Emery with a smile.

It wasn't returned.

She stopped outside number twelve and jutted her chin towards it. "That's his."

"Have you ever been inside his home?"

She gave Fallon a withering look. "Now why the bloody hell would I want to do that?"

"Only asking, Mrs Noble, is it?"

"It is. And no, I haven't."

"But you know he's away?"

"I'm only guessing. I haven't seen him."

"Nor his girlfriend?"

"Not since last week. She calls every Friday. Without fail."

"Every Friday?"

"Without fail."

"So, she was here last Friday?"

She sighed and, folding her arms, nodded towards the door again. "Aren't you going to try it?"

Grunting, Fallon did so and stopped.

The door opened.

The back garden was a mess. Clearly, Howarth was not a gardener. The lawn was overgrown and overtaken by weeds, choking the little path, which wound its way to the rear entrance. Fallon followed it as best he could, pausing only to peer through the grimy window of a small outhouse. Shaking his head, he continued towards the back kitchen. He tried the handle and again, the door opened. He looked at Emery over his shoulder.

"Stay here with Mrs Noble will you, Constable."

"Is that wise, boss? I mean, shouldn't we—"

"Just stay here," said Fallon and went inside.

The kitchen smelled strongly of fried onions

and, on the cooker, sat a blackened frying pan, the remnants of Howarth's last meal clinging tenaciously to the surface. Fallon touched the pieces of onion and found them to be soft. As he turned to move on, he noticed the half-full coffee cup. Folding his fingers around it, he gasped and something cold gripped his guts. The cup, in contrast, was warm.

Careful now, forcing himself to move slowly, he stepped into the hallway. Ahead was the front door. To his left the stairs leading to the bedrooms and on his right the doors to the front and back rooms. Both of these doors were open.

From where he stood, Fallon could quite clearly make out the two legs lying on the front room carpet. He rushed to where the man lay. Blood leaked from a deep wound in his head, and, pushing all thoughts of procedure aside in his desperation, Fallon felt for a pulse, found one, and immediately did his best to save the man's life, screaming, "*Emery, get in here now,*" as he worked on the chest.

Less than an hour later, the ambulance crew admitted Howarth to hospital. It was then a matter of waiting.

Emery took it upon himself to patrol the corridor, impatiently pacing up and down whilst behind closed doors the surgeons battled to save their only witness's life. Outside, Fallon stood staring at the grey sky, smoking. A gaggle of young nurses brushed past, heads together conspiratorially. He watched them, wishing he was twenty years younger. Perhaps even then he wouldn't have flashed them a smile, but at least he had his own teeth back then.

"Boss, the doctor's ready."

Throwing away his unfinished smoke, Fallon followed Emery into the depths of Victoria Hospital. Like so many people, Fallon hated hospitals, associating them with death. How many times had he confronted the final moments of someone, their life slipping away? His father was the last. Maybe his mother would be next. And witnesses too, victims, perpetrators. Too many.

"Thank you, Doctor," he said before the man in the white surgical coat said anything. They shook hands. "What can you tell us?"

The doctor was endlessly tall, a large head perched on narrow shoulders. Middle-aged, experienced, he appeared worn out, heavy black rings under his eyes. "He's strong, which is what probably saved him. But, he won't be able to answer any of your questions for at least two days, maybe longer. He's lost a lot of blood. But what you did, pressing that cushion against the wound, you probably saved his life."

"I was fortunate to be there at the right time," said Fallon, picking up Emery's big eyes staring directly at him. He shrugged. "Do you think there might be brain damage?"

"Too early to tell, but I'd have to say almost certainly. How extensive, we'll just have to wait and see. I picked a lot of bone fragments from his brain, Detective. A single blow, delivered with enormous power. I'm not a forensic scientist, but it's my opinion that his attacker was disturbed, which stopped whoever it was from delivering a second, lethal blow."

"Disturbed? In what way, in the head? Insane?"

"No, no, not that sort of …. No, I meant literally – whoever did this was interrupted. Another blow or two would have killed him, so he's lucky. True, he would have bled to death without your timely intervention, but I don't think a murderer would take the risk of him recovering."

"Yes, yes I've considered that. Perhaps he saw us coming or heard us, and made good his getaway before I entered the house. The coffee mug was still warm." He looked at Emery. "All right, thank you again, doctor. Two days. We'll hope for the best."

"That's all we can do, I'm afraid."

Another shake of the hand and Fallon left, with Emery next to him. Both stood outside the entrance. It was raining.

"You think that's right, boss? That the killer saw us and rushed off before he could finish him?"

"I reckon so."

"But we didn't see him. He must have moved fast."

"Do a sweep, house to house, see if anyone saw anything. Perhaps a neighbour was looking out of their window. We might strike lucky, and God knows we need it. I've worked on murders before, but nothing like this. No witnesses, no clues, no reason as far as we're aware."

"Perhaps Howarth knew his killer. Perhaps he was part of a team that murdered Janet."

"Possibly, and his partner got anxious about our interest, they argued, et cetera, but I'm not sure. It could be that the killer got wind of our investigation and followed Howarth intending to murder him as a sort of insurance policy, in case he remembered anything significant." He shook his head and lit up another cigarette. "We need to find his girlfriend. She visits every Friday that woman said, so we'll post a Bobby in the street from early Friday morning until such time as she calls. Then we'll bring her in and see what she knows."

"What if she doesn't show?"

"Then we're back to square one, aren't we?"

"Boss, Howarth is a big guy. Strong. Have you seen his hands? I wouldn't want to get into a ruck with him, so I think he must have known his killer. Unless he was a monster, I don't think he could have overpowered Howarth, and, to hit him from behind must mean Howarth felt secure enough to turn his back."

Fallon smiled. "Emery, you're enjoying this secondment, aren't you?"

Shifting his gaze, Emery shrugged. "To be honest, yes I am."

"How would you like to be permanently assigned to C.I.D.?"

Emery gaped at his superior. "Boss... I mean, *sir,* are you being serious?"

"I'll talk to the Super, if you like. You're doing all right, Constable. I like the way you think."

"Thank you very much, sir."

"If we crack this case, I think it'll be down to our teamwork more than anything else. I like bouncing ideas off you, keeps me focused." He pulled up his collar. "Now, let's go back to Pelham Road and interview that busybody of a woman again. I suspect she knows a great deal more about our Mr Howarth than she's let on so far."

THE BULLIES

CRAIG'S SENSE of guilt over what happened to his dad never left him. Sometimes, he would lie in his bed, racked with despair, crying silently to himself. Mum never knew, of course, because Craig never told her. How could he? If she knew the truth she would disown him, of that he was certain.

The months after it had happened crawled by and Craig somehow learned to cope, even though a single day did not pass without him thinking of his dad. The tiny photograph of his dad standing at the bus stop at the top of the street, stuck down on the wall with sticky tape, was his favourite, but every time he looked at it the tears would come.

Occasionally, when he felt strong enough, he'd stand in the garden shed, breathing in the scent of wood shavings, eyes roaming across the workbench,

Dad's tools still there as if he'd only just recently put them down. It was Dad's domain, every Saturday he'd be there, working away at something. If Craig closed his eyes and thought hard enough, he could believe his dad was there. But Dad was gone. Dead. He remained, however, the most wonderfully creative and skilful craftsman Craig had ever known.

That morning, Craig found himself at Billy Baxter's house. In something of a daze, thoughts clogged up with the past, he'd wandered aimlessly along the streets and now, here he was. He gave a little start when he became aware of where he was, Instantly, the window cleaner's words came back to him, causing him to question, to ponder. Why was Billy so angry? Was it because Craig had scaled the wall to his garden, or something else? Everything about that house, the garden, even the man himself seemed so sad. Something had happened to him, something massive, to make him so aggressive.

Confused, not understanding why he was there, he turned around to begin his return journey home when he saw him. Baxter. Stooping low in his front garden, he had not yet noticed Craig who quickly flattened himself against the adjacent wall. He waited, listening to the old man wheezing and puffing as he worked away. After a moment, Craig chanced another glance.

Baxter shuffled as if in pain, bent over, an old

man, wizened, joints already swollen, making the simple act of walking difficult. To underline his discomfort, he pressed the flat of his right hand against the small of his back. Craig, so close he could hear him breathing, close enough to see the scar running down the side of his face, a feature he hadn't noticed before.

Baxter stopped, a sixth sense perhaps causing him to turn. Their eyes locked on each other.

"You," was all he said, but it was enough, and Craig was running head down, not daring to glance back but hearing the words nevertheless, *"You come back here, you little swine! I'll bloody well murder you when I get my hands on you!"*

But he wouldn't be getting his hands on him today. No way. Craig ran, and the only thing on his mind was how Baxter's scar seemed to pulse as if it were alive.

He berated himself for ending up at Baxter's. He thought too much, dwelled on things he could not change, and unconsciously wandering to the old man's house was a mistake. It scared him a little, at how easy it was for him to wander off in his own head. All he'd accomplished was adding to Baxter's anger, his conviction that Craig was nothing more than a lout, a vandal, a 'little swine'.

He decided to go into town, do some window shopping. *Bookland* was the Mecca for his interests and he spent a lovely hour sifting through the novels on the shelves, promising himself he would buy one at the weekend, he spent what little money he had on a small paperback *Western*. A mere two-and-six, the story appealed and it was so short he could probably read it in an afternoon. Then, as he stepped outside he froze.

Three faces glared directly at him. Craig's stomach lurched, but he could not move, legs of lead, so heavy, they welded to the ground.

Adam Crossland stepped up close, all leery lopsided grin and blackened teeth. "Well, well, look who it is."

Craig measured him with his gaze. Samantha Lloyd, who stuck to Crossland like flypaper, lingered in the background with another boy called Keith Roberts. Craig thought Keith Roberts was all right and had never had any trouble with him, in school or out. Craig suspected that the only reason he hung around with the other two was because he fancied Samantha, like just about every other boy. She was no Melanie, but with her endless legs and those enormous eyes, she was irresistible. As he stared, she snarled, forcing Craig to look away.

"What you up to then, Craig?"

Samantha and Keith came up alongside Crossland. Samantha was smiling, without humour, mocking him. "Where's Raymond? Where's your boyfriend?"

Craig saw red, "Why can't you just shut your face, Lloyd!" he spat.

As quick as lightning, and without any warning, Crossland punched Craig in the stomach, folding him like a penknife. Clutching his abdomen, gasping for breath, Craig crumpled to his knees as he fought to swallow down the bile rising into his mouth. Through swirling mist, he felt, rather than saw, Samantha picking up the novel. "Ah, what's this? Playing cowboys and Indians, are we?"

Through his tear-filled eyes, Craig glared at his tormenters and croaked, "It's a novel, Samantha."

"Ooh," piped up Samantha, sounding smug, as if she had uncovered some terrible secret, "you like all that leather and rawhide do you, Craig? Does Raymond know? Does he dress up for you?"

They all laughed at that and Craig wanted to roll over and cry with the shame of it. He was alone, defenceless, no friends to help. All of it was his fault. The tears burned his eyes. He reached out to snatch back the paperback but before he could, Crossland gripped him by the collar and hauled him to his feet. "Help me with him, Keith, we're gonna have some fun with this little fella."

Still reeling from the blow, breathing proving difficult, strength nothing but a memory, Craig offered up no resistance. He surrendered, allowing the two boys to drag him along between them, whilst Samantha skipped in a circle, pretending to shoot them with a pretend six-gun, whooping and yelping at the top of her voice.

He sagged in their grip, feet trailing along the ground and, head snapping from side to side, he hoped to catch a friendly figure, a neighbour, anyone that might stop and intervene. But nobody did. The enormity of his hopelessness crushed him and, defeated, his chin fell to his chest.

They took Craig to the disused railway tracks that ran along the bottom of Craig's street. Well away from any prying eyes, they dragged him to the edge of the cutting, a drop of some twenty or so feet yawning below. They threw him to the dirt. Hitting the ground hard, Craig wheezed in a few breaths, flattened his palms against the hard, sandy soil, and tried to raise himself. Before he made a mere six inches, Crossland kicked him in the side, dumping him to the ground again to taste the dry soil. Craig writhed, spluttered, and whined whilst Samantha whooped with laughter and shot out taunts of, "Hit him harder, Crossie, hit him in the jacks! He's a weed, Crossie, a little baby weed." Her words hurt more than any blow. But he wasn't going to give any of them the satisfaction of seeing him cry. Suck it up, he told himself. Dad would want him to be brave, the window cleaner, Melanie…

He rolled over and saw, through blurred eyes, Keith standing a little way off, gnawing away at his fingernails, frightened and uncertain. Craig knew he wasn't like the others, so why didn't he speak out if he didn't want to be a part of this? A word, a gesture, anything to put a stop to what was going to happen.

What was going to happen soon became clear. Crossland pulled Craig to his feet wrenching his arm behind his back, roughly twisting it. A strangled cry, more struggling, all useless, Crossland too strong, too determined. He put his other arm around Craig's throat in a sort of wrestling hold and motioned Samantha over. Cackling with glee, she eagerly did Crossland's bidding and together they carried Craig to the edge of the cliff.

This was madness – were they going to throw him off the cliff edge? Too late he put up a desperate fight, his one free arm flaying wildly, kicking, twisting, yelling, "Let me go, let me go!"

Craig's tiny, pathetic voice brought nothing but further bouts of laughter from Crossland's mouth.

Enjoying himself, he hissed, "No chance of that, little Craig. All you got to do is plead for mercy. Beg us not to do it Craigy-boy. Beg for mercy!"

"Beg Craig," joined in Samantha, holding Craig firmly in her grip, her lips slack and wet, a thing possessed. "Beg, or we'll throw you over."

Tears sprang from Craig's eyes, more from frustration than fear. No matter how much he fought he could not break their grip. "You're mad you are, Crossland. Both of you are mad! *Let me go!*"

"Just say 'mercy'. Go on, say it." Crossland jarred Craig's arm further up his back. Pain, like a knife seared through him and he squealed. This was more than mad, this was a nightmare. Another jerk, and he felt his eyes roll up into his head. He was going to faint.

"Go on Craig," laughed Samantha, bringing her face close to his. "Just say the words." She put her lips tight against his ear, her voice soft, a mere whisper. "You know you want to, don't you? All of this will stop, if you just do as Crossy says. Do it for me, Craig. You can't say no to me, can you? I know you fancy me like mad, so if you say it, I might let you kiss me afterwards. You'd like that, wouldn't you, to kiss me? I know you would, so I'll let you. I'll let you kiss me, Craigy. So just say it..." She pulled her lips from his ear, her voice loud as a banshee as she shrieked, "Say *mercy*."

Craig wanted to, despite the pain. He wanted to do her bidding. Her voice, like that of an angel, a beautiful, kind angel. If only it was just her, he'd do it without any hesitation, the thought of obeying her, surrendering to her so delicious. God, those lips. He'll do it, he'll say whatever she wants. Anything. Anything for her …

But then he caught sight of Crossland, slavering like a demented wild thing, out of control. Craig snapped his face away, his resolve hardened. Squeezing his eyes shut he forced himself to remain quiet, determined not to give Crossland the satisfaction of watching him suffer.

"All right then, you little shit, over you go." Crossland rammed his knee into the small of Craig's back, forcing him to the ground. Pushed flat on his face into the broken, hard dirt, Craig's mouth filled up with soil. Coughing and gagging, he tried to turn over but, in a sudden flurry of violent moves, they lifted him. He saw Samantha in front, gripping his wrists, grinning, that lovely mouth no longer so lovely. A snarl. A rabid dog's snarl. Someone else, it had to be Crossland, taking him by the ankles. Craig felt his bowels move, the terror total. As the stink rose to his nostrils, the two bullies carried him to the cliff edge.

He saw it all mapped out before him in his mind's eye, their awful plan, but he dared not believe it. No one could do something like this – if they put him over the edge, he'd be killed. What was it, a twenty-foot drop? Thirty? This wasn't bullying, this was murder.

They upturned him onto his back. As he peered to the sky, their faces grinned down at him, jungle animals, savages. Samantha let go and suddenly, disorientated, Craig's view changed as a series of flashing images danced before his eyes. Crossland, it had to be him, holding his left ankle, dragged him closer to the edge, the tiny stones and jagged pieces of debris beneath him cutting and scratching at his back. Another hand, Samantha's, took the right ankle and they dangled Craig over the edge of the cliff, head first.

The world was upside down, his wits all over the place, a kaleidoscope of swirling hills and fields and sky. No, not sky, earth. Or something else. More rocks. Struggling to focus, he had no sense of anything, just an overriding sensation of total, absolute dread. The rush of blood to his head made him feel giddy and confused, concentration impossible, the one, dominant sensation the horrible sickly feeling building in the pit of his stomach. Distant voices called out, high-pitched, excited, but from where they came he had little idea. He saw the ground far below. The rocks, jagged, dangerous. He'd be amongst them soon, smashed to pieces, skull cracked open, his blood spewing out. Colours danced in front of his eyes, the pounding in his ears so loud. He tried lifting his hands, to wipe away the mist, ward off the dancing, throbbing light, do anything to get a clearer view or find some way of getting free, but he failed. He was moving. From side to side. Dear God, they were swinging him from left to right, his tormentors both cackling like the crazy, vicious monsters they were.

He knew the end was close, all strength and resistance draining away. Bile came into his throat, burning, making him cough uncontrollably. He retched, tears sprouting from eyes no longer able to see. He farted, loudly. The others screeched with maniacal glee. He felt the wetness in his pants, knew he'd pissed himself, and worse.

"Beg for mercy, you dirty little shit," screamed Crossland, a tightness in his voice. Frustration mixing with anger. *Do it or we'll drop you!*

But they didn't. They held him and Craig knew, through the clouds of fear invading his senses, that all he had to do was hold on. Dad would want him to hold on, to never surrender. Better to fall, to die amongst those rocks. Better that than to give into these fiends.

Unconsciousness beckoned. He was slipping down into a dark, fathomless tunnel and it felt so good, so warm and inviting. But then, as his mind lurched towards blackness, he was hauled upright. Dragging him away from the cliff edge, they left him in a heap on the ground. He lay gasping, forcing in great gulps of air, clawing at the earth, the earth he loved and never wanted to leave again. He was safe, the soft, moist soil between his fingers so good. He loved it, wanted to kiss it and stay there forever. Good, sweet earth. Never again would he take it for granted. Closing his eyes, he sobbed.

Something hard and heavy slammed into his ribs. Strong hands wrenched him onto his back and there was Crossland's face, lips drawn back over chipped and blackened teeth. If Craig thought this might be the end, he realised he was mistaken. This was just the precursor to another, perhaps even more terrifying round of torture. "I'm gonna make you suffer," growled Crossland before he drew back his fist ready to strike. Craig closed his eyes, held his breath, preparing for the blow to land.

"*That's enough,*" came a voice from somewhere nearby.

Everything stopped. Nobody moved. Nothing happened. Craig cautiously half-opened his one eye to see Crossland standing, turning to his left.

Cautiously, Craig sat upright and wiped the sweat and tears from his face, the fog clearing from his garbled mind. He dared not believe the trauma was ending. This was nothing but a pause, an interval before they hung him over the edge again. He shuddered, struggling to control his thoughts, to come up with a plan, a way of escape. As he trawled through his options, he became aware of the raised voices. An argument. Crossland and someone else. Craig shook away the last remnants of confusion and turned to look.

The other voice belonged to Keith. Keith, who had remained silent for so long, had, at last, let common decency take control. "No, enough is enough," he was saying, "and I'll not let you do this." He came into focus, pushing Crossland out of the way, stooped down and smiled down at Craig's. "Are you all right?"

"What d'you mean, is he all right?" Crossland's voice crackled in fury. Now it was his turn to push, and he knocked Keith aside. But Keith was not Craig. He was bigger, older, and when he stood up and planted his feet wide, it was clear that for him at least, the game had gone a step too far.

"I mean what I say, Crossland, this is stopping right now. You're a nutcase, you are. What do you want to do, *kill him?*"

"Maybe I do, yeah. I hate him and I'm going to make him suffer, so you'd better get out of the way before I knock your teeth out."

"Is that right? You can try it if you like, but you

won't find it so easy. I'm telling you now, before something awful happens, to let him go."

"You make me, you yellow-belly."

For a second or two, nothing happened, and then Keith charged, head down, straight into Crossland's guts. The two of them smashed into the dirt, grappling in a mad tangle of arms and legs, trying to gain the advantage, to get on top of the other. Samantha was beside herself, jumping up and down, whooping with glee, shooting them with fingers and thumbs. "Smash him, Crossie!" she shrieked, possessed with some uncontrollable lust for more violence.

Craig watched open-mouthed. The two boys seemed about equal in strength and skill, first Crossland getting the upper hand, then Keith. Fists cracked against bone and flesh, but neither gave way. Craig looked at Samantha's macabre dance. She was consumed by what she saw and, checking for an escape route, he took his chance and ran.

He had no idea where he was going, he just knew he had to get away. Not looking back, he paid no heed to the shouts and cries behind him, pumping his arms and legs as fast as he could, He bounded over rocky outcrops, leapt over gorse bushes, and scrambled between tiny pathways, not slowing down despite his lungs screaming, fit to burst. He put as much distance as he could between himself and the living nightmare behind him.

He reached a high hedge, a sort of natural barrier between the broken ground where his nightmare played out and another, probably private area. Without pausing, he pushed through, not caring if sharp, twisted branches scratched and cut across his arms and cheek. And then, suddenly, he stumbled free and stopped, hands on hips, breathless, a stitch in his side.

He stood on the fringes of some sort of enclosed garden. No, more than a garden, an allotment, garden sheds and greenhouses, well-manicured plots of land over-laden with a myriad of green plants. Cabbages, broccoli, lettuce, perhaps potatoes and carrots too. Craig scanned the view, seeking out a possible escape route. At any moment Crossland could be on him again and everything would start up where it left off.

Over to his right, some men were digging. He dismissed the notion of asking for their help, set his eyes straight ahead, and took a few uncertain steps.

A man shouted to him to stop, to hold up. He ignored him, he had to. Crossland must have overcome Keith by now, would soon be renewing the hunt. With time pressing, Craig continued, ignoring further shouts, and spotted a gate ahead. Reaching it, he fumbled with the latch, hands shaking, sweat dripping into his eyes. He had to get away. If Crossland arrived, anything might happen ...

He clawed open the latch, and made his way down a set of stone steps, steps he recognised and his heart sang with the knowledge. They led to the bowling green which was part of the social club at the bottom of his street. The social club of which Dad was once a member. It was always busy, busy with people enjoying their afternoons playing bowls. Someone there might recognise him, protect him from Crossland.

Images of the bully's gloating face, of what had happened, caused Craig's strength to drain away. His legs buckled under him and he reached out to cling onto the rusted handrail. He couldn't manage another step. He'd run faster than he ever believed possible, adrenalin giving him the powers of an Olympic athlete, but now he felt drained. The realisation he was so close to safety washed over him, and he crumpled, sat on a step and gave up a silent prayer of thanks.

He sat there for a long time, not daring to move. He stank, he knew that. The shame of soiling himself welled up, to mingle with the stench of faeces and urine. What they'd done to him, what they'd forced him to endure was beyond anything he could ever have imagined. How was he supposed to move on from this? When Ray asked him what he'd done that day, what should he say? How to retell the story without making himself out to be such a … Such a what, a coward? He'd stood up to them, hadn't he? But the truth of it was he hadn't fought back. Not once. He'd shit himself with fear. Nobody else would have allowed themselves to do that. Not Ray, not the window cleaner, not Melanie. Dear God, what was he supposed to say to her?

Shaking, he stood up and made his way down the steps, taking them one at a time, afraid he might slip. Reaching the door at the foot of the steps, he pushed it open and walked on. His eyes blurred, lungs screamed, but his head gave him most concern. It was as if someone had stuffed it full of cotton wool, a thick, muffled feeling pressing in on his senses, pressure building in his ears. He needed to stop and gather his wits, regain some strength. He made for a nearby bench and flopped down, bent himself double, took deep breaths, and struggled against the urge to vomit.

A hand came down on his shoulder and he jerked upright. A man's concerned face, a face he thought he knew but couldn't place. He couldn't remember anything. Only Crossland, and what he'd done. "Are you all right, sonny?" the man asked, voice hollow as if he were talking from the far end of a long, dark tunnel. Craig tried to search for the words to explain, but they would not form. Nothing worked. He no longer listened, no longer cared. All he wanted was to go down that tunnel, follow the voice into the warm blackness. The silence. It all seemed so wonderful.

So, he allowed himself to slide, and it felt glorious.

He was unconscious.

CONFESSIONS

HE BLINKED his eyes open several times, wincing at the light, and slowly his surroundings came into focus. The smell hit him first; not a nasty smell but comforting, the warm, rich aroma of hay and sweet compost. He looked around. A small room, wooden walls, every available space filled with gardening implements of one type or another. Through a grimy window, sunlight struggled to filter through. But the thing that took all his thoughts was the pain, all down his side, and slowly, piece by piece, everything fell into place. The memory. The shame.

Someone had draped a rough brown blanket over him and he realised, with a start, that he was naked beneath it. Was this another bout of sadistic torture conjured up by Crossland and his acolytes?

With renewed panic gripping him, Craig sat bolt upright.

A heavy hand came down on his shoulder. And the voice. As before, kind, quiet, concerned. "It's all right, son, you're quite safe."

Craig stared. Silhouetted by the light from the window, the shape of a man. And others, bunching up close. Three men, all dressed in identical dark blue overalls, check shirts and caps, faces etched with worry. The first man moved away from the light and Craig saw his face, recognised it, and felt his testicles clench with a new level of fear.

It was Billy Baxter.

Cocking his head, frown deep, he studied Craig for a long time. "I wasn't sure before, but now I see your face ... I know you, don't I?"

Struggling to remain calm, Craig shook his head. For a long drawn-out moment, Baxter stared before drawing in a sharp breath. "I'm not sure ..."

Another cleared his throat. "Who is it, Billy? Do you know him?"

Baxter shook his head but didn't seem convinced. Something akin to a smile developed along his mouth. "You've had a bit of a shock," he said. He didn't sound angry. He should have done, thought Craig, if he realised who this dirty, terrified boy was. Was his concern a sham, a piece of play-acting for the benefit of the others? Or a trick, to put Craig off his guard? For now, those eyes, so worried, soft, with no anger, gazed down at him. Every few seconds, a tick played in the corner of his eye as if he struggled with something, and this worried Craig. Perhaps he was beginning to remember. Craig forced a smile of his own. "I'm okay," he said. "Where am I?"

The three men filled the cramped shed, their size intimidating, but Baxter most of all. Given what he had gone through with Crossland, Craig should have felt secure and safe. He didn't. He knew only one thing – he had to get out, get out into the air, as far away from this place as possible. Crossland would be about, searching, intent on revisiting upon Craig all the horrors of being tipped over the cliff edge once again, but that seemed as nothing compared to what he knew Billy Baxter would do when the truth finally dawned on him. Would the others step in, ask questions? *Why was he here, what was he trying to do, what did he want?* The next step, to call the police? Craig had trespassed after all. It was a total mess.

Too many thoughts and images flew around for him to think coherently. He rubbed his eyes and sniffed. "I want to go home," he said, voice small, scared.

"Of course you do," one of the others. A big, friendly giant. "Here, try and drink some of this. It's hot, sweet tea. It'll help you get your strength back."

"You've had a rough time," said another.

"Those others was it?" the big man asked. "Two boys and a girl? They came running in here like a pack of wild dogs. Been fighting too, by the look of them."

"Little one had a bloody nose," said Baxter, who never took his eyes off Craig, studying him.

Craig nodded his thanks and sipped at the scalding brew. Refreshing him almost instantly, he grinned and took a bigger mouthful.

"Did you do that to him did you?" the big man asked. "Did you punch him?"

Craig shook his head, "No, they had a fight between themselves."

"Why was that then?" Baxter put his hands on his hips, his expression beginning to change. "You've got a few bumps and bruises yourself. Were you a part of their gang? What were you all doing up here, in our allotment?"

Craig caught the sharpness in Baxter's voice. The atmosphere became charged, all too fast and all too readily from compassionate to abrasive. Craig didn't like it. His feeling of being trapped grew more intense.

"Why did you come in here?" The accusing tone, growing stronger, Baxter's face took on a dark look. The eyes narrowed, the mouth becoming a thin, cruel line.

The others seemed to sense Craig's discomfort and the third piped up, "Now then, Billy, take it easy on the lad. You can see he was not part of any gang. He's only a little fella." The man smiled towards Craig. "I reckon they was chasin' you, isn't that right, lad?"

Craig nodded, watching Baxter over the rim of his mug as he took a longer sip. He could see the burning intensity in the man's eyes, Baxter's memory growing clearer.

Chuckling, the big man put a large hand on Craig's shoulder. "There, you see, I told you it would be something like that, Billy. What were they doing to you, lad? Hurting you?"

"They were holding me over the cliff. By my feet."

A sudden, shocked silence followed. The second man cursed under his breath as the big one stood up to his full height, face twisted into a cruel scowl. "The little...I can't believe anyone could do such a thing! Are you sure you're all right? Listen, we knew something bad had happened. We took off your clothes and it was obvious... Well, we couldn't leave you in that state. Don't worry, we've put them in a bag so your mum can wash them when you get home. We'll lend you something for you to wear when you—"

Baxter's harsh voice cut in, "Why would they do that?"

Craig looked at him. If Baxter did recognise him, that would explain everything. His change of mood, his suspicions, looking for the bad in people, no matter who.

"Perhaps it was their way of having fun," suggested the other.

Craig swallowed hard. "Yes, yes it was. Because..." He struggled to find the words, to try and make sense of what happened, not only to the men but to himself. He pulled in a breath, "Because they just did. They're bullies, mister. And bullies like to hurt you."

The same man went to speak again, but Baxter gripped his arm, cutting him off before he could speak, and leaned forward, face so red Craig thought it might explode. "I remember you now! It's all coming back to me – you were in my garden." Baxter glared, eyes bulging, teeth gnashing as the spittle frothed from his mouth. "It *was* you, wasn't it? You're the one who broke into my bloody garden, you little shit."

The other man tugged free his arm. "Here, hold on Billy, no need to talk to the lad like that. He's clearly had a dreadful shock and he needs to go home."

"I'll help him on his way," said the big man. "You

123

back off, Billy. He's terrified and he's been through enough."

"Like bloody hell," roared Baxter, a rabid dog now, hackles rising. He waved a clenched fist in front of Craig's face, his temperament changing in an instant. "You're here to steal again, I know it."

"I'm not," said Craig, flinching away from Baxter's distorted face and threatening gestures, "I swear to God I'm not."

"I'll bloody well make you wish you'd never been born," and the fist came back in readiness.

The big man was there first, grabbing Baxter's arm and swinging him around to face him. "I said *enough*, Billy." The words were delivered calmly, in a low, controlled voice, but the threat lurked at the edges.

Body trembling, Baxter stepped away, sullen, defeated whilst the big one looked at Craig once again. That smile returned. "Come on, lad, drink your tea and I'll walk you home. Do you live far?"

Craig shook his head. His eyes met Baxter's. "I'm sorry about going into your garden," he said in a small voice, "I was only trying to get my ball back."

"Well, why didn't you knock on the door?"

"Come on, Billy, I've asked you – not now."

"Just hold on a minute, Bob," spat Baxter, scowling at the big man, the one Baxter called Bob. He swung his glare back to Craig. "I reckon they put you up to it, that lot that had you by your feet. They put you up to coming into my garden, as some sort of dare or something, and you failed, so this was payback. That's why they did what they did, isn't it? As a punishment."

"It wasn't like that, I—"

"What was it they wanted you to do? Eh? Break into my house? Steal something from me?"

"Billy, leave it now. You can see he's not thinking straight."

"You mind your own damned business Bob Bewdsley. You don't have to suffer these little tykes kicking their ball against your living room wall every minute of every blasted day. Have you any idea what it's like, trying to sit down to read the paper having that damned thing slamming against the wall, time after time after time? Have you? No, of course you haven't, because you live up on Cliff Road and they don't play up on Cliff Road, do they."

"Billy, he's only a kid."

"Stuff you, Bob. I've had enough and I'm going to teach him a bloody lesson."

"No you're not," said Bob, facing Baxter again, dwarfing him, "If what he says is true – which I think it is given the state of him – he needs to be at home, resting. So what if he went into your precious garden, the garden you couldn't give two figs about?

Eh? That gives you no right to talk to him like this, no right at all. He's a kid."

"Get off your high horse, Bewdsley. You may think you know it all, but you don't."

"Come on you two," said the other man, stepping between them. Let's just get the lad home, yes? He's had a hard time and he doesn't need any of this. Look at him, he's terrified."

"I couldn't care less if he was the Prince of bloody Wales. He has no right to ruin my life." Baxter turned his blazing eyes towards Craig. His mouth opened in a vicious snarl and he was about to say something more when he stopped.

They all stopped.

Reeling backwards, the words slapping across his face like blows, Craig crumpled, head in hands, and broke down in tears.

"You mustn't pay any attention to him, lad," said Bob Bewdsley as they tramped up the hill towards Craig's home.

The tears no longer streamed down Craig's cheeks, but inside his stomach twisted and squeezed, making him feel weak and uncertain. "I didn't do anything bad," he said, his voice shaking. "I just went to get the ball back."

"Yes, I know that lad."

"I kicked the ball over his wall, you see. I didn't mean to, but the others, well, they told me I had to go and get it back. And his backyard door was locked, so I had to..." He sniffed, and Bob handed him a ragged handkerchief. He dabbed at his eyes. "I wouldn't have done those things Mr Baxter said. I wouldn't have stolen anything, honest."

Bob came to a stop at the end of Station Road. He looked across the road to Holden's corner shop, reached inside his pocket and brought out a two-shilling coin. "Go and buy yourself an ice cream, lad. Or a drink. It'll make you feel better." He pressed the coin into Craig's hand and smiled.

Staring at the coin, Craig shook his head. "No, no, it's all right, I can't take your money, mister."

But Bob simply smiled that gentle smile, "Of course you can. You go and get yourself an ice cream and then I'll tell you something about Billy Baxter that might help you make some sense of all this."

Inside the shop, alone at last, Craig moved slowly towards the counter. Mrs Holden was sat on a wooden stool, engrossed in a copy of 'My Weekly'. Standing watching her, Craig did his best to fit the pieces together. Bob Bewdsley was Ray's dad. Had to be. He lived in Cliff Road, as did Ray, and hadn't Ray mentioned that his dad's name was Bob? He was sure of it. He scrolled through his memory, searching to pick out what Ray had told him some years ago as they sat on a park seat near the lake.

"We went to Conway last summer," Ray was telling him, "and me da took us to the castle. Ever been to the castle?" Craig had shook his head. Holidays or visits held no interest for him anymore so he stayed silent, swallowing down thoughts of his own dad. "It's brilliant. Da says he's going to make me a castle. Yours made you a sword didn't he?" Craig nodded without looking at his friend. "Thought so. My da made me one and now he'll make a castle and it'll be brilliant. Me da can make anything. When it's finished, you can come round ... but only when me da is not there. He doesn't like visitors." Craig looked up for the first time, fixing Ray with a quizzical look. "Me mam says it's because of what he did in the war. He doesn't like noise. I heard her say, 'Oh Bob, one day it'll be all right,' but I don't think he heard her because me mam, she's got a funny accent. Me mam's nice, but me da ... Well, I can always bring the castle to you because he'll make it in pieces. He showed me the plan in 'Homemaker' magazine."

"Are you wanting something?"

Craig snapped his head up, Mrs Holden's voice bringing him back to the present. Smiling, he ordered an ice cream.

So yes, Ray's dad's first name was Bob. But he

wasn't a Bewdsley. Couldn't be. Silly thought. It was weird though, something of a coincidence to have two Bobs in one small street. On balance, that's all it could be, a coincidence because Bob Bewdsley was nothing like Ray's dad. Bob Bewdsley was all right with noise. Of course, he was!

They sat on a bench at the start of the strip of grass that ran along the outside of Hillbank playing field. Craig ate his ice cream whilst Bob stretched his long legs, waiting quietly for the right moment to speak. As the last piece of ice cream cone disappeared into Craig's mouth, Bob asked, "I'm not sure how much you know about Billy Baxter?" Craig shrugged. "That's answer enough, and I wouldn't expect anything else."

"I know he scares me."

"He scares a lot of people."

"You? Does he scare you?"

Bob smiled. "We go back a long way, me and Billy."

Craig liked Bob. Trusted him. He was a kind man, one of the few grown-ups he knew who was willing to listen. He felt he could tell him anything. Almost anything. He cleared his throat, "That doesn't answer my question. Bob."

A cackle of laughter. "No, I suppose not. He's difficult to get to know, but I know him well, and no, he doesn't scare me. He's a loner. Not many people talk to him or care to for that matter. Stan – that was the other bloke in the shed back there – well, him and me we just say hello to Billy every now and again when we happen to be up at the allotments together. Even though I've known him since forever, apart from our interests in gardening, we rarely speak." He folded his arms across his chest, "No one *really* knows him. He was in the war, had some terrible experiences by all accounts. He never talks about it, but rumour has it that something bad happened to him over in France. When he came back, he got married, to his childhood sweetheart. Then… No one knows exactly what happened, but we suspect that he told her."

"Told her? Told her what?"

"About what happened over there. Soon afterwards she left him."

"You're joking?" Craig felt his eyes widen. "What, she left because of what he did in the War?"

"Seems like, although no one actually *knows*."

"Can't you ask her, his wife I mean?"

"Ex-wife. No, no one can, because she's left. Left the town. Gone to London, working in the Civil Service down there, so people say."

Sitting forward, hands clasped on his knees,

Craig stared at the grass. "It must have been bad. What he did."

"Aye, I think it must have been. Bad enough for her to have left him anyway. After that, he sort of went to pieces. Got drunk, got into fights, arrested a few times. Then he lost his job. This would be ... ooh, Nineteen-Fifty I think. Not sure, exactly when, but around that time."

"But that's eighteen years ago. He's still angry?"

"I don't suppose it would matter if it was seventy years ago. Some things don't ever heal, lad."

"But..." Craig shook his head. Despite doing his best to decipher this new information he wasn't doing well. "The way he is, bent over like an old man, that's because of what he did back then? He can't be *that* old, can he? I mean, the War? How old would he have been then? Twenty-five? Thirty? He looks the same age as..." Craig screwed up his mouth, feeling awkward. Had he gone too far? There was a fine line between being friendly and overly familiar – even rude. "Sorry, I didn't mean ..."

"You mean, me and Stan?" Bob laughed, "Aye, well, Billy Baxter looks as old as Stan, who is almost seventy, that's for sure. The truth is, he's only fifty-two or three is Billy Baxter."

Fifty three? An old age for sure, Craig thought, but not an old man. Fifty-three ... Uncle Eric, his mum's brother, was fifty and he didn't look as old as Billy Baxter did.

Bob broke into Craig's thoughts. "The sad truth is he's ill. Very ill."

"You mean, seriously sick with something?"

"Aye. He's got a thing called angina." Craig frowned. "Bad heart," explained Bob. "Too much smoking and too much drinking. The man's digging himself an early grave."

"Why doesn't he stop?"

"Because he doesn't care. He's got nothing to live for, so he just keeps on punishing himself. The strain of what happened has taken its toll. I think the real cause of all of this is guilt. Guilt at what he did."

Craig chewed away on this thought but couldn't think of anything that was so bad that you would simply give up on life. At no point did he ever contemplate such a thing, despite what happened with Dad. Depression, guilt, yes, but never wanting to end it all. What Baxter did was way beyond imaginings. It made Craig's own feelings of guilt over what *he* had done seem trivial by comparison. "It must have been terrible what he did, don't you think?"

"Aye, I do. He never speaks of it. Never. I doubt he ever will because whenever anyone tries to coax something out of him, he simply clams up." Bob shook his head, resigned. "No, he's a man who is lost. Lost in his own despair."

INTERVIEWS

WHILST A TEAM of officers went from house to house, Fallon sat in Mrs Noble's living room, drinking tea, waiting patiently for her to return with the promised plate of biscuits. She appeared slightly more spruced up than last time. For one thing, her stockings were no longer bunched around her ankles. In a fair light and with the help of a few double whiskies, Fallon thought she might pass as attractive. But then, as she sat opposite and smiled, he put such an idea aside. Putting down his cup, he helped himself to a biscuit and produced a postcard-size photograph. "The girl that visited Mr Howarth. Is this her?"

Adjusting her skirt, Mrs Noble leaned forward, took the photograph, her fingers brushing Fallon's for a second more than necessary, and studied the image with genuine interest. "No. Is this recent?"

"It's a photograph of Janet Stowe, the girl found murdered some days ago. As far as we know, it was taken at the start of her studies."

"She's too young. The woman who came most Fridays was older, more mature." She cocked her head, sucking in her bottom lip, concentrating. "Definitely not her. The other one, she ... Well, she was more like one of them hippy types. Bows in her hair, that sort of thing. Not like this girl, with her trim little blouse and neat hair."

Grunting, Fallon took the photograph back and held it in his forefinger and thumb. "Hippy type?"

"Yes. You know what I mean, colourful, mismatched clothes and..." She stopped when Fallon produced a second photograph, a group of girls this time, all eager smiles and one of them giving a 'V' peace sign.

"This is Janet with some of her college friends. They all started the course together ..."

Frowning, Mrs Noble drew this second photograph closer, studying it carefully. "It's difficult to make out, but ..." Pressing her lips together, eyes hovering over each of the six girls standing side by side on a manicured lawn, she shook her head. "It's difficult."

"Yes, well, I do understand, Mrs Noble, but if there is anything else you can tell me about this woman visitor – what time she arrived, how long she stayed. Did Mr Howarth ever mention her, perhaps?"

"We rarely spoke, Inspector. A brief 'good morning' every so often. He was a private man."

"And yet you seem to know a fair bit about whom he entertained."

"Well, he made no secret of it. He'd come running down the path, hugging her, lifting her off her feet, and her squealing and giggling like a little schoolgirl. I remember she had bright red hair, dyed of course. You could tell. *I* certainly could."

"Anything else? You said she wore a mismatch of clothes?"

"Big, flowery skirts and frilly blouses. The sort students wear."

"So," he gestured towards the photograph she still held between her fingers, "she could have been one of these girls?"

"Perhaps, but it's not very clear." She held out her hand and studied the photograph again, taking more time. "I'm not certain, but …" She tapped one of the girls. "It *might* be this one. She hasn't got red hair here. Mousy. But, she certainly seems familiar."

Fallon moved closer. "This one?" He pointed to the image she indicated and she nodded. It was the girl making the 'V' sign. He took the photograph and returned it to his pocket. "Thank you very much, Mrs Noble. You have been a great help."

"I don't see how Inspector. I haven't told you very much at all."

"On the contrary, Mrs Noble, you have told me a great deal."

She did not appear convinced. At the front door, she smiled. Fallon shook her hand and went outside. As the front door closed behind him, he stood, heart pounding and adjusted his collar as heat rose to his cheeks.

The girl Mrs Noble recognised was Millie, Janet Stowe's flatmate.

Back at the station, Fallon threw his raincoat over his chair, patted through his pockets for his cigarettes and sighed. "Stan, give us a fag, would you?"

A pasty-faced man busy battling with an old Olivetti typewriter tutted and threw him a carton of Benson and Hedges. Fallon took one and was about to light it when Emery came bounding up to him, red-faced, breathing hard.

"Did as you said, boss. Got some interesting bits and pieces."

"Then bloody well tell me," snapped Fallon, lit

his cigarette and slipped the carton into his jacket pocket.

Pulling out his notebook, Emery quickly found the relevant page. "Her name, in the University records, is Clovis, but her *real* name is Baxter."

"Why did she change it?"

"Don't know. She said she didn't have to tell me, that it was her business."

"Seems a bit defensive."

"Oh, she was much more than that, boss. She wanted to know what the 'bloody hell are you doing snooping around about me for'," Emery's weirdly exaggerated impersonation of the girl's voice brought a smile to Fallon's face, "so I just left it at that. She's what you might call a man-hater, boss."

Fallon collapsed into his chair. "All right. So, she visits Howarth every Friday, she's changed her name, and her lesbian lover was Janet Stowe."

"She likes it both ways."

"Did she tell you that?"

"No. I just—"

"Well, don't *just* anything. There could be any number of reasons why she visited Howarth. We'll go and see her again, the both of us this time, and if she starts getting shirty, we'll bring her in. In the meantime, have a look through the electoral roll for anybody named Baxter in the local area. It's a bit of a long shot, but you never know."

"Will do boss."

"Hey boss," came a voice from across the room. Fallon turned towards it. Stan pulled a face, "Finished with those fags?"

"Fags?" Fallon drew on his smoke then studied the glowing end, "Barely started, mate. Barely started."

UNLOOKED FOR CONFRONTATION

THAT WEDNESDAY, Craig, his mum and Aunty Ida, took the bus down to Park Station where they caught the train to Liverpool. Something of a weekly ritual, Craig immersed himself in the atmosphere of Central Station, the noise of the great locomotives filling the air, billowing gouts of smoke spiralling upwards to the blackened roof. He recalled the last journey his family made down to Conway. The hubbub of people as they milled about, expectation and excitement crackling in every outburst of laughter, children giggling, running between stressed-out parents, laden down with luggage. Whistles shrilled, loud rasps of steam from funnels and between the great wheels heralding the initial grind of wheels on tracks as locomotives eased away from the platform, soon picking up speed towards the valleys and mountains of Wales. Dad was with them on that last journey, a journey from which he'd never returned.

After lunch at the *Kardomah,* as a reward for his patience, Craig was allowed some precious moments in *The Hobby Shop* and the model railways displays upstairs, but all too soon, Mum appeared at his shoulder. "Come on, we have to go."

"Mum," he said distantly, "do you think I could go round to Uncle Eric's one day soon? Talk to him about model trains and stuff?"

"I don't see why not, but I'm not sure if he's into all that model business anymore."

"Oh. I just wanted to ask him for some advice, that's all."

"Advice?"

Ignoring her, Craig stared in awed silence at the sections of beautiful train layouts displayed in large wall cabinets. Dreams took over his thoughts, dreams of rolling hills and winding tracks, of model locomotives chugging through the wonder of a tiny world he had created. If only it could become a reality.

He didn't emerge from his dreams until his mum's voice shouted, "Bye Ida, see you next week," and he found himself standing on a street corner just minutes from his home. He had no recollection of the journey home.

The first indication he had of the man's approach was when he barked, like an angry dog, from the opposite pavement. "Excuse me, madam, I'd like a word with you!"

He crossed the road, pulling a small, wiry terrier behind him. "Oh God," groaned Craig.

Billy Baxter, out of breath, glared as the dog ran around everybody's heels, tail thrashing into shins. Mum bristled. "Can I help you?"

Baxter twisted his face into a scowl. "This one broke into my garden, climbed over the wall, upset my dog, then yesterday, I caught him in my allotment, up to more mischief, and when I confronted him he came up with some cock-and-bull story about bullies chasing him. Said the same thing about him breaking in, lying about others *forcing* him. I've had enough, and I'm *warning* you that if you don't keep him under control, I'll inform the police. That is if you can control him. Is he even yours?

"How dare you accost me in the street," shouted Craig's mum, face turning a deep puce colour. "I've a good mind to call the police myself."

"Good, I wish you would, then this little so-and-so would get what's coming to him."

"I didn't break into his garden, Mum," Craig interjected, his own anger rising.

"You know damned well you did, you little liar."

"*Excuse me!*" erupted Craig's mum, face scarlet, eyes bulging. "If my son says he didn't break into your garden, then he didn't break in. You need to go and blow off steam in the pub, which is probably where you've been most of the day anyway if the stink of your breath is anything to go by."

"How dare you!"

"How dare *I*?" She jabbed a rigid finger at him, "I don't know what your problem is, but my son is not a thief, burglar or anything else you want to label him as."

"Then what was he doing in my garden?"

"I told you," said Craig. "I was looking for the ball I kicked over your wall."

"Likely story."

"Likely or not," said Craig's mum, "if he says that was what he was doing, then I believe him. So should you and not be so quick to judge."

Chest heaving, she pulled Craig away and marched down the road. Craig shot Baxter, who stood face ashen, lips a curious blue colour, a glance. "I think he's ill, Mum."

"I couldn't give a tuppeny damn if he was about to drop dead – horrible little man that he is." At the *Boot Inn,* she swung Craig around to face her. "How do you know that man?"

"I don't know him, all I did was kick a ball over

his garden, *by accident*. He's a nutcase, shouting and screaming the way he did."

"And what about that business at the allotments?"

Looking away, Craig fought down the urge to flee. How to tell her the whole story of what Crossland did to him? The humiliation, the admittance of fear... He took a breath and let it all come out in a rush. "We were playing, down at the railway cutting, and some boys came, and they weren't nice, and I had to get away because I didn't feel good about it. I just ran and I didn't know where I was, and before I knew where I was, I'd run across his allotment and Baxter shouted at me and that's all. I promise."

His mum looked at him. "You didn't break anything? Any of his flowers or vegetables? Nothing at all?"

"No, Mum! I was lost and I ran through into his allotment by accident. That was it. I just wanted to get away from those boys, but he thought I'd done it all on purpose. He's just a nasty, mean old man."

"Mmm ... He's not *that* old, but he certainly is mean and nasty, Billy Baxter is."

Craig gaped. "You know him?"

"I know *of* him. You're not the first to have had their fur singed by Billy Baxter, and you probably won't be the last. Come on, let's get home and you can read your new book."

"And Uncle Eric? You'll talk to him?"

She shook her head. "How do you manage it, eh, you young people? How do you put things straight out of your minds so quickly? Didn't you hear any of the things Billy Baxter called you?" The anger left her voice as she ruffled Craig's hair. "Yes, all right, I'll talk to your Uncle Eric, don't worry."

As they resumed their walk back home, Craig couldn't help turning his mind to the many questions he had about Billy Baxter – his bitterness and anger, so chewed up inside over what had he done back in the War, so terrible that it could turn him into such a vicious, uncaring old sod.

MORE BLOOD

BEFORE VISITING Millie for another interview, the two police officers took a diversion to Victoria Central Hospital in response to a call from the doctor dealing with David Howarth. In the corridor outside the ward, they met and spoke.

Emery couldn't keep the impatience out of his voice: "He's awake?" Fallon tutted and shot him an annoyed look.

"He came around about two hours ago," said the surgeon, "sitting up to tell us he was hungry." He laughed. "He said he needed a bath, so he went and had one."

Fallon piped up before his overly eager assistant could ask anything more, "Can we talk with him?"

"You can try, but I'm not so sure you will get that much out of him."

"Oh? Why not?"

A shake of the head. "I said there might be some brain damage. I was right. It's his memory. It's gone."

"Gone?"

"He doesn't even remember his own name."

Deflated, they later left the hospital and drove across the peninsula to Millie's flat. Neither spoke. They'd tried. Calm, patient, voices low, reassuring, but there were no responses, just a glazed look in Howarth's eyes, a lop-sided grin. No recollection. Nothing at all.

Emery parked the car and switched off the engine. Without turning, he said, "What do we do now, boss? Millie's not going to be very forthcoming, is she? And without Howarth's evidence ..." He let his words filter away. Outside, cars drove past, tyres slushing through the puddles left by the recent rain. Large Edwardian semi-detached houses lined the street, rooms converted into bed-sits, populated with students, grim and grey net curtains hiding what went on inside. Fallon shuddered. "This is an alien world for me," he said, staring through the window, putting off going inside for as long as he could. "Students. Education. Not things I know a good deal about."

"Well somebody does, boss. Somebody knows enough about it all to murder Janet Stowe."

"That's not quite what I'm getting at, but ..."

Turning, Fallon stared grimly at his younger colleague. "You think that might be the reason she died because she's a student?"

"Not necessarily, but there could be a link. A jilted lecturer perhaps? A horny student buddy who got mad about being rejected?"

Unconvinced, Fallon grunted and looked again at the house in which Millie Clovis shared a room with the now-deceased Janet Stowe. "Until we get something out of our friend Millie, we really are barking up the proverbial tree. We'll have to take it easy, so you leave the questioning to me."

"Whatever you say, boss."

On the second-floor landing, a young man of around twenty or so rushed past, out of breath, grinning his apologies, "Sorry, late for Cubism."

Frowning, Fallon watched the young man plunging down the stairs. "Cubism?"

Emery shrugged. "Some art thing, I think." He stepped up to Millie's flat door and gave it a tentative knock.

"She might know," said Fallon, reaching for a cigarette, "being an art student."

Emery knocked again, put his ear to the door, listened. A few seconds crawled by. He knocked again.

Stepping past, Fallon pounded on the wood with his fist, "*Millie, come on, we need to talk!*"

Emery gaped at him and Fallon jutted out his chin. "What?"

"Take it easy, you said, boss."

"Yeah, well ..."

A groan from within. A tiny voice, "Go away."

"Doesn't sound too good," said Emery, voice low.

"Probably drunk. Or worse." They exchanged a glance and Fallon raised his voice once again, "Millie this is important. It's about your friend, David Howarth."

The response was a prolonged silence and just as Fallon's impatience got the better of him and he pulled his fist back to unleash another barrage, the bolt released, and the door inched open.

Both men stood and stared, speechless.

She peered out at them through eyes bruised and swollen from an obvious battering. Smeared blood covered her puffed-up lips. Pulling the door open wide, Millie stepped back and waved them inside.

The room was a mess, furniture up-ended, papers, books, and broken glass littering the floor. A small space, the room contained a large single bed, covers now ripped apart, cotton sheets shredded, pillows burst open, feathers spilling out in sporadic piles.

"Jesus," breathed Emery and Millie stumbled backwards and flopped down on what remained of the bed. Emery crossed to her, disregarding Fallon's previous orders, all of that forgotten now. "What the hell has gone on here?" He sat down next to her. All her former hostility gone, she looked at Fallon.

"It was Fender. The one Janet met in that sleazy bar over in Liverpool."

"Fender?" Fallon took a step closer. "What did he want?"

"Answers. He burst in like some wild animal," she said without preamble, holding the detective's gaze with eyes seeping with tears. "He just came straight in and hit me, smashing me to the floor where he kicked me, over and over." To give emphasis she pulled up her blouse, wincing at the effort, and showed the bruising. Both men gasped. "He wanted to know what I'd told you, who else knew about him and Janet, who else knew about *him*, as if anyone would give a damn about the little shit." She dropped her hands, pulled out a tissue, dabbed one of the swellings on her cheek, which had split as she spoke and now bled freely.

"You need to get checked up," said Emery.

"I'll be fine."

"When did this happen?" Fallon again, always on duty.

"An hour. Maybe a little more. I was asleep, thought it was the postman because I'm expecting a package. So I didn't ask. I didn't think. I should have done. I'll never do it again."

"Millie," said Fallon, voice growing a little quieter, "I need to ask you about David Howarth."

Downcast, she stared at the tissue in her fist. "It was nothing. Sex. Nothing more."

"But you're ..." Emery let the question hang there. The unease grew, becoming a palpable thing.

"Janet," she said slowly, tentatively. "I'd never ... When we first met, it was like a light going off in my head. Men, I'd known plenty. All of them arseholes, all of them obsessed with performance, ramming away, no affection, no tenderness. Janet, we got on so well. Her love of art, her knowledge, like a bloody encyclopaedia. That's how it started. Late-night chats in the Uni bar. I didn't think there was anything else until she invited me back here one night and ... Well, the rest is history."

"But you still needed the attention of a man."

Her face came up, eyes narrowing. "Only the one. David. He's like no one else. He's tender, loving. And big." She gently wiped away a trail of blood from the cut. "If you understand me."

"You met with him once a week?"

"Yes. It worked for both of us. He never said he wanted more. I think he guessed that there couldn't *be* more. He knew about me and Janet, you see." The two police officers exchanged a glance. She saw it, shook her head violently. "No. No, it wasn't him that did the murder, if that's what you're thinking."

"He was at the canal," said Emery quickly.

"Canal?"

"Where Janet's body was found."

Her eyes widened, the remnants of her self-confidence seeping away. For a moment, it seemed she might break down, but she rallied herself, sniffed and blew her nose. "That doesn't mean he murdered her, does it? A coincidence, nothing more."

"How can you be sure?"

"Because I know him. He was a big man, but he was gentle. So gentle." She shook her head again, "Besides, he didn't know anything about Janet, not even what she looked like."

"You said he did," said Emery quickly. "Just now – you said Howarth knew about you and Janet."

"Yes, but nothing specific, just that I had a girlfriend."

"He could have seen her," said Fallon. "He knew where you lived, he could have come here and—"

"No. He didn't come here. Never. He didn't know my address."

"You always met at his place?"

"Yes. Pelham Road. A nice house."

"Once a week?" She nodded.

"Howarth has also been attacked," said Emery. He stopped when Millie's hand flew to her mouth, all her pain and trauma forgotten. "Oh, Jesus. Is he all right?"

"It's a little touch and go," said Fallon, "but he'll live."

"Oh my God. Where is he?"

"Wallasey. He's recovering well, but he's ... Millie, listen to me, we need you to be straight. He's hurt, it's not life-threatening but his memory ... The doctors have assured us it's only temporary, but his memory is impaired. He doesn't even remember his own name."

Shaking her head, tiny groans seeped out from her broken mouth.

"Can you think of anyone who might have done it," said Emery gently.

"It had to be Fender. It's obvious."

"But why attack Howarth, Millie?" She shook her head again, no words, just more groans. "Boss, I think we should call an ambulance now, don't you?"

Fallon agreed and went back to the car to call it in.

When he returned, Millie was lying down on the bed and Emery was doing his best to find more than one mug. The kettle was on the hob. "Making tea," the constable said as Fallon came up close. "She's in shock, and those bruises ..." He looked at her over his shoulder. "That bastard. When I get my hands on him, I'll—"

"Howarth didn't know where she lived, but Fender did. And if he got out of Millie Howarth's address before he clubbed him …"

"Bastard," breathed Emery. He threw a teabag into the single mug.

"You wait here for the ambulance. Call me when you are at the hospital and I'll come and pick you up."

"Where are you going?"

"Where do you think?"

"Fender's? You can't go alone, boss. The man's a fucking nutter."

"So am I, son. So am I."

Emery returned to Millie's side, carefully placing the tea on the floor. Her huge eyes were staring into space, tiny spasms pulsating across her mouth. Fender had hit her hard and soon the swelling and bruises would make her look like the punch bag that he used her as. "We'll bring him in, don't worry. You'll have to make a formal statement so we can charge him." A slight nod, an acceptance of reliving the horrors. "Did he say anything else, Millie? Any clues as to why he would beat you so badly?"

"Nothing, but it was difficult to make out anything he was saying, to be honest …"

"Yes, I understand that, but anything about David Howarth, Janet, anyone?"

"I can't …" She dragged in a breath. "His voice, it was muffled, and I was scared, the way he broke in."

She broke down and, unconsciously, Emery put his arm around her. "I know. It must have been horrible. The way he hit you, it's understandable that you couldn't make out exactly what he said."

"No, no," she said, recovering a little. "It wasn't that. He wore a mask."

"A mask?"

"No, not a mask, one of those full-face Balaclava things, with just the eyes showing."

"A full-face …"

"Yes. Like a bank-robber."

"Oh my God," gasped Emery, already looking around the room as if he was slipping into some sort of a fit, "Where the hell is your phone? I need to tell the station, warn Fallon."

"Warn him? I don't understand. Warn him about what?"

"He's gone to question Fender. But it's not Fender, it's someone else!"

A MODEL OF THE PAST

THEY SAT in Uncle Eric's workroom at the bottom of his garden. Brick-built, with carpet and white-lined walls, covered in paintings, old posters and cut-out pictures from magazines, it felt like a small house. On the shelves, of which there were many, books of all shapes and sizes, of every military subject; ships, aircraft, army history, together with volume after volume of uniforms, stood in untidy heaps. Whilst Craig scanned the titles, Uncle Eric delved amongst a collection of crates and boxes. "Lost something, Uncle Eric?"

"No, no, I'm all right." He sat back, holding an immaculate, unopened box in obvious delight. "Here it is, *Triang* double-O scale, four-six-zero steam locomotive with tender! Just look at that."

As Uncle Eric turned away to begin a new

search, Craig inspected the model more closely. Pristine, never taken from its box, it gleamed as if it were new.

"I only collect them," said Uncle Eric's muffled voice as he dipped his head into the depths of another box, "I'm not a railway modeller."

"Mum bought me a book."

"Eh?"

Craig raised his voice, "*Mum bought me a book.*"

Uncle Eric re-emerged, another locomotive in his hand, "Sorry. Didn't get that. About a book, or something?"

"A book of plans." Craig took the proffered model and gazed at it, noting how different it was from the first.

"That's a tank engine."

Craig frowned. "It doesn't look much like a tank to me. I want to drive a tank when I leave school."

"Not an army tank. Bah...it doesn't matter." He stumbled around the workbench, sat down next to Craig and picked up the first locomotive. He peered as if seeing it for the first time. "Beautiful isn't it? Sorry I can't show it running. I tell you what I have got, though," he said with a sudden thought, "something you might like." This time he didn't root through the same boxes but instead pulled out another carton from beneath the bench. On the cover was an illustration of a British World War Two tank.

"How about that, eh? Model kit of a Churchill." He carefully opened it up and extracted pieces of plastic sprue. As if slipping into his own world, unaware of anyone or anything around him, Uncle Eric took to carefully snipping off fragile-looking pieces of plastic with a pair of sharp cutters. Craig watched, absorbed.

Time drifted by, Craig unaware of how long he sat and watched the model slowly taking shape. At last, after some considerable time, Uncle Eric sat back grinning in triumph. "There. Done. Almost made itself it did. Clever these model makers."

"When do we put the tracks on?" asked Craig.

"Tomorrow. It has to be thoroughly dry before I do that. What do you think?"

"I think it's wonderful." He gently turned the turret round. "And everything works!"

"Funny old thing the Churchill. Great big tank, little tiny gun." It was his turn to move the turret around with his fingertip. "Imagine that coming up against a Panther."

"What's a Panther?"

"One of the main German battle tanks of World War Two. Excellent machine." He again dipped underneath the bench and brought out s small, sealed plastic bag with a card masthead running across the top. "You can have a go at this one if you like. When you've finished it, bring it back and we'll paint it."

Craig studied the packet. "What is it?"

"Spitfire. RAF fighter plane of World War Two. Go on, take it home, you'll enjoy it."

Craig spent the rest of that afternoon completing the model, surprised by how easy it was to build. He was flying it around his bedroom when his mum popped her head around the door. "I thought you were into model trains?"

"I am. Uncle Eric showed me some of his. Lovely they were."

"So why did he give you a model aeroplane?"

Craig shrugged, not having thought about it all that much. "Dunno. I watched him make a tank, and he gave me this." He placed the aircraft on his bed. "I'm glad he did, though. I've never done anything like this before, I feel really chuffed with myself."

Mum smiled. "Well, just so long as this bedroom doesn't become like his workshop. I've seen the amount of junk he's got in there."

"It's not junk, Mum, it's his models. It's all good stuff."

She pulled a face, not convinced. Craig had the sneaking suspicion that she was quietly laughing at him inside.

. . .

The following day, as Craig set off to see Uncle Eric again, he made a slight detour to look through the window of *Hobbies*, the tiny shop behind Woolworth's. Pressing his nose against the window, he drooled at the display, wishing he had the money to buy something. As he looked he saw, reflected in the glass, someone he knew. His heart leapt into his throat. Whirling around, he beamed as Melanie crossed the road and walked towards him. As she drew closer, her smile froze, replaced by a deep frown of concern. "What the hell happened to you?"

Craig unconsciously touched the bruising on his face. The heat rose from under his collar. "Oh, you know…nothing really."

She craned forward, inspecting him. "No, I don't know, Craig. Have you been in a fight?"

He withered under her harsh gaze. "Sort of."

"Sort of? What does that mean?"

She sounded like a schoolteacher accusing him of something and he wished he could put a bag over his head. If he had a bag. "I just got into a scrap with some other boy, that's all."

"I don't like fighting," she said stepping back. "I didn't think you were like that."

"No, I'm not!" A sudden urge to pull her close came over him, convince her of his honesty. To do just that, he said to himself, he had to be completely open. "All right, I'll tell you. There were three of them. A boy called Crossland and his girlfriend—"

"Samantha? Yes, I know her."

Craig gaped at her. "You *know* her? How?"

She sniggered. "It's not rocket science, Craig. She was in the year below me at school. I had a little ...what should I say ... a little scuffle with her myself."

"You mean a fight?" He gazed at her in awe. Wearing a white blouse, short blue skirt, and high heels, she looked like a junior executive. He couldn't help but stare, mesmerised.

"Not exactly a fight. More like a slap."

"She slapped you?"

Her head tilted to one side. "No, Craig, *I slapped her*."

"Ah, I see ..." This girl was more perfect than he could ever have hoped! His eyes drifted over her, drinking her in. He swallowed hard. "Are you going somewhere, somewhere special? I mean, you look, you know, you look really nice." His face burned.

She laughed. "Wow, is that a compliment?"

"I...Well, yes, I suppose it is."

Her hand stretched forward and his stomach turned to liquid as she gently caressed the swelling on his cheek. Her voice, when it came again, sounded a long way off, floating on the breeze, at once cool and warmly comforting. The words she spoke didn't matter, only the wonderful sensations they brought. A delicious glow spread through him as her fingers delicately drifted over his skin. He closed his eyes and believed himself to have come before the gates to Heaven...

"Craig, are you listening to me?"

Snapping his eyes open, he jerked his head up. "Eh? What?"

"I said I've just been for an interview for a Saturday job, but I don't think you heard me."

Her hand fell away, the moment shattered. "Yes, yes of course I am listening. It's just, you know, this..." He gave a tiny, self-conscious giggle and moved the back of his hand over the area she had caressed. "Sorry, but it was so ... You know."

"You're funny. Listen, I have to go. Why don't you call into the shop," she turned and pointed to the rear entrance to *Woolworth's*. "I'll be there all day this Saturday. Come and see me." She turned and smiled at him again. "If you want to, of course."

"If I *want to*?" He shook his head, the smile spreading across his face. "You try and keep me away!"

Her eyes held his for a moment and then, without another word, she walked away, leaving him to stand and watch her, honing in on that oh-so-short skirt, those legs and the way her hips swayed... He blew out a long breath, his head filled with nothing but white clouds and images of her as wonderful new sensations and feelings spiralled around inside him, turning his stomach mush. Melanie. How could such a wonderful girl be in the least bit interested in him? But she was and that was all that mattered.

Looking again into the shop window, those objects that only minutes before had filled him with such joy, now seemed childish and insignificant somehow. She had invited him to visit her on Saturday, and he resolved to ask her out on a date. The cinema, a walk in the park, some window shopping followed by a doughnut in one of the town's cafes. Flushed with this new-found courage, he raced to his uncle's, his legs bouncing with excitement. By the time he arrived at the front door, life felt better than it had for an age.

Uncle Eric placed a plate of chocolate biscuits and a glass of cream soda before him. Craig drank the soda down in one, without a pause for breath.

"Whoa, Craig, you were thirsty."

Smacking his lips, Craig's nose wrinkled as the bubbles invaded his nostrils. "Yeah, I was. Thanks." He laid the empty glass down on the workbench and munched down a biscuit. "Can I ask you a question?"

"Depends what it is." Craig stared and Eric laughed. "Only joking – of course, you can ask me anything you like."

Relieved, Craig studied the remains of the biscuit in his fingers. "Have you ever been in love, Uncle Eric?"

Eric gawped and flopped down in his chair. "*Love*? Dear God, Craig...what a question."

Craig paused in the destruction of a second biscuit. "Sorry, I didn't mean to annoy you."

"No, I'm not annoyed. A little surprised, but..." He rubbed his face. "Love? That's quite a thing, Craig. Quite a thing. Well, what can I say, it's...I remember there was a girl some years ago. I had hopes things might develop between us, but, well, life is a funny old business. It never goes in the direction you hoped for, at least not for me it doesn't. She didn't, or couldn't, commit to a relationship, despite my wanting to. The world was all over the place back then anyway and even love suffered." He stared down at his biscuit, untouched, perhaps forgotten as his memories took hold. "I wrote to her for a long time, but it fizzled away. Besides, she had moved back to Germany with her parents, so it wouldn't have worked."

"Germany? When was that, during the War? Were you in the War, Uncle Eric?"

Within a heartbeat, the atmosphere changed,

the workshop walls seeming to press inwards. Uncle Eric, who always struck Craig as a cheery, happy-go-lucky sort of person, stiffened and grew serious. He put down the uneaten biscuit and ran a finger across the model he made the previous day. "Yes," he said in a quiet voice, "I was a regular, Craig." He pushed the unfinished model tank away, picked up the grey, plastic tracks, and studied them. "I served right the way through. I was at Dunkirk."

The silence hung heavy over them both, his uncle far away. Feeling uneasy, thinking he had unconsciously upset Uncle Eric by trawling up difficult memories, Craig attempted to change the subject and picked up the tracks. "How do we fit those?"

Uncle Eric didn't answer. Instead, he stared into the distance. "I lost three friends on the beach. Good mates they were. That morning, we'd been to a prayer service. We were coming back when the plane came from nowhere, strafing the sand. I was hit in the arm, but managed to roll away. My mates weren't so lucky." He ran his hand through his hair. "I was twenty-two. I'd joined up in 1937, just a year before the Munich Crisis. Didn't have a clue about any of that, just knew that being a soldier was a good life, a secure job with steady pay. I never believed I'd actually end up fighting anyone. That all changed of course, after war broke out. My regiment was shipped to France and pretty soon we realized just how bloody awful it was going to be. The Germans were incredible fighters, tough and well led and we knew almost straight away we were in for a good hiding. After I left hospital, I spent some time at home, but all I could think about was getting back. But there was no 'getting back' because the ruddy Germans had conquered all of Europe. Found myself on a slow-boat to North Africa. Stayed there for almost the rest of the War, working on engines – I was a mechanic. Then came Normandy, and I found myself back in France, only this time things were different and it was the Germans' turn to get pushed back." He laughed to himself briefly. "Funny thing is, I only ever fired my rifle in anger once. Weird, isn't it?" He smiled at Craig. "Fighting in a war is nothing like the things you see in the films, Craig. It's a lot worse."

Later, with the sun shining bright, they took a turn around the garden, Uncle Eric showing his nephew the ornamental pond he was building. It seemed that Uncle Eric could make virtually anything. Just like Craig's dad.

As they peered down into the water, Craig took a breath, preparing himself to chance another question. "Was my Dad in the War?"

"Your Dad? Goodness me, no! He was only born…nineteen thirty-one I think. Your Mum would know. She's a year or so younger than him. We had different dads, your Mum and me. Mine was killed in a mining accident when I was about five. Can hardly remember him now."

Shocked by this revelation, Craig pressed on, curiosity taking firm hold. "I'm sorry, I never knew about any of that." Eric shrugged. "Why can't you remember him?"

"I was only a little boy. Not like..." he smiled warmly, "Craig, I know what you're getting at and you mustn't worry – you'll *never* forget your dad. He'll always be with you, in here." He tapped himself around the heart.

Nodding, Craig bent down and ran his fingers through the cool water of the pond. "I hope not," he said with feeling.

On their return to the shed, they worked quietly on their respective models, Uncle Eric whistling tunelessly, whilst Craig applied enamel paint to wings and fuselage. His attention unfortunately was on too many other things to do the model Spitfire justice. The recount of his Wartime experiences must have been painful for his uncle. Old memories, remaining dormant for years, unearthed by Craig's probing. How many years had passed since nineteen-forty? Twenty-eight. Half a lifetime thought Craig. For events to remain so vivid, they must have festered inside him for so long. Losing three friends, in such horrific circumstances, Craig didn't understand how Uncle Eric could put that aside, to smile, talk, continue as normal. Except for this one time, he always appeared so cheerful and with a jolt, Craig considered if the pained memories *he* had of his Dad and what had happened would ever fade. The idea was not a pleasant one. His dad meant everything to him and not having him around was a constant sore, a pain that would not go away.

Gathering up his courage to ask the question he'd been chewing over for a long time, his hand trembled as he tried to paint. "Do you know Billy Baxter, Uncle Eric?"

Stopping, Craig's uncle looked up from under his brows. "Why do you ask that?" His voice sounded strange, hollow, the mention of the gruff old man's name bringing a chill to the air.

Craig shifted in his seat. "Just wondered."

Eric rested his chin in his hand, contemplating his model with unwarranted intensity. "I'd known Billy before the War," he said slowly, in much the same tone as he had when regaling his Wartime story, "but lost touch with him when I joined the army. I'd heard he'd been called up around 'forty-one, but I later learned that he had actually volunteered. He was slightly older than me, by about six years I think. I never came across him during any of the campaigns until D-Day. He was a tank driver."

Something as heavy as a brick hit Craig in the chest. "*A tank driver?*" He nodded towards his uncle's model. "Did he drive Churchills?"

"Shermans more than likely," Uncle Eric replied, voice distant. He didn't volunteer any further information. For some time, eyes hooded, he fell into deep thought. "Coming from the same area of the country doesn't necessarily mean we'd serve in the same unit. There were so many men from all over during the Normandy campaign …" His voice drifted away for a moment. "We met up after the War. The town was putting on some big celebration to welcome us all back and there was a dance down at the Tower Grounds. Couldn't believe it when I saw him." He shook his head, and Craig was shocked to see his uncle's bottom lip trembling. "He'd lost his right leg late in the War. Invalided out."

So that was it, the reason for all the anger. Poor old Billy Baxter had had his leg blown off during the War. There he was, a young man in the prime of his life, giving up everything he knew to go and fight for what he believed to be a just cause, and the only reward he received was the loss of a limb. No wonder he was so angry at everyone and everything, blaming them all for what happened. "That answers a lot of questions about why he is the way he is."

Eric frowned at him "You know, being such a grumpy old man."

"Is that what he is?"

"Well, that's how he seems. Some people have told me to steer clear of him, and the way he spoke to Mum in Liscard … If we'd known … If *I'd* known." He carefully placed his model kit on the worktop. "God, I feel guilty now."

"Guilty? Why on earth should you feel guilty?"

"I should have treated him with more respect, been more understanding. I thought he was just a bitter old man. But he's not old at all, and now, with what you've told me, I understand why he looks the way he does. I can't imagine what that must be like, to have lost your leg, *in a war*. Those first moments, when it happened, the disbelief, the shock," he shook his head and looked down, the shame brimming up. "I can't begin…"

"Craig, don't be so hard on yourself." Eric put his hand on Craig's shoulder. "No matter what the reasons, he has a reputation. A bit of an 'odd-bod' if you like. A loner, short-tempered, even nasty. But since the night of the welcome-home dance, I don't think I've spoken another word to him, so what do I know?"

"Bob talked to me about him."

His uncle's hand dropped from Craig's shoulder. "*Bob*? You mean Bob Bewdsley?"

"Yes, I met him the other day up at the allotments. He knows Billy, and he told me—"

"Craig, you must stay away from Bob Bewdsley, you understand?"

Craig felt ice gripping him around the testicles, spreading upwards in a surge. Uncle Eric's face grew dark, the anger raging in his eyes. "I said *do you understand!*"

Shocked, Craig rocked back, more afraid than when Crossland dangled him over the cliff's edge. "Uncle Eric, what's wrong?"

Ashen-faced, Eric clawed through his hair, "You have to promise me Craig that if Bewdsley speaks to you again, you tell me. Understand?" Craig nodded, hardly able to breathe. "Good. You stay away from him. Far away."

"I will."

"All right then." Eric took a few deep breaths to calm himself, aware of the effect his outburst had on his nephew. Craig's eyes were watering, his face pale. "War changes you, Craig, you have to understand that. Everyone changes in different ways, sometimes for the better, sometimes for the worse. I've seen ordinary, mild-mannered blokes turn into rabid monsters and big, tough nuts crumple like tiny children, sobbing uncontrollably. All any of us can do is put our heads down and get on with it." He straightened his back, squeezed his nephew's shoulder and grinned, the amiable uncle slowly returning. "I'm sorry, I didn't mean to frighten you, but … Listen," he leaned forward, "let's get these models finished, then I'll make us some jam sandwiches and another glass of that cream soda you like so much."

A few hours later, after he said goodbye to Uncle Eric, Craig wandered home in a sort of dream, eyes glued to the pavement, feet heavy. As he walked, he pushed away the memory of how maniacal Uncle Eric had become with the mention of Bob Bewdsley. Images of tanks rumbling across open fields, of guns blazing, shell-bursts, explosions, fires leaping out of broken, twisted hunks of blackened metal replacing his fears and he lost all sense of direction and time. When he finally emerged from his reveries, he found himself standing a few doors away from Billy Baxter's home. The street appeared quiet, houses on both sides silent, their windows like accusing eyes, angry at his intrusion. He felt sure Baxter would erupt from out of his door at any moment, finger waggling, face red, more words of abuse. Quickly now, Craig pushed on, eyes dead straight, determined not to look towards the gruff old man's home. If he did catch sight of him, maybe he could give a tiny 'hello', allow Billy Baxter to see there were no bad feelings, that Craig was not such a bad person after all. If he were honest, however, he hoped he wouldn't see him.

And then, as if materialising out of the air, there he was, appearing from behind the front garden wall. Craig gave a jump of surprise and went to move on.

Baxter, shirtsleeves rolled up, cap pushed back, leaned on a garden rake, and wiped the sweat from his brow. Too immersed in his work, he did not notice the young lad inching away on the other side of the wall. Until Craig decided to face his fears and convince Baxter of the truth of what happened at the allotment. He stopped and turned. And froze.

Billy Baxter stood glaring at the small blond-haired youngster standing in front of him. "You," he hissed, throwing down the rake, face livid with rage, "what the *hell* are you doing here?"

Craig, stunned, took a step back and held up his hand, "Mr. Baxter," he gushed, "please, I'm only passing."

The frown grew deep as Baxter's eyes narrowed, "How do you know my name? Been asking around, have yeh?"

The accusation seemed ludicrous, of course, he knew his name! Seeing how furious he was, Craig decided to lie. "No, nothing like that, I promise."

"More lies. Your mother needs to know the truth

about you, lad. What are you doing here? Come to have another look at what you can steal?"

"Please, Mr Baxter, you've got it all wrong," said Craig, frantic now, his voice straining to fever pitch. Craig wanted to build bridges, not tear them down. Resigned, he realised there was nothing he could ever do or say to make this man change his opinions.

"You'll find out how wrong *you've* got it all if you don't clear off." Baxter, closer now, took a wild grab at Craig from across the wall. Craig skipped nimbly out of the way, too quick for the old man. Baxter cursed and brought up his bunched fists. "I hate you kids. All you do is make noise kicking your ball, swearing, causing all sorts of mayhem. You have no respect, *no respect!*" His face grew redder, swelling like an over-inflated football. Horrified, Craig realized this was more than mere anger. Something else was happening. Baxter's features crumpled, face screwed up like a church gargoyle. Clutching at his chest, he teetered backwards, breathing laboured. His arms flayed about, searching for support, but he was like a blind man, and, groaning and spluttering, he dropped to his knees.

Craig recognised what this was, and he vaulted the wall. He planted himself next to Baxter as the old man writhed on the ground. "Have you any pills?" Craig demanded.

Baxter nodded, waving his left hand towards his jacket lying in a heap on the grass. Frantic, Craig searched through the pockets, found a little silver pillbox, opened it and took out one of the tiny pills. Baxter grabbed it without a word and popped it into his mouth. He sank into himself, and Craig watched, waited. The minutes crawled by, Baxter stretched out on the ground, breathing growing more shallow and controlled. The redness gradually left his face, the wheezing retreated, eyes losing their bleary, unfocused glaze. He released a loud, prolonged sigh and glanced over to Craig, nodding once. "I'm all right," he said simply and managed a thin smile.

Craig remained wary, not sure if Baxter might turn into a mad demon again. The encounter at the allotment, the way the old man became a raging beast, was not something Craig wanted to repeat. He waited, without speaking, preparing to run if needed.

But Baxter didn't become a wild beast again. Instead, his smile broadened. "Thank you," he mumbled, words which must have proved difficult to utter.

Craig helped him to sit up. A long moment wriggled by. "Why did you do that?" asked Baxter in a weak, uncertain voice. "Why did you help me?"

Craig shrugged, embarrassed, not sure how to answer. "Oh … you know."

"That's just it," said Baxter, "I *don't* know. I've been horrible to you, lad. Then you go and help me like that." He put his fingers across the bridge of his nose and squeezed hard. "I feel awful." He dropped his hand, and appeared sheepish, a little ashamed. "I've got angina."

Craig didn't say anything, not wanting to reveal what Bob had already told him. "That's to do with … the heart?"

"Yes. My poor old ticker's not too good. Too many fags. I've tried to give the damned things up, more than once I can tell you, but I can't. Damned things have got me truly hooked."

"But," Craig prepared himself for an onslaught as he added, "they could kill you."

"Oh yes," smiled Baxter, "they'll do that all right." He went to stand. Taking his arm, Craig helped him to his feet. "Thanks. You're a good, lad. I misjudged you, I think."

"I didn't try to steal anything when I went into your garden," said Craig, in a mindless rush of an explanation. "Honestly, I swear to you. It was just the ball, it went over and my mates egged me on to go and get it. I couldn't just … I couldn't say 'no', how could I? I'd never live it down. I'd be taunted forever if I'd have done that."

A grin. "So, you were forced to do something you didn't want to do?" Baxter looked at Craig, measuring him with a penetrating stare. "I can understand that. Done it myself a number of times. But what about the allotment? Who was egging you on that time?"

"That was something different ... I was being chased. Some bullies had gotten hold of me and I'd managed to get away. Going through your allotment was the only way I could escape from them. I didn't destroy anything, I wouldn't do such a thing, I promise." Craig held his breath, wondering if his explanation would have any effect at all.

Baxter looked down at the ground, bottom lip stuck out. Craig could see that the old man was grateful, but there had to be a limit to his good nature. He turned to leave, but Baxter's hand came down on his shoulder. Something crossed between them, something that took Craig by surprise. Kindness, understanding. Acceptance.

"I know you wouldn't do that," Baxter said quietly, eyes moist, gentle. "I can see you're a good boy and I regret not seeing it before. If you can find a way, I'd like you to forgive me for the way I've been treating you, the things I said. Your mother too. I'm sorry."

Shocked, Craig, not knowing what else to do, stooped down and picked up the rake. He forced a smile and handed it over. "You need to take care of yourself, Mr Baxter," he said. "A friend of my dad's, Roy Emerson, he had pills like yours. I saw my dad trying to help Roy the day he collapsed." He left it there and scrambled over the wall. He stood on the far side, and Baxter's eyes locked on his without any sense of reproach. "I could help you, Mr Baxter, with your garden. I've always loved plants and stuff, so if you want, I could come over at weekends, cut the grass, do the weeding." He noted how sad Baxter's smile was, but at least it was a smile. Another smile and then Craig headed towards his home. At the corner, he paused and turned. Baxter, still standing, slowly raised his arm and waved. Craig's heart swelled, and he returned the wave. At last, with amends made, he walked home, relief mingling with happiness.

His mood changed to anxiety as, nearing the entrance to the alleyway at the back of his house, Craig spotted Bob Bewdsley standing on the corner as if he were waiting for him. He stepped in Craig's way and, without preamble, growled, "You've been talking with Baxter, haven't yeh?"

Craig went to speak, then stopped. Uncle Eric's words came home to him in a rush and he saw now what his uncle meant. This was not the Bob he'd talked to the other day. Then, he'd been kind, understanding. This was a different Bob. His t-shirt, stained with sweat, and something else.

"You keep away from him," continued Bewdsley, eyes flashing, intense, even threatening. "He may seem like he's old and feeble, but believe you me, he isn't. What he did, all them years ago, he should be locked up. So you keep away. Understand? Don't listen to his stories, because they're not true. None of them." He leaned close and glared. "I'm warning you. Keep away."

Without another word, Bewdsley strode off, leaving Craig breathless and scared.

And wondering why there was blood on the man's shirt.

PIECES THAT DON'T FIT

FALLON STOPPED off at a nearby off-license to buy himself a carton of cigarettes before he parked up outside Fender's apartment block. It was dark by now and no lights shone in any of the windows. Resigned, Fallon used his lighter to illuminate the barely legible names of the occupants. Finding Fender's, he pressed the buzzer and waited.

He took a glance at his watch, again using his lighter and cursed the fact that the only lamp in the street was not burning. He shook his head. Eight o'clock. He lit himself a cigarette and gave the buzzer another push, this time angling his head to listen out for the sound of the distant bell.

There was nothing.

Cursing, he pressed all three of the other buzzers. After a pause, a short, rasping click saw the door wheezing open as if pulled by invisible hands. Fallon stepped into the darkened hallway. It stank of wet dogs and stale urine, a smell he couldn't recall from his previous visit, but then that was in daylight. Everything seems cleaner in daylight.

From somewhere on the first floor, the tired, anxious little voice of an elderly woman called, "Hello?"

"Police, madam. Don't be alarmed, I'm here to talk to Mr Fender. Do you know if he is in?"

A door closed, followed by silence. Fallon waited. "Madam?"

He groped along the wall to his left, searching for a light switch. There was none. Maybe on the right. He turned.

A shape loomed out of the darkness. Before Fallon could react, a fist slammed into his midriff. The air belched out of him and he dropped to his knees, struggled to straighten and received a hefty kick in the side for his efforts. He crashed against the wall, hands coming up in a vain attempt to ward off any more blows. Through a watery mist of pain, he put his back against the wall to try to slide upright. Something blurred. Another punch, but he was ready now, blocked the blow and swung a right cross of his own, hitting nothing but thin air. Dazed, but not debilitated despite the kick, a surge of anger gave him the strength he needed. Crouching in his best Jack Dempsey style, he prepared to mix it with his attacker. If only he could see.

Retreating, the assailant yanked open the door, allowing Fallon his first decent look at him. Big man, moving slow with heavy, lumbering steps. Fallon leapt forward, gripping the man by the shoulders, hauling him back into the hallway. Twisting in his grip, the man thundered another fist into Fallon's guts. Then a left, a right. Damn good punches. A boxer, or similar. Fallon went down and stayed down, the blood leaking from his nose, and he rolled over groaning as whoever it was disappeared into the night.

He felt rather than heard someone close. The faint whiff of a cigarette, not his, which lay forgotten but still burning on the floor. The light went on and he flinched away from the glare, hand coming up to shield his eyes.

"Ooh my, you don't look too good."

"Call the police," Fallon said, giving it his best effort to try and sit up. But the lights were flashing before his eyes now and he knew he should stay still. "And an ambulance," he managed before he fell backwards into a huge, gaping hole of inky blackness.

"Looks like all of this was for nothing, boss."

Emery stood with his back to the sink, arms folded, watching the ambulanceman gently dabbing at Fallon's swollen face with an antiseptic-drenched piece of lint.

They were in the old woman's kitchen. She was making their second cup of tea and making plenty of noise about it. She handed one over to the ambulanceman, who smiled politely and shook his head. Shrugging, she gave the tea to Emery instead.

"So, you didn't get a decent look at him at all, boss?"

Fallon grunted and the ambulanceman applied a sticking plaster to the detective's left eyebrow. "Keep this pressed against your nostrils," he said, giving Fallon a fresh piece of lint. "It's not broken, but it'll swell up nicely tomorrow, together with your eye." He turned away without another word and left.

"Nice man," said the old woman.

"An angel," said Fallon and took the next mug of tea. Making a face, he sipped it, found it to be very palatable, and took a bigger mouthful. He looked across at Emery. "It was too dark."

"I have to say, boss, I did tell you not to come here on your own." Fallon gave him a look and Emery continued, unabated. "You think it might have been Fender?"

Fallon shook his head. "Too big. And he knew how to punch." He stretched his back and winced when he touched his ribs. "Kicked like a mule too."

Emery finished his tea and smiled at the old lady. "Do you know if Mr Fender has many visitors, madam?"

"The odd girl or two, I suppose. The only reason I know that is because of all the shouting that went on here a few nights ago." She turned her gaze on Fallon. "I'm not one to gossip, you understand. Usually, this building is very quiet. Everyone keeps themselves to themselves. Sometimes I pass Mr Fender on the stairs, but we hardly ever speak."

"But this one night ...?"

"Well, I heard them. Screaming at each other they were. Then I heard a terrific bang and I went out to see, and she comes running down the stairs, hand to her face, crying her little heart out."

Pulling out the photograph of Janet Stowe with something of an effort, Fallon showed it to her. "This girl?"

Instantly the woman's eyes grew wide. "Oh my ... Yes! Yes, that was her, Inspector. How did you ..."

"She was found murdered some way away, Mrs ...?"

"Connery. Betty Connery. Murdered? Oh my, poor girl. You don't think ..." This time her eyes grew wider still. "You don't think Mr Fender ...? Oh my Lord!"

Fallon did not wish to alarm her further. He returned the photograph to his wallet. "When was the last time you saw Mr Fender?"

She took a moment to regather her wits. "I think it was that night. The night this poor girl went running down the stairs, like a scalded cat. He came after her, you see, leaning over the top landing, shouting down at her, "Tell that bitch she's next." She shrugged, "Or words to that effect."

On the way up to the top floor, Fallon was forced to stop several times, hand pressed against the near wall, head down, gulping in air. After the third time, Emery cleared his throat, "Boss, don't you think you should let me and a couple of Bobbies do this?"

Turning, Fallon's face took on an expression that was beyond pain. "You think I'm too bloody old for this, or what?"

Recoiling slightly, Emery put up his hand. "No, boss. Not at all. But ..."

"Just come out with it why don't you?"

"I ... All right, sir. I don't want to say 'I told you so', but in the circumstances ... Sir, it really wasn't wise of you to come here on your own. You should have waited, called in some assistance."

"He took me by surprise. You may think I'm past it, son, but believe you me – I-m not."

"I never meant that, Sir. All I'm saying is—"

"For your information, I'm fifty-four years of age. I'm out of condition, I smoke too bloody much and I live on my own and my life is *shit*, but don't ever think that I can't do this bloody job because I can. You understand me?"

"Yes Sir, of course. But I—"

"Good, now let's go and call on our Mr Fender, shall we."

Emery took a deep breath. "Sir, something Millie said. Her attacker wore a Balaklava, to disguise his features."

"But it was Fender, so why would he want to disguise his face?"

"Exactly, which is what I wanted to tell you. It couldn't have been Fender. Millie knew Fender, didn't she, so why wear a disguise? It wasn't him, boss."

Mulling this over, Fallon stood frowning as he looked up to Fender's floor. "Or possibly he was trying to confuse her into thinking it was somebody else." He looked at Emery again. "And us." In a renewed spurt of energy, he bounded up the remaining stairs, leaving Emery trailing behind him.

Outside Fender's apartment, Fallon tried the handle, then pounded at the door with his fist. He looked at Emery. "Get a couple of those big lads waiting outside to come up here and break down this door, would you?"

"Sir, we haven't got a warrant, we could be jeopardizing the case."

"I've been assaulted. We have justifiable cause. Get those two Bobbies up here *now,* or I'll break it down myself."

After a few seconds of indecision, Emery disappeared downstairs. Fallon went to take a cigarette, thought better of it, and returned the carton to his pocket. Another rattle at the door handle and he shouted, "Fender. This is Detective Inspector Fallon. Get this door open or we'll break it down."

As he suspected there was no reply. He banged on the door for one last time and then Emery was behind him, breathing hard, two burly uniformed constables accompanying. "Put your shoulders against this door, lads. You're acting on my orders."

Both men grunted and set to work, launching themselves at the door, slamming their solid shoulders into the equally solid door. After half a dozen or so determined attacks, they stepped away, defeated. The door remained firmly closed.

"Here, there's no need for you to be doing all that," came a voice.

A small-framed man dressed in white shirt and dark trousers came up the stairs, cigarette dangling from his mouth, a bunch of keys in a gnarled fist.

"I'm the caretaker if you like," he said. He stepped up next to Fallon and, without looking at the detective, picked out a key from the bunch and placed it in the lock. "You're taking full responsibility, Mr Policeman. All right?"

"Just get it open."

A grunt and the man did so.

The door swung open.

A small side lamp, standing on a tiny table next to a wall-mounted phone, gave off a weak glow, barely strong enough to illuminate the narrow hallway disappearing into the depths of the apartment. "Hello," shouted Fallon. His voice came back to him, confirming his suspicion that it was empty. Aware of the others close behind, he moved deeper into the apartment, confident of no more sudden attacks.

The first door on the left hung open but in darkness. He slipped his hand between the edge of the door, feeling for a light switch. He found it and the room burst into brightness. A small couch, table, covered in magazines and newspapers, pushed up against the wall. A television turned off. An ashtray, overflowing with stubs, the smell of stale cigarette smoke hanging in the air. Nothing more.

Returning to the hallway, there was a room straight ahead. Another to the right.

"That's the kitchen," piped up the caretaker.

"Bathroom is off it. To the left is his bedroom. One-bedroom flat. Nice if it wasn't for the smoking."

Fallon gave him a look then pushed open the bedroom door.

Again, no light and again Fallon found it and switched it on.

Stretched across the bed lay Fender, completely naked, eyes wide open, a necktie around his throat, clearly dead. Emery pushed past his superior and checked for a pulse nevertheless. The caretaker groaned. One of the constables laughed. "Bloody hell, has he got any tackle there, boss?"

"Shut up," snapped Fallon and turned away. In the hall, Emery came up to him. "That's put the cat amongst the proverbials."

"Question is, who killed him?"

"Hunches, boss? Guesses?"

"The same guy who smacked me around more than likely but apart from that, I don't know."

"Then we could be stumped, boss."

Fallon had no answer to that. Ramming his hands deep in his pockets, he decided to walk home. It had been a long night.

LITTLE DOG LOST

SATURDAY MORNING, the sun shining, Craig stood at his bedroom window and looked out towards the neighbouring houses. The holidays dented the usual feelings he harboured for Saturday morning, the sense of freedom and expectation they brought after a week at school. This day, however, Craig had something special to look forward to.

He could see Melanie.

After a quick breakfast, which he barely tasted, Craig popped his head into his Nan's room. Sat in her chair, knitting and humming a long-forgotten tune, she didn't look up as he lingered close to the door. "Off out are we?"

"Yes, Nan. I won't be long."

A smile crept over her face. "It's nice seeing you

happy for a change," she said. "I worry about you sometimes."

He wanted to tell her his exciting news about his meeting with Melanie, crawl onto her lap, hug her, just like he used to do when younger before the world became a very terrible place. But he knew those days were sadly long gone. He rustled up a smile. "There's no need to worry about me, Nan. I'm fine. I'll see you later."

He closed her door softly, her voice drifting to him from inside the room. "I love you, Craig."

His stomach lurched. Would she still love him if she knew the truth about what happened with his dad? All the love in the world couldn't undo what he had done. One day, he would have to tell her and everyone else. But not today. Today the present, with all its hopes, pushed his dark thoughts aside.

He walked to the shops, the sunshine easing as clouds collected overhead, and he hoped it was not a signal, a portent of bad things to come. People shuffled by, oblivious, lost in their own worlds, another normal day. For them of course, because for him today was special. Reaching Woolworth's, heart thumping in his chest, pessimism slipped away and expectation grew. His step quickened as her face filled his thoughts.

He found her at the rear of the shop, stood on tip-toes, readjusting some mixed-up toys. She didn't notice his approach. He waited and drank her in. She looked fine in her smart new uniform, a one-piece, floral patterned overall.

He coughed and she whirled around, surprised, off-balance. She clutched at the boxes to save herself from stumbling.

Craig reacted, stepped in and caught the boxes before they fell. He held them whilst Melanie gathered herself and beamed her relief. "Wow, Craig. Don't do that." She pushed the boxes back into place and, for a brief moment, her hand brushed against his.

He felt the heat on his cheeks. "Sorry, I didn't mean to startle you."

Her smile helped his embarrassment slip away, but not the joy of feeling her soft, warm skin on his. "That's okay. What are you doing here?"

"You said for me to come and see you, so I thought...Well, you know. Here I am."

"Well, that's nice of you, but my break isn't until eleven. Why don't you come back then? I've got twenty minutes, we could go to *Sayers* if you like."

He wanted to scream *If I like? Of course, I'd like to! I like you, I want to take you out, walk you along New Brighton Prom, watch the sunlight play with your hair, hold you and kiss you.* Instead, he gushed, "Yes, yes of course." Smiling, he left the store at a run.

With almost a whole hour to kill, he wandered aimlessly, window shopping, stopping to buy a chocolate bar before continuing towards Central Park. It was quiet, hardly anyone about, and the first raindrops fell. He turned to go, he saw the little dog and froze.

It was Baxter's dog, no question. When it saw him, it stopped, something like recognition flickering across its face. Crouching down, he gestured for it to come closer. "What you doin' here, boy? Where's your master?" Cocking its head, the little dog regarded him with uncertainty, tail twitching a little. It refused to move closer, clearly uncertain. He needed a treat but only had the chocolate to offer. He snapped off a piece and held out his hand enticing the little dog to come forward.

Resistance was futile in the face of such a delicious morsel and it moved within striking range. Craig took his chance and scooped it into his arms. Desperate to escape, it wriggled like an eel but soon its attention centred on another piece of chocolate. He prepared to take him home.

A cruel voice, close by, mocking and full of glee brought him up sharp. "Well, well, if it isn't lovely little Craigy."

Samantha stepped into Craig's line of vision. He

gasped. Dressed in the tightest jeans he thought he'd ever seen, he could not turn his eyes away, intoxicated by her, all thoughts of Melanie or anyone else disappearing in an instant. Her breasts pushed against her white t-shirt, bare arms of burnished bronzed so smooth, wisps of golden down across her forearms, hair cascading to her shoulders framing that face. As her eyes held his gaze, her smile widened, relishing the effect she had on him.

His stomach yawned with desire for her. If she asked him to run away with her, he'd do so in a breath, leaving everything and everyone behind.

A shape moved beyond this angelic vision and Craig's heart fell. A little way behind, finishing off his cigarette, stood Crossland. In that instant, all desire disappeared, replaced by overwhelming guilt. Melanie's face rose in his mind. Wasn't it Melanie he wanted? Longed to be with? Yes, yes it was. Samantha, so seductive, but so cruel. Vicious. Was that her appeal? Her dominance, her power? He didn't know. His mind swirled with confused emotions. Hastily, he looked for an escape route, or a friendly face to help him. There was no one, the entire population of the world seemingly disappeared to leave him alone and vulnerable.

"We've got unfinished business, you little shit," said Crossland coming closer.

Craig did his best to remain calm. But then

Samantha leaned forward, her perfume wafting over him, and almost sent him into delirium once again. She tickled the dog under its chin. "He's lovely, Craig. Is he yours?"

He stared into her face. How could she be so lovely and so horrible at the same time? "No. I'm looking after him for a friend."

Her face grew reflective, eyes concentrating on the dog, but glazed, as if she were remembering something, looking back to memories. She was mesmerizing.

"Sam ..." he whispered.

She didn't flinch, continuing to tickle the dog, a curious half-smile lingering on her lips. "I had a dog once ... Lovely he was."

"Sam, please, can't you ..."

All at once, Crossland pushed Samantha aside and shot out his hand to grip Craig by the throat. His face loomed so close Craig could smell the stink of tobacco on the bully's breath.

"I'm going to make you squeal."

"Please Crossland," Craig managed, unable to move, the dog in his arms struggling to get free.

"Ah, what's the matter Craigy," mocked Samantha, that coldness returning to her voice. "Don't you want to play?"

"I'm going to kick your head in," hissed Crossland. "I hate you. You think you're so bloody smart, don't you, eh? Well, you're not. I'm going to kick you all the way into next week, then I'm going to get your wimpy friend and do him in as well."

The grip tightened. Craig yelped.

And the dog attacked.

It moved so fast, Craig could do nothing to prevent it from springing forward, teeth clamping around Crossland's fist. The bully, mouth open wide, screeched with pain. He yanked his hand free, the dog's teeth ripping through the skin, blood seeping from the ragged wound.

Samantha, shaken, stepped away, fists crammed into her mouth, eyes wide with fear. Crossland crumpled to the ground, eyes tight shut, tears sprouting, teeth grimacing as he tucked the bloodied hand under his armpit and rocked himself backwards and forwards, uttering a stream of curses.

"Oh shit, shit, shit," wailed Samantha, and she ran to her boyfriend's side, throwing her arms around him, holding him tight.

Craig watched and a new sensation surged over him, at once surprising, but revelatory. She actually cared for Crossland, despite him being the vilest creature alive. A surprising new sense filled him. He didn't care. Triumph replaced his fear.

Samantha turned her face to his, tears running

down her face. "Craig, for God's sake, do something!"

Samantha's appeared like a little girl, lost and frightened.

"*Please* Craig, help him!"

Craig didn't hesitate. He worked quickly, pulled free his belt from his trouser loops and, fashioning a sort of lead, attached the dog to the nearby railings. He tugged out a handkerchief from his pocket and applied a makeshift bandage around Crossland's wound. "Put pressure on this, Sam, It'll stop the bleeding."

She turned her big round eyes towards him. "Craig …"

"Victoria Central is just around the corner, we can get him there and they'll give him a jab."

Crossland reacted, face draining of all colour. "A jab? What the hell do you mean, a jab?"

"Anti-tetanus. It's just a precaution."

"Anti what," mumbled Samantha, clearly in distress, eyes wet with tears, lips trembling.

"It doesn't matter," said Craig. "Come on, let's go."

Afterwards, with Craig nimbly deflecting the nurse's questions about how Crossland had received the bite, Craig stood with Samantha outside the hospital's main entrance.

"I'm sorry, Craig," she said all of a sudden.

"For what? For making my life a misery?"

"For everything. I didn't ..." She looked down at her feet. "You're all right you are, Craig. I never really knew you before now, but ... I'm not Crossie's girl, you know. We're just mates."

"I didn't know."

"I'm no one's girl." Her face came up. "But I could be."

His stomach pitched over. He stared. The moment lingered. Then, the dog pulled and Craig, grateful for the diversion, said, "I'd better go, I have to take him home."

Her fingers brushed over his arm. Hadn't Melanie done the same? "Thank you."

He swallowed hard, conflicting emotions raging throughout his body. Melanie. Samantha. All these months, *years* of having nobody and now ... He forced a smile and rushed away.

In his doorway, Baxter stood speechless, open-mouthed at seeing Craig standing on the step with the dog. Smiling, Craig released the dog from the belt, the little rascal bounding straight into the house, yapping noisily, desperate for a drink or a meal.

Craig watched him go. "He was up in the park," he said in answer to Baxter's bemused expression.

Baxter scratched his head. He wore a thin shirt, sleeves rolled up over his biceps. Craig could see the bulge of muscle there. Baxter was tough, no doubt about it, but the skin was blotchy and unhealthy looking, tinged with prominent blue veins.

"What was he doing there? I left him in the garden."

"He was just running around, barking at everyone, having a lovely time. I thought I'd better bring him back."

"Well, that was good of you. He's always getting out lately, but I never thought he'd stray that far. It's all my fault because I can't walk him anymore so he gets frustrated. Things aren't going too well."

A sudden idea seized Craig. "Why don't I take him out for you, Mr. Baxter? I'm on holiday and I've got lots of free time. I know I said I'd keep your garden neat, but I can walk him too."

Billy Baxter thought for a moment, then beckoned Craig to come into the house. "I've just put the kettle on. I've got some cake somewhere too. We can talk about your ideas over a nice brew if you like."

Craig followed Baxter down the hall to the living

room. "Sit down," said Baxter, moving some old magazines and newspapers to clear a space. "I'll go and make that tea. You like tea?" Craig nodded. "Right, I shan't be long."

If he thought Uncle Eric's room was amazing, then what he saw all around him was like a scene from the Arabian Nights.

A small, cramped yet snug room, crammed with a lifetime's accumulation of memorabilia, bric-a-brac and dust. Lots of dust. There was a frenetic feel about the place, bits and pieces of all manner of things tossed anywhere, with no real order or plan. Shelves bulged with an assortment of books and magazines, whilst others carried models. Above the mantelpiece, thick with dirt, rested an old musket, another propped up against the wall, accompanied by a sabre. In a display cabinet, there were other things – a couple of old helmets, bayonets, a pistol and model soldiers. He pressed his nose up against the glass and recognized them as Napoleonic figures, an accompaniment to the helmets, muskets and sabre.

Everywhere Craig looked, there was an object of interest, be it bygone weapons, books on military history, or ornaments. One, in particular, on a shelf, half covered by some old pieces of curled-up paper, caught his eye. A small whimper of memory played around his head and he moved closer to study it.

It was another figurine but unlike the others. Craig recognized the uniform as German. It was an officer studying a map. The urge to pick it up was almost irresistible. Immaculately painted, right down to the minute brass buttons on his jacket, even its eyes had coloured irises.

A cough made him turn to find Baxter returning with a tray full of cups and plates. He beamed. "I see you've discovered my little Ludendorff."

He set the tray down on a low table and heaped sugar into the cups. Craig sat on a threadbare armchair. "Ludendorff?"

Baxter handed over a cup of tea, went to the shelf, and extracted the model from between the papers. "I'll clear this place up one day." He grinned and sat down on the accompanying armchair, turning the figure around in his fingers. "General Erich Ludendorff, architect of the March Offensive in the Great War." He held the figure up to the light. "Introduced a whole new concept of warfare, and he almost won. Fortunately, he didn't quite manage it." He held out his hand. "Have a look. I'm pleased to see you're interested."

Craig carefully took the figure. He weighed in his hand. "It's heavy"

"Yes. A lot of metal in that."

"You have so many things, Mr Baxter." He squinted at a display of framed faded photographs, depicting a battle tank, together with several soldiers. Blurred faces peered out at the world, smiling, assured, more like holiday snaps, not captured moments from a war zone. And they clearly were from war, as in the background ghostly glimpses of ruined buildings loomed, burned-out vehicles standing in mangled, blackened clumps and, as he looked harder still, bodies, lying twisted and broken on the ground.

Baxter sat without speaking, sipping his tea.

When he finished, he got up and crossed to the far corner and a desk, almost totally submerged in papers. He sifted through the detritus and returned with a few pieces of crumpled paper in his hand. "I started making some notes," he said, "I had a crazy idea that a local newspaper would like to hear my story. That was in nineteen sixty-four. The Echo was doing an anniversary piece about the D-Day landings and I thought they might be interested, but I sort of lost the courage to send it in. I've kept the notes, though." He smoothed out the sheets across his knees. As he gazed at them, his voice dropped, "A young journalist came to see me lately. She said she was writing a piece about the War and, well, you know how it is, she …I think she had second thoughts about seeing it in print. A little too graphic for her readers perhaps."

"Graphic? In what way?"

"Too much gory detail. Wars a bit like that."

"I was talking to my Uncle Eric. He was at Dunkirk. He said he only got to fire his rifle once."

"Your Uncle Eric?"

"Yes, he said he knows you. Eric Dawson."

"Eric Dawson is your uncle?"

Baxter appeared incredulous, sitting aghast, staring at the papers, shaking his head. "Well bloody hell! What a small world this is." His face came up. "Yes. We knew each other, before and during the War. What did he tell you about us?"

Craig paused, something about Baxter's change of tone causing him to check the retelling. He chose his words carefully. "Not much at all really. Only that he was a mechanic, helping maintain tanks."

"Is that what he told you? Helping to maintain tanks?"

Clearly, something was developing here, something which made Craig uncomfortable. He remembered Bob Bewdsley's words about Billy Baxter. And Uncle Eric's about Bewdsley. The three of them knew something none of them wanted Craig to know about. He drank his tea, giving himself some time. "Yes. That's all."

Baxter nodded his head. "Well, well. Eric Dawson. Who'd have guessed it, eh? But yes, there were many blokes like him, who didn't fire their weapons. I'm not one of them, though." He looked at the papers again, lost in thought. His chin began to tremble and, as he turned the papers over, his gnarled hands shook. Craig waited, thinking the details must be shocking, even after all these years. "Could you read it to me?"

Baxter looked up, mouth down-turned. "I don't need to read it, lad." He tapped his forehead, "It's all up here. It'll never go away." He breathed a sigh and then, quite unexpectedly, he screwed up the sheets into a tight ball and hurled them across the room. "They'll never go away."

A heavy silence settled down over them. Shocked, Craig struggled with what to say next, something to change the mood. He glanced across to the cabinet and the soldiers "Those models, they're cavalry regiments aren't they?"

"Tanks were the new cavalry," said Baxter, voice flat. "That's why I've got them. As a link."

Nodding, Craig put down his finished cup of tea. He gazed down at the Ludendorff model, stood up and carefully placed it on the mantelpiece. He should go, he thought. He'd trespassed too long into this bitter old man's world.

Baxter stared at him, mouth a thin line. "I'll tell you a story if you like. My story. It's not pretty and I've only ever told it to one other person in my life." He closed his eyes for a moment and when he opened them again Craig saw they were wet with emotion.

"It's all right, Mr. Baxter," said Craig quietly. "You don't have to tell me anything."

"No," Baxter said, voice hard, determined. "I want to! I misjudged you, lad, and I don't want you to do the same with me. I'll keep it brief, but it's something I think I have to do, especially as this year is the twenty-fifth anniversary of when it all happened."

Those old mixed emotions of Craig's stirred around inside once more. Confessions, the very thought terrified him. He didn't know if he should feel privileged or afraid. Either way, he knew he wanted to hear the story so he sat down, and waited for Billy Baxter to recount his story from the War.

CONFESSIONS

BILLY BAXTER CLIMBED to his feet and picked up one of the photographs. Craig leaned towards it and saw four smiling men clustered around a big ugly tank. Billy held it with great care like it were a treasured heirloom. "This was us; my tank crew. I was the driver and took the photo. That's why I'm not in it." His finger pointed out each figure in turn. "That's Wally, the commander and this," he tapped the face of another, a tall and angular-framed young man exuding supreme confidence, "is Paul Noble. Nobby, obviously. Gunner. Next to him is Stan. Stan Fellows, the loader. And finally, we've got here someone you already know."

Frowning, Craig studied the photograph closely. "Who?"

"He looks a little different now. But that's Bob. Bob Bewdsley. He was the co-driver and just about the best mechanic there was. I'm not sure what Eric said to you, but your uncle was in the infantry, a support unit that travelled along with us. Bob was our only mechanic."

Craig dared not say anything about his last meeting with Bewdsley, but he recalled it now and a chill ran through him. If Bewdsley and Baxter knew one another in the War, why was there such animosity between them? And why had Uncle Eric lied? Why would he say he was a mechanic when all along he was a soldier, a fighting man? "Yes, I recognize Bob from the allotments. So you…"

"I was the driver, of Churchills up until this point when we got delivery of the new, shiny Shermans. I'd done a few weeks of orientation work but essentially, we were untried in combat. In the beginning, the Sherman seemed a good tank and we felt safe in it. Not as safe as in the Churchill, mind, but the Sherman's gun was better, and we knew that if we came across any Panzer Threes or Fours we'd do pretty well."

"I helped my uncle build one of those Churchill tanks." He noticed Billy frowning. "A model, I mean. A plastic kit. To be honest, he made it and I just watched. But afterwards, I went home and built a Spitfire he gave me."

"I've never made a model like that." There was a hint of Billy being impressed.

Craig felt emboldened to reveal a little more, "But my real love is soldiers."

"Ah, soldiers? That's how come you know so much about those Napoleonic blokes"

"Yes. I've got hundreds. Not like the metal ones you have, not like the Ludendorff. Mine are plastic. Timpo, Lone Star, a few Britains."

"Do you think you'd like to be one, when you grow up?"

"A soldier?" Craig paused. An unsettling feeling of embarrassment came over him, given his ambitions and Baxter being a tank driver. "Maybe," he said but didn't go into any more details.

"Tanks ..." Billy's eyes clouded over, the memories stirring. "Panthers, they were the thing we dreaded most. Panthers were something else." He shook his head and sat back, reached inside his pocket and brought out a crumpled packet of cigarettes. Craig eyed them with distaste. Baxter caught his look and raised his eyebrows. "Yes, I know. I shouldn't. These damn things are killing me, lad."

Incredulous, Craig felt the rush of anger coming to his face, "So why do you still smoke them? You're ill, Mr Baxter. You shouldn't smoke them, not at all."

"You're right, and I know it. But..." Billy shrugged. "Truth be known, I'm not exactly sure myself. I've got more than an addiction, it's almost like bordering on ritual." He looked at the packet and slowly put it back. "If it makes you uncomfortable..."

"Passing over one cigarette isn't going to cure you, Mr Baxter."

"No, but it's a start. You never know, I might be able to give them up completely."

Craig shifted in his seat, unimpressed. "So, these Panthers..."

"Panthers...First time I saw one, my God, I couldn't believe it. The most beautiful thing I'd ever seen."

"Beautiful? How can a tank be beautiful?"

"This wasn't just any old tank, lad. The Panther was just about the best tank there was, on any side. I fought the damn things." He seemed to drift away again, the years coming back. "Since the day we'd landed on Normandy, I'd had this horrible sick feeling rolling around in my guts, every blasted moment of every blasted day. It was fear. I was stinking with it. We'd come in off the beach with little opposition and made our way inland. We saw lots of burned-out vehicles, plenty of dead people, but no Germans. We believed we'd missed all the action.

"As the days went by, the absence of German soldiers made us careless, I suppose. Motoring down those lonely lanes, nothing to see but high hedges, open fields, the occasional farm, everything deserted, our advance became more like a drive in the country. A vanguard, the brigade commanders said we were, our job to scout ahead of the main battle group, reconnoitre the land, ensuring it was secure for the main units following up. It was so quiet it felt as if the enemy was already long gone, the danger past.

"We carried on like that for mile after mile, and the farther we went the more complacent we became. When came across the first village, we stopped and looked. It was more of a hamlet really, a few houses clustered around a small square, overlooked by a rundown farm in the distance. A commander from another tank gave it the once-over with his binoculars, turned around, gave us the thumbs up and off we went. We were in a troop of three tanks. The lead tank went down the single street. Silent as the grave it was. That should have given us cause to be more alert, but like I say, we hadn't seen sight nor sound of anybody all along the way. We didn't know but hidden behind a wall was a seventy-five millimetre anti-tank gun. None of us saw it because it was camouflaged with all sorts of rubbish and we got a bloody rude awakening when it opened up on us, I can tell you." He sat back, studying the photograph at arm's length. "The first shell went straight through the turret of the lead tank as if it were made of cardboard. Struck dumb the rest of us were. I saw the shell, like it was in slow-motion, streaking through the air, going through that Sherman like it wasn't even there." He put the photograph down and blew out his cheeks, his voice taking on a low, distant. Tone. "Wally was screaming at Nobby to get the gun around. I had my eyes glued solid on that other poor tank because I saw another shell hitting it. It shook for a moment, then the whole damn thing blew up. One minute there, the next, engulfed in flames, a black, burning wreck."

From somewhere Craig heard the soft, slow chime of a clock, its mournful sound seeming to fit the mood. Baxter's words painted a terrifying scene and Craig's voice, when he found it, was little more than a croaked whisper. "What about the crew?"

"Not a chance. All dead, every one of 'em. That seventy-five, as we learnt quickly, made mincemeat out of Shermans. A Churchill would have withstood it, but as I sat in that damned bloody Sherman, I realised I was no longer safe and snug. I snapped out of my daze, rammed the tank into gear, and drove as fast as I could to the right, trying to create a difficult angle for the seventy-five. I wasn't thinking, I was reacting, and the streets were too narrow, nothing more than paths between the closely built houses. Forced to stop, I struggled to get the

Sherman into reverse, try another exit, but all I'd done was make us into a perfect target. Those seventy-fives were easy to move, and I knew the Germans were already making a beeline for us. The street was …ooh, I'm not sure…twenty feet wide, perhaps? Anyway, there wasn't much room to manoeuvre, and as I tried to reverse, Wally screamed at me to stop because the third tank was close up behind us. We were boxed in."

"Like a bottleneck."

"Yes, a bottleneck, that's exactly what it was. Anyway, Nobby, bless him, managed to aim our gun at that seventy-five. I could see the German crew working hard, trying to line us up for another shot. I battled with the gears and managed to inch the Sherman around, flanking the gun, and I saw the crew frantic, arms flapping, doing their best to get us in their sights. Then Nobby started firing. Now, that is *really* hard to do that is, firing a tank when it's moving. Virtually impossible. I don't know how he did it, but on the third round – the *third* round, mind you – he hit it. Went up like a firecracker. Then the other tank raked through the whole area with its machine gun. It only took a minute or two before it was all over.

"Wally radioed to H.Q. and they ordered us to find cover and keep quiet. There were plenty of Germans around, H.Q. said, and we had gone too far forward. Infantry were on their way to give us support, and until they arrived, we had to wait.

"Well, we waited all right, for almost twelve flaming hours. The other tank parked up in the farmhouse barn on the hill making it virtually invisible from the outside. Meanwhile, I managed to position our tank out of sight behind a little house and Bob draped a tarpaulin over us. Only the tip of the gun was showing. We felt pretty secure after that.

"Anyways, when the infantry finally arrived, I saw one of them was your uncle. Bob and me, we were almost dancing, so happy to meet up with someone from our hometown. By then, it was getting dark, so we stayed put until morning. We had no time for breakfast before continuing on our reconnaissance, much more cautiously now. We weren't going to be caught out again. Despite that, it was when we came to the next village that my life changed, Craig. Changed forever." Without warning, he creased up, engulfed by a bout of violent coughing, his body shuddering with the effort, face red.

Craig winced, gripping the chair's arms, watching as Baxter's face, now puce-coloured, creased up with the violence of his coughing. "You don't have to tell me any more, Mr Baxter, not if it's causing you distress."

Pressing a fist to his lips, Baxter shook his head,

his breath coming in short gasps. "Call me Billy." He patted his chest and winked. "I'm all right. Craig, it'll pass."

Not waiting, Craig rushed out to the kitchen and returned moments later with a glass of water. Smiling, Baxter took and drank it down. He grinned. "Thank you, Craig. Listen, what I'm about to tell you, I've only ever told to my wife before. Ex-wife that is. But I need to tell you because..." He looked away, clearing his throat for the umpteenth time. "When I told her, you see, she...Look, I want you to understand. War is just about the worst thing there is. It changes you, you see. You become less than human, doing and saying things that you wouldn't normally do or say. Because you know that at any moment, and I mean *any* moment, a bullet or a bomb is going to end your life, so you live on instinct. You don't think, you just do. You understand?" Billy Baxter's eyes seemed to be pleading. "No, how could you?" Baxter reached out and, to Craig's astonishment, ruffled the boy's hair. He smiled. "Everyone thinks I'm a grumpy old sod. Well, I suppose I am. I've got no friends, got no one at all. I just live here, on my own, apart from my dog, doing my garden, tending my allotment. I go down the pub, but nobody talks to me. Not even Bob ..." He stared into space as if the mention of his old comrade's name plunged him into a deeper chasm of despair. "What makes things worse is that I'm ill, as you know. I look old, Craig. Act old, too. Sometimes I find it difficult to get out of bed in the morning. The doctors, all they say is to stop smoking, give up the drinking...but they're the only things I've got left. It's my heart...you know that attack I had when you helped me? They're getting worse. The doctors said they would. But I'm not bothered, Craig. Not bothered at all because everything I ever had has gone, and everyone that ever loved me is dead or has left me. I've got nothing to look forward to anymore and knowing all my best times have already gone is the most depressing thought there is."

"But you *have* got things to look forward to... Billy. This story, you could write it all down again. A book. You could write a book."

"No, I won't be doing that. Let me tell you why, Craig. Let me tell you the part of my story that my wife thought was so awful that she left me. Yes, that's right. She thought I had done something so dreadful that she couldn't stand to be with me anymore. What was it she said, *'I thought I'd married a good man. Instead, I have married a monster!'* And with that, she packed her bags and left and took my baby girl with her." He looked over to Craig with eyes cloudy with grief. "I think you'll do the same, Craig. You'll not want to know me anymore, not after what I've told you."

Craig said nothing because he was no longer sure. All he knew was that he had to hear the truth. He sat back. "I'll do my best not to judge you, Billy. I promise."

"You're young, Craig. You haven't known pain, not the sort of pain I've had to deal with."

A sudden need gripped Craig, an urge to tell his own, painful story. He wanted to make this man understand that his life was not the only one filled with despair and misery. He thought of how he could retell it, without in any way diminishing Billy's own story. But before he could even open his mouth, Billy went and returned the photograph to its place on the wall. He studied it for a few quiet moments, then looked over his shoulder. "Perhaps… perhaps I've said enough for one day." He raised his hand to cut off any objections. "Truth is, I'm not feeling up to it right now, Craig. Why don't you call again tomorrow, if you can? Would that be all right?"

Craig nodded his head but couldn't keep the disappointment from his voice as he muttered, "Yes, of course." Having built himself up for this moment of revelation, all he felt now was frustration. "I could come and take your dog out if you like," he said.

Billy smiled and nodded. "Sounds good to me." And almost at once, the smile returned to Craig's face.

FIGHT

CRAIG HAD NO SOONER REACHED the end of the street than he saw him. Bob Bewdsley, standing, feet planted wide apart, clenched fists on hips, face set in a mask of cold, barely contained fury. Craig stopped, experiencing that horrible clenching around his scrotum, wondering what was wrong. He didn't have to wait long. Bewdsley marched forward, jaw set, face livid with rage. Stepping right up next to him, he jabbed his finger hard into Craig's chest. "I thought I told you to stay away from Baxter."

This close, dwarfed by the man's size, the fear overwhelmed him, the strength leaving his legs. As Craig fell back against the wall, he blurted it all out in one blast, "I was only taking his dog back. I found him, up in the park, and I knew Billy would be worried, and he was, and he asked me in and gave me some tea, and ..." He stopped, gulping in a huge lungful of air and steadied his racing heartbeat. Despite his fear, he held Bewdsley's glare. He'd faced down Crossland, he wasn't about to be intimidated again. "Anyway, why do you ask? What is so wrong with me—?"

"I told you he is a bad man," said Bewdsley, voice quivering, that wildness playing around his eyes. "I'm not going to tell you again, you hear me? *You stay away from Billy Baxter.*" He jabbed Craig again in the chest, forcing him backwards.

"There's nothing wrong with him," said Craig, clutching at his chest. "He's just misunderstood, that's all. What happened to him, it's made him—"

"What do you mean, *what happened to him*?" Something snapped in the man's demeanour, greater even than his anger. Something like panic. Could it be he was afraid of Billy Baxter? Gripping Craig by the throat, Bewdsley pulled him close. "What did he tell you? *What did he bloody well tell you?*" Shaking Craig, he sprayed spit, his body quaking with fury. "Tell me, you little shit!"

Craig snapped his head away. He was just like Crossland, only bigger. A bully, and Craig hated bullies, now more than ever. Trying desperately to tear himself free of the fist holding him, Craig realised within seconds there was nothing he could do, Bewdsley proving too strong. A long sigh of despair rattled from his throat. "Let me go!"

This pathetic show of defiance led Bewdsley to apply more pressure and his fingers squeezed hard around Craig's throat. "Tell me, or I'll wring your scrawny neck!"

Spluttering, Craig slapped and beat away at Bewdsley's hold, but nothing short of a mallet smashing over his skull was going to deter this monster. He sagged in the man's grip and perhaps it was this that forced Bewdsley to release the pressure, albeit a mere fraction. Coughing, Craig wheezed, "He didn't tell me anything, all right! Nothing. He told me to call again tomorrow when he'd tell me what happened to him in the War!"

"The *War*?" Bewdsley, breathing hard, tilted his head, frowning. "What about the War?"

"I don't know. He's going to tell me tomorrow."

"You don't go there, you hear? You stay away. The man is a lunatic, understand me? A raving, bloody lunatic. He'll tell you a pack of lies to disguise the truth of what he did. Baxter's a liar."

Despite the fear, or perhaps because of it, Craig reacted, drew a breath, summoning all his courage, all his bloody-mindedness. "But you *know him*, Mr Bewdsley. You were there, during the War, in France. You were part of his tank crew – you *know what happened*."

As if hit between the eyes, Bewdsley froze, mouth half open, lost in a dark and terrible place. He released his grip, strength draining away, and he seemed to collapse within himself. "Oh Jesus …"

"Mr Bewdsley," said Craig, overwhelmed with relief but resisting the urge to rub his throat lest it should spark off another assault, "what happened back then? Why is it so terrible?"

"I …" Blinking rapidly, Bewdsley slowly recovered his senses, his voice returning to normality, or as close as he could. "I don't want you listening to those stories, you hear me? They're all lies. *Lies*. He'll make it out that he's the victim, you see. The injured party. But he's not. After he told his wife, she ran off. With his daughter Millie. That's how bad it all was. But he'll not tell you the truth, Craig. He'll blame it on me, that's what he'll do. And it wasn't me – it was *him*."

"I don't understand. What was him? What did he do?"

But Bewdsley was no longer listening. Dazed, as if punched, he slouched off without another look, leaving Craig to massage his already swollen throat and consider that whatever Billy Baxter had to tell must be terrifyingly awful.

It was only as he neared home that he remembered he was meant to meet Melanie for her break.

Panic surged through him and he broke into a run, not stopping until he reached Liscard.

Woolworths was not a big store, and he saw her almost as soon as he burst through the door. She turned towards him, her eyes blazing. As he approached, throwing out his arms, he plunged into his explanation, "I'm sorry Melanie, I tried to get here sooner, but—"

"It's all right, Craig," she said coolly, her anger disappearing. "It's not as if we're girlfriend and boyfriend or anything."

He reeled, her words hammer blows into his heart.

"We'll have other days, but for now I have to get on. I'll see you later."

Buoyed up with a mixture of courage and desperation, he pushed aside his usual bashfulness and blurted, "Yes, later! I'll see you at five-thirty."

He swung away before she could reply because he knew what she would say. And he didn't want to hear it. Not now. Not today.

Finding a bench, Craig, vaguely aware of the shoppers milling all around him, put his face in his hands and tried to make some sense of the dreadful series of events that had ripped through his day so far. Coming across Crossland again, Baxter's revelations, Bewdsley's scary reaction and missing the meeting with Melanie. He imagined her waiting for him in *Sayers,* foot tapping with annoyance. Of them all, this was the worst. He sat back, unconsciously touching the welts across his throat. Yes, even worse than what Bewdsley had done to him. He'd let Melanie down, maybe lost any chance of making a go of things with her. When he met her later, he'd explain everything about what had happened. Except for Crossland. Nothing about him though because then he'd have to mention Samantha. No, best to leave her out of it, for now at least.

At closing time, standing across the street from the shop entrance, he saw her saying her farewells to her colleagues. As she turned to go home, she spotted him, her anxiety obvious as any anger she may have felt was replaced by something else – a look of panic.

He didn't hesitate, he needed to make her understand. Crossing over to her, he did his best to present a brave front, face serious, mouth a thin, hard line. "Melanie, I have to explain to you what happened today, why I didn't come to meet you."

"Craig, it's not—"

He stood not three feet away, swallowing down his natural shyness, pulling in deep breaths, determined to explain. "Yes, it *is* important, because I need to make you see. I couldn't get away to meet you, because of what happened." He studied her face, the way her eyes bulged, her bottom lip trembling a little. He frowned, realizing this was not panic after all, but fear. And it was growing. Something caught her attention behind him. Craig turned.

A boy, maybe eighteen or more, tall, razor-cut dark hair, wearing a plain white shirt and blue jeans, held up by braces, watched them. His face reddened as he stepped closer. "*Meet you*? Who the hell is this, Mel?"

Standing close, Craig had a better sense of just how big he was. Not just in height, but in his build. His arms, shoulders and forearms bulging with ropes of muscle.

"He's a friend, Danny. That's all."

Danny scowled at Craig, measuring him from head to foot, and snarled. "Clear off, you little fart."

Craig stood his ground, not with bravery, but through sheer confusion. He frowned at Melanie, hoping for an explanation. She seemed to be about to speak, but then Danny interrupted, right hand clamping around Craig's throat, almost lifting him off his feet. The third time that day, he realised in disbelief.

"I don't know who you are," this maniac hissed into Craig's face, "but I'm only going to say this once, so you better listen – I see you anywhere near her again, and I'll kill you, understand?"

Craig squirmed in Danny's grip. How could he *fail* to understand? He nodded limply.

Melanie's voice came from somewhere far away, "Danny, please—"

"You shut it," Danny screamed, turning his contorted face towards her, drawing back his hand as if to strike.

He didn't know how, and he certainly didn't know why, but Craig twisted himself free of the grip and threw out his arm to block Danny's blow. He acted from some deep-rooted sense of gallantry perhaps, but as soon as he reacted, he realized his error. Melanie yelped and stepped away as Danny swung around and, in uncontrolled rage, slammed his fist into Craig's stomach with the force of a steam hammer.

Craig retched as the air exploded out of his lungs. Head filled with a swirling grey mist, throat burning with the vomit rising from within, he crumpled, knees hitting the pavement hard. He floundered, unable to focus, moaning, wheezing.

Steel fingers caught him by the collar and picked him up, Danny's hot breath close to his ear, the voice, in contrast, like ice. Cold. Merciless. "I'll do for you. Open your gob again and I'll do for you!"

"*Oi!*" came a voice from a thousand miles away, "You leave him alone."

Craig, released from the grip, slumped on the

pavement, rasping in air, desperate to keep the rising nausea at bay. Through the mist of pain, he looked up, saw Melanie sobbing, managing to mouth 'sorry'. He forced a smile, shook his head.

A movement to his left grabbed his attention and he saw, in disbelief, the owner of the voice stepping up to them. The window-cleaner. He shot Craig a questioning glance, reached down and helped Craig to his feet. "What's going on here? This heap of shite causing you a problem?"

Rigid with uncontrolled anger, Danny struggled to form the words, "What's it to do with you?"

The window cleaner turned with infinite slowness, his voice low, dangerous. "He's a friend, now back off before I bounce you down the street."

Danny's mouth fell open. "Oh yeah? Bit of a hard case, are you?" He sniggered. "You're past it mate, go and find somewhere to lie down before I knock you down."

Craig saw it but could hardly believe it. Maybe three or four blows, fast and accurate. *Bang,* from out of nowhere, the first blow struck the side of Danny's jaw, wobbling his entire head as if it was connected to his neck by a spring. Stunned, incredulous, Danny tried to raise his arms. *Bang,* the second punch straight under the right eye, the force of it again rocking the head back and forth. Danny took the first two blows well, despite his head jerking like one of those punch balls you see in the fairgrounds. The third blow, however, was different. It thundered into his ribs, Danny's body bending, crumpling like an aluminium tray. Craig saw the look of disbelief on Danny's face. He was in more trouble than he could ever have imagined.

The look wasn't there for long.

The left fist came around in what Craig knew was a hook. It connected high up on Danny's temple.

Melanie screamed and ran to his side as Danny went down like a sack of potatoes.

Not even out of breath, the window cleaner grunted and shot Craig a concerned look. "Are you all right?" Craig blinked a few times, looked from his saviour to Melanie, saw her upturned face, those eyes so full of hatred. Yes, *hatred*. What the hell was wrong with her? Hadn't he tried to save her by putting himself between her and a crack in the face from her horrible boyfriend?

From out of nowhere, a short woman appeared, bristling with indignation. Face bright red with anger, finger-wagging, mouth curled back over gritted teeth, she directed her vitriol not towards Craig, not even at the window cleaner, but at Melanie.

The nightmare became a reality then, even more terrible than before.

Melanie broke down, tears tumbling down her face, "Mrs Penwright, I can explain, please let me—".

"I'm sorry, Miss Lewis, but this can't be allowed to happen. You're still wearing your overall, for pity's sake! We have the company's reputation to consider, and here you are—"

"It's not like that Mrs Penwright, I really didn't—"

"No, no, *I'm* sorry. You're representing the company, Miss Lewis. On Monday, you can return your overall and I'll give you your wages for the week, but I can't have someone like you working for us anymore."

Craig heard every word and watched Melanie's face collapsing into tears, the hopelessness complete. Danny on the ground, moaning, cradled in her arms. If he didn't suspect already, Craig now knew for sure that any chance he may have had to find a tiny piece of happiness with Melanie had been well and truly ripped up and thrown to the wind.

MAKING NO SENSE OF ANYTHING

THEY SAT at the bar of the Nelson Hotel in Grove Road, neither of them saying much, Fallon staring into space, Emery into the bottom of his glass. Pubs at lunchtime are not always a good choice, every drink seeming like a double. There were few punters around, but they generated enough noise to prevent either police officer from noticing the approach of another. Both jumped at the voice, "So this is where you are, sir."

It was Taylor, the second police officer on the scene of the Janet Stowe murder. He was out of uniform, doing his best to look casual in tweed jacket and dull brown chinos and failing.

"Not your usual haunt this, is it sir?"

Ignoring him, Fallon motioned to the barman

for a refill, holding up three fingers and nodding towards their newcomer.

"What's brought you here, Marcus?"

Taylor turned to Emery without expression. "Been thinking about Millie. Millie Baxter. I found her dad."

Fallon stopped, reacting with interest to what Taylor said. "We were going to have a look through the electoral roll, Taylor. You didn't have to—"

"I know that sir, excuse the interruption. He isn't on the electoral roll. He's never registered, but something came up, sir. A report. From the allotments behind Saint Luke's church. An old bloke by the name of Stan Prentis went up to Manor Road, made a statement about a boy."

"A boy?"

"Yes, sir. A young lad chased into the allotments by some bullies. Seems he ran into there trying to escape. Mr Prentiss did his public duty, sir. Saved us all a lot of time and bother."

"What's he got to do with Baxter?" asked Emery, thanking the barman with a nod when the fresh drinks arrived.

Taylor took up his glass, drank, smacked his lips. "It was in the old boy's statement. He was there when this boy came running across their plots. A William Baxter and another bloke, Robert Bewdsley, they were there too." He took another, larger drink. "I've got their addresses, sir."

The others exchanged a look. Fallon, nodding with appreciation, rolled his untouched glass in his palms. "Well done, Taylor. Impressive."

"Thank you, sir. I took it upon myself to go and see Mr Prentiss, sir."

"Oh?" Fallon swivelled around to face the young constable full on. "That shows a lot of initiative, Taylor. Why did you do that?"

A small shrug, an awkward smile. "I thought perhaps he could shed some light on it all because something in his statement ... The way Baxter was with the boy, sir. Angry. No, more than angry – *enraged* is what Mr Prentiss said. Bewdsley stepped in, protecting the terrified boy."

"All right, so tell us what you learned when you went to see Prentiss."

"He told me some very interesting things, sir. How Baxter and Bewdsley had served together in the War, Baxter being sent home wounded. He'd lost his leg. Mr Prentiss told me about what happened shortly after the War, with Baxter's wife. She left him, taking his daughter with her. Millie."

"Well done, Taylor!" Fallon's gratitude obvious, he beamed and rubbed his hands together, "Well done indeed."

"Thank you, sir, but it was more good fortune than anything else. If Prentiss hadn't come in ..."

"Well, he did, and that's all that matters. Drink up boys, and let's go and see these gentlemen. Emery, I want you to go and interview Bewdsley."

"Eh?" Emery turned a surprised face from Fallon, to Taylor and back again. "What's he got to do with it?"

Was there a note of jealousy in the young policeman's voice, Fallon wondered. The fact that Taylor had come up with the goods whilst Emery hadn't? Smiling, Fallon rolled his shoulders and pulled on his raincoat. "Give him Bewdsley's address will you, Taylor? You can come with me."

Beaming, Taylor finished his drink, winked at Emery and ripped off a page from his notebook. Sliding the paper across the counter, he strode after his superior officer, leaving Emery to contemplate the three glasses in front of him, and especially Fallon's, untouched and forgotten. "A little like me," he said aloud, took the glass and drained it.

AND ANOTHER

THE NEXT TIME Craig called on Billy Baxter, he found the old man in a sombre mood, quieter, more reflective. In addition, there was a further change about him, one that seemed to reflect Craig's own depressed feelings. Filled with images of Melanie holding Danny so close, sleep had proved impossible and now his body ached with fatigue, coupled with the punch he'd received in the guts.

Billy stood in the doorway, forming a very real barrier to any attempt to enter. Confused, Craig said, "I've come to take your dog out, Mr. Baxter. Remember?"

Face creasing, clearly, Baxter did not remember. A trickle of an awkward, confused smile developed followed by a slight shake of the head.

"I found him at the park, Mr Baxter. I brought him back here for you."

"Billy." Slowly the lights came on. "Call me Billy." Disappearing into the house for a moment, he returned with the little dog on its leash. Craig stooped and rubbed the dog behind its ears as Baxter said, "His name is Skipper."

"Skipper," Craig rubbed the dog more energetically, "that's a good name. I'll take him up to the park, if that's okay? Give him a run."

Without waiting for an answer, Craig trotted down the street with the little dog leaping with excitement beside him, relieved to leave the man's bleak demeanour behind.

Deciding on the shortest route to the park, Craig tried his best to keep his thoughts clear of the previous day's events. They refused to budge. After the fight, the window cleaner, or Gary as he had finally introduced himself, accompanied him home. They stopped at the gate and shook hands and Craig watched him. Once inside, ignoring his mum's shouts, Craig went to his room, lay down on the bed and stared at the ceiling. Melanie. She was all could think about. He'd lost her, if he had ever had a chance of being with her. There would be no more liaisons, no more tickling sensations in the tummy, nothing more to look forward to.

Taking Skipper out for a walk helped. The little

dog put everything into perspective. There were other things besides girls, he chided himself. How long had he known her for? Less than a week? He needed to get a grip, recharge his batteries and *stop* worrying!

Outside '*Bookland*' he tied Skipper to the railings and nipped inside for a quick browse through the paperbacks. His interest sparked by Billy Baxter's story, he purchased a novel about the Second World War. Outside, as he bent down to stroke Skipper, he caught a movement out of the corner of his eye, and his blood ran cold when he saw who it was.

Crossland, leaning against the wall outside the coffee shop, one foot propped up against the bricks as he peeled away a chewing gum wrapper. Craig knew it was a play-act, Crossland doing a bad job of miming. Stomach tightening, Craig scanned the street and spotted the other monster, Samantha, waiting to pounce.

He groaned. All he'd wanted was a quiet day, to enjoy the park with Skipper, to somehow erase the memory of Melanie and Danny.

He jumped when the little dog barked, pawing at his legs. It broke the spell and Craig, eyes set dead ahead, marched in the direction of the park where, if luck was with him, enough people would be around to prevent the bullies from doing anything terrible.

Hopes faded as he went through the gates. The weather, dull and grey, thick with the promise of rain, meant few people milled around. A solitary old man walked his dog, which growled at the sight of Skipper whilst, down at the lake, a fisherman, huddled in green coveralls, stared blankly at the float bobbing in the water. A bomb could have gone off without causing any reaction.

Skipper tugged hard at the lead, desperate for freedom. Craig stooped to release him and groaned. They blocked all three exits from the lake, Samantha and Crossland joined by Keith. Surprised, Craig stared at this most reluctant of bullies wondering what had caused him to become part of their gang once again. Then he saw Samantha, leaning against a tree, hair cut short like a boy. She wore a clean, newly pressed pink, check shirt tucked into tight blue jeans, and Craig understood. Craig's eyes roamed over her, his throat tightening. Why couldn't she set herself free from the bullies, just smile, be ... *nice*? In another world, he could ask her out, forget Melanie, be Sam's boyfriend.

He sniffed. More stupid, idle fantasies. He dragged the back of his hand across his nose, crushed by the hopelessness of it all.

Giddy, weak-kneed, he watched Crossland's swaggering approach, a huge grin splitting his face from ear to ear. Craig, realizing there was no chance of escape, sank under the weight of his defeat. Perhaps enjoying the prospect of seeing his victim squirm, Crossland's pace increased.

"Hello Craig," said the bully, stopping an arm's length away. Craig did not reply. Crossland pursed his lips and smiled down at Skipper. He rubbed his bandaged hand. "He's not yours, is he?"

The dog growled and Crossland backed off, wary. Yanking Skipper backwards, Craig gave his best hard stare and said, "What do you want, Crossland?"

"It's like I said last time – before this little turd of a dog interrupted me. We have some unfinished business, Craig my mate. There's going to be fun times ahead, for you and me."

Craig felt his insides melt, but still managed to stand without swaying. Brave or stupid, he couldn't work out which but knew only one thing – this menace had to stop. "I'm not going to beg for mercy, Crossland, if that's what you think. You can do what you want, but I'm not going to give you the satisfaction, so you may as well forget it."

"Brave words, little Craigy-boy. Wonder if you'll be so brave when I've knocked your teeth out and have my boot pressed down on your throat."

As if understanding the words, Skipper growled, louder this time, more threatening. Craig saw something flickering in Crossland's eyes, a mirror to his own fear. "Why can't you just leave me alone?"

Having already experienced Skipper's teeth, Crossland hesitated. Perhaps another dose would see him off for good. Frowning, Crossland glared uncertainly at Skipper. "That dog doesn't like me."

"I wonder why."

Anger flashed over Crossland's face, as the sarcastic remark bit deep. "I'm going to kick your teeth in, Craigy-boy, even with your dog here."

"I know you will, but I'll fight you, Crossland. You and your cronies. I'm not going to be such a push-over this time."

Crossland gaped, then laughed. "Fight me? *You?* Do me a favour, Craigy, you haven't got a clue about fighting."

"You tell that to Danny."

Craig almost cried out at his own pathetic, impulsive attempt at playing the big hard case.

"Danny who?"

And that was it, right there. *Danny who*? Because Craig didn't have a clue about Danny's surname. He turned his gaze to the surrounding fields. Almost at once, all his anxiety and fear disappeared, as if they had never been there in the first place. Striding across the grass came Ray, arms swinging, a bounce in his step.

Keith and Samantha came over at a run. "It's the other one," Keith gasped, nervous.

But Samantha's mood seemed to lighten. "It's your boyfriend, Craig – Ray-*mond.*"

Crossland narrowed his eyes. "I've always wanted a pop at Ray-*mond,*" he said, a hint of relish in his voice.

Samantha giggled. "Oh yeah, have a pop Crossy. Then I'll have a pop at little Craig here." She reached out, put her fingers under Craig's chin and tipped his head back. "You'd like that, wouldn't you, Craig? For me to have a pop at you?"

Craig gazed at her. Did she mean it, was this nastiness a sham, a performance for Crossland? He hoped so. There was something about her, an unseen power, the thrill of surrender intoxicating. He was about to breathe, 'Yes please,' when Skipper snarled and lurched forward. Samantha shrieked and Craig, snapping back to reality, pulled the dog back.

"Nasty little—"

"Give it a rest, Sam," snapped Crossland, eyes turned to the far side of the lake. "We have things to do."

From across the dappled water, Ray called out Craig's name. There followed a silence, and no one moved. It reminded Craig of a classic Western movie scene. The gunfighters staring at one another from opposite ends of the street, hands hovering close to their six guns, the music playing in the background, steadily building to a crescendo ... and then, all hell burst loose

It was Keith, the voice of reason from before, who moved first. He sprinted around the lake, fists bunched, head down, a charging rugby prop-forward and Ray ran to meet him. They slammed into each other with a sickening, hollow thud. Falling, they grappled like two desperate wrestlers. A mad flurry of kicks, punches, attempted holds, scratches and bites ensued, both struggling to gain the upper hand. First Ray, then Keith, grunting, rolling on top, pushed back, pinned down. Neither could gain the advantage.

Next to Craig, Samantha shadowboxed lefts and rights, punctuating her blows with grunts. "Go on, Keithy," she shouted. Craig watched in awe, her features so fine, prominent cheekbones, lips so soft, skin so smooth. Could this be the same girl who had held him over the cliff edge, who took so much pleasure from his discomfort, his terror? She caught his look and then did the most incredible thing, something he never believed possible at such a moment – she winked.

Behind him, Crossland roared and he charged forward, arms stretched out, snarling like a wild, enraged beast. Without thinking, Craig let Skipper go. The little dog charged, yapping and growling, hurtling itself towards the bully, snapping at his heels. Crossland in a whirl of flaying arms and thrashing legs tried to keep the dog at bay, but Skipper, tenacious and brave, was not to be put off by a few ill-placed kicks. As Craig watched those sharp white teeth sink into Crossland's ankle, heard the bully screech. Moving close, Samantha's voice floated into his ear. "I never wanted this, you know."

He turned to her, her face so gorgeous, eyes welling up. "What?"

"I never wanted to hurt you, and I don't mean what I say about Raymond being your boyfriend." She dragged in a breath. "I like you Craig, I really do. You're clever and funny and I wish… I wish everything was different. I don't want to do these terrible things, but I have to, you understand? I'm part of the gang, Crossy's gang. That's all there is to it. If I was on my own, things would be different, and you and me, we could … I wouldn't…" She shook her head and smiled. "I'm sorry, Craig."

Confused, not understanding anything, Craig wondered if her words held even a semblance of truth. Nothing made much sense anymore. With the world going wild around him, he had neither the courage nor the strength to decide what to do. Amidst all the confusion, however, he knew he should say something if nothing else than to tell her how crazy she made him feel. He held her gaze and stepped past her. He had to help, Ray. And Skipper.

Skipper, growling like something possessed, had Crossland's trouser bottoms firmly in his jaws. Craig was about to step in when something hard cracked across the back of his head. A searing, intense explosion of pain almost made him vomit. A deafening clanging of bells exploded inside his head and he reeled aside, losing his balance, his limbs so very heavy. He buckled as the ground began to move, rearing upwards to swallow him. Not even the sound of Skipper's maniacal barking could penetrate his senses now. Lightheaded, confused, vision blurring, he thought he saw the grass, felt its dampness beneath him. But nothing mattered anymore, only the sweet, irresistible desire to sleep.

POLICE, ALWAYS THE POLICE

"I DON'T KNOW what I can tell you," said Billy Baxter, showing the two plain-clothed policemen into his living room. "Tea?"

"We just have a few questions, sir. Nothing to concern yourself with." The man smiled and Baxter waited. The younger of the two policemen sat down, the other nodded towards an ashtray. "We won't have tea thank you, but can I smoke?"

"Suit yourself."

Smiling again, the older policeman lit his cigarette and stared out of the French window towards the garden, the early evening bathing it in an auburn glow. "I'm Detective Inspector Fallon. This," he waved his hand towards his younger companion, "is Constable Taylor. We're here to talk to you about the murder of Janet Stowe."

Outside, beyond the front door, someone was repeatedly slamming a car door. A horn blew. Voices raised. Then a silence. Silence in the room too. Tumbleweed quiet.

"Did you hear me, sir?" Fallon turned and stared directly into Baxter's grim face. "This is a murder investigation and we'd—"

"Murder?"

Fallon shot a glance towards Taylor. "Did you know Janet Stowe, sir?"

Looking from one man to the next, Baxter appeared in a sort of daze and dumbly shook his head, went to an armchair and fell into it. Stunned, unable to speak, the expression 'shell-shocked' might have come to mind. He sat staring into the distance as the seconds dragged by. Eventually, he seemed to rally himself. "Yes. I knew her."

Fallon joined Taylor on the sofa. Neither spoke. They simply waited until Baxter told them what he knew.

"She visited me a number of times, the first perhaps six months ago. Less maybe. I don't remember. Bold as brass she was, stood in the doorway, chin stuck out, daring me to tell her to bugger off. I didn't. Instead, I asked her in. She sat there, where you are now, and she asked me questions."

"Questions?"

"She was some sort of journalist, so she said.

Trainee, I think. Said she'd found a journal and wanted to ask me about it."

"A journal?" Baxter nodded. "Did she say where this journal came from, what it contained?"

Baxter shrugged, collapsing within himself. He fumbled for a cigarette, fingers shaking so badly that Fallon had to lean over to light the smoke for him. "Mr Baxter, however painful this is, you have to tell us. Like I said, this is a murder investigation."

"Yes, yes, I understand." He blew out a stream of smoke and watched it float upwards to the ceiling, a ceiling stained brown with accumulated nicotine. "It was something one of my pals kept in the War, you see. Notes, memories, that sort of thing. She said she'd found it by accident but when she read it she had to know." He looked from one policeman to the next. "Know if it was true. I confirmed it, of course. At first, I thought that was all it was, that she merely wanted some background information for a piece she was writing about local war heroes, but when she came again she was different."

"In what way different?"

"Angry. She sat right there, where you are and told me she knew everything."

"Knew everything?" interjected Taylor. He stopped when Fallon gripped his knee.

Baxter, ignoring what passed between the others, looked at his hands. "She told me she knew all about what I'd done, that she'd learned it from my daughter. And, if I didn't cough up a thousand quid, she'd write the truth in her newspaper, tell everybody everything."

Taylor's voice crackled with enthusiasm, "So she was blackmailing you?"

Fallon sighed and, shaking his head, smiled across at Baxter. "Forgive my colleague, Mr Baxter. He's somewhat impetuous."

"He's almost right," said Baxter, not looking up from his hands, "only trouble is – I haven't got a thousand pounds. I told her so. She didn't believe me, of course. Started ranting on about how I'd be prosecuted under the Nuremberg War Trials, maybe even the English courts. I didn't know if that was true or not, but when I told her some home truths about the man she got the journal from, she grew quiet. Very quiet. First of all, she said I was lying, that I was just trying to cover my backside, but I showed her some letters. When she compared them with what was written in the journal, she went white, started swearing, and stormed out. That was the last I heard of her."

"Wait a moment," said Taylor, forever keen and eager. "What letters?"

"Letters which proved that what she thought was the truth, what she'd read in the journal, was nothing but a bunch of lies."

"I don't understand," said Fallon. "Janet Stowe thought she could blackmail you because of something she'd read in a journal and which Millie confirmed to her?"

"Millie?" Baxter's face drained of colour. "You mean ... what has Millie to do with anything?"

"She was Janet Stowe's flatmate. She knew of Janet's investigations about what she had unearthed in the journal. What was it, Mr Baxter?"

"You don't need to know."

"I'm afraid I do, Mr Baxter. Like I told you – this is a murder inquiry."

"The reasons she died can't have anything to do with what I showed her. Those letters can't be why she was murdered."

"All right, even if that were true, she now knew the truth. Perhaps the killer took it upon himself to finish her off, shut her up because he was involved. Involved in something pretty awful, Mr Baxter."

"I wouldn't know."

"But you can hazard a guess, surely."

"I know about how her body was found from reading it in the Echo. I didn't once believe it had anything to do with what I'd told her. I still don't."

"Why not?"

"Because ... Ah, Jesus, I need that bloody cup of tea even if you don't." He stood up and went out, leaving Fallon to give his colleague a quizzical look.

Taylor chomped his teeth a few times. "You think he did it?"

"Taylor, you're beginning to sound like Emery. You did well getting this old boy's address, but let's just stop the detective work right here and now, all right." He shook his head. "He no more did it than I did. *But* ... Millie must have told Janet something that caused her to come around here and try and blackmail Baxter. My hunch is the perpetrator got nervous, angry, violent and poor Janet ended up getting herself murdered by the owner of the journal."

"And you think Baxter knows who this perpetrator is?"

"Almost certainly."

The prolonged buzz of the front doorbell stopped Taylor from further speculation. The two policemen waited whilst Baxter went to the door. Voices fired off with machine-gun rapidity, then Baxter returned to the room, flustered, scared. "It's my neighbour. Something is happening down at the park. They've got my dog – and Craig!"

A face, vaguely recognizable, brought him a curious sense of comfort. As features mingled and melded together, they formed a familiar shape. Concerned eyes, narrow and piercing, lips a thin, pale line. Craig forced a smile before the fog rolled in again and he gave himself up to the liquid warmth of it all, resistance disappearing and he slipped away once more.

As he drifted into soft, inviting arms of sleep, someone shook him by the shoulder. He wanted them to stop, let him sleep. It was so lovely there, so soothing. A voice, urgent yet so far away, broke into his consciousness. *"Craig ...Craig wake up!"* A voice of no importance. Only sleep was important now.

The hands forced him to stir. He tried to knock them away, angry at them for rousing him from his beautiful dreams. Dreams of Melanie and Sam, watching them walking away from him, those jeans so tight.

Despite the fuzziness, the world gradually came into focus. A strong hand cupped itself behind his head, easing him upright. He moaned. Pain, a burning rush across his skull. Wooziness engulfed him again, his head lolled, and they lowered him gently back down.

"Craig?"

He recognized the voice now. A gruff, barbed voice, capable of cruel, harsh words. But not this time, not now.

"Craig?"

His eyes sprang open, but the glaring brightness burned into his brain, forcing him to turn away. A hand yanked his face forward again. Billy Baxter's face filled his vision, deep lines of concern cut into his face. "Are you all right?"

Craig tried a grin. "I think so." Gingerly he touched the pulsing spot at the back of his head, pulling his hand away almost at once as an electric shock of pain hit him. Tiny traces of blood were on his fingertips. "What happened?"

"It was that girl," spat Billy Baxter, helping Craig to his feet. Billy held him as Craig swayed, legs wobbling, not yet able to support his weight.

"Girl?"

"She hit you on the back of the head with a piece of wood. The ambulance is on its way. Try not to worry."

The girl? Craig wanted to scream. All the doubts about her words were true. She lied. The impact of her lies hit him with more power than her blow to his head. "You mean, Samantha?"

"Is that her name? I wouldn't know. Blonde girl, pretty. What the hell's she doing mixed up with the other two, I've no idea. But she hit you. Craig. She told the police exactly what happened. Listen, don't be thinking of all that. Like I say, the ambulance will be—"

"I don't need an ambulance," said Craig, a new resolve restoring his courage

"You might have concussion. Best to be sure."

Craig, not yet sure of where he was, saw people

milling around, people he didn't recognise, gawping at the sight, the heavy, dull buzz of their conversation as they soaked up the drama, relishing the gossip they could spread. "I'm all right, I promise. Just a bit groggy. Police you said? What police? Why are they here?"

Billy helped him over to a bench and lowered him onto it. From somewhere, Skipper came yapping, tail a blur and Craig's heart leapt. Grinning, he bent forward and ruffled the dog's neck and throat. "Thank God he's all right. It's coming back to me now. There was a fight and … Oh, Billy, I thought they'd hurt him, for sure."

"Nah, he's tougher than he looks. Besides, I think your bully-boy mate came off worse. He'll be needing the hospital as well, I shouldn't wonder."

He found he could focus now. There they all were. Crossland and Samantha, sitting dejectedly on another bench, Keith standing just to the side, his face a picture of bruises and bleeding cuts. Farther away, stood Ray. Ray, his friend, his saviour! Craig wanted to go to him, hug him, thank him, ask him a million questions about what had happened.

But next to Ray stood a tall man, writing something in a notebook.

"Billy," whispered Craig, not taking his eyes from Ray and the man. "Billy, is that…"

"It's the police, Craig," said Billy. He stood as two

uniformed officers appeared. Not police this time, although their black surge made them look almost identical. "Just sit still, there's a good lad, I've got to go and talk to those two. They're park wardens, and I need to tell them what's happened."

Craig was no longer interested. Crossland took his attention now, and the other, older man, in a shabby raincoat, talking to him. As he looked, Craig couldn't believe what he saw.

Crossland was crying.

HOME IS NOT ALWAYS HOME

"I'LL MAKE you something to eat," Ray's mum said, fussing like a moth around a lamplight. She stroked her son's eye, applied more witch-hazel to his bruises, and a dab of iodine to the cut on his bottom lip. "That policeman was nice. Very young. So polite. He said you saved Craig. Says you might get your name in the papers."

"Please, mum."

"You mustn't be so modest, Raymond. If you hadn't gone there when you did, they might have killed him."

"That's just silly."

"Well, the nice policeman said they might have killed the little dog." She hugged him, squeezing him so hard against her ample bosom he cried out and she pulled back, appalled. "Oh Raymond, I'm sorry, I didn't mean to—"

"Mum, please. Policemen are not nice."

"Well, this one was. Are you feeling better, because if you need any—"

"*Mum!*"

"All right, all right. I´ll get you something to drink. We have cherry-aid. You want some?"

Ray nodded and watched her go to the cupboard underneath the sink. "Dad told me that police are not to be trusted, that all they want to do is nick you."

"Nick?"

"Arrest you."

She grimaced as she tried to open the bottle. It was new, freshly delivered that morning. Ray, a big lad, reached across and, with the merest flick of his wrist, screwed off the black top. She poured the wildly fizzing drink into a glass. "He shouldn't say such things," his mum said sitting down at the table. "The police are there to help. They helped you, didn't they?"

"Mum, I don't want you to tell Dad about what happened."

She tilted her head. "He's away on business for the moment, Raymond. He won't be back until the middle of next week." A smile. "Perhaps by then all those knocks will have disappeared."

"So you won't tell him?"

For a long moment, she seemed to consider this, weighing up whatever reasons there might be for not giving her husband the details. "Let's hope the police don't call again when he's here."

"I'm sure they won't."

"Let's hope not."

This time it was Ray who hugged his mother, pressing her to him. "Thanks," he said into her neck. He knew all too well that if his dad did know, the response would be horrific, as it was two years ago when the police brought him home after that incident in Peter Toner's. Sometimes the memory of those blows forced him awake at night and, when he heard his dad mooching around downstairs, the fear gripped hold of him by the balls and squeezed him until he cried out, muffling his voice in his pillow.

His mother's voice cut into his thoughts. "How is Craig?"

"I don't know," said Ray, disengaging himself from her arms. "They were still waiting for the ambulance when the police brought me home. I hope he'll be okay, but Samantha really clocked him one, I can tell you."

"*Clock?*" She giggled. "I sometimes think I will never master this English language."

He joined her, laughing and the mood lightening at last. "Clock. To hit. She hit him across the back of the head with a bit of tree branch, I think. Laid him out flat."

"She's a terrible girl."

"No, it's Crossland, he has her in his control. She's frightened of him."

"A bully. All bullies should be given a piece of their own – what do you call it – a piece of their own medicine?"

"A dose. A dose of his own medicine. Yes, you're right, Mum. He should. Somehow, I don't think we'll be seeing much of him from now on. Not too sure about Samantha, though. I think Craig likes her. A lot."

"Oh my, that's not good."

"She is good-looking."

Her face dropped, "Oh my, Raymond! What are you saying?"

"Mum," he reached over and squeezed her hand, "I'm not a little boy anymore and neither is Craig. We're fifteen. Next year is our last year at school. Girls ..." He turned away, jawline reddening. He stood up, touching his lip, testing it. "I'm going to my room, listen to some music. If Dad calls, you'll not—"

"I told you, Raymond, I won't tell him anything. He'll only worry anyway."

He stared at her. She didn't know anything

about the beating his dad had meted out, closed fists, real punches slamming into his ribs, careful to avoid the face. Ray wondered what her reaction might be if she knew the truth. Not only of the beating but of that night when Ray had seen the girl. In bed. With his dad.

Alone in his room, he lifted the lid of his record-player, and gently lowered the stylus onto the forty-five. He sat back as the sound of Manfred Mann's 'Mighty Quinn' filled the room and for a few, blissful moments, he could forget.

IN A BROKEN CHURCH TOWER

SOON AFTER ARRIVAL, an ambulance man shone a tiny pen torch into his eyes, asked him to roll them around, look left then right. Someone had telephoned Mum. She had rushed down from work, still in her grey overall, ashen-faced. The tears spilt down her face as she put her hands on his shoulders, careful not to touch his bandaged head. Billy stepped up and eased her away, talking with her, and she kept glancing over, a tiny smile, a raised hand. Craig returned it with a 'thumbs-up' and that seemed to help, her shoulders relaxing.

"Do you feel sick?" the ambulance man asked.

"A little."

"But you haven't *been* sick?"

He shook his head, attention drawn to the plain-clothes police again, the way they seemed to be speaking in harsh tones at Crossland and Samantha. They were too far away for Craig to pick up the words, but he saw their expressions, knew it was serious. Samantha sat slumped on a park bench. Keith, next to her, pinching his nose, blood dripping onto the ground. They'd taken Ray away and he wondered where to.

One of the policemen exchanged some words with the ambulance man before stepping closer. He squatted down on his haunches, stern-faced. "You're going to be all right, son," he said. "She could have split your skull wide open, stupid girl as she is. We'll be taking them to the station, and you'll have to come along later and make a statement."

Craig saw it played out in his mind. Charges made, a court appearance perhaps. Crossland would probably get some sort of detention, and Samantha…She'd said she was 'sorry', so why had she hit him? He believed she was sincere, but she wasn't. Right now, sitting like a little lost girl, he couldn't believe she had done what she did. She was staring into the distance, no doubt wondering why her world had become a nightmare, as did Craig. "I don't want to," he said in a small voice.

"You *don't want to?*" The policeman appeared puzzled. "What do you mean you don't want to? You're not in trouble, son. It's only so we can get a better picture of what went on here."

All of a sudden, Mum was there with Billy close behind her. "Craig, we're going to make a complaint," she said, voice trembling with a mix of anger and worry. "They can't get away with this."

"Your mum's right," said Billy. "They need to be taught a lesson."

"They already have," said Craig, and he met the policeman's eyes and held them. "My dad always said you have to learn lessons the hard way, and I think that's what they've done."

"Craig!"

"No Mum," he smiled at her. "I think they know what they've done. Especially Samantha. I want this to be over, Mum. That's all. Over."

The policeman seemed annoyed, and clicked his tongue, "I'm going to talk to them, put the fear of God into them..."

"But tell Samantha..." Craig shook his head, "Just tell her, I understand."

Mum seethed, hands on hips. "Well, *I* don't understand, Craig. I don't understand you, or any of this!"

"I do, Mum. That's all that matters. I see it now. She told me, you see, told me she felt trapped inside the gang. I don't think she wanted to hurt me, not like this. Let's just forget it and go home."

As he made to leave the lake, he saw the policeman wagging his fingers at the defeated bullies, all of them crying. Samantha's eyes met his, and even from this distance, he could see that silent 'thank you' written there. That made him feel so much better.

Another policeman, one in ordinary clothes, told Craig's mum they needed to speak with him further but, due to the trauma, it might be best to delay the conversation. Mum didn't seem happy but didn't press him over what they might ask him and Craig, for his part, told her he needed to go back to Mr Baxter's to check on the little dog. She wasn't going to budge, he could see that, and she insisted he rest, so it wasn't until the following morning that he called around to check on Skipper.

The little dog wasn't well. Craig could tell that just by looking at him. He lay on the sofa, flat out, Craig slowly stroking his tummy. Across from them, Billy Baxter watched, in a dream-like state. Neither had spoken for a long time, not since the previous day. After the police had told everyone off, Craig had gone home for a hot drink and a lie-down. That morning, Mum eventually gave in to his pleas to go and visit Billy, and little Skipper. Now, here they all were, not a word passing between them. Stroking the dog, whose big eyes seemed so mournful, Craig's anxieties grew. At some point in the melee,

Crossland must have succeeded in kicking the little terrier somewhere bad and now Craig was sure there was something seriously wrong.

Observing them, concern etched into every crease of his face, Baxter sighed. "I should never have let you take him out," he said. "I should have realised... But them bullies, they shouldn't have done what they did. To you, or to Skipper."

"I'm sorry, Mr Baxter. If I'd known they were around, I wouldn't have taken him...I'm sorry."

"No, no, I'm not blaming you, Craig. I'm blaming them. It was their fault." He looked out of the window, his attention drawn elsewhere for a moment. "A week or so ago, I *would* be blaming you. You've taught me a lot, Craig." He padded out of the room, leaving Craig to continue tickling Skipper's tummy. From the kitchen, he heard the clanking of teacups, of water pouring into a kettle. Although he had not asked for tea, Craig was grateful for the time he had alone. Billy Baxter was acting strangely, and not solely because of what happened at the lake. There was something more, but Craig could not fathom what it might be. His old anger returning perhaps, but this time directed towards the bunch of bullies. Concern for Skipper ... That expression on his face, as if he were looking back, bringing up memories... could it be the story he'd left untold?

Baxter returned with a tray full of steaming cups

of tea and a plate overloaded with chocolate biscuits. Reluctantly, Craig left Skipper's side and settled down in an armchair. They drank tea and Craig munched down the biscuits. "I'm glad they're in trouble," said Baxter with feeling. "The policeman told me that they are going to press charges. There will be a court appearance. The girl is going to be charged with GBH."

Grievous Bodily Harm. Craig, appalled at this news, felt his stomach tighten. "I didn't want that, I told the police I didn't want to press any charges."

"The police have other ideas, Craig. Sorry, it's out of your hands. That boy, Crossland? He's been in trouble before, has a bit of a record. The girl will get a warning, but *him* ... He may even end up in Borstal, who knows. She came round to see you, so your mum told me."

"Who did?"

"The girl."

"*Samantha*?" He couldn't believe it. She had actually gone to his house? "When was it, I don't remember."

"You were asleep. Your mum was furious, sent her away."

"Mum never said..." The thought of Samantha coming to see him, to check that he was all right... He put his tea down. "I think she wants to change,

Billy. I don't believe she's all that bad, not really. She told me she was sorry."

"Was that before she hit you, or afterwards?"

The words were as sharp as a knife blade. Clearly, Baxter was not convinced of Samantha's Road to Damascus conversion, but what could Craig say to change the old man's mind, what answer was there to give? He shook his head. He hated the thought of Samantha receiving a punishment, even if it was only a warning. He was sure she hadn't meant to hurt him so badly. The ambulance man had repeated that he was extremely lucky not to have suffered a fractured skull. Surely, Samantha never intended for such a thing to happen? Craig said as much.

"You're too forgiving, Craig."

"How can anyone be *too* forgiving? What's done is done, and they realize it, Crossland and the rest, so what's the point—"

"The point is they should be punished for what they did."

"But they have been, already. Especially Samantha – I don't think she'll be hanging around with Crossland from now on."

"Craig, they need ... " He shook his head and rubbed his chin. "Ah, what's the point? Who knows, what you say may well be true..." He kicked his heels against the carpet, eyes downcast, struggling with something. "Craig."

Craig looked up, catching the serious tone in Billy's voice.

"Listen…if anything were to happen to me … would you, do you think …" He pulled in a breath, "Would you look after Skipper for me?"

Craig went to speak but checked himself, a mix of anxiety and confusion bringing a tremor of trepidation to run through him. "What do you mean, Mr. Baxter? If *anything happens to you*? Like what?"

"It's Billy, Craig, don't forget. Call me Billy." He drained his cup. "I'm not going to be around forever, and Skipper's only a young dog. I found him, you know. Stray he was, rooting around in the compost up at the allotments. Silly little thing. Cute though. I couldn't resist him. Took him to the vet to get him checked over and they told me he wasn't much more than about six months old. I had another dog … Alsatian he was. Lovely thing, but I couldn't control him on the lead. He was so strong."

"What happened to him?"

"Bob took care of him. Bob Bewdsley. You remember Bob."

Flashes of him, the threats, the promise of violence simmering under the surface. How could he ever forget him? "Yes, of course. So, he looked after your dog? Your Alsatian?"

"Yes. Although to be honest, I haven't seen much of him since ... probably because Bob's away a lot. He owns some other properties and has to look after them. Anyway, Skipper was nowhere near as hard to look after." He shrugged. "I couldn't bear to think of him ending up in some rescue centre, given away to a bunch of people I don't know. I'd much rather he went to someone who cared for him, who knew him." He smiled. "Like you."

None of this was what Craig wanted to hear. He looked down at the little dog, stretched out, relaxed and content. Whatever Crossland had done, the danger seemed to be over. Clearing his throat, uncertain how to proceed with what was churning him up inside, Craig went for the direct approach. "Could you finish that story for me," he asked quietly.

Billy stiffened a little, "Craig. I don't think that's such a good idea."

"Please. Look, I know you think it'll turn me against you, but it won't. I won't judge you, not like ..." his voice trailed away. He didn't dare voice the thoughts developing in his head.

But Billy knew, and he said it, "Not like my wife did, you mean. Well, you're right enough there. She judged me, true enough. Wouldn't listen to my explanation. She felt betrayed, I suppose you could say." He sat back in his chair, stretching out his legs.

A rumbling developed in his throat. "I don't feel half so bad today," he said, almost to himself. "Knocked the fags on the head."

"Really?" Craig beamed. "But that's great, Billy. You'll start to feel so much better from now on, trust me."

"You think so? I'm not so sure. I took up smoking when I was *ten* Craig. Ten. Never stopped since then, never felt I could, or that I wanted to. That's another thing you've taught me."

"So, why are you being so morbid then?"

"Morbid?" Billy laughed. "Where did you get a word like that from?"

"Reading. I read a lot."

A silence followed. Craig felt Baxter scrutinizing him as if for the first time. "I always thought you were something of a reader. You're very special, Craig, do you know that? In so many ways – the way you are with that girl, for example, how you've forgiven her. That takes courage that does, a lot of courage."

"I don't think it's courage, it's just…" He felt awkward. He'd seen the look on Samantha's face, and that was enough. She was frightened, not only of what was going to happen to her but of what she'd done. They must have told her how close she'd come to causing him serious damage. "I think … I'm not sure what I think, but I know she has changed.

People can change, like you Billy. I'd like to hear your story because, in a way, it might help. Help me."

"Help you?"

"Yes, with how I think about things. So, maybe ..." He shrugged.

Billy sighed. "You seem troubled, Craig."

"No, I'm okay."

Billy went to say something more, but stopped, saying only, "Nah, doesn't matter." He clapped his hands together, "All right. If it's the story you want, I'm just going to have to take the risk. But try and remember, Craig. This was in wartime. I was very different then. We all were."

Craig sat back and waited. Skipper, no doubt feeling put out that the tickling had stopped, opened one eye, gave a grunt, and then promptly fell asleep. Craig's attention centred on Billy now, and what he had to say.

They moved out into the garden. It was a lovely day and Craig was grateful to be in the fresh air. Sat on the patio, Craig looked towards where, not so very long ago, the football had lodged itself under the wheelbarrow. So much had happened since then. Old wounds well healed.

Billy poured orange juice into a glass brim-full

with ice. He winked, "I think you'll enjoy that slightly more than tea."

Craig smiled and took a sip. "Delicious," he said and waited for what he knew was to come.

Baxter stretched out his legs, folded his hands over his stomach and looked into his past, recounting the details of the horrors that forever changed him, his voice low, reflective, and laced with emotion.

"I left off telling you about the seventy-five-millimetre causing chaos amongst our troop. I'm now going to continue with when our infantry arrived and decided to stay and support us. Almost immediately, they fanned out around the tanks as we left the little hamlet. We crossed open country, trying our damnedest not to out-pace them. Tanks without infantry support are sitting ducks so we moved at a slow speed until eventually we came to another little village. It wasn't like the last one. It was utterly destroyed, the buildings reduced to rubble, huge potholes all along the roads. A whole battalion of Germans might be lying in wait for us amongst the debris, so we moved in slow. One structure remained intact – the bell tower of a ruined church. We parked up and I peered through the driving slit. There was something not right about it, I could feel it in my water. Call it sixth-sense if you like but a terrible premonition of something awful about to happen overtook me. I felt sure the Tommies accompanying us would sense something, but they didn't seem in the least bit concerned as they picked their way through the broken buildings. Wally even felt confident enough to stand up out of the turret. Now Wally hardly ever did that, but he was laughing and joking as if the danger was gone, that we may as well be on holiday. It was that sort of atmosphere and for a moment I almost believed him." He paused, eyes dark, remembering. "Then the shot came, ending all of those feelings in an instant."

Leaning forward, deep in thought, Baxter rested his arms on his knees.

"I didn't know what had happened at first. Everything stopped, like a freeze-frame in a movie. It lasted for no more than a couple of seconds before everyone started screaming. A bullet had hit Wally and it was bad. I mean, *really* bad. It was a sniper you see and the bullet had hit him right in the head. He was dead, of course. I couldn't see him, but the others were yelling, telling me to get out of there. Soon machine guns were opening up, the Tommies scurrying around like ants as they ran in all directions.

"I slewed the tank around, brought it to a halt, and got out. I don't know why, don't ask me. It was against every procedure we'd trained for. You're safer in the tank than out, unless it was on fire, of course. But I wasn't about to worry about any of that malarkey. So far, there had been no anti-tank fire, and I felt sure there wouldn't be any. A lone sniper, hidden away, with orders to delay the enemy for as long as possible, that's who this was. I wriggled my way through my escape hatch and looked up and there was Wally. I say 'Wally', but the thing hanging there, a hideous lump of bloodied flesh stuck in that turret was nothing like the friend I remembered." Baxter ran a hand through his thinning hair, his voice quaking as he continued. "His whole head had gone. I didn't know what to do, I was confused, frightened. Then I saw Bob, scrambling outside too. We looked at one another, both of us gawping, trying to come to terms with what had happened. One minute Wally was there, the next just a headless corpse. I'm sorry to say I threw up. That was what saved my life."

Listening intensely, shocked at what he heard, Craig barely mumbled, "What? Being sick saved your life?"

Baxter nodded, "Yes. It came over me in a great wave and I couldn't help myself. As I bent double, I heaved my guts all over the ground just as another bullet whizzed overhead and slapped into the tank's hull, right where I was only moments before. Some dirty great sergeant slammed into me like he was playing rugby, and we went to the ground in a heap.

He pushed me behind some rubble, and we lay there, breathing hard. He had a Sten gun with him, a sub-machine gun that is and all I had was my sidearm. I nudged him and told him to hand over his gun. He was an enormous bloke, but he must have seen the look in my eyes. Without any argument, he gave me it and I immediately took off, keeping low, weaving this way and that, as fast as a whippet. Three or more shots whizzed overhead. I felt them burning through the air like hot streaks before I rolled behind a bit of cover, where a bunch of Tommies were crouching. They told me two snipers were firing from different positions and moving after every shot. Then Bob appeared, a look on his face the like of which I'd never seen before. A man possessed he was, eyes wide and wild. It chilled me to the very core of my being. He smiled. Can you believe that? He actually *smiled*. Like he was enjoying the thrill of it all, I guess but something else as well. He was relishing the thought of killing them. We'd come all the way from the Normandy beaches, and throughout Bob was so quiet, in a deep sleep, but now everything came to the surface, the manner of Wally's death making him snap."

He paused. His hands were shaking. Despite his desperation to hear the rest of the story, Craig waited, not wanting to push the old man too hard.

He knew exactly what it felt like to relive such hurtful memories.

Without prompting, Billy took up the story again, voice monotone, almost dreamlike as if he were in a sort of trance "The Tommies set up a Bren and began strafing the top of the bell tower where they believed the snipers to be. Bob prodded me in the shoulder. 'I want to find Wally's killer,' he said and without any hesitation, he broke cover. I sprinted after him, careless of the soldiers' warning cries behind me and we both leapt over the rubble, making straight for the tower.

"We must have been blessed that day because we reached the base of the tower without so much as a graze. I stood flat against the wall, sucking in the air, and all I could think about was Wally. He was my mate, my best mate, Craig. He'd always tell us stories about his life back home, his wife, Joan, and his little lad Michael. He'd pass his photographs around and we'd all listen patiently to him as he reminisced about them. We must have heard those stories a hundred times, but we didn't care. Some of them were so funny. He could tell great jokes about how things that had happened. We laughed so loud our guts ached. We were so glad to be alive and together. So now, with it all gone, a kind of mist came down over us. Certainly, it did with me. I remember standing there, feeling first sad, then angry. Angrier than I've ever felt before. I could see Bob felt the same. With sweat and tears streaming down his pale face, his hands holding the Sten shaking uncontrollably, there was no doubt he was close to falling apart. Both of us were so full of hatred for those damned snipers – there was no honour with them, just a cold-hearted determination to kill, with no thought for those they killed. It's the same as being in a tank. You're distant from everything, detached but the big difference, of course, is that drivers don't kill. Neither Bob nor I had fired a single shot in anger since coming onto the beaches at Normandy. All that was about to change.

"Bob set off and soon out-distanced me. I followed cautiously across the twisted heaps of mangled stone and jagged metal where many shells had blown huge holes into the walls. Reaching the stairs, which were mostly intact, I caught a glimpse of Bob disappearing at the top. I heard the Sten rattling off a burst of fire, then another. If I had any fear, at that moment they all disappeared. I ran, taking the stairs two at a time, not knowing what I'd find, or caring.

"I paused about half-way up and shouted for support from the others and before long several Tommies joined me. We edged up and at the top, we saw a massive, gaping hole where once the tower connected to the rest of the church, with the open sky above us. Wooden planks crossed the gap, like the bones of the building. A shape moved over to my right. Not knowing where he was, I screamed for Bob to take care, that those bastards were close. As one of the Tommies covered us with the Bren, the rest of us plunged into the guts of the ruined church.

"All I could think about was how like a sitting duck I was and expected the sniper to open up at any moment. But there was no shot, only the sound of Bob's Sten again. I ran on, the other Tommies close behind. We were in the rafters, I think but there was so much rubble everywhere it was difficult to pick out any details. We were perfect targets and then, as I moved towards another clump of cover, a bullet pinged off a fallen buttress, ricocheting away to hit the bloke to my left in the face. He fell, screaming like blue murder. I'd seen plenty of blokes who'd been shot, and I knew the difference between a killing wound and one that kept you on the ground, wounded. He was going to be all right, but I'd seen where the shot had come from and I indicated where the sniper was. Motioning to the others to outflank him, I slithered over the rubble.

"A tall bloke got down next to me and fired off short bursts, shouting he could see the sniper. 'There he is, there he is!' Squinting through the shadows, I saw them."

Chest sounding tight and wheezy, the effort of retelling his story was proving too much. Baxter paused and poured himself some juice. He drained the glass in one and sat back. Refreshed, a renewed purpose crossed his face. "There were two of them. The Tommies had managed to block off any exits and we had them cornered. When some of the Tommies shouted to them to come out, they gave up, hands high in the air, rifles thrown down. As I came up, they had their backs to me and I heard one of the Tommies, who had his rifle trained on them, saying something. He then did the strangest thing. He pushed the muzzle of his rifle toward the nearest sniper, put it under the rim of his helmet, and tipped it off.

"I just stood there, not believing what was there before my eyes."

He stared, studying his empty glass.

Craig couldn't contain his impatience and cried out with the suspense, "*What*, Billy? What was it you saw?"

Baxter's eyes bored straight into him. "It was a girl."

The seconds passed, allowing Craig time to digest this revelation.

"She had beautiful flaxen hair tumbling down to her shoulders. The other blokes gasped and when I stepped up and looked at her, I was just blown away.

She was incredibly pretty. Huge, saucer-like eyes of the clearest, palest blue I'd ever seen. Freckles, a little snub-nose…She couldn't have been more than, I don't know, seventeen or eighteen, maybe less. I couldn't speak. This was the first enemy I'd seen close up. I'd always thought of them as hardened veterans, skilled soldiers, fanatics. Our instructors had told us about the Waffen-SS, and especially the *Hitler Jugend* but nothing prepared me for seeing that girl. I didn't think there were girl soldiers. Later I discovered that many were used to operate anti-aircraft guns but as for fighting on the frontline, that was something that just didn't happen."

"So what was she doing there?"

"I didn't know, at the time.

"I turned at a commotion behind me to see Bob, holding a small young lad by the collar in one hand and the sniper rifle in the other. A boy about your age I would say, his helmet far too big for his head. Bob shoved him forward to join the girl. They both stood there, defiant, the look in their eyes sending a chill down my spine. Their eyes were lifeless, no fear at all, just a horrible, total disdain. Dressed in light brown, camouflaged smocks, they bore the Nazi eagles of the *Hitlerjugend SS* and on their left sleeves. Indoctrinated withNazi crap, prepared to do anything to defend the *Fatherland,* they summed up everything terrible and awful and *sick* about that whole, damned war." A sudden bout of hoarse coughing seized him. Fist over his mouth, Baxter struggled to take in several sharp gasping breaths until the moment passed. It was something which he seemed well used to and gave it no mind. With his breathing under control again, he continued. "At that moment, I couldn't give a damn if they were six or sixty. All I knew was that they had shot my mate Wally and it would probably have to be me who wrote the damned letter to his wife and...and his boy...I couldn't get that out of my head, you see. What that was going to do to them, his family. How were they supposed to carry on?" He pressed both hands against his face, speaking through his fingers. "Everyone was stunned to see them. We had no idea the snipers would be kids, how could we? Just two brainwashed kids, their love of Hitler the only thing they cared about. Bob, he was ..." He shook his head. "I told my wife what I'm going to tell you now. It's like this. I should have walked away from them, those kids. I should have just let the Tommies take them prisoner but I didn't. Over and over, I kept seeing images of Wally's boy, Michael, asking his mum when his dad would be home. I was shaking so much, I was out of my mind with rage. Clenching my teeth, I brought up my gun and cut that girl in half, keeping my finger on the trigger until I'd emptied the whole magazine into her." He put his knuckles against his mouth and the tears slowly tumbled down his cheeks. "I was on fire. There was no reason for anything I was doing anymore, no rational thought, no conscience. I took my gun by the barrel, swung it like a baseball bat, and cracked it across the boy's head. He went down like a sack of spuds. He was crying. Screaming. God help me, Craig. God help me…" He looked up through the tears, "I just kept on hitting him again and again until…Oh, God."

"And nobody tried to stop you?"

Billy Baxter was no longer listening. Unable to hold anything back, he broke down, body-breaking sobs shuddering through him as all the pain, anger, and almost certainly guilt, poured out unchecked, uncontrolled, and unending.

MISPLACING THE PIECES

THEY SAT AROUND A LARGE, bare table in a chill, windowless office just off the main squad room. It was late afternoon and their attempts to make headway in the case were proving limited. Taylor joined them after an hour or so and, sensing the mood, sat in silence. Emery got up at that point, put his head out of the door, and called for tea. He received a sharp look from a passing uniformed female constable, a reaction that brought much amusement from Taylor. "I'll get it," he said and squeezed past. Fallon saw him slipping his arm around the WPC, who giggled.

"Seems he has a way with the ladies," he said.

Emery rolled his eyes. "He's a pratt."

"Is he? He came up trumps with Baxter. Besides, I thought he was your mate."

A grunt for a reply.

Fallon studied him, then said, "Let's try again to move on."

Emery leaned back in his chair and flipped open his notebook. "I went to talk to Bewdsley but he wasn't home. Spoke to his wife. Nice, very attractive. Spoke with a slight accent. She couldn't tell me much, only that Bewdsley and Baxter had served together in the War, that this *thing* Baxter did, it seems to have caused a huge rift between them. They were polite to one another but at a distance. Baxter's ex-wife, she was badly affected by it, turned Millie against him, caused her to change her name."

"Any clues as to what 'this thing' might be?"

"She didn't explain, only that it was bad. Bad enough to force the wife to leave him."

"An affair maybe?"

"Something more than that, it has to be. I mean, it might be linked to an affair, but there has to be an added element."

"The fact that Baxter knew Janet Stowe worries me."

"Me too. Bewdsley's wife says that Bob knows all the details so I'm going to try again. He has some industrial units out of town, she said. He's got something to do with haulage, but she didn't say what."

"If we can link Janet Stowe with this story, of

what Baxter did, then maybe we have the bare bones of a motive."

"You fancy him for the murder?"

"Maybe. I didn't, but ...We'll know more when we go and see him later on. And the boy. How does he fit in with everything?"

"Maybe he doesn't."

"Yes, but maybe he does. I've telephoned the mother and, after a lot of persuasion, I convinced her we needed to have another chat. Maybe he knows Janet Stowe too."

"Jesus, if he does ... What about Howarth, and Fender? Where's the link, boss? Where's the thread running through all of this?"

The door eased open and Taylor came in carrying a buckled, cheap metal tray with three cups and a sugar bowl. "I was thinking just the same, sir." Smiling, he settled the tray onto the table. He caught his colleagues' bemused expressions. "About the thread, sir. I went back to Mr Prentis."

Fallon heaped sugar into his mug. "Who?"

"The old boy who first reported the incident up at the allotment. As I told you, he mentioned Robert Bewdsley, as well as Baxter. I thought about that, went through the records, and called a friend of mine down in London."

Emery sat upright. "You did *what*?"

Taylor laughed at Emery's outburst. "My old

friend Vincent from Hendon. He joined the Met. They are accumulating a mass of criminal records from around the country. Apparently, their Chief Constable, a Mr Harwood wants to create a sort of nationwide central database of—"

"Just get on with it," snapped Fallon, taking a sip of his tea. He shuddered and stared with distaste into the bottom of his mug.

"Bewdsley moved to Swanage after the War. He was originally from Bromborough, but he didn't come back here straight away. He'd met someone over in Germany. A girl whom he brought back with him from over there and they—"

"Is this actually going anywhere, Taylor?"

"Er, yes sir." He looked at his tea, then at Fallon before releasing a low sigh. "This idea of a nationwide sharing of resources and records is a long way from being established, but Vincent managed to find some interesting stuff about Mr Bewdsley."

"All right, enough of the drama – what's the score with this Bewdsley?" Emery was growing more irritated. "I thought we were looking at Baxter?"

"Nothing on him, I'm afraid," said Taylor. "Not in any national archive anyway. Nor the military police. Baxter has an exemplary record, both during the War and ever since. He's not known to us, not for anything, except for the fact that he was invalided out. Lost his leg."

"Well that's interesting," said Fallon. "He could hardly have carried an adult woman down to the canal could he!"

"But Bewdsley could," interjected Emery.

"Is what you found interesting enough to warrant further investigation, Taylor?"

"Oh yes, sir," said Taylor with a grin. "Very much so, sir."

A quick double-take before Fallon threw out his arms, "Do you want to enlighten us, or what?"

Taylor flicked through his notebook. "He got into some bother in Swanage. Grievous bodily. Got three months. Came out, stole a car, smashed it into a tree, lucky to get out alive. Suspended for six months, lost his license, all of that. Interesting thing is, he wasn't drunk. His wife, the girl he met over in Germany, took out a private lawsuit. Apparently, she was in the passenger seat, said he was trying to kill her."

"Why would he do that?" asked Emery.

"Because she'd been carrying on with someone else. He was the one Bewdsley beat up, put in hospital. Spurred on by what Vincent told me, I dug deeper. I went to Chester, Liverpool, as well as here. Everything I found, I passed on to Vincent for the database they're creating down there at the Met."

"How about passing it on to us," commented Emery, shaking his head.

Ignoring him, Taylor pressed on. "I discovered that after the car crash, he totally lost it. Wrecked a local pub, beat up three other guys, ex-squaddies. In the court case that followed they testified about what they knew he'd done in the War."

"What *he'd* done?" Fallon shook his head, bewildered. "What do you mean by that?"

"He'd killed someone unlawfully in the War, so these guys said. They didn't say anything at the time because ... Well, it was War, I suppose. These things happen."

"Exactly," said Emery. "How can you 'unlawfully kill' someone in a war?"

"Lots of ways. Haven't you heard of My Lai?"

"Who?"

"Never mind. Even back then, in World War Two, there were rules that, as a soldier, you were supposed to follow. The Nazis chose to ignore them but, for the most part, Allied troops followed the Geneva Convention. There were one or two high-profile exceptions, of course, but nothing like what happened from the other side."

Fallon said, "So what had he done?"

"He'd shot two kids, sir. Murdered them in cold blood. Prisoners they were. The Geneva Convention was meant to protect prisoners of war. Britain had signed up to it, and was very proud of its adherence to its laws."

"Kids, you said." It was Emery's turn to look bemused. "Kids aren't POWs, are they?"

"These were. They were members of the *Hitlerjugend*. It's all in the file I've collated, sir I've shared it with Vincent, and he added everything he knew and gave me a copy."

"Quite a character this Vincent," said Fallon.

"If this national criminal archive gets going, sir, it'll help us all do our jobs a lot better."

"Big *if*, Constable."

"Yes, sir. Unfortunately."

"All right," said Fallon. "So, what have we got? Three old guys who were at the allotment with the boy, Craig. One of them is a bloody nutcase, the other knew Janet Stowe because she...What? Attempted to blackmail him? Over this incident that happened in the War? Bewdsley, from what you say. committed something pretty awful in the War, and it was bad enough to throw him into a rage when those ex-soldiers mentioned it to him in a pub in Swanage."

"No, not Swanage, sir. He'd left Swanage by then. This was in Cheshire. Royal British Legion reunion do. Lots of men from all over the area got together for the twentieth anniversary of D-Day. Nineteen sixty-four."

"And now we're coming up to the twenty-fifth anniversary," said Emery.

"Passed it," said Taylor. "June that was ... But get this, sir." Taylor turned his smiling face from one to the other. "What he did, Bewdsley? Shooting those two kids? Twenty-five years ago, this August. Two weeks' time."

"So, you think he might go berserk again?"

"He could do, sir, if somebody mentions it. He lives here now, sir, along with Billy Baxter, although they're not neighbours. We've discovered they know one another, and they share the secret of what happened." He leaned back, waving his notebook in front of him, the victor's trophy. "Because Billy Baxter and Bewdsely were in the same bloody regiment."

"So, whatever they did, they were in it together." Fallon put his chin in his hand, thinking hard. "And Janet Stowe finds out about it from Millie, and decides she wants to make a bit of money ...And Bewdsley, given his history of violence, won't take too kindly to that, so ..."

"What about Fender, sir?"

Fallon looked towards Emery. "I don't know. We need to work out how he's involved because I think he is. Howarth perhaps found out something too. Maybe ..."

Fallon brought his hand down with a slap on the

table. "Emery, go and see if you can get hold of Bewdsley down in that warehouse, or whatever. I'll go and chat with Millie, get the truth out of her about Fender and Howarth, what their connection is, or was. Taylor, find out everything you can about what happened in the War with these guys. Go to their regiment, find out the details."

"How am I supposed to do that, sir?"

"How should I know? Ask your bloody friend, again. Maybe there's an Army Central database-thingy-archive."

"I doubt it, sir."

"Imperial War Museum," said Emery. "They'll know. They'll have loads of stuff about D-Day, what with the anniversary and all."

"Brilliant," said Fallon, standing up. "You get on with that. I'll also talk to Craig again, find out what he knows about these two old men before I go over to see Millie. Oh, and Taylor. This tea," he pulled a face, "it's bloody awful."

COLD AND DARK, HOT AND BRIGHT

ROLLING INTO THE LARGE, debris-littered warehouse car park, Emery sat behind the wheel and studied his surroundings. A cluster of single-storey concrete blockhouses to his left, windows with grills, the glass smashed long ago by malcontents looking for something to fill their time. Graffiti across the front-facing walls, some of it vaguely artistic, most scrawled abbreviations and declarations of love to Julie or Mary and 'I'll drop my knickers for you Lloyd!' At the end, an even lower building with an outer iron staircase clinging to the side, leading to a square concrete blockhouse on the roof, which almost certainly served as the office. To the right, piles of rusted, twisted metal objects and heaps of wooden pallets leaning up against a flatbed trailer, but no cab. No vehicles.

This place was dead, unused and Emery wondered why Bewdsley's wife would think her husband continued to work here. An ageing haulage business no longer operational. Perhaps she never visited. Curious, he checked his notebook. The address was as it appeared. No mistake this was the correct location. Sitting back, he lit himself a cigarette and smoked it down to the stub before he stepped outside.

Instantly, a blast of chill wind flapped at his jacket and he pulled it closer, buttoning it up tight. He contemplated getting back inside and driving away. Fallon would not question him, but something tugged away at his natural need to know. Hands in pockets, he walked over to the first building, checking and rechecking the others as he went, and tested the door. Peeling paint, warped woodwork. Locked. He rattled the handle, but it would not budge. Another check across the silent car park. Although it appeared deserted, the wind groaning through the dereliction his only companion, he felt eyes boring into him. A shiver ran through him. Trying to shrug these feelings off, he moved to the next door, which was hanging from rusted hinges. Taking a breath, he put his shoulder against the rotted woodwork. With little effort, it burst open.

Gaping before him only darkness, the thick smell of dank, dead years catching the back of his throat. Grimacing, he groped forward, barely enough light from the grilled windows to allow him to find a route through the gloom. Nothing barred his way, no crates or boxes, no tables or chairs. The area, devoid of anything save some pieces of shattered glass from where the vandals had thrown stones through the windows. He went out again, blinking at the sunlight.

He wondered how long it had remained empty. A little research back at the station should give him some answers, a call to the Inland Revenue perhaps. Someone would know.

With these thoughts, he moved across to the staircase, tested it with a bout of rigorous shaking and, reassured of its stability, he began the ascent. Never one for heights, he kept his face forward, gripping the steel handrails firmly, the sound of his boots clanging on the iron steps amplified alarmingly in the silence of that eerie, forgotten place.

Reaching the roof, he paused, scanned the open vista around him. Fields, as forlorn as the complex, flanked by low trees and bushes, marshland beyond. He struggled to get his bearings. Moreton lay somewhere over to his right, to his left Hoylake, but only if you were familiar with this area. You could just as well be anywhere. A sudden, unnerving thought seized him – he should have called in his arrival to the station, kept them aware of his whereabouts, or the approximate location at least.

Shrugging off his unease, the concrete office caught his attention. No vandals had assaulted the windows and the door was well painted. It could well be the last remaining functioning building in the entire complex.

From beyond one of the tiny windows, a faint yellow glowed. Someone was inside. He gently rapped on the door, calling out, "Mr Bewdsley? It's the police. I'd like a word please, sir." Emery waited. Again, he used his fist, more insistent this time, to pound on the door. Emery sucked in a breath and, levering down the handle, was surprised to discover it was unlocked. He gently eased it open.

A table, papers spread haphazardly across the surface, with more on the floor, lay before him. To the right a metal filing cabinet, top three drawers open, cardboard folders poking out from a rack of others. Someone had been here, searching through the records, but records for what, he couldn't be sure.

An oil lamp, the origin of the glow, hissed from atop a sagging bookcase filled with lever-arch files. He scanned the printed labels on the spines. They were of years, ranging from Nineteen Fifty-Seven to the present. Over seven years' worth of business records arrayed along three shelves. He noted how Sixty-Two and Three required three such files each.

Preparing to tug one of them free, he heard something moving behind him and turned.

The empty office glared back at him. It might have been the wind, he decided, causing the staircase's old rusted bolts to groan in their housings on the wall. They were solid when he climbed, he reminded himself. Easing himself across the room, Emery went to the open door and listened.

Nothing but the wind came back at him. He released a long, low sigh and swung around to return to his searching.

A sound. Shuffling feet. A low expulsion of breath.

He had no time to turn again.

The blow hit him with immense power across the back of his right thigh and he squealed, dropping to the ground as he clutched at his leg. A booted foot cracked across the side of his head and he fell sideways, skull cracking against the office door well. Dazed, Emery brought up a hand in a pathetic attempt to protect him from further blows but the attacker swatted away his feeble efforts, lifted him to his feet, and slammed his knee hard into the policeman's groin.

A horrible, sickening world of red enveloped him, the pain so intense it sent his senses reeling.

Vomit roared up into his mouth and he retched, hanging in the attacker's arms, unable to offer up any sort of resistance. Defeat complete, he could do nothing as a fist erupted across his jaw. He fell and lay on the floor tasting the sick and the blood in his mouth, wishing it all to end.

Barely aware of someone stepping over him, he heard papers ruffling, the slamming shut of cabinet drawers, the growing frustration of the searcher underlined by violent cursing. From out the corner of one swollen eye, Emery saw a large man throwing papers on the floor, pulling out the lever-arch files and anything else, piling them up into a heap in the corner.

Snarling, the attacker took Emery by the back of the collar, hauled him across to the pile of debris, and threw him on top of it. Taking the oil lamp, he went to the door and hurled the lamp into the corner, where it shattered, igniting the paper and cardboard in a flash of blue-white flame.

Emery wanted so much to move, but he could not. He lay there, whimpering, as the flames lapped around him, building in intensity, tendrils of fire spreading across every part of the room. Soon flames licked at his trousers and arms and he screamed. No one heard him, his attacker already making good his escape.

OF GUILT, KISSES AND HOSPITALS

CRAIG CAME from the kitchen onto the patio and placed a freshly brewed cup of tea carefully beside Billy before he sat down. It was early evening, the air growing muggy. A light breeze rustled through the trees and somewhere a blackbird sang its last plaintive song of the day. The mood was sombre.

Craig's head hurt, but he tried not to let it show. Billy Baxter seemed in far greater pain than he was, and this concerned him. He remembered when Baxter collapsed, the desperate hunt for his pills. And now, as if to underline his worries, Baxter coughed and spluttered, face turning puce, body racked with violent hacking. He pounded at his chest, trying to clear some sort of a blockage. After several seconds, breathing easing, he managed a sip of the tea, visibly relaxing.

For a long while, both sat and listened to the evening. Craig longed to hear the conclusion to the story, but he could wait. The trawling up of bitter memories was a sort of torture. "I lived with what I'd done in silence for the rest of the war," he said suddenly. Pricking up his ears, Craig listened expectantly. "None of the other lads from my tank ever asked me what happened. I doubt if I could have told them. The girl's face haunted every waking and sleeping moment. If I was hoping for some release on my return after the whole filthy business was over, I was wrong. When, some years later, I found the courage to tell my wife, the nightmares truly began. She listened in silence at first, turning paler with every word. I remember her sitting there," he jerked his thumb behind him in the general direction of the house, "and it was like she'd seen a ghost. When I'd finished, she said nothing and I thought she'd fainted, but her eyes were open. I leaned forward and touched her knee. Instantly, she flew up, screaming, wild, out of control, telling me to leave her alone, that I was a monster, that I should have told her all of this before our wedding." The sadness rimmed his eyes. "How could I have done that? I'd never told anyone that story, not a living soul, allowing it to brew way down deep inside. Even after peace had returned to Europe and I'd gone to see Wally's wife and son, I didn't give any details. How crass would that have been? I told them *lies*, Craig. To protect them. Especially Michael. I told them how we'd entered the village, how a stray bullet killed Wally, how we'd done our very best to save him … I left out all the details of what really happened, of what I'd done to avenge his death. Now here was my wife, accusing me of being inhuman. She said I was no better than the guards at Belsen, that to kill *children* was the action of a monster, not a soldier. She may well have been right, I don't know. Anyway, I spent the first of many nights on the couch after that. I tried time and again to make her understand but she never spoke another word to me, not even a good-bye when she got into a taxi some days later and left me for good, taking our daughter with her. I never laid eyes on them again."

Not even the blackbird's song, so beautiful in the still air, could lighten the ominous mood, which settled over them. Craig felt he should offer words of comfort, of understanding. True, it was a horrible story, but, as Billy himself said so many times, in war, people do the most awful things. Nothing could ever excuse what occurred in the death camps; that was not a reaction to an event, ill-judged and spontaneous, but a carefully thought-out plan of mass murder. There was no comparison between Billy's actions and the Holocaust. As he said, it was an act of revenge, one which gnawed away at him, leaving him a tired, sick, dejected old man, racked in guilt and regret.

When at last he spoke, feeling almost apologetic for disturbing Billy's grief, he said, "Billy, it was an unreal situation. You'd just seen your best friend killed—"

"They were children, Craig. It was unforgivable. I should have let the authorities deal with them. But I was so full of hatred, you understand?" Craig nodded because he did understand, better than Billy could appreciate. "I'd never killed anyone before, and after that *baptism*...I never fired my gun again. That was the first and only time. I have to live with what I have done, together with the consequences."

Craig had no answer to that. Perhaps the Army disciplined Billy when the truth emerged but seeing the effect the re-telling had taken out of him, Craig thought better of asking. His wife's reaction, to leave him, to call him a monster, liken him to what they did in the camps...Perhaps she was more angry at not being told sooner than at what Billy actually did?

"I know what you're thinking," said Baxter after a short silence, "because everyone thinks the same. I'm Billy Baxter, and I'm a nasty piece of work.

You're thinking what I did to those young people was as natural to me as walking down the street is to you."

"No, Billy, I'm not thinking anything—"

"Perhaps you're right. Perhaps everyone is *right*. I really am a bastard." He stood up, his face drawn and tired. "You should go now, son. I'm all done in, and my chest feels like the inside of an exhaust pipe. Why don't you call round tomorrow and we'll talk about something a lot more interesting – Skipper." At the mention of his name, the dog lying flat out on the carpet, cocked an ear, but not a lot else. "You could take him for another walk, if you want to."

"Yes. I'd like that, Billy. Thanks." He ruffled Skipper's neck and made his way quietly to the front door. He paused, a sudden thought seizing him. He turned towards Billy, standing there in the hallway, dejected, small, fragile-looking. "Billy. Bob Bewdsely."

A visible change came to Baxter's demeanour, face hardening like carved granite. "Bob again? What about him?"

"He … He's spoken to me."

Baxter looked at the carpet, defeated, tired of doing all that he could. "Craig, you have to stay away from him." His eyes clouded over with sadness. "Promise me you won't *ever* talk to him again."

Craig stood his ground. "That is exactly what he said I should do with you, Billy."

"Ah, Jesus ... I knew it. I knew he'd do that."

"Billy ..." Craig reached out to gently touch Baxter's arm. "What is it? What's going on?" The old man's eyes came up, wet with tears and Craig crumpled inside. "Oh my God, Billy. What is it between you?"

"I can't ... Craig, I'm sorry.... Please, please don't hate me."

"Hate you? Billy, what are you talking about – of course I won't hate you!"

"I can't, Craig ... I can't tell you the truth. I couldn't tell my wife and I can't tell you."

"The truth? But you've just ..." He stopped, the thought developing in his mind that there was more to tell, that Baxter's story could well have been just that – a story told to mask the reality of what happened. Craig's hold on Baxter's arm tightened. "You mean what you told me ... it wasn't the truth?"

"It was a kind of truth ... I'm sorry." He pushed past Craig and went to the front door. "Call around tomorrow, Craig. Please." He opened the door.

Both cried out in shock at the man standing there in the act of pressing the doorbell.

"Afternoon Billy ... Craig. I've just popped around for a few questions," said Detective Inspector Fallon, stepping inside without another word.

In the living room, Fallon watched as the others shuffled in behind him. "So, Craig. How are you?"

"What do you want, Inspector?" interjected Baxter. The air crackled with tension.

"All right," said Fallon, remnants of his smile disappearing. "I'll get straight to it."

"I wish you would."

"What do you know about a Mr Robert Bewdsley?"

Craig stiffened and Fallon caught it, that non-too-subtle change. He arched an eyebrow.

"He's a mate, that's all," said Baxter.

"Yes, you know one another from the allotments, is that it?"

"Yes. We meet up every weekend usually. Why? Has something happened to him?"

"No, nothing like that, just some inquiries. Do *you* know Mr Bewdsley, Craig?"

"Only from when he helped me."

"Ah yes, with the bullies? That was kind of him, wasn't it? Is he a kind man, Craig?"

"I think so."

"Have you seen him since he helped up at the allotments?"

Craig looked at Billy, whose scowl grew. He turned again to Fallon and shook his head.

"Good." The smile returned, but only for a moment. "Perhaps you also know Mr Bewdsley from the Royal British Legion, Mr Baxter?"

"The Royal ... What have they got to do with anything?"

"Well, you're ex-army, aren't you?"

The stillness intensified. Baxter's voice sounded chilly. "I was in the army, yes."

"And you served with Mr Bewdsley, didn't you, in the same regiment?"

A tiny tremor ran along Baxter's cheek. Fallon's unblinking eyes bore into him. Caught in the spotlights, frozen with indecision, Baxter merely shrugged. "We may have done."

"Oh, I think you can be a little more certain than that, Mr Baxter. You served together, in the Royal Tank Corps. You were at Normandy, making your way through the Bocage, a fighting unit, living cheek-by-jowl with the other members of your crew, one of whom was Robert Bewdsley." His smile broadened as he turned his attention towards Craig. "Wouldn't you say so, Craig?"

"The boy knows nothing," snapped Billy Baxter, stepping in between Craig and the policeman. "You have anything to say, you say it to me. Craig helps me with my dog, takes him for walks, and that's it."

"But you lied to me, Mr Baxter, didn't you?

About Bewdsley. You *do* know him … Very well, I'd say."

"All right, what if I did bloody well know him. We were in the same bloody tank together. What's that got to do with anything?"

"Well, it might have quite a lot to do with our investigations, Mr Baxter. Quite a lot." He pulled in a breath. "And what do you *really* know about Janet Stowe? Your daughter Millie told her about what happened in the War, didn't she Mr Baxter? That's why she came here and she tried to blackmail you? But letters she found proved that whatever happened over there had nothing to do with you and so she planned to blackmail Bewdsley. That's about the gist of it, isn't it?"

"You don't know what you're talking about," growled Billy, face glowing with rage. "You know nothing about any of it!"

Turning to look at his friend, Craig saw Baxter's face draining of all colour, the redness turning white almost in an instant. Suddenly the strength seemed to leave the old man's legs, and he fell, smacking his back against the sofa with a sickening crack, and Craig screamed.

IN THE COOL OF THE EVENING

MUM SAT ACROSS FROM CRAIG, sitting at the kitchen table head in hands. "Is it still hurting you?"

"A bit. But it's not that."

"No," she said, with that tone mums put on when they know full well there is more to be said. "I didn't think so. Is it Billy Baxter?"

He dropped his hands, furrowing his brow. "How did you know?"

"Because he's a horrible little man and you shouldn't have anything to do with him." She turned away when she saw Craig's appalled look. "All right, I'm sorry, I shouldn't have said that. I'm happy he helped you the way he did up in the park and he seemed genuinely concerned. I got to talking..."

"Talking?" What would Billy Baxter talk to his mum about? He asked her.

"You, of course. Seems you have common interests, like you and your Uncle Eric. He told me about how interested you'd been, about his photographs, his *things*. So, I told him a little bit about you, your soldiers. He seemed a little angry when I told him about those soldiers you'd ordered, how they hadn't arrived, and how upset you'd been."

"The Greek hoplites? Why did you tell him about them?"

"I didn't see how it would do any harm. It seemed to, I don't know, make him *think,* but about what, I couldn't say. To be honest, Craig, he seems to have some sort of hold over you and I'm not comfortable with it. I don't like him."

"I know that Mum, but I want to know *why* you don't like him. What's he ever done to you?"

"Me? Well, nothing *personal*…I just know about what he's done to others – look how he was with us when he met us in the street. Like a raving lunatic."

"Is he?"

She frowned. "Eh?"

"A lunatic, Mum. Do you think he really is a lunatic?"

Her expression changed, panic welling up in her voice as she reached across, clutched his hand, and squeezed it tight. "What's he done to you? What's he said?"

"Nothing." The heat spread across his cheeks, causing his eyes to water. Angry, he pulled his hand away. "How can you say that? You always think the worst. You just don't understand."

"Well, perhaps you should tell me."

He knew she was right. He should tell her, unburden himself in just the same way Billy had to him. What happened with Dad had tarnished Craig's life ever since. But if he told her, her reaction could be the same as Billy's wife. He couldn't blame her if she disowned him, threw him out, put him up for adoption, or any number of other, terrible things. He'd always believed it would be best not to say anything, keep it well hidden, allowing it to simmer. Billy's confession, however, brought something of a change of heart, gave him a new surge of courage to face up to the inevitable consequences. Not today, however.

"You visited him at his house, haven't you?"

That accusing tone again. He shook his head. "He's had another attack."

"What? Oh my God, how? When?"

"While I was there. He was telling me some more stories, about the War, and the policeman came, and he—"

"*Police* man?"

"Fallon. The detective. He was so cross, Mum, started laying into Billy and then ..." He dragged in a shuddering breath. "Billy collapsed and Mr Fallon called for an ambulance whilst he ..." A tear rolled down his face. "He gave Billy mouth-to-mouth. I thought he was going to die but Mr Fallon saved him! He brought Billy back."

"That's awful. What happened next?"

"Ambulance came and took him away. I wanted to go with him, but Mr Fallon said I should come straight home."

"Why didn't you tell me about all this as soon as you got in?"

He shrugged. "I don't know, Mum. I'm ..."

She squeezed his hand as the first tears came. "It's all right, Craig. There's clearly a lot more going on than you've told me so far, especially this police business. This is more than just a gang of bullies beating you up, isn't it."

He looked at her, amazed at how intuitive she was. He needed time to work out how he could tell her. "I'm tired, Mum."

"Yes, of course you are. You go and get ready for bed and I'll bring you up some Horlicks if you like."

"Yes, I'd like that."

"In the morning, you can tell me all about it."

She patted his hand. Craig mumbled a few excuses and shuffled up to his bedroom.

Rain pounded against the window, high winds elevating the noise, causing Craig to wake up. He pulled the covers over his chin, hating a storm at night more than anything, his mind consumed with all sorts of invading monsters and demons, their unearthly groans filling the darkness.

Eyes wide open, Craig thought he heard something else. Not the pounding of nightmarish hands against his door, or the screech of claws raking along the windowpane, but something else. Not the product of his fertile imagination, but something real. Breathing. Low, laboured. The sound of something waiting, waiting to pounce.

He daren't move. The presence lingered at the foot of his bed, filling the room and not only with its sound. Craig could also smell it. Damp, musk, the odour of a body soaked through to the skin, of clothes ringing wet, clinging, dripping pit pat, pit pat onto the bedroom carpet.

Fear like a living thing enclosed around him, freezing his mind. Lying as still as possible, feigning sleep, hoping the presence would grow restless, give up its intentions, and drift away again into the night.

He heard it move. A single footfall, a heavy tread squelching into the carpet fibres.

"Craig?"

A deep voice conjured up from the bowels of a hellish black hole of despair and dread. A voice of something inhuman, of something that meant him harm.

He daren't move and squeezed his eyes tight shut, his heartbeat pounding in his ears so loud he felt sure that whatever it was would hear, rip him from his bed, devour him, murder him.

Oh sweet Jesus, he said to himself, *please make it go away. Please make it go away!*

"Craig, listen to me ..."

There was something familiar in the voice, the way it rattled in the thing's throat. Before he could put a face to it, its words gargled again, "Listen ... you stay away, you hear. You stay away from Billy Baxter and you do *not believe* what he says."

Suddenly, its hand reached under the bedclothes to grip his leg, the voice close, threatening. "Stay. A. Way."

Yelping, careless of the consequences, Craig lashed out, throwing back the blanket, and yelling, "*Mum!*"

He saw it, a black smudge, a shadow in the dark, turning, dipping through the bedroom door, and disappearing into the gloom. He heard it padding down the stairs, the back door opening, unoiled hinges better than any alarm, and out it went into the night.

"*Mum!*"

She came in like a Dervish, arms flapping, scrambling for the light, hair tussled, eyes wild with alarm. "Dear God," she said, rushing to him. She held his trembling, fear-soaked body. "What is it?"

Clinging to her, breathing her in, thanking God for His help, he struggled to find the words.

"Was it, a nightmare?" With some effort, she managed to disengage herself from his arms and leaned back to study him. Wiping away hair plastered with sweat from his face, she forced a smile. "Oh Craig, my darling, you have to try and—"

He took a breath as he found the strength to speak. "There was something in here, Mum."

She wiped away more hair, stroked his cheek, calming him. "I'm here now. This damned weather, it's ..." She turned to the window as a blast of wind shook the glass. "It's only the wind, darling. You have nothing to be afraid of. If you like you can—"

The crash of the backyard door slamming against its frame caused her to jump. Another slam. Then another.

"Damn," she moaned, standing up, "I thought I'd bolted it ..."

She went to get up but he grabbed hold of her arm and stopped her. "Mum. There was something here."

"There couldn't have been, darling. It's your

imagination, the wind and the rain they can make you—"

"No, Mum. It wasn't my imagination, I promise. Someone was in here."

"Craig, how could there have been? Listen I'll go and make us both a cup of tea, then we can—"

The words choked in her throat as she turned to go. A hand flew to her mouth. As he got out of bed to stand beside her, Craig followed the line of her sight and saw it too.

The unmistakeable imprint of muddy shoes on the bedroom carpet.

The uniformed police officer came in shaking his head. He took off his cap with deliberate slowness and levelled his unblinking gaze toward Craig. "Are you sure you didn't recognise the voice?"

"Positive."

"Whoever it was has well and truly gone."

"There were muddy footprints," said Craig, determined not to be ignored.

"I know, son. And we´ll investigate don´t worry." He turned to Craig´s mum, who stood in the corner wringing her hands, her face taking on a grey, gaunt look in the sharp bright light of the kitchen. Outside the rain continued to come down in sheets. "We take things like this very seriously, madam. I assure you we'll do everything we can."

Replacing his cap, he gave a tight smile and left. Both Craig and his mum watched the tiny patrol car disappearing into the night.

"Thanks, Mum."

"What for?"

"Believing me."

She put her arm around him and held him tightly to her side. "Of course, I believe you. That footprint ... Someone was in here."

"But who, Mum?"

"He warned you, so you said."

"Yes. 'Stay away'. But what did that mean? Stay away from what?"

"It's obvious, isn't it?" She blew out a sigh. "Not a 'what', but a 'who'."

He turned his face to hers and recognised that look. He knew exactly who she meant, and probably who the intruder did also.

COLD CONFUSION

FALLON WAS on the phone when Taylor came through the office. His superior gave him a nod and continued to mumble monosyllabic replies into the mouthpiece. Taylor crossed to where an old kettle stood, frayed electric cord promising instant death at any moment. He switched it on, threw a tea bag into a brown-stained mug, and waited for the water to boil.

"That was Chief Superintendent Lawson," Said Fallon, moving up next to his younger colleague. "He's becoming slightly anxious." He shook his head. "I went to see Craig but found him at Baxter's so I killed two birds with one stone, so to speak."

"That sounds good, Boss. So how come the Super's getting anxious?"

"Because Baxter fainted whilst I was interviewing him, bashed his head, and had to go to hospital. He's all right, they made him comfortable and are keeping him in for tests. The Super thought I might have been a bit heavy-handed. Told me to calm down a bit. How about you?"

"I'm still waiting to hear something from Emery, about Bewdsley. He's been away quite a while boss and he hasn't called in."

"He will, when he's got something."

"In the meantime, I thought I could pay a call to Millie, find out what she knows about Howarth and Fender as well as Janet."

"What's your thinking on that?"

"Howarth and Fender were friends."

"Close, you think?"

"Possibly. I'll try and get her to open up."

"Break down her defences, eh?"

"Sort of."

Pulling a face, Fallon leaned closer and tapped Taylor on the jacket lapel. "You watch out, son. D'you hear me? A woman like that …"

"How do you mean?"

"I mean she's a bloody viper. I saw the way Emery was looking at her when we went there. She's seductive, feisty, would probably give you the best time of your young life, but trust me – she's poison. She'll eat you up and spit you out, mark my words." The kettle came to the boil and Taylor quickly poured the water over his teabag. He kept his back to Fallon as the older detective continued. "I had a woman like her, years and years ago. Just like you, a young copper on the beat, I was following up on a report she'd made about a couple of suspicious-looking so-and-sos casing the street from inside a white van. She'd got the number and we found 'em. Nice bit of detective work, thanks to her. Name of Rosa. Pretty. Half-Asian she was, with legs that …" He shook his head but could not help but smile. "She took me to her bed and, I'm not telling you no porkies, she was *amazing*. I literally skipped home!" Chuckling, he pulled out a chair from under his desk and sat. "Problem was, three days later, when I called again for seconds, her husband was there. Huge he was. He told me she'd confessed everything and that if I didn't pay them two hundred pounds, he'd beat me to shit and then deliver me to the Chief Constable and finish my career there and then."

"But how could they prove it?"

"He was in the wardrobe, wasn't he? Took photographs. She'd set me up, the bitch."

"Holy shit … What happened?"

Fallon shrugged. "What could I do? I paid up. He still hit me, mind you. Bloody hard, right in the chops." His hand ran over his chin, wincing as he recalled the blow. "I can still feel it sometimes."

"And the photos?"

"I got them back. Negatives and all. But, from that moment on, I've steered well clear of any intimacies with members of the general public."

"I'm sure she's not like that. Millie, I mean."

"No, probably not, but you'll be careful, won't you, son?"

"Yes, boss. I will."

Taylor contemplated his senior officer with a newfound sense of respect. Nobody knew much about D.I. Fallon, apart from the rumours. That he was a workaholic, always got his man, did not suffer fools, all of the usual stuff. But the man himself remained something of an enigma. Perhaps this case would bring them closer, develop trust between them. Trust. Taylor drank his tea. Such a thing could help in the promotion stakes if Emery didn't get in the way of course.

Sometime after eleven the following morning, he took the two flights of stairs to Millie's bedsit and stopped on the landing. A faint whiff of fried bacon reminded him of how hungry he was. He went to move, noticed Millie's door a little way to his left gaped open by a few inches, and froze. Cold tendrils spread through him and he edged closer, alert, listening. Fingertips pushed the door open. Its hinges creaked, sounding unnaturally loud in that empty and lonely hallway. "Millie?" The sound of his own voice startled him and he hesitated, waiting, wondering what might have caused her to keep her door open. Had she seen him arriving? Or had fate brought him here just a few moments too late? Stealing himself, he took a step inside.

The dishevelled, cluttered room glared back at him, the bed empty, clothesthrown back to expose the rumpled bottom sheet. Her bathrobe lay on the floor and, in the corner, on a small, stained, unstable table, a steaming cup of coffee, an untouched bowl of cornflakes beside it.

But it was the robe that took most of his attention. Perhaps a dozen spots of blood were spattered across it. Getting down, he touched one with his small finger. Still wet. His stomach rolled over horribly and a faint moan of despair escaped from his lips.

WORDS WITH FRIENDS

CRAIG SPENT most of the day in his room, staring at the soldiers strewn out across the floor. The Greek hoplites had failed to arrive again. He felt miserable and, worse still, his head pulsed constantly, the horror of the night before refusing to leave his thoughts for long. He longed to visit Billy, and also check on Skipper, but his mum outright forbade him to go. So, here he sat, fed up.

Through the haze of his thoughts, the doorbell rang, and he heard Mum's angry voice. He went to the top of the stairs to take a look and could not dare believe what he saw. The bottom of her blue jeans gave the game away and, unable to suppress a cry of joy, he bounded down the stairs, eager to see her in all her breath-taking loveliness.

Except Samantha looked dreadful, hair matted

and unkempt, eyes red-rimmed with tears. When she saw him, her features brightened, but only momentarily as Craig's mum hissed, "I don't want you here."

Craig tried to push past her. "Mum, *please.*"

"No Craig, I've had enough. You give in too easily, that's your problem." She jabbed her finger at Samantha. "You come around here again, and I'll have the police on you."

"No, Mum, I want to talk to her!"

"Well, you can't!" She slammed the door shut without giving Samantha another glance.

Craig seethed. "She's been here before, hasn't she and you didn't tell me! Why not?"

Her face grew puce. "Craig—"

"I want to speak with her, and you can't stop me."

"You see if I can't!"

But before his mum could utter another word, Craig was already racing down the far end of the hall, through the kitchen and into the backyard. He didn't stop, despite his mum's desperate cries, until he reached the bottom of the rear entry, not caring if he'd angered her or what the consequences might be.

He caught up with Samantha at the corner of his street, took her by the arm, and pulled her around.

The tears streamed down her face. "I'm so sorry, Craig. I never meant—"

In one heart-pounding moment, all his indecision and lack of confidence disappeared, and he pulled her to him and pressed his mouth against hers. At first shocked, Samantha responded, her lips soft, giving and they kissed for what seemed a lifetime. When she slowly stepped back, eyes wide, the tears nothing but a memory now, she breathed, "Wow."

"It's me that should be sorry, Sam. We're both trapped, but together I think we can set ourselves free."

"You don't hate me?"

He smiled and leaned into her, running his hands through the back of her hair, folding his lips over hers once more. She tasted like honey, of clean air, of summer evenings laced with the tang of fresh fruits. "Does that feel like hatred?" he asked.

"Oh God, Craig, no!" She was grinning, but almost at once her expression changed to one of panic. "I must look a complete mess," she said, attempting to flatten her wild, unkempt hair.

"You look beautiful," he said and took her hand. He led her along Station Road and there, on an old rotten bench, he sat her down. He took her hand in his, staring at her fingers, picking each one up to gently caress it as he spoke. "I'm not angry at you,

Sam, for what happened. I don't want you to be afraid anymore. I know it was all to do with Crossland, the control he had over you."

She pulled out a tissue and pressed it against her nose, a nose that looked sore and red. "How can you know that? Every time I saw you, I was so nasty, saying such horrible things."

"Was that because you wanted to, or because he told you to?"

"I hate him. I've always hated him. He's so horrible, never seeing any good in anything. We never laugh, just do things that hurt others. Like you. I tried to tell you so often, to explain, but ..." She sniffed. "God, the number of times I wanted to grab you and ..." She chuckled and he leaned over and kissed her cheek. For a long time, she stared at him. "You're so nice, Craig, and handsome." Her cheeks grew red.

"*Handsome?* No, I don't think I'm hand—"

"You are Craig, you just don't know it. And that," she added, the back of her hand running over his face, "makes you even more attractive."

Craig studied her features, her high cheekbones, the dimples, those lips ... An ache developed in his heart, and it thumped hard against his chest. "Sam," he began, throat thick with emotion, "I'd like us to be more than friends. I want us to be together. You know, go out."

There was a moment when he feared she would burst into tears again. "You mean it?"

His arm, as if of its own volition, wrapped itself around her shoulders and he held her very tight.

On his return, he found his mum seething with rage, but she couldn't say anything as Ray was waiting in the living room. "He's been here a while," explained Craig's mum. "He insisted on waiting here until you returned."

She went out and Craig immediately went to his friend, overcome with joy that at long last their friendship was rekindled. That was the hope, anyway, a hope realised when Ray showed Craig the book he'd borrowed a book from the library. "It's by a guy called 'Donald Featherstone' and there's rules about how to play *real* games with model soldiers. I thought it would be good to give them a try."

Later, as they played with the soldiers up in Craig's bedroom, his thoughts kept returning to Samantha, and every time he did, his heart leapt. He had never felt happier and, beaming from ear to ear, he manoeuvred his troops, rolled the dice, and destroyed Ray's forces with glee.

"You seem cheerful," said Ray, packing away his casualties.

"I'm just happy all that mess with Crossland is over with."

"You do know, if I'd have known what he'd done, I would have knocked him out long before."

Craig smiled. "Yeah, I know that, Ray. And thanks for coming to the lake when you did."

"That Samantha too. What a bitch she is, to have smacked a piece of wood around your head and then—"

"No, no, Ray, she was only doing what Crossland told her to do." He caught Ray's bemused expression and backtracked a little, not wanting to reveal his newfound feelings for her, at least, not yet. "It was all him, Ray. I don't blame Sam, not at all."

"*Sam?* Sounds to me you've gone soft on her."

Ignoring his friend's questioning stare, Craig busied himself tidying up his soldiers, hoping his cheeks weren't burning too brightly.

"Craig."

He stopped, turning his face to his friend, and saw a look he hadn't seen before. A look of anguish. "What is it, Ray?"

"I wanted to tell you something, but I just didn't know how to go about it. I'm sorry. All this," he waved his hand over the Featherstone book, "I think it's great, but I'm not in the mood for it."

"Ray," said Craig, sitting down next to his friend.

"Just tell me. Is it Samantha? I remember you telling me that you thought she was—"

"It's nothing to do with her."

"Okay, so what?"

Chewing at his bottom lip, Ray's voice took on a strange, frightened tone. "It's my da. He came home from being away, and him and me mam, they had a row. They've always had rows but this one was really bad. It was about our dog, I think. Me da, he'd brought it home a few months ago, a lovely big fluffy Alsatian. I loved him. I've never had a dog, you see. But then, he disappeared."

"Disappeared? You mean ran away?"

"I don't know, but I heard him telling me mam that he was gone. ... Craig, I need to tell you some things, things which I've never told anyone, but I have to. I *need* to."

Afterwards, when Ray went home and the soldiers all packed away, Craig did his best to take his mind off his friend's revelations. He wrote a letter to one of the model soldiercompanies he'd noted from the Featherstone book and requested a catalogue. Wandering down to the post-box to post it, he found the postman already there, filling his sack. Craig handed him the letter, hoping this time his request, unlike what happened with the hoplites, would result in something concrete.

For a long time, Craig stood and watched the little red van as it disappeared down Station Road. He recalled how he sat with Samantha, held her hand, kissed her over and over. Before they parted, she asked him to phone her and arrange to call at her house. She lived alone with her dad. Craig, a little nervously, assured her he would.

But there was something even more pressing than visiting Samantha to deal with, something which refused to go away. Craig's decision to confess what he had done, brewing since yesterday when he almost revealed it all to his Mum. Now, with all that had happened, it was almost unbearable to contemplate.

Ultimately, Billy's words caused him much soul-searching. He'd witnessed how guilt gnawed away at the old man, bringing more pain than the actual act itself. An identical situation for himself, he mused. He could no longer try to deny it. As for the aftermath, what had Billy's story brought? The revelations hadn't soured Craig's feelings for the man, but they had certainly changed them. Would it be the same with Mum? Billy showed enormous courage in telling his story, together with trust and hope. Trust that Craig would understand, at least some of it, and hope that Craig would remain his friend.

Both parts proved true, so Craig would have to do the same; find the courage, prepare himself for the fallout. He closed his eyes. One thing remained unchanged, above all else, despite the horror of what had happened on that terrible day when those young people had died in that most awful of wars; Billy Baxter was his friend.

He walked home, taking his time, running through the permutations of what he was about to do, the remnants of indecision clinging on tenaciously. If Billy had shown the courage to unload his guilt and sorrow onto his friend, shouldn't Craig unload his to his own mum? Surely of all the people in the world, she had the right to know the truth? Yet, she had been so angry when Samantha had called. Her anger would be the first obstacle to face.

He decided the next time he went to take Skipper out, he would recount his own story to Billy. He'd be shocked, of course, but perhaps relieved that there was someone else who had guilt to live with. But Mum...she was a whole different matter.

He found her in the kitchen, washing dishes. She stopped, aware of his approach, and her shoulders hunched, but she didn't speak. Craig retreated a few steps and glanced at the table, bare with nothing prepared for tea. He sighed, then jumped when Mum threw down the tea towel, swung around, and glared. "So, decided to come back after all have you?"

"Why wouldn't I come back?"

"Because of what I might say – because of *her*. It was only Raymond being here that stopped me. How dare you ignore me, Craig! I was frantic, had no idea where you were going, what would happen. For God's sake, she hit you over the head!"

"She was confused, frightened. She didn't mean to—"

"You can go to your room," she said. The look on her face clearly showed the conversation was closed.

His bedroom felt lonely and cold. Even his soldiers didn't help. He sat and gazed into nothing and wondered if his roller-coaster of a life could get any worse.

He didn't know for how long he sat and stared, but when his mother came in, the spell broke and they looked at each other, neither prepared to give way. At last, she blew out her cheeks. "Your uncle Eric rang."

"I didn't hear the phone."

"Whilst you were out," fists on hips again, a loud blast of air, "with *her*."

"Mum, please, I just want all this to end."

"Well, so do I. That's why I asked Eric to talk to you. Well, to be honest, it was he who suggested it.

He wants you to meet him at the club. He's training there."

"Now?"

"Yes. Holidays, he gives private lessons. He said you should go as he has something important to tell you."

Heart leaping, Craig jumped to his feet. It must be the hoplites, it had to be! He went to bolt out of the room, but she caught him by the arm.

"Craig, I wouldn't mention anything about last night."

"Last night? Why not?"

"Well, Eric, he has something of a temper. He might put two and two together and make five."

Frowning, he gently tugged himself free. "All right, I won't say anything. But Mum," he drew in a deep breath, preparing himself to ask the question that would inevitably bring back the horror of the intruder, " who do you think it was that broke into our house?" He saw her eyes lowering to the floor. "I think you should have told the police about any suspicions you may have."

"Craig, I'm not absolutely sure that what you saw or felt was real."

"What? And the muddy footprints, who made them? You saw them, and so did the policeman."

"Yes, and I saw the bottom of your trainers too."

Pressing her lips together, she cocked her head and gave a thin smile. "Go and talk to your uncle, he usually makes sense."

ALONE WITH MILLIE

THERE WAS no telephone in Millie's room, so Taylor decided to dash down to the corner and make the call using the public telephone box there. He was already running before he barged straight into her as she came through the main door.

"What the bloody hell—" Knocked back into the hallway, the loaf of bread and carton of milk she held spilt to the floor. "You're a bloody idiot," she said angrily, stooping down to retrieve the fallen goods, but he was there first, red-faced, suddenly looking and acting embarrassed. She shook her head. "Idiot," she said again, but without the venom this time.

"There was blood," he said.

She snatched back her breakfast things and went into the flat with Taylor close behind. She spoke over her shoulder, "I cut myself," she held up her left index finger, suitably bandaged, blood seeping through. "I got up late, famished as usual, and rushed to slice the last piece of bread." She threw down the loaf and showed him the remnants of the previous one, nothing more than a ragged, misshaped hunk as evidence. "Never was much good at slicing bread." Reaching over, she picked up the electric kettle, swilled it, and put it under the tap. "Why are you so worried anyway, Mr Policeman?"

He shrugged, turning away awkwardly from her gaze, Fallon's words making so much sense now. She oozed sexuality.

Switching the kettle on, she crossed her arms and watched him. "Tell me."

"Emery." She frowned. "My colleague. Has he been here, to talk to you?"

"No, not since last time. Why? You sound worried."

"I am, a little. He hasn't called in and that's a bit, you know, unusual."

After some minutes of neither of them talking, the kettle clicked and Millie poured steaming water into two cups, tea bags waiting. Without asking, she heaped in the sugar, splashed in the milk, turned, and handed him a mug, chipped around the edge, stained down the sides. Taking the tea, he sat and drank.

"I'm not sure if I should ..." She watched him over the rim of her mug. "Janet. Everything has happened so quickly, without warning. Her death, I mean. And how I feel about it all."

"I don't understand."

"I thought I loved her."

"You *thought* you loved her?"

"Maybe that's too strong. I *did* love her, but perhaps not as much as I thought. Before she was ... Hell, I can't even bring myself to say the bloody word."

"Murdered?"

"Yes. Murdered. Jesus, how many people get to say that, eh? About a loved one, someone close? That they were murdered? It just doesn't seem real. I mean, I know it *is* real, but it's hard to come to terms with. You must deal with it all the time."

"No. Not at all. This is the first time I've been involved in a murder investigation. Before this, I was just a copper on the beat. I just happened to be the first on the scene when it was called in. It's Fallon, Chief Inspector Fallon who is leading it all."

"The other guy who was here with you, the first time you called? Emery? He struck me as being a bit of a moody sod."

Taylor laughed and, finishing his tea, stood up. "You were saying, about Janet?"

"We were rowing a lot. Something was changing between us, perhaps the excitement had gone out of what we had, I don't know, but ... I had been having sex behind her back and she got to find out about it. We argued. I fired off about Fender, she came back at me about David. How come, if we cared so much about one another, we still needed cock? There was other stuff too." Finishing her tea, she went over to where the bread still sat in its wrapper. She busied herself cutting several slices with a great deal of care.

"Other stuff?"

"All right, Mr Policeman, let's get this out of the way, okay?" She swung aroundknife in hand. "We were both fucking men, okay. So don't judge."

"I'm not. I wouldn't." He flopped down on her bed. "If there is anything you can tell me, which will help."

"All right."

She went to the small fridge and took out bacon, laid it into a frying pan, and placed it on the 'Baby Belling' grill. "What my mum told me, about my dad ... what he did. I told Janet. I was drunk, depressed, and it all poured out, as it does. She listened and I felt good about that. A relief, just to get it out, to share it with someone, someone who I cared for. Trusted." She placed the bread on plates, reached into a cupboard, and found a small bottle of tomato ketchup. The bacon sizzled. She moved it around the pan with a wooden spoon. "Well ... You know she was a trainee journalist?" Taylor nodded. "They must teach her things, how to find out stuff, who to talk to. Anyway, she found out where my dad lived. Went there, started threatening him." Sniffing, she pulled out a handkerchief and wiped her face. "I shouldn't let it get to me, but it does. Why would she go and see him, after all this time? She never said anything, only that she'd been so angry with me for what I'd done ... I was furious, told her about David, how he gave me what she didn't – comfort. I talked to him as well, but his reaction was one of understanding."

"What did you tell him exactly?"

"Same as Janet. About my dad. What he'd done."

"And what had he done?"

"He'd killed some children in the War. Executed them, my mum said. He's a war criminal, and he's never been brought to book. Perhaps he should be, I don't know. I don't care, but Janet should never have gone to see him."

With the bacon cooked, Millie piled the rashers on a plate. Taylor arranged some on bread, splattered it with ketchup, and attacked it. They both ate in silence, grease and tomato sauce trailing down their chins, their eyes locked on one another.

Breakfast finished, Taylor wiped his mouth with his handkerchief and carefully placed the plate on the floor. "I'm wondering if she might have told Fender?"

"About my dad? Maybe."

"Perhaps that's the link, you see. Janet finding out this story, confronting your dad, telling Fender."

"And David?"

"Who knows? Somebody murdered Janet *and* Fender."

"And bashed David's head in. Perhaps it was the same person who did it to them all."

"But David was at the scene. So, he knew the murderer, perhaps he even assisted in the disposal of her body."

"That's ... No, he couldn't have."

"Why not? You didn't know him that well, did you? A weekly visit. Be honest, how well do you know him, outside of bed?"

"Not at all."

"So ..."

"But, he couldn't ... No, it's just too much to even consider. He couldn't."

"Did he know Fender?"

"No. If he knew what Fender had done he'd—"

"Kill him?"

Her eyes widened for a moment before she returned to her sandwich, mopping up the last of the tomato ketchup with a final piece of crust. "I think you could be right about there being a connection, but it's not the one you say. If I were to guess, I'd say there was someone else involved in all of this."

"Yes. Could be." He hesitated in telling her about Bewdsley, deciding to keep it in reserve, waiting for the right moment to reveal all. "Do you know if Fender ever visited your dad?"

She popped the final piece of her breakfast into her mouth. "I don't know. Why would he?"

"If Janet told him? She was telling him something, something which caused him to come here and knock you about." Without warning he took her hand in his. "Millie. Tell me."

"Shit," she said and looked into the distance. "You're like a bloody terrier."

"She did tell him, didn't she? And he came here to find out the details. But why? Why would he do that?"

"Blackmail." She looked at him. "He cooked up a plan to blackmail my dad. I wasn't having any of that. Even though I hated Dad for what he'd done, it was a long time ago. I saw no point in raking it all up again, so I had a go, told him to get out, to leave both myself and Janet alone. I started pushing him out and that's when he hit me. I fell, split lip, blood dripping and it seemed to spur him on. Give him a thrill, seeing me like that. He put the boot in, the bastard, two or three times then punched me. I guess he thought I'd cave in, tell him what he wanted to know, but I didn't. He came here to find out all about it because Janet wouldn't tell him."

"Why not?"

She carefully mopped up the remaining grease from her chin with her tissue, balled it up into her hand, and stared. "Because she was already dead."

PLAYING THE DETECTIVE

FROM OUTSIDE, Craig could hear the solid thump of bare feet against the wooden floor, the raucous *kiais* followed shortly by laughter. Uncle Eric's voice sounded gleeful as he said, "Brilliant Hugh!"

Easing open the door, Craig slid inside.

The hall, or *dojo* as it now served, was large, floor well-polished, ceiling high, strip lights suspended by chains giving off a glaring light. To the right, a stage, curtains drawn back. A multi-functional space, used by Uncle Eric to train his karate students twice weekly, and private students, such as Hugh, every Wednesday and Friday,

"Craig!"

He looked up to see his uncle striding towards him, looking faintly comical in his white *gi*, the black belt tied loosely around his waist. He ruffled Craig's hair.

"Mum said you wanted to talk to me. Is it about the hoplites?"

"The hop…? No, no, it's something else." He swung around to speak to his student. "Well done today, Hugh. See you next time." He stepped away and bowed, Hugh doing the same before he shuffled off and disappeared through a door in the far corner. Eric took Craig by the elbow and led him over to the stage. "Thanks for coming, I just needed to ask you something."

Unable to show his disappointment, Craig let out a long sigh. "Always questions – everybody asking me bloody questions."

"Hey, steady on, I've never asked you anything before."

"No, but… Uncle Eric, I just want things back to normal. Like they used to be when Dad was alive."

"Yes, of course you do. Listen, about that Billy Baxter, he's not a nice bloke. He might even be dangerous."

"Dangerous? In what way?"

"The War, it changed him. It changed all of us. We saw things no one should ever see or experience. You forget your humanity, you understand?"

Frowning, Craig wondered where all of this was leading. "I think so," he said slowly.

"In that church tower, after what had happened, it was like entering into another world, a nightmare world. Those kids, the boy especially, he was the one—"

"Hold on, Uncle Eric," interjected Craig quickly, "you mean you were *there*?"

His uncle's eyes grew large as if, for the first time, he suddenly realised what he had said.

"Thank you, *sensei*," came a voice.

They both looked up to see Hugh clutching a holdall, beaming.

"Yes, thank you, Hugh," said Uncle Eric, unable to keep the relief from his voice. Stepping away from Craig, he pumped the man's hand. "Yes. Next time."

Hugh left, giving a slight nod to Craig before he went out into the evening air.

"Uncle Eric, I think you need to tell me—"

"Craig," returned his uncle, face growing severe, all his usual *bonhomie* gone, "I want you to steer clear of Baxter. Your mother doesn't like it and neither do I."

"Steer clear? But he saved my neck up at the park."

Red-faced, lips drawn back in a snarl, his uncle rushed up to him, finger-wagging, "You do as you are told! I *know* Billy Baxter, all right? I know what he's capable of."

"So you saw him kill that boy?"

His uncle rocked backwards, hand clamped across his mouth. Stifling a scream perhaps.

"Uncle Eric, if you know the truth then you have to say."

"Go home," was his only reply before he whirled around and marched off to the same door Hugh had emerged from.

Perplexed, Craig went outside. His bus wasn't for another twenty minutes, which gave him plenty of time to think.

They rowed again that morning, Mum furious, at one point slamming her fist down on the kitchen table. "I talked to your uncle last night, and he's not happy at all with your attitude."

"It's nothing to do with him. It's nothing to do with any of you!" Craig, close to tears, had announced he was going to see Billy Baxter, to honour his promise of taking Skipper out for a walk. "Dad would understand. Dad would let me go and see him."

"No. He'd agree with me. He wouldn't want you to have anything to do with that man. Ever since you met him there's been nothing but trouble. I let you go and see him last time and look what happened. That could have been you in the hospital, Craig."

"No, he fainted, that was all." He bit down hard

on his lip, not wanting to lie but not wanting his mum to become any more annoyed. Billy had been 'clinically dead' for almost two minutes.

"Well, whatever, I think it best if you keep away. For the time being, until all this nonsense dies down. I'm sick with the worry of it all."

"But I *promised*. I'm only taking his dog out. Billy's sick, Mum. He's finding it hard to cope."

"Yes. You're right – he *is* sick. Sick in the head. What he did is beyond belief."

"You have no idea what he did. You're only listening to gossip and rumour, and you're believing it."

"Eric told me all about it."

"Uncle Eric? Ah yes, he knows quite a lot, doesn't he?"

"More than you think. Uncle Eric has been a town councillor for over twenty years, and he knows a lot of people. Clever people, people in the know."

"What does that mean?"

"It *means* he can find out a lot more about what goes on in this town than almost anyone else. He's preparing to be our MP in the next election. He doesn't lie!"

"Meaning Billy does?"

"I believe he's hoodwinked you."

"You don't know what I know."

"He's brainwashed you, that's what he's done. All

that nonsense about soldiers, using his dog to get to you. And after what happened in the park—"

"If it wasn't for him, I'd probably be dead."

"Don't be so stupid. I told you I'm grateful for his help, but that hasn't changed my mind about him."

"They kicked his dog. That Crossland kicked Skipper, nearly killed him and I want to go and see if he's ok. Mum *please*."

She stood, breathing hard, the anger etched into every line of her face, but also the inner conflict. Craig waited. He saw the fight raging within, her distrust of the man, struggling to overcome her natural attitude, her love of animals. He touched her arm. Chanced a smile. Puppy dog eyes. "If he touches you, so help me …"

"He won't. We're friends, Mum."

"I want you back here by tea-time. You hear me? No later."

Gushing, he kissed her cheek. "I love you, Mum."

"And when you get home, I need to talk to you about that Samantha girl."

He went to speak but stopped himself. Conversations regarding Sam could wait. Right now, he needed to go to Billy, find out if everything was all right. With him and with Skipper. So, he kissed his mum again and exited the house at a run.

He left by the back gate and jogged down into

Station Road, moving past the bench where he'd spoken to Bob Bewdsley.

And where Bob sat right now.

"Going to Billy's?"

Craig stopped. Perhaps he shouldn't have done so, but there was something in the man's tone which trucked no argument. So he stood still, out of breath not merely from the running but from the fear twisting through him. What did he want?

"I asked you a question."

"I'm taking his dog out."

"I warned you, didn't I, to keep away. I told you what would happen."

"Mr Bewdsley, please, please listen to me. It's got nothing to do with Billy, I promise you..." Here it was again. The pleading, the attempts to persuade. Just as he had with his mum, but this time ... This was on a totally different level. Fear laced through every word, every gesture. "It's only his dog. I'm taking him out for a walk, that's all."

"If I find out you've been talking, I'll skin you alive. You understand?"

Throat gripped in terror, panic swelled up from his bowels. Larynx crushed, but not by this man's hands, by sheer fear. No hope of forming any sound, not even a whimper let alone words. Craig nodded, wanting so much to run away, knowing he couldn't. He didn't have the strength. But he also knew he shouldn't. The consequences would be too awful.

Scowling, Bewdsley stretched out his legs. "If you say *anything* to *anybody*…"

He left the words dangling, no need for further development. Craig knew what he meant. The threat. The promise. Despite it all, something uncontrollable spread from within, giving him not so much a boldness as an irresistible urge to confront this dreadful man. "Was it you who came to my house?"

Bewdsley paused, Craig's words seeming to plunge him into confusion for a few moments before a deep frown slowly developed. "Come to your house? I´ve never been to your house. Maybe I should though, tell your mother that it would be better for both of you if you—"

"No one else would need to break in, would they?"

"Lad, you're pushing it and I'm warning you—"

"I'm not afraid of you and if you keep threatening me, I´ll tell the police *everything*."

"You do that and I´ll break your neck!"

He meant it. Craig knew he meant it, the cold glint in his hard eyes unmistakeable in their intention. Looking straight ahead, Craig moved cautiously away, taking his retreat one step at a time until he broke into a jog. He daren't look back. Concentrating on the road ahead, his gait lengthened into a full run, not stopping until he was outside Billy Baxter's front gate.

Inside the house, beyond the door, Skipper set up a loud series of barks. The door opened and Baxter stood, smiling initially, then frowning. "Craig? Are you all right?"

He stepped out and Craig almost fell into his arms. "Billy …"

"Come on inside," Baxter said, taking him around the shoulders whilst scanning the street. "Come on in and tell me what the bloody hell is going on."

Ten minutes or so later, the story told, Baxter stood by the mantelpiece, fingers drumming on the surface, face to the French window, biting down on his bottom lip. "That bloody Bob Bewdsley …"

"Billy, please don't say anything to him. You're not well. The hospital said you needed rest."

Swivelling slowly around, Baxter measured Craig with a piercing look. "He has no right to be frightening you like that. But don't worry, I'll stay quiet. He's up to something, I can feel it."

"What do you mean? Why is he so concerned about me talking to you? What's he afraid of?"

Billy Baxter's face took on a pained expression. "He's afraid of a lot. A lot."

"But why?"

Shaking his head, Baxter stepped away from the fireplace, resolute now. Determination bringing a different kind of rigidity to his body. "I'm going to find out what the hell is going on. You go home, Craig. Come back tomorrow."

"No, Billy. I'm coming with you."

"You mustn't. Your mother would—"

"Mum's not expecting me until tea-time." He looked to Skipper, lying beside him on the sofa, and tickled him under the ear. "I'll take Skipper out tomorrow."

Baxter set a brisk pace, marching in a military style, arms swinging, jaw set hard. "Killarney Grove," he said when at last he stopped. "That's where he sometimes stays. In the corner house, overlooking the old rail track, where they're building the new tunnel approach road."

"What are you going to do? You can't just walk up to him and confront him, can you?"

"I'm not sure if there's anything else I can do."

"Shouldn't we think about this first, then come back?"

"What's there to think about, eh? I always knew it would come to this, but I don't want you involved, Craig. It's too dangerous."

"Billy, you're scaring me – dangerous? Why is it dangerous? Why is he so angry at me, at you?"

"It doesn't matter."

"But it does, Billy. You told me that after your wife learned about what happened, she left you. Took your daughter with her. Has that got something to do with it? Does Bewdsley have some sort of hold over them?"

"Why would Bob Bewdsley... It doesn't matter. Look, I'm going to talk to him, that's all. Tell him to leave you alone. None of this has anything to do with you."

"He's frantic that you don't tell me anything. But you already have. And Bewdsley, he had something to do with it, didn't he." It was a statement, not a challenge, laced with doubt, but as soon as Craig uttered it, he saw the change in Billy's face. That reluctance to meet him in the eye, the uncertainty, the quickening of the breath. "Billy, what you told the police? That inspector? You said something about that girl coming round, and you showed her a letter."

"She came to see me with a diary she'd found."

"A diary? About what happened back in France? Does it mention Bewdsley?"

"Shit." Baxter grabbed him by the arm and quickly pulled him away, going into a nearby front garden, ducking down out of sight. "It's him," he whispered.

Craig wrenched himself free but said nothing. He chanced a quick look from where he squatted behind the gatepost. Bewdsley, dressed now in black blazer and grey slacks, had his head down, going through his wallet as he emerged at the bottom of Kent Road and strolled away in the general direction of the main road.

"Where's he going?"

"I don't know." Billy grabbed him again and swung him around up close. "I'm going to follow him, find out what he's up to. You go home, Craig."

"I don't want to. Not until you tell me the truth."

Eyes rolling to heaven, Billy shook him. Violent. Painful. Craig swallowed down a cry, hand unsuccessfully trying to release himself from Baxter's grip.

"Listen to me. He *was* involved, all right. When that girl came to see me, to have it out with me, I saw him standing outside. Him and some other fella. When she left ... Craig, go home. I'll tell you it all when I get back. Trust me."

"Girl? Janet Stowe? Billy, what did she tell you that put her in so much danger?"

"Jesus, don't you *ever* do as you're told?" He shoved Craig into the open, sending him sprawling across the pavement. Craig lay there, rubbing his arm, tears forming, and Billy Baxter set off, following Bewdsley, never looking back.

For a long time, Craig lay there, hurt that this so-called friend could be so violent, so angry. He remained there until the owner of the house where they'd sheltered came out, saw him, tilted her head and said, "Aren't you Craig?"

That was enough to spur him on and he raced across to the back entry and made his way to, what he hoped was, the safety of his own home.

But he wasn't quite safe.

Not yet.

No sooner had his hand closed around the latch to his backdoor than he felt rather than saw the figure stepping up close to him. For one awful, sickening moment, he believed it to be Bewdsley. Somehow, he'd been able to double-back, unseen, and here he was, confronting him again, scaring the life out of him.

But it wasn't Bewdsley. It was Crossland.

"Oh God," murmured Craig, both hands coming up to protect him from the blows soon to rain down on him. "Please. Please don't hurt me anymore."

In response, the unbelievable happened. Crossland's eyes grew moist before sprouting tears. They tumbled down his face. His shoulders bunched, body juddered, and in snatched, yawning groans, voice bleating, he said, "I'm sorry, Craig. I'm sorry."

He fell into Craig's arms. Craig, bemused, not knowing what to do, held him gently and waited. Consumed with surprise, uncertainty but mostly a toe-curling embarrassment, he checked the entry to ensure no one was there, but they were alone.

After a few awkward moments, Crossland stepped away snivelling and blew out a long sigh. "Ah shit, Craig, sorry." He sniffed loudly, face red. The great bully, the great fighter, belittled, defeated. "I … I want you to know, I'll never bother you again. I'll never bother *anyone* again. I was horrible to you and I'm so …" His face came up, red-rimmed eyes staring. "I'm so ashamed."

"Don't be. Honestly, it's okay."

"No, no it's not. I've learned my lesson. I know you refused to say anything, about what I did to you. Hanging you over that ledge. You had every right to dob me in, but you didn't and I can't tell you how grateful I am, because … My dad, he would have killed me. Beaten the shit out of me. Anyway. That's it. What you did, it changed me. For the better. Just so you know." A weak smile followed, then a gentle slap on the shoulder. "I know we'll never be friends, but, if ever you need anything. You know, you just … You know."

"Yes. Thanks."

"I've been watching you, waiting for the right moment." He nodded towards the end of the entry, where it opened up into Station Road. "I saw that guy from the allotments talking to you. I don't like the look of him, Craig."

"Billy? No, he's a friend. No need to worry about him."

"No, not Billy Baxter. I know Billy Baxter. He was down at the lake, remember? He talked to me afterwards, got me to thinking. Me and Sam."

"He talked to you? What about?"

"Life, I suppose. How it's too short, that we should try to be kind. That we could have killed you, and then what would have happened … He made a lot of sense but no, not him. The other one."

"Ah. Bob Bewdsley, you mean?"

"Do I? I don't know his name. But I've seen him around, watching Billy's house. Talking to some other guy. Nasty looking pair. I know their sort. I've grown up with people like them. You have to watch him, Craig. I mean it."

"I will, Crossie. Thanks."

Smiling, perhaps relieved amends had been made, Crossland went to move away and then stopped. "Oh," he said, face to the ground, the redness returning to his jawline, "about Sam."

Craig's stomach lurched and he tensed, half-expecting the Crossland of old to return. "I didn't … Look, she and me, we're just—"

"It's all right," he said, cutting Craig off. He

laughed. "She told me. Told me you'd kissed and that she liked it. That she wanted you and her to … The thing is we were never really boyfriend and girlfriend. Not like *that*. Not like you and her are now. So …" He nodded, leaving the rest of his comment to drift away in the air. "I'll see you around, Craig."

Head down, hands thrust deep into his jean pockets, kicking at the occasional stone, Crossland shuffled off into the distance. For a long time, Craig stared at the former bully's back. Sam had spoken, and told him that she liked the kiss? He ran a hand over his face. He should have felt a tinge of the embarrassment he felt earlier, but he didn't.

He felt elated.

TREADING WATER

MUM MET him as he came through the kitchen. Her face drawn, pallor grey. Concerned, Craig frowned. "What is it?"

"The police are here, Craig."

He wondered when it was all going to stop. Every time he thought things might be getting better, the horrible queasiness returned. He remembered Billy telling him of the same thing happening to him during the War. A horrible constant churning inside his guts, breaking down his resilience. It happened with Melanie and her skanky boyfriend Danny, and now the police, erasing his good mood after seeing Crossland. He sighed. "What do they want?"

"The usual. More questions. They're in the front room."

Fallon. Etched into his brain, he knew the man's name now. The other one was an unknown quantity. Much younger, slim, thin almost, hands too big for his wrists, clasping them together like he was in a church. Perhaps they should be. A confessional. Craig sat down.

"This won't take long," said Fallon. "We didn't get a chance to finish our conversation last time, did we?"

They waited. Craig waited. Mum moved somewhere behind him. She cleared her throat. "Craig? Answer the policeman please."

"I suppose not."

"Mr Baxter is all right, yes?" Craig nodded. Fallon shifted position, looked at companion, and shrugged before turning his smile towards Craig. "I checked in with the hospital and they released him early."

"He's alive because of you. Thank you."

Fallon's face flushed slightly. "Just what anyone would do really. We'll need to go and see him again soon, of course, but for now, it's you I need to ask something. Does he ever mention his daughter, at all? Millie?"

"Not really."

"What does that mean? Not really?"

"Hardly ever. Maybe once."

"All right. Did he ever mention her with regard to Janet Stowe?"

"The murdered girl?" He shook his head.

"Craig," it was the one with the big hands. He spread them out, like two fans, fingers splayed, inviting him in. "Did he ever tell you what happened to him in the War?"

Craig swallowed hard, glanced at his mum as she sat down. "Go on, Craig. If you know something, tell them."

"He told me what happened, yes."

Another exchange of looks. The man with the hands smiled. "Did he mention anything about Mr Bewdsley?"

It was like a huge cell door slamming through a large, open space, shutting him in, closing off all means of escape. He heard it ringing, heard the bolt engaging. No way out now. The enormity of his predicament overwhelmed him and he sat rigid, desperate for this to end, for him to be in bed, under the covers, safe. Alone.

"Craig?"

Blinking, he turned from the man with the hands to his mum and back again. "Bewdsley. Yes. He was at the allotment. He helped me before I got friendly with Billy."

"Bob Bewdsley," said Mum. Leaning forward,

she took Craig's hand but her eyes remained on the policemen. "What's he got to do with all of this?"

Arching a single eyebrow, Fallon, eyes bright with anticipation, asked, "You know him?"

"Of course, I know him," she said curtly. "Not to speak to, but I know *of* him. He has a temper, but he's a decent enough sort. My brother knows him better than anyone, I think."

"Your brother?"

"Eric Dawson – *Councillor* Dawson. You may have heard of him."

Fallon sat rigid, face revealing nothing. "Yes. Naturally."

"He's the one to speak to about these men. He's had dealings with lots of ex-soldiers."

"I'm sure," said Fallon and turned his gaze to Craig. "What did Billy say Bob Bewdsley had done in the War?"

"Nothing." His voice like a mouse. Unconvincing.

"Nothing? Are you sure about that Craig?"

"He said Bewdsley was there, that he saw what happened."

"And what did happen, Craig?"

"You should ask Billy."

"I'm asking you, Craig. What did Mr Baxter tell you about what he did in the War – specifically."

Mum's hand squeezed his. He snapped his eyes

to her fingers but he didn't pull away. Something like a squeak forced its way from his throat. "My Dad was killed, you know."

This time the silence fell much heavier than that cell door. The atmosphere crackled with the tension.

"Craig ..." Mum's voice, splintering as it had when it happened. "Craig, this is not the time."

"They held me over a ledge," said Craig quickly, "Crossland did, by my ankles. That's what made me think of it because my Dad, you see, he fell over a ledge. Fell to his death."

"Craig—"

"Perhaps we should come back," said Fallon, smiling at Craig's mum. Slapping his knees, he made as if to stand.

"He told me he murdered two children," said Craig breathlessly, his eyes locked on Fallon's, challenging him to interrupt. But Fallon didn't. Instead, he settled back into his seat and nodded. "He said his unit had come under fire and one of his best mates got shot. Billy lost it, he said, went out of control and killed them. Children. No more than fifteen. Prisoners. He knew he shouldn't, but he was so ... *Angry*. Revenge. He wanted revenge. He murdered them. A boy and a girl. After he told his wife, she left him, taking Millie with her. Much later, Janet Stowe got to hear of it and came around to confront him about it, tried to blackmail him and that's all I know."

Silence stretched out as everyone inwardly digested Craig's words. At last, Fallon cleared his throat. "Nothing about Bewdsley?"

"No, I—" Craig stopped, unable to say anything about the threats, the terror of those moments gripping him. Slowly, his mum snaked her arm around his shoulder and pulled him close.

"I think that's enough now, Inspector," she said.

Agreeing, the two policemen stood up. "Thank you," said Fallon. "We'll see ourselves out."

It wasn't until he heard the front door close that Craig crumpled into his mum's arms and sobbed.

FITTING THE PIECES

THEY GOT the call as they fell into the car, the radio crackling, the operator's voice sounding vexed, annoyed nobody had picked up sooner. Fallon made a few perfunctory remarks, not wanting to grovel or sound apologetic before he stopped, almost as if some unseen hand had yanked him upright and listened in numbed silence. He dropped the radio mic back into its cradle and stared.

"What is it? Sir? What's wrong?"

Fallon slowly turned, his expression of one close to apoplexy. "There's been a fire, out near Meols. Firemen got there and found a car. It's Emery's."

"Oh shit. What the hell was he doing out there?"

"No idea." He turned the key and the Mini's engine fired up. "There's no sign of him, or at least I hope there isn't."

"I don't understand."

Taylor's superior stared into the distance, voice dropping to a whisper. "They found a body inside the building, burned beyond recognition."

On the way, another call came in and Fallon took a quick detour, dropping Taylor off at Victoria Central Hospital before continuing on his own to Meols. Alone in the tiny Mini, he tried to keep his mind clear, but nothing could shake the feeling of impending doom enfolding him, smothering any meaningful thoughts. He drove in a sort of thick fog, barely registering traffic and road signs. By the time he rolled into the wide, open field in front of the burned and gutted buildings he was feeling sick with dread.

The body – if it could be called such a thing – was wrapped in thick black polythene. A nearby ambulance had its rear doors wide open, waiting, like the entrance to another realm, one infinitely darker than this. Fallon could not imagine a worse existence than the one in which he currently moved through.

"We couldn't determine anything," said a voice and Fallon turned to see a middle-aged man in a charcoal grey suit standing in front of him looking sheepish. "We might get something from his dental records."

"Fingerprints?"

The man shook his head. "Nothing. Burned to a crisp. Sorry." A slight raising of the eyebrows, "Do you think you might have known him?"

Fallon nodded in the general direction of Emery's car, standing there like a faithful dog waiting for a master who would never return. "The owner of that car, a colleague of mine."

"Ah." The man shifted his weight from one foot to the other. "I'll have something for you in the morning, Inspector ...?"

"Fallon. Manor Road police station."

"Yes. Of course. I'll get it to you as soon as I can."

Firemen were treading cautiously through the smouldering timbers of the building. One caught his eye, pulled a face, and shook his head. Defeated, Fallen swung away and tramped back to his car.

Some twenty minutes later, Fallon walked along the hospital ward and found Taylor marking time, looking sheepish. "What's going on, Taylor?"

"The ward sister greeted me when I got here, to let me know Howarth had woken up and seemed pretty coherent. The only thing is, I wasn't the only one waiting."

"Let me guess – Millie."

"How did you know—" Taylor recognised that superior look on Fallon's face and sighed. "She said she wanted to know if he was all right. Then, she told me some fairly amazing stuff, sir."

"Tell me as we walk down to Howarth's ward."

"It seems Janet Stowe had attempted to blackmail Baxter, but Baxter had convinced her it wasn't him. She'd told Fender about what Millie had said. Fender got angry at this new complication. He was desperate for money, saw Baxter as an easy target. Apparently, when he said he wanted to go and get the truth out of Millie, Janet stopped him, wouldn't give the address. They used to meet up in a nightclub over in Liverpool. A place called 'The Lonely Extra'. A right bloody dive. It's a pick-up place. Anyway, it hires out rooms in the back and that's where they, you know. Did it."

"Did it?"

"Had sex."

"Even though she was a lesbian?"

"Bi-sexual. so Millie says. They both are – *were*."

"So, he knocks her about, to find out what Millie knows?"

"Not yet. First, he goes to confirm what Baxter has said is true. He wants to see this diary, this proof. It's there that he meets Bewdsley. Bewdsley's seen Janet at Baxter's. He confronts Fender, wants to know what's going on, why he and Janet have been talking to Billy."

"And Millie told you all this?" Fallon pulled a face. "You must be on awfully friendly terms with her all of a sudden. I warned you about her, son. You're playing with fire."

"Sir, nothing is going on." He paused, gazing towards the entrance to Howarth's ward. "It's this conversation with Bewdsley which makes Fender convince himself he can blackmail Baxter, that Janet has lied to him, that she wants the money for herself. First, he tries a clever approach. At least, he believes it's clever. He goes and talks to Millie."

"Knocks her about as well?"

"Yes. He plans to go and threaten Baxter, get some money out of him, but Millie stands up to Fender, tells him he has no right to be blackmailing her father, regardless of what he's done. They struggle, he loses it and, well, we know the rest. He then decides to teach Janet another lesson."

"He murders her?"

"Millie doesn't think so. But in between Fender visiting Millie and going back home, Janet disappears. We know what happens then."

"So if Fender didn't murder her, who did?" Fallon sighed and his expression changed, growing clearer. "Bewdsley! He believes they know the truth, that *he* murdered those kids, not Baxter. So he does for Janet, then later Fender."

"But … Sir," Taylor didn't look convinced. "All right, it's a terrible thing and all, but, killing those kids, even if he did, what difference does it make now? I mean, no court in the land would convict him. He's got form. He's not going to be bothered if the news got out, is he? I mean, probably in the eyes of everybody, those kids deserved it. It's not worth murdering for, is it? And certainly not twice."

They stood in silence as the everyday life of the hospital carried on uninterrupted around them. Oblivious, lost in thought, they mulled over Millie's words until at last, Fallon took a breath, ballooned his cheeks, and said, "You're right. Absolutely right. There's something else going on here, son. Something which would lead to murder. Question is – what."

"Can I ask what happened at the fire, sir?"

"We don't yet know." He clapped his hands together, changing the mood. "All right, let's go and see what Mr Howarth can tell us, shall we?" Ignoring the young constable's pained expression, Fallon stepped up to the ward door.

Answering the doorbell, Craig's mum stood, unsure, not quite believing who she saw standing on her doorstep. "Who is it, Mum?" Craig came bounding down the stairs and stopped.

"Can I come in?"

She stepped aside after the slightest of pauses and Billy Baxter crossed into the hall, assenting his head at Craig, standing at the foot of the stairs. "Is it Skipper?"

"Eh? No, no, he's fine. I just wanted ..." He looked at Craig's mum. "Can I talk to him?"

"What about?"

"Something I've found."

"Not more bloody soldiers, is it?"

"Soldiers?" Frowning, Baxter looked from her to Craig who nodded frantically. "Yes. Soldiers. Those Greek hoplites."

Muttering under her breath, she waved him further in, closed the door, and waltzed down the hallway to the kitchen. "I'll make tea."

Craig led him into the back room, eager to hear what all this was about. He knew for certain it wouldn't have anything to do with any Ancient Greek soldiers.

"I followed him," said Billy without any preamble. "All the way over to Liverpool."

"He didn't see you, did he?"

"I thought he had at one point, but I'm certain he didn't. Not a good look anyway."

"So where did he go?"

"A club. Special sort of club. Not a particularly nice place, if you get my meaning."

Craig didn't, but he let it go. "Is it important?"

"I'm not sure, but it's strange he should go there. He was clearly a member because he went straight in. I waited outside, maybe for two or three hours. Decided to come home in the end."

Craig was about to say something when his mum came in with a tray bearing two mugs of hot tea and a plate of biscuits. She set it down on the dining table, gave them both a look, and went out.

Munching on a biscuit, Craig took a sip of tea before he spoke. "This place, the club. What was its name?"

Billy drank, licked his lips, and said, "The 'Lonely Extra'."

'WHO TO PULL IN FIRST?'

"I DON'T WANT you upsetting him," said the nurse, standing, arms folded, severe and uncompromising.

"That's not my intention," said Fallon. "How is he?"

"He seems fine. He wanders around a lot. As if he is looking for something. Other than that, you'll have to ask his doctor."

"Wanders around? You mean, in the wards?"

"Always going for a bath. It seems an obsession with him. He can often be in there for hours."

"I see." But Fallon didn't. He thought for a moment.

"He's still not well, so keep it brief. I'll let the doctor know you're here."

"Thank you."

She flounced off and Fallon nodded to Taylor. "Given what she said, best if I interviewed him alone."

"What's the thing about baths, sir?" asked Taylor.

"No idea. Maybe he'll tell me, but it's probably of no importance, a symptom of his amnesia I suppose. Either way, we don't want to upset him unduly, so wait for me here."

Taylor didn't argue, despite the look of disappointment on his face.

In his private ward, Howarth sat up in bed, a pile of pillows behind his back. There was a newspaper across his lap and he drummed a pencil against his bottom teeth. He stopped as Fallon stepped closer.

"Hello Mr Howarth, how are you feeling?"

"A little better." Frowning, Howarth laid down the pencil. "Do I know you?"

Fallon pulled out his warrant card. "D.I. Fallon. We have met, but …" He smiled, went to the window, and looked out. "Good that they kept you in here. A bit of privacy."

"They need to monitor me … I'm sorry, Inspector, I'm very confused but is there a problem? What is it you want?"

"Millie Clovis." Turning around, Fallon looked directly towards the big man sitting there with hands like plates, head far larger than it should be. Perhaps back in his school days, the other kids would call him Herman Munster. Perhaps people still did.

"Who?"

"You still can't remember? She's your girlfriend, Mr Howarth. All right, not the regular type of girlfriend, but even so. She'd visit you on Fridays and you were always happy to see her. Attractive girl. Wears big flowery skirts, hippy type things, flowers in her hair, but maybe she's never been to San Francisco."

"I'm sorry, I haven't got a clue what you're talking about. San Francisco?"

"Forget that part. Just concentrate on the girl. Millie Clovis. Her dad fought in the War. Killed some kids he shouldn't have. She told you all about it."

"Well, if she did ... Inspector, I'm sorry, but none of this is—"

"Someone hit you over the head. You were lucky they didn't kill you. We think you must have known who it is because nobody in their right mind is going to go up against you. You were an M.P. A Military Policeman?"

"Yes. I was. Malaya. Then Aden."

"You saw action?"

"Lots. More than I wanted."

"So, you remember all that, but you don't remember Millie?"

"I'm sorry, Inspector. Like I say, everything is confused and blurred. Vague."

"Or selective."

"I beg your pardon?"

Shaking his head, Fallon stepped up to the bed. Howarth seemed relaxed, unruffled. "What about Fender and Bewdsley? Janet Stowe … You must remember her?"

Not a flicker crossed Howarth's face and he remained as impassive as if Fallon had told him about the weather. "Those names mean nothing to me, Inspector. I'm guessing they are connected to the murder investigation?"

"How do you know about that? Your memory coming back, or are you simply playing with me, Mr Howarth?"

"No, Inspector, I'm not playing at anything." He picked up the newspaper and folded it to reveal the front page, and the headline, 'Police remain baffled'. "It's all here, Inspector. Janet Stowe. The name, if it rings a bell at all, is in my head because of this report. But I don't know anything about Millie, Fender, or Bob Bewdsley. So, if you don't mind, I feel somewhat tired. Perhaps you can come back in a day or two and I might be able to help you. If things get clearer." He tapped his head. "In here."

Fallon was about to speak when the door opened and a tall, sanguine-looking man of about fifty came inside. The stethoscope dangling around his neck announced who he was. "Inspector?"

"I'm just leaving." Fallon looked again at Howarth, that large, cheery smile beginning to get on his nerves. "I'll be back in a day or so."

"I'll be here."

Outside again, Fallon took in the expectant looks of his younger colleague. He shook his head and strode towards the exit.

Once outside, he lit up a cigarette and blew the smoke skywards. "He knows," he said, "but he's not saying anything. He's using his memory loss to great advantage."

"You don't believe him? That it's real, his loss of memory?" Fallon shrugged, exhaled smoke, and looked grim. "So, who do we pull in first?" asked Taylor.

"How can we pull in anyone? I'll go and call on Baxter again, you do another sweep of Howarth's street. Show photographs of Baxter, Fender, and Bewdsley. See if anybody recognizes them. Our original thought has to be correct – whoever hit Howarth knew him. He let his assailant into the house. Howarth is covering it up."

"For what reason, boss?"

"Because they were both involved in Janet's murder. We know it took two of them to put her into the canal. Howarth was there and gave us a description of someone he saw, someone with red hair and a dog."

"Bewdsley has red hair," said Taylor, "but no dog."

"And Baxter does have a dog but is not red-headed." Fallon blew out a stream of smoke before he threw the stub to the ground. "Do the sweep. If anything turns up, get in touch. I'll talk to Baxter again. Then, if there's nothing, we'll meet up at the station and think about who we should pull in."

Fallon disappeared across the road, heading through the side streets towards Baxter's. It would take him the best part of half an hour to reach the old man's house, but he didn't appear to want a lift.

Taylor lost himself in thought, knowing the case was leading nowhere. A sudden urge to march back into the hospital and confront Howarth gripped him.

It was an idea that lasted mere seconds before he went back inside, resolute and determined.

CONFESSIONAL

FALLON STOOD IN THE CONSERVATORY, gazing out across the garden. Behind him, Billy Baxter and Craig sat on the sofa, waiting.

"I spoke to your mum," said the policeman keeping his back to them, "and she is perfectly fine with me interviewing you again, Craig. So, no worries, okay?" He turned, smiling.

Craig didn't feel much like smiling at all. Far more comfortable with a scowl, he turned away from Fallon's gaze, preferring to stare at the carpet.

"What can you tell me about Robert Bewdsley, Mr Baxter?"

Craig felt Billy tense beside him. He glanced, from his friend to the policeman. "Bob Bewdsley?"

If Fallon was surprised that Craig had been the

one to speak, he didn't show it. "You met him, didn't you, Craig? At the allotments?"

"Did Stan tell you that?" piped up Billy Baxter. "A great one for gossip is Stan, ever mindful of his civic duties."

"Stan Prentis? Yes, he went to Manor Road Police Station, gave a statement. We've used what he said to deal with those bullies, the ones who attacked you, Craig."

"Yes," said Craig, dejected, surrendering to the inevitability of it all.

"But that's not why I'm here," said Fallon, crossing to an armchair and sinking into it. "Janet Stowe, Mr Baxter. I think you need to tell me how you knew her."

Baxter sat in silence. "You already know that Inspector. She was a reporter, asking questions. That's all."

"What can you tell me about her murder, Mr Baxter?"

"Nothing, except what was in the newspapers."

Fallon's gaze shifted to land on Skipper, stretched out in front of the fire. "Is that your only dog, Mr Baxter?"

Craig didn't like the way the conversation was leading. He squeezed Baxter's arm. "Billy? What is he talking about?"

Baxter looked blank. Fallon's face reddened. "I

have to caution you, Mr Baxter. This is a murder inquiry, if you are found to have been withholding evidence then I will have no option but to—"

"No," said Craig. "No, it won't come to that. Billy. Tell him what you know. *Please*. Whatever it is, I won't hate you. I'll understand. I will, I promise you."

"Craig," said Fallon, "you really don't have to--"

"It's all right," said Billy, sniffing loudly. "It's all right. Craig ..." He turned to his young friend, smiling, but a smile full of sadness, regret. Pain. "I couldn't tell you everything, Craig. I couldn't tell my wife. I couldn't."

"You mean there's more to the story? About what happened?" Baxter nodded. "Why couldn't you tell me everything?"

"Because of Bob. We made a promise, you see, a pact."

Fallon leaned forward. "Mr Baxter, if you could just—" He stopped, Craig's outstretched hand, palm forward, cutting him off.

"Just tell us, Billy. Tell us about what *really* happened."

"I lied to you when I gave that story to you. I lied to you just like I lied to my wife, and look where that got me."

"But why would you lie?" Craig's eyes grew wide. He shot a glance toward Fallon before he turned again to Baxter. "Tell me the real story, Billy."

Baxter, clearly struggling with how to proceed, put his hands over his face and blew out several, ragged sighs. Eventually, he dragged his hands away, a bleak look descending over his features. "All right," he said at last.

They waited, knowing this confession was to prove a painful one. A truthful one.

"We were in the Bocage. Rolling up from the beaches. We had men with us, infantry. We were on high alert, and then the bloody tank broke down. We couldn't believe it. We had to get out. Tommies were laughing, calling us lame ducks, useless, bloody amateurs. We ignored them. Bob was on it. Great mechanic he was. There was sand, you see. It had somehow worked its way into the gearbox. He stripped it down, cleaned it, while the rest of us sat down next to the tracks, smoking, watching the infantry passing by, ignoring their jibes. Pretty soon, wewere alone. Just us, the crew, Bob, shirt off, covered in oil and grease working on the tank engine. I wanted a piss, so I went off into the hedgerows." His fingers raked through his thinning, wispy hair. "Stupid. Our orders were to never to leave the tank. But it was such a beautiful day and the birds … Anyway, I went over, pulled out my Little Fella, and that was when it happened. Three of 'em emerging from the thick undergrowth. Young bastards, they were. Schoolboys but hardnuts. Faces like maniacs, taut, wide-eyed, like they were on the drugs those hippies use."

"What, marijuana?" Fallon shook his head. "They didn't have that then, did they?"

"God knows what they had, but they were on something. Their eyes were as big as plates. It was obvious they were fanatical, that they could fight all day and all night. I saw it. In their faces. But I also saw they were uncoordinated like they were in a sort of daze. I was in the hedge, taking a piss, and I saw them on the other side. Running towards me. Two of 'em with an LMG, the third with one of them Panzerfaust jobbies. I screamed and Bob ..." He shook his head. "I don't know where he came from, but he fell on top of me, flattening me to the ground as that bloody Panzerfaust shot above me and exploded against a tree beside our tank. Nobody was hurt, thank God, but it would have blown me in half if it hadn't been for Bob ..." A big sniff. Baxter blew out several breaths. The retelling seemed to be taking a lot out of him. "He took out his Browning and shot those bastards. One, two, three. Just like that, *pop, pop, pop*. I've never seen a man so cool, so ... And he was grinning. He asked me if I was all right, then he strode across the field. One of them German boys, he was screaming in pain from where the bullet hit him. Without a blink of an eye, Bob put another shot through his head, and that was that. Something seemed to have snapped inside him. All of his pent-up fear, rage, *hate* I suppose, it all came spewing out, and from that moment he changed."

Craig looked across to Fallon, who sat, hands clasped together as if in prayer. Neither spoke. There was nothing to say.

"After that, we got the tank going and ... I told you, Craig, about the village, with the church tower and the snipers? It was Bob, not me that killed them. And he didn't do it in front of everyone either. He found them, you see. Whilst the rest of us, me and them Tommies, were rummaging around, Bob found them kids. I thought I saw him, way over in the distance and I ran over to him, telling the infantry to stay low, to keep looking.

"I found him in a far corner, well away from anyone. He had his Browning against the girl's head, a sniper rifle in his other hand, and the boy ... The boy was on the ground, and Bob's foot was pinning him down by the throat. The lad was squirming, hands grabbing Bob's boot. Bob, he turned to me and I saw that look. Jesus, that look. He smiled at me and, without even looking at her, hit that girl across the jaw and dumped her to the ground. I saw Bob's foot press down on that boy. He pressed and pressed and ... Oh Jesus..." He covered his face again, his voice a wail of despair, every word wrenched from his memory. "A Tommy came up. Don't ask me why or how." His hands dropped. "This poor bastard, couldn't have been more than nineteen I suppose. He saw Bob's boot on that lad's throat, and he shouted, 'What the bloody fuck are you doing, you fucking maniac!' And Bob, he shot him."

"Shit," said Fallon, gaping, voice barely audible. "He shot the Tommy? Dead?"

"Yes. Single shot, through the head. He used the sniper rifle. Yeah. Bob, he reacted real quick, had already got it in his head what to do. Ignoring me, he got down and put a bullet into the boy. I backed off, hands up in the air, believing I'd be next and Bob just looked at me. 'You say anything, Billy Baxter, and I'll fucking kill you too. I saved your fucking life, you bastard. So you keep your mouth shut, you hear me? You keep it fucking shut and we're even.' And I knew what he said was true, because he had saved my life, and I did owe him."

"But he'd murdered one of our own."

Billy looked into Fallon's stricken face. "Yes, and

I have lived with that knowledge all my life, Inspector." He sat back, head up, staring at the ceiling. "It didn't end there. Another Tommy arrived, took it all in, and told Bob to back down. He knew him, you see. Knew him from before the War. He took the rifle and turned to me and, without a moment's pause, shot me through the leg."

"He did *what*?"

"I was invalided out and the story went around that the boy had shot both me and the other Tommy before Bob got to him."

"Who was it who shot you?"

Billy's eyes clouded over and his voice, when he at last answered, had taken on a new tone. Fear gripped him. "I can't tell you anymore. If I do, I'm dead, and so is Craig."

"Wait a moment," said Fallon, leaning forward, barely under control, looking as if were about to spring forward. "You're telling me that two former British soldiers cold-bloodedly murdered not only enemy prisoners but also one of their own?"

"That's about the size of it. When the others came up, despite me writhing on the ground, I told them it was me who'd shot the boy after he'd killed that Tommy and Bob had finished him. Later on, when I was all patched up, I made a full report to the Company Commander, embellishing the story still further. Bob stood behind me in the mess tent. I made out as if everything was down to me. And that was the story I told my wife and the story I told you, Craig."

"But why tell your wife anything at all, Billy?"

"Because after the War Bob found out where we were and he wrote to her, the bastard. Asked her if I'd told her what happened to us in Normandy. He was terrified, you see. Terrified that I'd tell her the truth. He wrote to me as well and he told me to stick with the old story, the lie. That he'd saved my life, but if I told the truth, he'd kill me. He said he'd have nothing to lose, once the authorities found out what really happened. I was scared. You understand? I was scared he'd murder me, so I stayed silent, told the lies. I told the same lie when my wife asked me."

"Who then left you," said Fallon. Baxter nodded. "She then told your daughter who has grown up thinking you are a monster."

"Yes. She's never been to see me, not even a telephone call in all these years. I tried to contact her, but ... I've lived with it, the shame of it, the lie I told. Ashamed of the fear I felt. Recently, I began to think I might be free of it, but then Bob ... He moved back here, see. I see him every day and every day I'm reminded of what happened, and the hold he has over me."

"But now you want to come clean?" Fallon considered Baxter for a moment before turning to

Craig. "Was it you telling this lie to Craig which has made you change your mind, Mr Baxter?"

"No. It was Janet Stowe."

"Janet Stowe, the murdered girl?" Craig shook his head. "What has she to do with it?"

"Ah shit ..." Billy's face crumpled as his hands dropped to his chest where he clutched at the material of his shirt. Breathing hard, the wheezing from his lungs grew more acute.

Craig, terrified that this might be the precursor to another attack, sat up and shot Fallon a worried glance. "Mr Fallon, Billy's not well. It's angina. Heart. I need to get his tablets."

"No, I'm all right Craig." Smiling, Billy patted Craig's arm. "Honestly, don't worry. I need to get all of this out in the open, off my chest at long last." He forced a laugh, which immediately turned into a violent cough. As Craig's concern grew, Baxter touched his young friend's arm. "I'm all right. Just couldn't resist making a joke ... Sorry."

Fallon shifted position, growing irritable. "Janet Stowe, Mr Baxter?"

"When she came here, she said she knew the truth of what had happened, that she was going to tell the newspapers. I told you, Inspector."

"So all that was true? She'd got hold of the real story?"

"Yes. She'd discovered Bob's journal. They were

sleeping together, apparently." A tiny chuckle. "Always was a bit of a lady's man. She confronted me with it, tried to blackmail me. But she'd only read a few extracts, I could tell that from what she said to me. I told her to get out, to get her bloody facts straight. When she questioned me about that, about what I meant, I got angry and I ... Jesus, I may as well tell you. I got her around the throat and made her tell me how she'd first found out about the story. She told me she'd been to see Millie who confirmed everything. That old lie, coming back to haunt me again. I knew then that I'd never be free of it. Not for as long as I lived."

Fallon stared. His face hard and sharp as flint, eyes fixed and penetrating. "So you murdered her?"

The room grew cold and Craig, having listened for so long, stared into a gaping black hole, full of sadness, betrayal, terror. "My God, Billy," he said, forcing the words out. "You killed that poor girl?"

"No!" Baxter sat upright, his anguish disappearing in that single, explosive word. "No, I bloody well didn't! I threatened her, yes. Told her I'd take her to the police, but I never bloody murdered her! What the bloody hell do you think I am?"

"Then who did?" asked Craig.

Nobody spoke and Fallon, sitting back in his chair, took out a cigarette and, without asking, lit it up. "All right. Let's just roll this back a little. Who was this other Tommy? The one who shot you?"

"I told you, I can't."

"Mr Baxter, whoever this person is, whatever the hold he has over you, you've told me so much, surely this one last piece won't cause you—"

"No, wait," interjected Craig. "There's another piece." Both men stared at him. "The girl. You said Bob knocked her out, but what happened to her?"

Blowing out a long sigh, Baxter gazed longingly at Fallon's cigarette. The Inspector, taking the hint, offered him one and lit it for him.

"Billy, for God's sake," said Craig. "You shouldn't be doing that!"

Shrugging, Baxter sat back and luxuriated at the feeling of the nicotine racing through his body. "To be honest, I don't know very much about all that because I was in a field hospital."

"He must have told you?"

"Oh yes, he told me all right. He brought her back, married her." A shocked silence descended over everyone. "And that's the hold he has over Bob, you see. The truth. If everyone knew, if his son knew. So, Bob keeps stum and does what he's told."

"It's that 'he' again, Mr Baxter," said Fallon. "You must tell me."

"I can't."

"I could arrest you."

"Then you're going to have to because I can't tell you anymore." He smiled at Craig. "I can't."

"I'll go back to the station, write this up." Quickly, Craig shot Fallon a glance and the policeman seemed to understand. "I'll be back, Mr Baxter, make no mistake." He stood up and Craig accompanied him to the front door, leaving Baxter to enjoy his cigarette.

"I'll do my best to find out who it is," Craig said to Fallon as he pulled open the door. "Just give me some time, please."

"Time is something I haven't much of, Craig. If what Baxter says is true, then you are in danger."

"I'll be all right."

"I'm not sure you will. I'll send a Bobby round later and he'll stay with you until we get to the bottom of this."

"Mum won't like that."

"She'll like it a damn sight less if something happens to you."

He stepped out, got into his Mini and drove away without another glance.

Back in the conservatory, Craig watched Baxter stubbing out the cigarette. "Those things will kill you," he said.

Without looking, Baxter forced a grim smile. "After today I think cigarettes are the least of my worries."

"Who was the other man, Billy? And why has he got such a hold over everyone?"

"Because he's powerful, Craig. He has lots of contacts, not all of them very nice. Bob might be mean and nasty, but even he is like a baby compared to …" He looked away. "I can't tell you, Craig. It would not only put you in danger, but it would break your heart."

Some fifteen minutes or so later, deep in thought, Craig walked slowly home, head down, taking the long route. Confused and disturbed by his tattered thoughts, he was no longer sure of anything anymore. After Billy's original story, he'd started out thinking what Billy had done was, in some way, understandable, but now …Now he wasn't certain of anything anymore. Could it really have been Bob Bewdsley? He remembered how different both men's reactions had been at the allotment after Craig had fled from Crossland. Billy, how he'd screamed and shouted and Bob so kind, comforting him. Then later, when Billy had come up and confronted Mum, those weren't the actions of a man depressed and alone, but those of a bitter, angry, and vicious thug. Maybe even before the War broke out, he'd been the same, the killing of Wally merely bringing his natural capacity for violence to the surface? Since then, of course, there were Bewdsely's threats. The chill his words brought to Craig was unlike anything he'd ever experienced. So, who was the innocent, and who the guilty party? This mysterious 'third man', who could it be? How could anyone ever know what really happened all those years ago, what were lies and what was truth?

Head filled with conflicting thoughts, he shuffled up to his front door and wondered if the answers would forever lay hidden beneath a mass of confusion and conflict.

Back at Manor Road, a bleak-looking sergeant approached, not daring to look him in the eye. "There's been a phone call, sir. From the medical examiner."

Fallon could tell from the sergeant's awkwardness this was going to be bad. He picked up his desk phone and dialled the number. "It's Fallon," he said, throat dry. "What have you found?"

He listened, each word slamming into him like nails hammered deep. When at last the report was over, he couldn't even summon the words to say goodbye and returned the phone to its cradle. Fumbling for a cigarette, he felt the eyes of the entire squad room boring into him. They all stood, expectant, preparing themselves for the worst. "It was him," he said, battling hard to keep the quivering from his voice and failing miserably. "It was Emery's body they pulled out of that building."

No one spoke. How could they, no words could ever convey the despair everyone felt.

A VISITOR

MUM STOOD IN THE HALLWAY, almost as if she were waiting, anxious to talk as soon as Craig came through the front door. She appeared agitated, drying her already dry hands on her pinny, "Oh Craig, where have you been?"

"What's up?" He knew there was something, sensed it in the heavily drawn lines of her face, her bunched shoulders, those eyes, so wide.

"We've got – I mean *you've* got a visitor."

Bemused, believing it was the police again, Craig went into the backroom, his grandmother's room. She was away visiting her sister but it still smelled of her. He guessed it always would.

"Hello, Craig."

Craig's mouth hung open.

Sitting there, larger than life, was his teacher, Mr

Forrester, the most hated man in Craig's entire universe.

"I'll get more tea, shall I?"

"That would be lovely," said Forrester with a smile and Craig's mum left the room. It seemed to Craig she couldn't get out quick enough. "Sit down, Craig. I want to talk to you."

Craig, however, wasn't having any of it. This wasn't school. This was *his home* and Forrester, staining it as he was by sitting there so arrogant, so pompous, was not going to tell him what to do. He stood, defiance mustered, his jawline set. He folded his arms and did not move. "What do you want, Mr Forrester?"

"I'd like you to sit, please."

"I'm not in school now. I don't have to do what you say."

"Craig, this is not something to do with—"

"This is my home, Mr Forrester. You can't bully me here."

"*Bully you*? Craig, it has never been my intention to … I'm sorry if you thought of me in that way."

"What do you want?"

All of a sudden, Forrester seemed very small, huddled up on the sofa, brown tweed jacket, dark green trousers, suede shoes, all old, crumpled, and well worn. No tie, the only part of his attire different to what he wore in school but no mistaking what his profession was. That loathsome air of superiority hung around him like a second layer of clothing. Crossing his legs, he clamped interlocked hands around his knees and looked towards an area to the left of where Craig stood. His self-confidence was showing the strain. "I want to speak to you, that's all."

"What about? Homework?"

"Craig! It's nothing to do with school."

"What then?"

He rocked backwards, undecided. "A couple of things."

Craig did not move. He had no intention of making it easier for this man, the man he hated with a passion that his mum would have found alarming. "What's the first?"

"Someone came to see me. Someone very concerned for your welfare, Craig. He got in touch with me through the Council, you see, and I went to visit him at the Town Hall. He spoke to me at great length and I knew something had to be done. So, here I am."

A hairline crack appeared in Craig's defences. Curiosity. It made him move, a slight inclination of the head, a narrowing of the eyes, a stirring in his guts. "Who came to see you, Mr Forrester?"

He sat up, hands released, "It was your uncle, Councillor Dawson."

Mum came in at that point, carrying a tray. Three teacups, milk jug, sugar bowl. Their best china, only ever used for special occasions. She stopped, sensing the atmosphere. "What's happened? Jim, have you told him?"

Craig blinked. His mother's voice, but her words making no sense. He looked at her. "*Jim*? Mum, what the bloody hell is going on?"

"Oh God," said Mum. "Craig, hasn't Jim – I mean *Mr* Forrester, hasn't he told you?"

"About Uncle Eric? No, not yet. Mum." He shook his head, his confusion deepening and the beginning of something far, far worse. "Why did you call him Jim?" He waited. His mum wrung her hands, Forrester stared at the carpet. "What's going on? Why is he here?"

"Oh God."

"Craig," said Forrester, standing up, offering a smile and, seeing it rejected, shrugged. "Mr Dawson came to tell me he was worried about you, worried that you might be in some kind of danger from Billy Baxter. He said he'd tried to warn you off, but that you paid no heed, so he wondered if I might ... Craig, are you listening to me?"

"Mum. I want you to tell me what's going on."

Forrester cleared his throat. "Craig, please, you have to listen to what I'm saying. Your uncle is very concerned. Mr Baxter is very—"

"Leave that for now, Jim," said Craig's mum, settling the tray down on the dining table with infinite care. She wiped her hands on the tea-towel stuck in the cord of her pinny but kept her eyes firmly fixed on the carpet as she spoke. "Craig. Mr Forrester and I, we've ... We've been seeing one another. Lunch times. Chatting. Getting to know one another. He's asked me out, for dinner and I'd like to know if that was all right. With you." Slowly, she brought her face up.

He saw the look on her face, wide-eyed and hopeful, but Craig felt he was going to scream. How could such a revelation ever be *all right*? He wanted to explode, to beat her about the face before turning his venom on this horrible man. Didn't she know what he was like, didn't she care that he made Craig's life a living hell? "*Dinner?*"

"Yes. Just so we can talk, you know."

"No, I don't know. What about Dad?"

"*Dad?*" She gasped, shot Forrester a quick glance. "Dad's ... Craig, it's been over a year now. I need to move on. And so do you." She reached to stroke his face, but he dashed her hand away with enough force to make her gasp and pull her hand back as if scorched.

"Don't touch me. How could you, Mum? How could ... with *him*." Suddenly, he was running, running away from both of them before he caught sight of him going to his mother, holding her, both their faces horror-stricken. It should be him who was horror-stricken. Forrester? Of all the men in all the world, why had she chosen him?

Tearing open the back door, he raced into the entry. He had only one thought, to go to Billy and tell him, tell him everything. No more secrets, no more lies. Those moments were gone. Gone for good. The time for the truth had arrived.

Blind, seething with anger, as he turned the corner, he ploughed straight into Bob Bewdsley's midriff. Catching Craig around the waist, Bewdsley turned him and slammed him against the wall. He pressed his face up close, his vile breath wafting across, smelling like something from a cesspit.

"Now then, you snivelling little shit, what have you been saying about me, eh?"

"Nothing," gagged Craig, struggling against the man's hold. "Let me go, you're hurting me!"

"I warned you. I told you what would happen if you told people."

"I haven't told anybody anything!"

"So what was that policeman doing at Billy's eh? Yes, that's right, I saw him. And not for the first time either. What did Billy say to him, eh?"

Kicking out, Craig snapped the toes of his shoe into Bewdsley's shin. It was a vicious crack, and Bewdsley yelped and released his hold, giving Craig the chance to run, head down, teeth gritted.

Without looking back, he knew Bewdsley was behind him, but how long could that old fart keep it up? Arms pumping, legs eating up the distance, Craig shot down Station Road, across Leominster, not stopping until he reached Billy's front garden. He vaulted the wall, and threw himself to the ground, chest heaving, throat screaming, lungs fit to burst. He lay there, wishing he was bigger, fitter, stronger. If he could just have a few minutes, he'd get to the door, rattle that knocker, get Billy out here. Billy, whom he doubted for so long, feared almost. Billy would know what to do. He could fix this. All of it.

The sound of approaching footsteps galvanised him. Awash with sweat, he got to his feet, taking in gulps of air. The front door was agonisingly close. Just a few steps, but the sound of heavy breathing looming up close behind him made him realise his means of salvation may as well be a mile away. He swung around, prepared to face Bewdsley down, perhaps kick up such a fight that someone, somewhere would be alerted to his plight.

"What are you doing in there?"

It was a woman, small and round, headscarf wrapped around her head, green mackintosh encasing her body, ample bosom straining at the buttons. She was peering over the wall, studying Craig with obvious distaste.

Craig, eyes on the road, searching for Bewdsley, ignored her and went to the door, setting up a terrific pounding on its surface with both fists.

"I'm calling the police," she said.

He turned, saw her about to move away, and blurted, "No, no please don't do that."

She stopped, studied him, uncertain now. "He's not in. I saw him taking his dog out."

"Oh no," said Craig in a small, frightened voice.

"I know you," she said. "You're the boy … You're the boy who takes his dog out, aren't you?"

Nodding, Craig turned his face skywards, the awfulness of everything crushing him. Billy should not be exerting himself. And Bewdsley, he would be here soon and nothing would matter anymore.

"He's bound to be back soon. What's the matter with you?"

"I'm all right. I've just been running, that's all."

"You frightened the living daylights out of me – I thought you were a vandal or something."

"It's all right, madam," came a voice, somewhat out of breath, "I'll sort this out for you."

Craig's heart almost stopped at the voice, horror gripping him as he stared helplessly towards Bewdsley, who stood on the other side of the wall, big cheesy grin on his face, kindness oozing out of every pore. The woman gave him a look, which spoke of trust, fondness, admiration, perhaps even a hint of something else. He touched her arm and she seemed to melt, eyes closing, mouth opening slightly. "Oh, thank you, Mr Bewdsley. You're such a treasure."

"Thank *you*, my dear. He's just a young lad who's confused and frightened. It's Billy, you see. Billy Baxter. Has some sort of a hold on him."

"Ah yes, yes I understand, Mr Bewdsley. Bad man that Billy Baxter."

"Indeed he is. But don't you worry now, I'm here. I'll sort it all out."

Face glowing, bosom heaving, she turned and waddled away, looking back now and then, beaming every time Bewdsley raised his hand.

Craig, pressing his back against the door, slid upright. "You bastard," he said.

"You watch that filthy mouth of yours," hissed Bewdsley, stepping over the wall and marching up to him. He gripped his arm. "I'll bloody well finish it for you."

"I'm not afraid of you," said Craig in a forceful voice, but inside his body pitched into the abyss, the bile rising, stomach turning to liquid. He knew it was hopeless to attempt another escape. It was over, but he was determined not to give this horrid man the satisfaction of seeing him squirm.

"Oh yes you are, and for good reason." He looked around. There was nobody there now, the street unnaturally quiet, and this seemed to embolden Bewdsley, who tightened his grip. "You're coming with me."

"I'm not going anywhere with you. I'll scream and I'll shout, and everyone will know what a—"

"You say a word and I'll kill you."

Craig saw the man's eyes, the rage burning there, and he knew he was capable of anything. Confirming his fears, Bewdsley brought out a flick knife from his pocket, one he probably had from his 'Teddy-boy' days. Pressing a button, the blade, as keen and as sharp as it was on the day it was bought, shot out. Craig shuddered.

"I'll slit your throat, you little shit. No more games, no more chances. You're coming with me and you're going to tell me what you've heard, and what you told the police."

"I haven't told them any—"

"Shut up. We're leaving."

Bewdsley lifted him off his feet, and Craig felt his bowels loosen. Where was this horrible man going to take him, what did he plan on doing? Thoughts became nothing but a blurred, wild, unfocused mess but through them, he saw another figure looming out of nowhere, his voice like honed steel, "Put him down right now."

It was him. His friend, Gary, the window cleaner! Sneering, Bewdsley turned, allowing Craig to slip from his grasp as he brought up the knife. "Piss off."

"Leave him alone."

Bewdsley gave a tiny mocking laugh and waved the knife. "Want some of this, dickhead?"

The attack came, swift and sudden, the window cleaner launching himself at Bewdsley and they both fell against Billy's front door, almost caving it in. Craig backed away as he watched them rolling around the front garden in a tangled mass of fists, and kicks. Gary was good and Bewdsley was old, but by God, he was tough. Tougher than anyone could have imagined. What was he, fifty? A little more. His strength matched his younger attacker's and when the knife flashed and the blade went in deep, Craig groaned more loudly than the window cleaner did. It was over as quickly as it had started.

Hauling himself upright, Bewdsley stared down at his stricken foe, writhing on the grass, clutching at his stomach as the blood flowed between his fingers.

"My God, you've murdered him."

"Shut it!" screeched Bewdsley and cracked Craig back-handed across the face.

Tasting the metallic tang of blood in his mouth, Craig staggered away. His eyes snapped to the window cleaner and knew he was in a bad way. "We must call an ambulance."

"I told you to shut it." Bewdsley stepped up to the front door, tried the handle and cackled when he found it unlocked. "Silly old fart," he said and went inside. "Has he got a phone?"

Craig went to Gary, wondering if he should try and stop the blood somehow. Hadn't he read somewhere about applying pressure? Furiously, he tore off his t-shirt, bundled it up into a ball, and pressed it hard against the vicious wound. He repositioned Gary's bloody hands over the t-shirt to keep it in place. "Hold it tight," said Craig and got to his feet.

"Oh Jesus," Gary hissed, eyes clamped closed, face screwed up into a ghoulish mask of pain, "it fucking hurts, man."

"Just keep the pressure on, I'll get help."

He went inside. The hallway, dark despite the daylight, daylight which seemed reluctant to advance into the house. Bewdsley's voice growled in the distance. He'd found Billy's phone and was calling an ambulance. Thank God for a small moment of sanity!

Except he wasn't calling the ambulance. Craig heard him talking feverishly to someone on the other end of the line and felt the fear overwhelm him.

"He's here and I'll bring him, but listen, there's a

problem...no, no, not that. Listen, it's some bloke, had a go and ... I don't know, just some bloke. I did for him, see. You understand.... Yes! I did for him, and now we have to cover this up ... All right.... Yes, ten minutes." He put the phone down and turned to see Craig. "You stupid little shit. If you'd kept your fucking nose out, none of this would have happened."

Shooting forward, he gripped Craig around the throat.

"Let me go."

"Shut up, you moron! It's you who's done this – *you*! We're going down the allotment, to end this crap."

"Allotment? What about—?"

"Fuck him. And fuck you. If you don't be quiet the same will happen to you, so you keep your mouth shut as we go."

Leaving the window cleaner writhing and groaning on the grass, his life's blood seeping out through the already-soaked t-shirt, Bewdsley frog-marched Craig through the streets. If anyone noticed, nobody intervened and Craig, unable to prevent the inevitable, knew that with every step the end of his life drew ever nearer.

. . .

Bewdsley kicked the door of the little garden shed open, almost ripping it from its hinges, and threw Craig inside. He crashed amongst a collection of garden hoes, rakes, and spades, which clattered over him, one of the heavy handles clonking him on the head. Holding his skull, he stared as Bewdsley slammed the door shut behind him, the whole shed shuddering with the violence of his action.

"You won't get away with this," said Craig, trying his best to sound brave, but all of his previous bluff and bravado was slipping away. "Please, Mr Bewdsley, I haven't done anything. I promise you."

"What did he tell you?"

"Billy? He …" He stopped. Was this the right way to go, the right route to take? Once Bewdsley knew, wouldn't he use that knife anyway and slit his throat? After what he had done to the window cleaner, he was more than capable. If not today, then some other time he would use that knife and … Craig wiped his face. He had no choice. "All right, I'll tell you."

"About time. You leave anything out and I'll—"

"I know what you'll do, you don't have to tell me again." His gaze drifted from the knife to the door. There was no chance of escape. He was trapped. A long sigh dribbled from his mouth. "Billy told me what really happened back then. Not the lie he told his wife, not the lie he's always told. He told me you'd saved his life, that he felt a debt of honour to you. So, when you killed that young sniper, he covered it up. He protected you."

"And what else?"

Craig stared. This was the moment, perhaps the sealing of his fate.

"He told me you killed one of the others – one of the British soldiers. How you covered it up, made out that it was one of the Germans responsible."

"The girl? Did he say anything about the girl?"

"Girl?" Genuinely confused, Craig trawled through his memory but could not remember any mention of the girl. It seemed obvious now – a huge omission. But why? "No, nothing about her except she was there."

Was that relief on his face? Bewdsley seemed to relax for a moment before he grew tense again, snarling, "He told the police all that, did he?"

Nothing else existed except for that single moment, the silence stretching out, the air chilled, tension mounting as the walls of that tiny, cramped, and rickety shed pressed in from all sides. Craig, uncertain what to say, what to do in the face of Bewdsley's hatred, his glowering stare, the clenched teeth, knew that once the truth came out, life would end.

"Mr Bewdsley, please. I'll tell them it wasn't true. I'll tell them it was Billy, that he was lying, that the truth is what he told his wife. You don't have to do this. Please, please..." Unable to hold himself in check, he broke down, sobbing uncontrollably, a small boy overcome with fear, brought to a place he never wanted to be.

If Bewdsley was moved by this plea, he didn't show it. He stepped forward, the knife large in his hand, and Craig saw it through his tears, and a single, elongated groan escaped from his lips.

He was about to die.

ARREST

FALLON SMOKED, tapping his foot impatiently. Beside him, Taylor scanned the street, watching intensely as the uniformed police swarmed around the house, blocking off all exits. Three panda cars were parked in a ragged line across the entrance to Killarney Grove, where Bewdsley lived, his house situated in the far corner.

"We have men down in the old railway siding, sir. We've had all construction work halted. If he's in there, he won't get away."

"We need every shred of evidence to nail this bastard, Taylor. I'm not going to have it all cocked up because a witness doesn't do their bit."

"I'll visit Millie myself and get her statement, so no worries there."

"And Baxter's wife?"

"Bobbies from where she's now living will be visiting her, sir. We've got it sealed tight."

"Let's hope." He blew out a final stream of smoke and threw the cigarette away, grinding it into shreds under his foot. "I'm giving these damn things up when this is put away."

Nodding in an unimpressed way, Taylor remained silent. Some fifty or so yards away, a huge constable pounded on Bewdsley's front door. He turned his face towards his superiors and Fallon nodded. Within a blink, three more burly officers charged, putting their shoulders to the door.

"We could do with a battering ram," said Taylor.

"We may not need it."

They both saw the door smashing inwards, one of the officers falling into the hallway, the others stepping over him, disappearing inside.

They waited. Fallon fidgeted, pressing the back of his hand against his mouth. "Come on," he whispered, impatience ingrained into every utterance. Hands shook as he ripped out another cigarette, clamping it between his teeth, the match striking across the box, flaring, going out. Taylor came to his rescue, his nerves much steadier and he brought a fresh match to the cigarette tip, lit it and Fallon inhaled deeply, gave a nod and then, before another word, the burly officer strode towards therm.

He looked grim, unable to hold Fallon's stare.

"He's not there, sir."

"Shit."

"You think he got wind of it, scarpered?" asked Taylor.

"I don't know," said Fallon. "Put out an A.P.B. whilst I go to see Craig. He might know something."

"And Baxter?"

"Yes. Him too. Get up there now. We have to move fast."

Stepping outside, a small band of woman stood, arms folded, raincoats and scarves on, florid faces staring furiously.

"What are you doing in there?" demanded one.

"Been shut up for years," said another.

"I hope you'll be tidying all that mess up," put in a third.

Taylor frowned. "Shut up? You mean—?"

"No one's lived there since old man Liggity passed away some years back. What's it got wrong with it?" she turned a quizzical face to her companions.

"Probate," said another. "That's what it's called. Probate"

Seized with panic, Taylor swung around to inform his superior just as Fallon stepped up to him. "It's all right, I heard." He measured the women with narrow eyes. "Ladies, this is a police matter, a very *serious* one at that."

"Ooh my, is it murder?"

"What makes you say that?"

"Been a few hasn't there. That young girl in the papers. Dreadful."

"Yes, so naturally, we have very little time to lose." Fallon gave them his best disarming smile. "Would any of you happen to know a Mr Bob Bewdsley?"

"Am I in trouble?"

"I doubt it," said Taylor. He'd raced across town as soon as they had discovered Bewdsley lived in Leominster Road with his German wife and son. Now, here he was, trying hard not to look at Millie's brown legs poking out from her flimsy nightgown. "You were doing what you thought best, and you didn't see any link with any of this to the murder."

"But if I'd said something …"

"She was already dead, Millie. You said so yourself."

"If I'd have warned her. Told her about Fender …"

"You couldn't have. It was too late."

She leaned forward, elbows on the table, face in her hands. "I was going to be next, wasn't I."

"I think so, yes. But Bewdsley wasn't thinking straight, all his reason and caution out of the window. As soon as Janet confronted your dad, Bewdsley got wind of it and felt certain the truth would out. So he acted. Him and Fender. We still don't know how they knew each other, but almost certainly Fender was trying to blackmail him. They did a deal, but it all went wrong and Bewdsley murdered him. That's my idea, anyway."

"You think this statement will help put him away?"

"Undoubtedly. We have a mass of evidence now. It's all come together. The guy's psychotic, what he did twenty years ago eating away at him. With the anniversary coming up, he just couldn't handle it any longer."

"Psychotic."

"Yes. He's spent more than one prolonged stay at Clatterbridge. Down at Diva too."

"Mental hospital? Jesus ... But Fender ...?"

"An opportunist, that's all. Desperate. Up to his eyes in debt. Janet gave him a way out of it all by showing him the journal she'd lifted from Bewdsley's place, but it all went pear-shaped because it wasn't your dad who killed those kids, it was Bewdsley. Both him and your dad have had to live with that truth in their own different ways." He smiled, tentatively closing a hand around one of hers. When she didn't flinch, he brought his other to join the first. "Your dad's quite ill, Millie. Probably brought on by the stress and strain of it all. He has angina and it's serious."

"I can't handle any of this right now," she said, avoiding his eyes again, not wanting to be drawn, not wanting to deal with the implications. "I've grown up thinking he was a monster. How am I supposed to reconcile myself to the fact that it was all lies, that he sacrificed everything, his life, his family, in order to protect that man – the real culprit. In a way, that was almost as reprehensible as the killings."

"Bewdsley had some sort of hold over him. He'd saved your dad's life. That's not something that anyone could forget, Millie, or ignore. Bewdsley reminded him of it every day, certainly after he'd moved back to the area … literally, just around the corner."

"Even so … To let Mum think that it was him. I can't forgive that. Don't ask me to."

"I'm not. I haven't got the right to even suggest such a thing."

Her face came up, eyes shining, bright with confusion, sadness. "You're not at all like a copper, do you know that."

"I'm not even sure I know what a copper is supposed to be like."

"Hard. Meeting life full in the face. Never shirking, never backing down. You're not like that at all. You're sensitive. You should be a priest."

"Jesus, Millie, I'm not sure about that!"

"A councillor. Maybe a social worker. Something, but not this. Besides, it's safer. I wouldn't have to worry so much."

"Worry? Why would you worry anyway?"

"Because I like you. And I'd like us to, you know, get to know each other."

"But you're ..."

"Thing is, all the men I'd ever known, they couldn't give a toss about me. Oh sure, in bed they were amazing, but out of bed," she shook her head. "You're different. I thought men were brutal, unfeeling, not interested in looking after me. I gravitated towards girls and found them so much more *giving*. Janet especially. I fell in love with her, but still craved for that strength, that need to be *had*." He laughed, gawping at her. "It's a primitive thing. I couldn't stand the farts, the stink, the disregard for my feelings, but I needed to have that intense physicality that only a man can bring. Well, at least as far as I'm concerned. Janet's lesbian friends were always wary of me, never convinced I was totally gay. Which I'm not."

"But neither was Janet."

"No, I know, and that's what surprised me about

their reaction. They seemed to accept her, but not me. Maybe it was jealousy."

"Jealousy?"

"Yeah, of what we had, me and her. We went everywhere together. Did everything. Holidays, nights out, theatres, cinemas, pop-concerts. Even when we went out in a gang, it was always me and Janet, holding hands, giggling like a pair of stupid schoolgirls."

"But you had Howarth. You visited him every Friday."

"He fulfilled that need I told you about." She smiled. "He filled it *very* well, if you must know. Just about the best I've ever had."

"Oh."

"Don't be silly," she squeezed his hands, which still held on to hers. "I'll go to the hospital and have a word with him. He's understanding. Like you."

Feeling the heat rising from under his collar, Taylor sat back, smiling awkwardly. "Millie, we can't ever—"

"I know, I'm teasing you."

Taylor studied her and noticed how frail she appeared, her inner strength ripped out of her leaving her vulnerable, small. "I can come with you to the hospital, if you like."

"No, it'll be fine."

"Why do you think he was down at the canal, the day Janet's body was discovered?"

"I don't know." Pressing her lips together, she leaned back, crossing her arms. "Perhaps it wasn't him."

"It was."

"Coincidence maybe."

"Hardly likely is it."

"I don't know," she snapped, agitated. She jumped up, went to her bedside cabinet and pulled out some cigarettes. She lit one up, smoked it, one arm across her chest, the other holding the cigarette close to her mouth, taking a drag every couple of seconds.

"Why didn't you mention anything about him in your statement?"

"Why? Because he had nothing to do with it."

"He was attacked. Either by Fender or Bewdsley, and we know he knew who it was because he let them into his house."

"They could've broken in."

"No. No sign of forced entry. He knew them."

"Jesus, you soon bloody change don't you – from priest to copper in one easy move."

"Are you protecting him?"

"What?" She snapped her head towards him. "Why the bloody hell would I do that? It's over between us, all right? Done. Finished. That's what I'm going to tell him."

"Millie, if he knew either of those two men, he must have met them and got talking. Perhaps he knew about the story your dad told? Perhaps he wanted a slice of the action?"

"What slice? My dad hasn't got any bloody money, has he. That's why Janet backed off. When she told me and we had that row, I phoned Mum. I had it out with her, told her the whole bloody lot. And you know what she did? She laughed. Yeah, laughed. And why? Because Dad hasn't got a bloody bean. Nothing. He lives in that seedy little terrace, surrounded by all his crap and all he gets is some sort of army pension. A pittance."

"How do you know it's seedy?"

Her eyes widened. "Eh?"

"You said he lived in a 'seedy little terrace', but you've never been there. Have you."

"No. Janet told me."

"Ah." He nodded and stood up. "When Inspector Fallon interviewed Howarth in the hospital, he let slip he knew Bewdsley." He sighed. "Later on, I went back to the hospital to try and figure things out."

"What did you do?"

Taylor cleared his throat. "It was something the nurse said about him being obsessive about baths."

"About baths? What has David taking a bath got to do with anything?"

"When Fallon told me about the slip, whether intentional or not, of using Bewdsley's first name, Bob, I started thinking. It just didn't add up. None of it. So, I went to take a look at the hospital bathroom Howarth always used. There was nothing special about it, just a normal, clean, bright bathroom with nothing much in there except the usual. There was a large, frosted window closed by a simple latch. Howarth's a big man, bigger than me, but I could get through that window easily, and I think he could too."

"Why would he want to do that?"

"Fender lived in Martins Lane. No more than ten minutes from the hospital. I reckon Howarth gathered some clothes and slipped out of that bathroom, made his way to Fender's flat, and killed him there. I also believe that Fallon disturbed him and received a smack for his troubles."

"You're letting your imagination run away with you. What possible reason could David have for murdering Fender? Fender beat me up, and yes it was terrible, but to kill him? I don't buy that. Besides which, how could he know Fender would be home that night?"

"He didn't. That's why he kept having baths, so he could go and check."

"But that would mean it was premeditated. If it was premeditated then he'd have to have motive, probable cause."

"I had a hunch. Not much of a one, but I thought there had to be a link between Howarth and the others. Yes, they all went to that nightclub, but there was something else. Howarth, he never struck me as the sort of guy who would frequent those places anyway. He was an M.P., military police, so I got onto the Imperial War Museum who, in turn, gave me a contact in the Army Museum. The guy I spoke to was very helpful, even though it's something of a mess over there. The museum is in Sandhurst at the moment, but they're planning on moving to a new, purpose-built building in Chelsea, but it's not yet ready."

"Mr Policeman, I'm not interested in where you went or what you did."

"They have records, and as Howarth was a regular, they have his service record. Malaya, Aden. It's all there. He was quite a lad."

"But he wasn't in the War, was he. He's too young to have been with my dad and Bewdsley."

"I know. That's what threw me at first. Fender, he was eighteen in Nineteen Forty-Four. Bewdsley and your dad around twenty-six, twenty-seven."

"So, there's no link between David and them, is

there? There is no way he could have known them. So, it must have been through the club."

Taylor nodded. "Howarth was born in Nineteen Thirty-Five. He was nine when Bewdsley murdered that kid and the soldier."

"Exactly. So why would he get himself embroiled in all this blackmail nonsense?"

"Because he wanted revenge."

Millie blinked, frowned, considered the words and looked perplexed. "Revenge for what?"

"We're coming up to the twenty-fifth anniversary of what happened to those men in France. We've already had all the necessaries for D-Day, but this particular anniversary, it's personal. Bewdsley murdered a British soldier and tried to lay the blame on those Germans." He took a breath and held Millie's gaze. "The man he shot was Howarth's father. Corporal Simon Howarth, 5th Battalion, the King's."

Stunned, mouth hanging open, Millie wrestled with the implications, the revelations.

"When Janet told him about the letter Billy Baxter had, Howarth started putting his plan into operation. His plan to kill them all."

Millie stared into a point somewhere in the distance. "But ... Why murder Janet?"

"He didn't murder Janet, but he knew who did. As your friend, it sort of spurred him on towards what he knew he had to do."

"Oh shit ..." Millie stubbed out her cigarette in the ashtray next her bed, grinding it right down to the unsmoked butt, tobacco shreds spilling out over the rim of the ashtray. She crossed to the window and rubbed a hole in the grime to look out. "I just don't believe he had it in him to murder."

"We'll go and see him together, you and me," said Taylor. He moved up behind her and turned her around slowly. He saw the tears in her eyes. "All right? We'll sort this out and then maybe you'll believe me."

"I do. I want to, but it's still raw, all of this. Janet, David. A lot's happened."

"So let's go and see him and put a line under it all, ok?"

"Yes, and then you can stop bloody well going on."

Smiling, the relief tangible, Taylor stepped away whilst she slipped off her bath robe and got dressed. He went to the door and opened it.

The shape filled the space, blocking out virtually all light from the corridor. Taylor gave a gasp of surprise but could do nothing to prevent something big and heavy slamming into his face, throwing him backwards into the room. Head swimming, a great cloud of black engulfed him and the last thing he heard was Millie's scream. Then something hit him again and there was nothing but darkness.

THE ALLOTMENT

BILLY SAW him from the end of the street and instantly tensed. Skipper, straining on the leash, made a lunge, his memory stirring. Something tempered Billy's immediate reaction to scream with rage, however. Something in the young man's expression. A mix of panic and fear.

"Mr Baxter," said Crossland, approaching at a half-run, both hands up. From this close Billy saw the sweat, the ashen pallor, the eyes laced with terror. "Mr Baxter, he's taken Craig."

Reeling back from the words, it took a moment for Billy to register their meaning. "Took him? Who has?"

"Bewdsley. I been watching him, watching him for ages and I saw him, with Craig. He's taken him to his allotment."

"Shit." Quickly, Billy Baxter raced up to his door as best he could, struggling to get the key in the lock. He pushed Skipper inside, the little dog resisting, barking. Billy gave him a shove, rolling him over on the carpeted floor. "Sorry lad, I have to go."

Swinging around, he saw the body lying in the grass. Staggering backwards, he pressed his hand against the wall to prevent him from falling.

Crossland had seen it too. The body, covered in blood. "Oh God, we better call the police, Mr Baxter."

Dragging his forearm across his brow, Billy said in a quiet voice, "How long ago did you see them?"

"Ten, fifteen minutes. Not long. But we have to – are you all right, Mr Baxter?"

"I'm fine." Billy grimaced, swallowing down the pain, not only from his leg which pulsed alarmingly, but from something like a vice gripping him around the chest. He fumbled inside his pocket, brought out the small, gold coloured box he always kept there and popped a tiny pill under his tongue. Almost at once, the pain subsided. His leg, that could wait. Taking a deep breath, he pulled Crossland with him down the street.

"What's going on, Mr Baxter?" came a voice from across the street.

"Nothing you need concern yourself with, Mrs Nugent."

Mrs Nugent, standing at her gate in the house opposite, bristled with indignation. Her headscarf appeared tighter than ever. "You've had visitors. There was a fight. I've phoned the police."

"Thank you, Mrs Nugent," said Billy, setting up a brisk pace with Crossland in tow.

"Where the devil are you going, Mr Baxter?"

Ignoring the alarm in Mrs Nugent's voice, he seethed inside that she'd spotted him. Bloody busybody, always sticking her nose in, and this was not the moment to be answering her. Not now. Not with Craig in obvious danger. Not with a dead body lying in his front garden.

"It was him, wasn't it," said Crossland, allowing himself to be pulled along like a little child. "Bewdsley. He killed that bloke didn't he."

Billy didn't answer. He set his jaw, and steamed ahead.

There was no one at the allotments. No sign of life. Usually there was someone. Stan Prentis almost always came up, to weed or potter about. Billy, a curious tingling running around the shoulders, pulled up sharply. Crossland, next to him, turned, peering into the old man's face. "What is it?"

"Don't know. Something. Listen, you scoot round the side of our shed. It's that one over there to the right, with the Brussel sprouts in front. You see it?" Crossland nodded. "Get down behind that big, blue water butt and wait, all right?"

Needing no further instructions, Crossland set off, half-bent and something in the way he moved reminded Billy of his time back in France, when it was he who weaved and dodged across the fallen masonry in that ruined church. He shuddered. Bob Bewdsley was there too, of course. And those kids. Two of them, just like now. Craig and Crossland, but no girl. No girl, thank God, because if there had have been, history would truly be repeating itself.

He tensed when he heard the footfall, and when he turned, not knowing what to find, his heart almost gave out and he slumped onto the ground, struggling for breath, gripping his chest, twisting the material of his shirt in his fist. "Oh Jesus," he groaned.

She got down next to him, her blonde hair brushing against his face. He was patting his pocket and she reached inside, brought out his pills and he took one and he looked into her blue eyes. "It can't be."

Her face, smooth as porcelain, creased into a smile. "I'm here to help, Mr Baxter," she said. "Crossie and me, we're friends, but Craig is much more than a friend to me, Mr Baxter. I'm here to make sure nothing happens to him." Taking his hand, she helped him to his feet.

"My God," he said. "You're her, the one from the park. I thought for a moment you—"

"I'm sorry I ever made you doubt me, Mr Baxter. I'm sorry for a lot of things and I'm here to put things right. Once and for all."

Shaking his head, doing his best to clear it from those wartime images doing their utmost to befuddle his mind, he peered over to the water-butt but instead found Crossland scurrying towards them, breathing hard. He crouched down, spluttering incoherent sentences. Baxter snapped, "I thought I told you to get behind that butt?"

"I couldn't," Crossland managed to say, lifting his head, tongue between his teeth, breath rasping. "I couldn't."

"Why not? I need you to hide there because if Bob is in there, we need to flush him out."

"It's the other fella."

Billy Baxter shook his head, bemused. "What other fella? What are you talking about?"

"What's going on, Crossie?"

Crossland reacted as if seeing her for the first time. "Sam! I told you to stay away."

"Tell me what the bloody hell is going on," said Billy, not wanting to raise his voice but the frustration so intense now he couldn't help it.

"There's a guy there. I think it's your other friend. I've seen him up here lots of times."

"Stan? You mean Stan?"

"I suppose I do. But he's there, stuffed behind the butt." He raked in a breath. "He's dead."

Mrs Nugent came across the road, ignoring the policeman's outstretched hand, warning her to stay clear. "I want to talk to the man in charge," she said.

Fallon, stepping away from the front door, paused to light a cigarette and caught sight of her beyond the ring of police officers blocking off the street. An ambulance pulled up, blue light rotating. "Can I help you, madam?" he said, stepping aside as the ambulancemen tended to the body. "Do you know this man by any chance?"

"His name is Gary Bogarde. He's a window cleaner, or at least he was." She turned away as the men lifted the body onto a stretcher.

"Have you any idea where Mr Baxter might be?"

"Yes I do," she said impatiently, grabbing Fallon by the arm and pulling him onto the pavement, away from the harrowing scenes going on in the garden. He didn't try to stop her. "He was here, with a boy."

"A boy? Do you mean Craig, madam? Small lad, wiry sandy-coloured hair?"

"No, no. I know him, that Craig. He's always here, taking out Mr Baxter's dog. He was here earlier, when the fight happened. No, this was another one. A big lad. Bit of a brute, but Mr Baxter took him away. Just like Bob did with your Craig."

"*Bob?*"

"Yes. Bob Bewdsley. He went off with Craig after he'd fought with Gary and then, quarter of an hour later, this other boy came alone and both he and Mr Baxter went off, leaving that poor man lying there." She shuddered. "They've all gone off to the same place I shouldn't wonder."

"There's only one place that can be," put in a local Bobby, appearing next to his superior officer.

The rear doors to the ambulance slammed shut. Fallon looked at his colleague and went to speak but thought better of it. They both knew immediately where that place was.

Bewdsley sat slumped against the wall, knees pulled up to his chest, staring at the wooden mallet in his hand and the blood which dripped from its flat surface. Craig watched but didn't speak. Earlier, when the door burst open and Stan Prentis came in, Bewdsley's reaction was instantaneous. The two of them fell to the ground and Stan, so much older, so much weaker, didn't stand a chance. He'd given Craig a moment, the chance he needed, to think, concoct some sort of plan. The abrupt, awful violence put paid to all of that.

Bewdsley dragged Stan's semi-conscious body outside. Craig heard the sickening, heavy thud of the mallet coming down on his head like a hammer on an anvil and understood what it meant. Murder.

After a second or two, he heard Bewdsley's grunting as if he were struggling with something. Craig took his chance, looked around the detritus of that cramped room, and found something. Something he could use, if the opportunity arose, which he hoped it would. Fear was giving way to hatred. Cold, calculating hatred.

Bewdsley came in, wheezing, blood spattered across his shirt front. Craig, wedged in underneath the workbench, as far from Bewdsley as possible, dared not move.

"There was no need for Stan to come here," Bewdsley said in a strange series of whimpers, almost as if he could not believe his own words. "I always liked Stan. He had nothing to do with any of this. Nothing. And now he's dead. Jesus, if I'd known he was coming here, I'd never have brought you here, but I had nowhere else." He stared sightlessly into the distance and a trail of saliva drooled from his lips, a rabid dog out of control. "If you've told the police, they'll be swarming everywhere like ants at any moment. It's you." A darkness came over his face, eyes as deep as night. Or hell. "You did this, you snivelling little shit." He drew back his arm and hurled the mallet against the workbench. Despite the protection the bench gave, Craig instinctively ducked. "Get out of there, do you hear me – *get out of there!*"

Crouching, Bewdsley slashed and stabbed with the knife, grunting with every movement, but Craig remained out of reach. Frustrated, enraged beyond control, Bewdsley put the knife in his waistband, got down on his knees and reached forward to grab him. He took hold of Craig in two handfuls of his shirt and wrenched him free, but Craig, instead of surrendering to the inevitable, took that longed for chance. He twisted in Bewdsley's grip and, as the man lifted him up, summoned all his strength and struck home with the screwdriver he'd found whilst Bewdsley was outside. It plunged deep into the man's inner thigh. Head thrown back, he roared like a stricken beast, lost his balance, and went crashing to the floor amongst a pile of old ceramic pots where he writhed in agony, the blood spewing over the screwdriver buried in his leg.

Stupefied, not only from what he'd done but from the effect his attack brought, Craig stood transfixed. Rolling from side to side, both hands clamped against the wound, Bewdsley tried to stifle the flow of blood, but it was useless; the screwdriver was buried too deep.

"You've done for me, you little shit," he said, a sudden, remarkable lucidity coming to his features. Pressed against the shed wall, he levered himself upright and drew the knife. "But I'll do for you too, don't you worry."

Bewdsley lurched forward, determination in every step, grimacing, the knife looking so huge in his fist.

With nowhere to escape to, Craig stumbled backwards until the wall stopped him and he could go no farther. He screamed, knowing this was it, no more chances, no more anything.

The door crashed open, the edge cracking against the back of Bewdsley's head, and suddenly the tiny room was filled with people. Some were police, others were those he knew. Billy, Crossland … And Samantha. He saw her and he collapsed to his knees, all of it gushing out of him, the relief, the horror. It was over and he was alive.

As several policemen struggled with Bewdsley, Samantha held onto him and, closing his eyes, he breathed her in.

She smelled so good.

THE WAY OF REVENGE

STEPPING out from the interview room, Fallon took a cigarette and was about to light it when he saw Superintendent Lawson approaching, one of his eyebrows arched. "It's all done, sir," said Fallon quickly as he, somewhat reluctantly, replaced the cigarette into the carton. "He's made a full confession."

"What, everything?"

"Seems so. Him and Fender murdered Janet Stowe. He made a big meal of telling me it was Fender, after he'd rowed with her over Baxter and the blackmailing. When she found out the truth from the journal and the letter, she was about to turn her attention to Bewdsley, that's when Fender lost it."

"So him and Bewdsley were close?"

"Very. They knew one another in the War. Served together for a while, after Baxter got shipped back home with his wounded leg. Apparently, they met up together on a regular basis in some seedy night club, a place called the 'Lonely Extra' over in Liverpool. A pick-up place. It's where Fender met Janet Stowe and Howarth first made contact with Millie Clovis."

"You've worked well on this, Fallon," he paused for effect before continuing, "after some gentle persuasion that is."

Fallon didn't react, despite wanting to. "Thank you very much, sir. We've got it all now. Full confession. He'll be going down for the rest of his natural. The boy's all right, Baxter will receive a caution … That letter he had. It was from one of the soldiers serving with the Fifth King's, much of which had been transferred to other units. He'd written to Baxter, telling him he knew the truth. That he was dying and needed to make some form of confession."

"Why didn't he tell the authorities?"

"Maybe he didn't think it would do any good. Anyway, it was this letter that Baxter showed Janet. It implicated Bewdsley, of course."

"So, she died because of something which happened twenty-five years ago. A War which is still claiming victims."

"It would appear so. Anyway, if it's all right with you, I'm off home. I feel like I could sleep for a month. Taylor can do all the bloody paperwork, wherever he's got to. We need to find him. He's a good copper Taylor – a bloody good copper. I'm recommending him for C.I.D."

"It's all up to the DCC, of course, but I'm sure given how you've handled yourself it'll all go through." He grinned. "I'll see you tomorrow, Inspector," and he left.

Fallon waited until he was certain Lawson was gone before he fished out the cigarette again. "This is the last one," he said to himself before lighting it up.

They sat in the dwindling evening light, she behind the table, Howarth on the threadbare sofa. Taylor, hands bound up tight with the cord from Millie's bathrobe, head lolling onto his chest, moaned, barely conscious. At one point, Howarth stuffed a handkerchief into the policeman's mouth and secured it with sticky tape. Lots of it. More than was necessary.

"You bastard," she said, her eyes glazed with hatred.

He sniggered, looked away. "That's not what you used to say. I remember you, lying there, legs spread, screaming, 'Fuck me David, fuck me'. Jesus. What a bitch you are."

"Why are you doing this," she said, ignoring his barbs, ignoring his arrogance. The way he sat there, Lord of the Manor. In control. Like he used to be, in bed.

"Because I have to. Do you know how many years I had to suffer the indignity of believing my father was killed by a pair of fucking kids? Violent psychopaths, they told me. Indoctrinated, brain-washed. As if that was a reason. My father. My mother used to send me to sleep with stories about him, you know that. She never met anyone else. Didn't want to. He was the only man she ever loved. And when I heard those two bastards ... when I found out that your precious Janet knew that it wasn't kids, it was that snivelling bastard Bewdsley and the fact you also *knew*—"

"I didn't know anything, David. I believed it was my father, Billy Baxter. I've always believed it. It was the story he told Mum. Nothing about your dad, that never featured in the story he told, I swear to you. Just the kids. Those two youngsters, a boy and a girl, killers. Indoctrinated, like you said. I had no idea of the truth."

"Even when Janet told you? Even when she came back here and told you what she'd discovered?"

"She didn't tell me the details."

"Yes she bloody well did! Don't lie to me, you bitch! I know the truth, I know that you knew what had really happened, that you kept it from me."

"I didn't know, I swear to you. Only until recently I truly believed it was my dad. If I'd known …"

"What? You would have told me? I don't think so. You played me for the idiot I was. And when you came to see me that night, Jesus, I was so happy. I thought you'd actually begun to love me, have some feelings for me other than a quick fuck. Wednesday night. Jesus, I was like a little boy and when you hit me, shit, you almost killed me."

"I wanted to."

"So, you see. There it is. You wanted to kill me because you knew that once I learned of the truth, I'd kill every last fucking one of you. Starting with your dad, who is the biggest bastard of all of you. He knew the fucking truth and he kept it buried, because of some pathetic feeling of honour. Bastard."

She turned away, pulled out her cigarettes and lit one up. She sat and smoked and Howarth studied the carpet, both of them knowing it was going to be a long night.

. . .

At Manor Road, Craig eased open the main door and sheepishly approached the desk. A large, burly desk-sergeant peered at him over the rim of his spectacles, laid down his pen and studied Craig with interest. "Yes, young man, what can I do for you?"

"Inspector Fallon."

The sergeant blinked. "What about him?"

"I'd like to talk to him, please."

"I see. Can I know what it's about?"

"The Bewdsley case."

Reacting as if this information was the most important he'd heard all day, the sergeant hastily lifted the telephone receiver at his elbow and dialled a single number. He waited, listening, whilst Craig tempered his impatience by studying the various posters on the wall, advising people about fitting seat belts and several other road safety notices, the 'Green Cross Code' being the one he most readily recognised.

"He's not in, I'm afraid," the sergeant said, replacing the receiver. "I suspect he's gone home after the shenanigans of the day."

"Could I leave him something?"

"Is it important?"

"It might be – for the case."

"For the case? Well, you'd better hand it over then."

Dipping into his pocket, Craig produced a brown paper envelope and smoothed it down on the desk. "It's the letters Billy received from an old pal. Mr Fallon knows about them, but he doesn't know what else I've discovered."

"I see." Sounding serious, the sergeant went to pick the envelope up, then hesitated. "What have you discovered?"

"There's another letter inside, from someone else. I think he'll find it interesting. I'll include a note, explaining."

The sergeant briskly tore off a page from his notebook and, together with a pen, gave them to Craig, who quickly wrote in a spidery flourish. He gave it to the sergeant and watched him fold it and place it inside the envelope.

"Thank you very much," said the sergeant. "Who shall I say dropped these off?"

"Craig. He knows who I am."

TYING THE KNOTS

DECIDING against barging into the flat, Fallon waited outside, overcoat pulled around his throat, crunched up inside his tiny Mini Clubman. News had come through that Howarth had escaped the hospital. An all-points bulletin meant he'd be apprehended before long. Everybody knew that. As an added precaution, Speke Airport had been shut down. The Belfast ferry port received similar treatment. Nobody was going in or out of Merseyside, Fallon had made certain of that. So now the waiting commenced and Fallon, parked outside Millie's flat, wanted the morning to rise so badly, so he could walk up there and drag Taylor out of her bed and tell him he was needed. Lucky bastard. Millie was as fit as any bird Fallon had seen. His ex didn't have those lithe limbs, that full, rounded arse, those breasts ... and that skin. Jesus. Brown as a nut. Maybe he should find himself a hippy, a student-type. Full of marijuana and free-sex. That's what he needed. Lots of free sex.

He groaned, ran a hand over his face. Taylor disappointed him. Stuck up there all bloody night whilst the whole effing world fell around everyone's ears. Like a decrepit old greyhound, run-down, past his best, sitting up all night, drinking coffee by the bucketful, waiting, waiting, waiting for the phone to ring, then the desk sergeant handing him Craig's envelope. That was a bloody clever thing the lad had done, to marry it all together the way he had, matching those pieces of evidence together.

He stretched out his legs and arms, groaning loudly as the joints cracked. He gazed at the small, grimy window that was Millie's only viewpoint of the world. A light went on. So, they were up, out of bed. He'd give them a moment to wash away their sex before he went up and told Taylor to put his trousers back on.

Lucky sod ...

At that precise moment, Taylor was feeling anything but lucky. He tried to reposition his legs, but Howarth had wrapped those up too. The beginnings of cramp developed in one of his calf muscles so he sat still, tried to relax and strained to listen.

"I never really thought I could kill any of them," Howarth was saying, talking to himself more than anyone else. "I'd shot an old guy back in Aden. He was selling cigarettes on a street corner. I saw the Sten hidden beneath the basket cover. I shot him, asked questions later. That was different I suppose. I reacted instinctively, doing my bit to save as many lives as possible. But after I'd discovered what Bewdsley had done, how Fender helped him, and then, when Fender attacked you, it made it easier I suppose." He looked at Millie, sitting smoking her umpteenth cigarette. "Why did you hit me?"

She flicked ash into the ashtray, adjusted her hair. "When Fender came here, he told me about how you two had bedded Janet. I couldn't believe it and went ape. At her and at you. So I went to your place, out of control. I wanted to kill you."

"You very nearly did. Thing is, I didn't bed Janet the way you were told. Not with Fender anyway. That was a lie."

"But you did sleep with her."

"Yes, but not in the way he described. I suppose he was hoping you'd do precisely what you did do – save him a job."

"I trusted you. You took away my identity, who I

believed I was. You and Janet. I also thought she loved me, but I was wrong."

"I'm not sure. I think perhaps she did love you, in her own peculiar way. She was a complicated character."

"And you fucked her."

"Yes. And it was amazing, I have to say."

Millie sniffed, put the back of one hand in her eye. "I don't need to know that."

"No. But, there we are. She was quite an extraordinary girl. I never meant ... Look, what you and I had, you always knew it was nothing serious. Yes, when you came to see me on that Wednesday I had hopes for something more, but deep down I knew you could never commit to me. Nor I to you. It was fun, but that was all." He pointed to Taylor, sitting there, glaring at him. "Besides, you have someone new now."

She spewed out a guffaw. "Do me a favour! He's nothing to me, a copper that's all."

"Don't you get on?"

"He's nice enough, but – look, you're going to kill him, aren't you? Then me?"

"Kill? Why would I want to kill either of you – I'm not a nutcase. I'm not a Bob Bewdsley. No, Millie, I came here to explain, that is all. Then I'll go. Try and get away. I didn't want any of this, but those bastards, they complicated everything. Bewdsley murdered my father, in cold blood. I didn't know about that, I didn't know about any of it. The last time I saw my father was the day he went off to war. I was eight years of age. I remember it as if it were yesterday, him standing there in his new uniform, backpack, shiny boots, rifle on his shoulder. He kissed my mother, ruffled my hair and off he went. I never saw him again. I cried for three days solid. So, when I overheard Janet and Fender talking together in that club, my mind got to thinking. A plan. I listened, intrigued, and I approached Fender afterwards. He was cautious at first, until I told him who I was. That my father had served in the War, that their story about Billy Baxter and what he'd done interested me."

"My dad's story never included anything about killing a British soldier."

"No, but the letter I received did. It was virtually the same letter that Billy Baxter showed Janet. It seems that his former mate from his old tank regiment was dying and wanted to make amends before he finally popped off. He'd witnessed it all, you see. Like your dad, I guess he felt honour-bound not to tell the truth until he was facing his end. Perhaps Bewdsley had some sort of hold over him too – he seems to have that with all of them. Including Fender." He pulled in a deep breath. "I wanted to kill your dad, because of his silence, but I changed my mind when I got that letter. All my hatred centred on Bewdsley then. Fender, he was nothing more than a hanger-on, but I hated him too, for what he did to you. What he did to Janet."

"David, wouldn't it be best to turn yourself in?"

"What, spend the next fifteen years behind bars? For ridding the world of a pair of miserable bastards? No, I don't think so."

"You'll never get away with any of it. You know that, deep down."

"I suppose so, but ... I'm going now. Listen, I know you don't have to but, perhaps in memory of what we had, could you give me twenty minutes or so before you let lover-boy here lose? I want something of a head start." He forced a smile. "I'm not a bad man, Millie. I never meant to hurt anybody, except for those two. Bewdsley murdered my dad and Fender tried to profit from it. I couldn't have let that lie. I hope you understand."

"Where will you go?"

"I don't know. Anywhere. Where they can't find me. I haven't got much money, but I've enough to get myself a plane ticket to somewhere. If can make it to an airport before they realise what I've done ... I'll need your car."

A tiny laugh and Millie turned, crossed to where her coat hung from a peg on the far wall, and pulled out a bunch of keys from the pocket. "I must be mad. I wanted to kill you, and now I'm helping you escape." She detached her car keys and threw them to him. "You'll need petrol."

For a long time, Howarth gazed at the keys, rolling them around between his fingers. "Thanks," he said at last and then he left, not stopping to give Taylor so much as a glance.

Millie went to the window and stared down into the street. After a few moments Howarth emerged and approached her car. Behind her Taylor strained against the cords holding him, voice muffled due to the tape covering his mouth. She ignored him. She'd give Howarth his twenty minutes, she decided. Perhaps a little more.

The sound of a car door slamming woke Fallon with a start. Panic gripped him and he twisted around to see a nearby car's interior light glowing, a large shape settling itself behind the wheel. A yelp escaped Fallon's throat, and he scrambled out into the sharp, cold air and ran across to the car.

The shape inside was big.

Very big.

Without waiting, Fallon pulled open the door and stared directly into David Howarth's face.

The man's fist struck out, hitting him full in the solar plexus. Retching, Fallon doubled-up, realizing, despite the pain, that he was in serious trouble. Before he could do anything, the shape loomed over him, the knee swinging up, connecting to his face, sending him flying backwards.

"David, no!"

Writhing on the ground, Fallon tasted warm, thick blood in his mouth. He needed to do something, make some sort of effort, so he rolled over as he heard the steady approach of footsteps.

"David, for God's sake," came a woman's voice, "just get the fuck away."

"You called them, you bitch!"

"No, I didn't. Don't be an arse. Jesus."

Fallon felt her kneeling down beside him, her hand cupping his head, lifting him. He wanted to say something, but he couldn't. He felt sure some of his teeth were broken.

"Get in the car," snapped Howarth.

"What?"

"Get in the fucking car."

"I'm not going anywhere with you – you're like a bloody lunatic. Look what you've done to him."

There followed a scuffle. Fallon saw the feet. She wasn't wearing anything on hers. Bare feet. Smooth, like the rest of her. God, Taylor was a lucky bloody sod.

Howarth's feet were booted.

Army boots they looked like.

Fallon didn't care anymore. All he wanted now was to sleep. Even the pain was receding.

Only sleep.

"Keep your hands off me," she said, ripping herself free of his hold.

"I asked for twenty minutes, you bloody bitch."

"I told you – I didn't call them. He must have been waiting for you. Soon there'll be others."

"Where's lover-boy."

"David, just go, please, before you do something you'll regret." She could see it in his face. He had already crossed the line. He said he didn't mean to hurt anyone, but he clearly did. Everything he'd told her was a lie. There was no other explanation. She knew where Howarth was going. "You're going to kill my dad, aren't you?"

"I told you, I never meant—"

"Even so, David. Even so. Look at you, you're out of control. You won't stop until they're all dead, isn't that true? What you told me, about the letter, your change of heart, it was all lies, wasn't it?"

"The letter changed nothing. Nothing at all. Your father had the power to put Bewdsley behind bars twenty-five years ago, but he didn't. He let him go scot-free. I thought I could let that go, but I can't.

I can't. I'm sorry." He took a huge breath. "Now get in the car – you're taking me to him."

"No, I'm not."

"Yes you bloody are, or I'll drag you there by your hair."

She heard the door, the sound of running feet. She swung around and yelped. "No. No, don't—"

But it was too late. All of it was too late.

Taylor charged, head down, crossing the tarmac at speed, slamming into Howarth's midriff like a prop-forward, driving the big man back against Millie's car with a shuddering smack. Howarth groaned and Taylor twisted, dipping low, avoiding the instinctive, defensive swing of one mighty fist. Baton in hand, he smashed it hard against the side of Howarth's knee. The big man gave a low grunt and buckled. Using all his strength, Taylor brought the baton down again, striking Howarth's elbow, the crack sounding sickening in the empty street. Millie screamed and Howarth crumpled.

"Jesus," said Taylor, stepping away, taking in gulps of air.

Millie fell into him and he put his arm around her and held her close. Howarth lay in a heap, nursing his shattered arm, eyes screwed up, teeth clenched. He wouldn't be going anywhere now.

. . .

The young nurse accompanying Fallon led him slowly into the reception area where Taylor waited. "Make sure he gets some rest," she said.

"I'll do my best."

Fallon, thanking the nurse, slumped into the seat next to his colleague. "I feel like shit."

Taylor, noting the swelling, the livid blue bruising, had to agree. "We got the letters back. They're a perfect match. The letterhead, it belonged to the company where Emery went, sir. We've almost got him."

"Yes, but not quite yet. I want you to go and see Craig. Tell him to lure him out so we can nab him."

"We haven't much to go on, sir."

"We can get Craig to wear a recording device. We're so close to bringing this to a close, Taylor."

"We'll need to have a whole team ready, sir. Surveillance and everything else."

"Lawson will sign everything off. This is huge, me old son." He brushed his swollen cheek with the back of his hand. "He was one hard bastard that Howarth."

"You should go home now, sir. Rest, the nurse said."

"I'll rest when this put away to bed. For now, I'll keep taking the tablets." Chuckling to himself, he climbed to his feet and went outside.

PROGNOSIS

THE FOLLOWING DAY, after listening to everything Detective Taylor told him, Craig went to Billy Baxter's. There was a strange emptiness about the house, which he detected from at least twenty yards away. He shivered, an awful feeling of foreboding pressing down on him as he stared at the upper-storey windows. He knocked tentatively on the door and waited. With no reply, he rapped on the doorknocker, the sound of it against the plate echoing through the house Nothing. Billy was not at home.

Thinking Billy had taken Skipper out, Craig turned, puzzled. It seemed strange, that after the events of the previous day, he would take Skipper for a walk. He again looked at the upstairs windows. They were dark, no signs of life. Mind made up, he moved quickly, following the path around the side of the house, and tried the back door. For a moment he pondered the idea of climbing over, as he had done all that time ago to retrieve the ball, but thought better of it. He didn't want any misunderstandings rekindled.

As he returned to the front door, his eyes focused in on something, which caused his concern to grow.

The milk bottle.

It stood there, on the step. Untouched.

Frightened now, Craig hammered on the door, certain something bad had happened. Visions of Billy lying on the floor after another attack gripped him. Surely, Skipper would be barking, letting the world know? No, calm down, think – Billy had gone out, and forgotten about the milk. It was a warm, summer's day. It would be rotten by the time he got back, but these things happen. Nothing sinister, or anything to be concerned about. As usual, his imagination had overtaken him.

"Is it Mr. Baxter you're after?"

He turned and saw the voice belonged to a woman, bent-double and swathed in a green raincoat, despite the Sun beating down. Craig recognised her and nodded.

"They've taken him away," she said, her eyes darting, checking nobody had heard this most terrible of secrets. "Early this morning it was. It was the little dog that did it."

Craig shook his head, confused. "I'm sorry? I don't understand – the little dog did what?"

"Well it was him – I assume it's a 'him', the little dog – it was him who was making all the racket, you see. He'd been barking most of the morning, then something came through the window and that's what made me come and see. I only live across the way there. I'm Mrs Nugent. I seem to remember seeing you quite a lot. You're Craig, aren't you? You were attacked by that horrible Bob—"

Craig's head started to swirl "What went through the window?"

"His shoe, lad. He threw it, you see, and smashed the window."

"It's a wonder you didn't see the glass." Another voice joined in. An elderly man, similar in size and shape to the woman, wizened and bent, shuffled up to give his contribution. "We cleared most of it up, but you never know." He placed his hand on the woman's arm, "Grandson is he?"

She shrugged. "Don't know, he wouldn't say. He's the one I've seen around here lots of times. Takes the dog out, he does."

"Must be the grandson. No one else would bother..."

Annoyed, Craig cut their conversation off, "Excuse me, I'm *not* his grandson. I'm his friend. Can't you tell me what's happened?"

The old man frowned, obviously not used to being spoken to in such a brusque manner by someone so young. He took in a breath. "He's gone to hospital. Victoria Central. The ambulance came after we'd called it."

Craig's temper brimmed over, and he barked his questions without any thought for hurting feelings. "But why – why has he gone? What's happened to him?"

The man and woman exchanged a glance. The man shook his head and sighed, and the woman, face like thunder, turned to Craig and said, in a hushed, conspiratorial whisper, "Heart-attack."

People, places, all of it a blur as Craig sprinted through the streets towards the hospital. At the little reception booth, the prim lady behind the screen took a long time before she gave him the good grace of a look of undisguised disgust. "Yes?"

Craig barked out Billy Baxter's name. She didn't flinch, peered at him over the rim of her glasses, licked a finger and leafed leaf through a wad of papers. Eventually, she pulled out a single sheaf, perused it before she returned it to its original place, then scowled. "Are you family?" she asked.

"Yes," he lied, adding before she had the chance to ask another question, "his grandson."

The receptionist frowned. "Where are your parents? Why haven't they come with you?"

Without pausing, Craig pressed on, "My Mum's at work and my Dad..." he shrugged his shoulders, made the most of the pause to add drama, "My Dad's dead."

She blinked. "Oh." For a moment her mask of officiousness dropped. "Here's the ward name," she said, scribbled it down and handed it over. Craig read it, and the receptionist added, "Straight through the main doors, then down the slope to the end. You'll find the wards there. Just follow the signs."

Craig set off, surprised at how easily the lies rolled off his tongue. As he neared the ward, already he was working out what he could say to his friend. The explanations he would give, the plans he had, the ideas for walks and talks, companionship.

But Billy, as Craig discovered as he stood at the threshold to the ward, wouldn't be talking to anyone, not for some considerable time.

There were four beds, three of them empty. In the far corner lay Billy, but not the Billy he remembered. The pallor of his face was of a dull, grey colour, his cheeks sunken, features sharp. Tubes ran from his arm and nose, with leads linked to a monitor blinking in the corner. A stern-faced nurse stepped up to him. "Here to see Mr. Baxter? Well, I'm sorry, but he won't be able to have any visitors for at least forty-eight hours. He's being transferred to an intensive care ward so it would be best if you came back in a few days to see what the situation is then."

"But can't you tell me what's happened?"

She looked at him, and her features softened a little as she spoke. "Heart-attack. Very serious, I'm sorry to say."

Craig lurched as if hit by a bus. He reached out for the door surround as his knees went weak and a horrible sickness rose from his stomach. This was how it had been when Dad died. Back then not only grief, but guilt too combining to make him feel giddy, detached from the world around him. Now, with the same feelings returning in a rush, his head span.

The nurse reacted quickly and helped him into a chair. She poured water from a jug by the bed and he sipped it. "Where are your parents?" she asked.

He shook his head. Intensive care? "Is he going to die?"

She placed a hand on his shoulder. "Listen, you just go home and come back in a few days. We'll be able to give you a better idea then. Try not to worry."

But he did worry. How could he not?

An enormous sense of responsibility engulfed him and the nurse, noticing his mood, knelt and patted his hands.

Craig, consumed by a myriad of conflicting emotions, tried to get to his feet, but his legs wouldn't respond.

"Just sit still for a moment," the nurse was saying.

Her voice sounded as if it were a long way off. Nothing else mattered anymore. But then, a new thought reared up. "Skipper," he muttered, "what about his little dog?"

The nurse looked at him blankly. "I don't know," she reached out to stroke his hair. "You just sit quietly for a moment. I'll go and get someone."

She padded off. Get someone? Who? The police? His heartbeat pounded in his ears. The one thing Billy would hate would be for Skipper to end up in a rescue centre. He had to find the little dog.

Moving quickly, head down avoiding stares, Craig slipped out of the hospital without anyone noticing. As soon as he was outside, he ran to Billy's house, but what to do? Where could Skipper be?

Desperation drew him to the nearest house. He rang the bell and waited. The man who eventually opened the door was middle-aged, his face a blank mask.

"I'm sorry to disturb you," Craig began, knowing he must have looked a bedraggled mess. He'd run all the way from the hospital and everything about him must have screamed despair.

"You're Billy's friend," said the man and Craig almost swooned with the relief. The man continued, "He's in hospital, had some sort of attack, and they—"

"Yes," Craig gasped. "I've just come from there, but it's his dog. I wonder…" He saw the man's eyes light up, and a surge of hope rose.

"His dog? Yes, they've taken him in, number twenty-three," he pointed across the street. "I think they have dogs of their own and—"

Craig was already turning away. He raised his hand in thanks and went straight to the other house.

This time, Craig recognized the man at once – the old man who, together with the little old lady, had told him of Billy's attack. As soon as he saw Craig, the man beamed, and from within came the hopeful, unmistakable sound of Skipper's bark.

Mum's face was a perfect picture. She'd always insisted they could never have a dog. Living on a main road would mean it could so easily run straight out into oncoming traffic and that would be the end of it. Now, however, as Skipper ran around her heels, the smile came broad and happy. "He's adorable," she said as Skipper sat back and looked up at her with those huge, pleading eyes. Craig knew it was a done deal. Mum, when it came down to it, was really just a big softy.

It was still early enough for Craig to run around to the pet shop and buy a few things with the couple of pounds Mum gave him. Soon, Skipper became the proud owner of a new collar, lead, bed, various toys and a week's supply of dog food. The man in the shop had been very helpful and supplied all the necessities.

Arriving home, he saw the car parked outside and stopped, the lump developing in his throat. Even before he opened the front gate, his mum was there, in the doorway.

"Is it Billy?" he asked, responding to her drawn, anxious expression.

"No, Craig. It's the police."

Without another word, he moved inside, his mum close behind. In the front room, Inspector Fallon sat, empty cup of tea on the table before him. He smiled but without a glimmer of humour. Across from him, equally as serious was Forester. Craig wanted to turn around and escape, but Mum blocked his way. Outside, in the backyard, Skipper's barks told him, if nothing else did, that his duty was here, in his home. So he breathed in and stared directly towards the policeman. "What's happened?"

Fallon shifted position, looked from Craig to Forester and back again. "The man who tried to attack you. Bewdsley." His expression became pained, almost as if the words he wanted to say simply would not come out.

So Craig helped him. "He's dead?"

A blink. A change to the direction of his gaze. "He was admitted to hospital earlier today after questioning. He made a full confession, admitting to the murder of Janet Stowe. We assumed he was also responsible for the death of Fender, but this was not the case. A man called David Howarth murdered Fender and was almost certainly planning on killing Bewdsley next. It was Howarth's father whom Bewdsley shot and killed back in the War. Craig ..." A heaviness developed in the air whilst everyone waited. "Howarth's under arrest, but we both know there's someone else and that someone might try to kill Billy."

"But Billy's in a bad way," said Craig quickly.

"We know. And we've got officers all over the hospital. He's safe, but we need to bring the other one out into the open. So, as Mr Taylor said to you on the phone, we need an opportunity to lure him out into the open. Can you do that?"

"I think so, yes."

A flicker of a smile. Brief, unconvincing. "The thing is ... Earlier on, Bewdsley was attended to and placed in a secure ward. There was every reason to believe he would make a complete recovery in order for him to go to trial. At some point, he told the officer guarding him he wanted to go to the bathroom. The officer accompanied him, but obviously not in the you-know-what." Forrester cleared his throat. Mum sighed. Craig simply looked. "Well, he locked himself inside and pulled out all of the stitches to his wound. The Bobby on duty didn't realise until he noticed the blood seeping out from beneath the cubicle door."

"He bled to death," said Craig.

A stunned silence settled. Fallon lowered his gaze. "Yes, Craig. He's dead. By the time the officer managed to get to him, it was over. He'd pressed himself up against the door, so the officer had to climb over the top of the door, and it was difficult and ..."

"I'm glad he's dead," said Craig and looked at his mum. "It wasn't Bewdsley who broke into my room though, Mum. You know who it was, don't you?"

She nodded. Craig could see her pain, and hear

it in her voice as she spoke, "I'm trying my best to find a reason why, but I can't."

"Find a reason for what?" asked Forester. He looked at Craig, "Who is this other person you're talking about? Inspector?"

Fallon merely blew out a breath, "You'll know soon enough. Craig, what can you do to make this all stop?"

"I'll phone Ray, tell him to meet me up at the Breck. Tomorrow at ten. I'll do whatever it is you want me to do. Right now, I'm taking Skipper upstairs. He can sleep with me tonight."

Nobody said anything as Craig went into the yard to collect the little dog. Scooping Skipper up in his arms, he went upstairs.

Sat in his room, with Skipper curled up at his feet, Craig felt more at ease than he had since Dad's death. He stared through his window, thinking of all that had happened and how much everything had changed. He tickled Skipper's ear, went downstairs again and, without bothering to ask permission, telephoned Samantha to tell her the news. The sound of her voice floated down the line like an angel's, and he arranged to see her as soon as he could. Replacing the receiver, he then dialled Ray,

"I need to tell you some things," he said.

"Craig. They rang to tell us – me and Mam – about my da. Craig ..."

Craig tried his best not to gulp. His suspicions were beginning to surface but he still wasn't absolutely sure. "Ray, your dad …"

"It's all right, me ma's told me everything. He'd even changed his name, his surname. It's like he was two different people. Craig, I'm so sorry."

Craig waited, listening to Ray breaking down. His best friend, his hero in so many ways, reduced to a snivelling wreck. He wasn't sure what to say, but he did his best. "Ray, it's going to be over soon."

"You mean it's not already?"

"Just a few things to tie off. Meet me at the Breck tomorrow, we can talk then."

"Okay, because I need to talk to you as well."

That sounded ominous, but Craig let it go, put the phone down and turned to see his mum standing there. Somewhere close behind her must have been Forester. "Life's going to get better soon, you see," she said.

Craig didn't reply but, no matter how much he disliked Forester, he knew instinctively her words were true.

THE HOPED-FOR END

THEY SAT on a bench in the old quarry, neither of them talking for quite some time. Ray had answered Craig's call to meet somewhere quiet and well away from prying eyes. Now they were here, Craig swallowed down his awkwardness, knowing his friend would speak when he felt ready. He'd been through a lot these past few days, perhaps as much as Craig, but in a different way. Loss, whatever its guise, was always hard to come to terms with, so Craig sat in silence and waited.

"I don't want you to think I knew anything," said Ray tentatively.

"I never thought that."

"I'm so fucking angry, Craig. Mostly at myself for not seeing it. I was blind, I guess, never thinking in a million that my da ..." He stopped, turning his head away.

Craig heard his friend fighting back the tears and he wished he knew what to say to bring him some comfort. But what could he say at a time like this? It must have taken Ray so much to come here, to say what he needed to say. "Ray, you helped me up in the park and that's something I'll never forget. You're a real friend."

"Am I?"

He still hadn't turned to face Craig. "Of course you are. No matter what."

Ray gave a little laugh, which helped ease the tension. "Was that what you wanted to talk to me about? My da? If I knew?"

"No, nothing about that. I never doubted you." Ray turned to him and gave a faint smile of encouragement. Reassured, Craig continued, "Billy's sick again, a heart attack, serious this time."

"So this might soon be all over?" Ray was about to say something else when, without warning, a shadow loomed over them. He went rigid. Craig followed his friend's wide-eyed stare to see their visitor standing in front of them, a wide smile in that genial, good-natured expression he always wore.

"Budge up you two," said Uncle Eric. Without a word, Craig shuffled to the side. "Beautiful day isn't it?" He looked from one to the other. "What you up to, eh?"

"What are you doing here, Uncle Eric?"

"Ah, well ..." He rubbed his hands before he sat back, arms stretched wide along the back of the bench, so close to touching them both. "Thing is, I need to have a little word, Craig. And to you too, Raymond. How's your dad? Spoken to him?"

"I'll never speak to him again," said Ray, in a faraway voice. He was staring at the ground, lost in his memories, his sadness.

Nodding, Uncle Eric's expression took on a seriousness that Craig had rarely seen before. "Yes, terrible business all of that. Are you coping all right, Raymond, with everything? Must be difficult."

Craig winced. Difficult? His dad killed himself! He went to speak but Ray got there first. "It was the lies mainly. All those years, using that other house to be with ...*women*. Changing his name, like he was living a double life. He broke me mam's heart. Mine too."

"I understand, Raymond, I really do. I knew him, of course, but even I never imagined how low he would sink. The whole thing is terrible. How is your mother?"

Shrugging his shoulders, Ray's voice grew even quieter. "Managing, just about. She probably feels the same as me – betrayed."

"Of course she does." He cleared his throat, threw a quick glance at Craig. "Time heals everything, Raymond. I know at the moment it's difficult to come to terms with, but in a few short years you'll find you'll able to speak with him again."

"Uncle Eric," said Craig, voice cracking a little. "Don't you know?"

"Know what?"

"Ray's dad, he—"

"We're moving away," cut in Ray. "Me mam's got a new job down in Shropshire. Working in a little café. It's not much, but anything is better than staying here." He looked across to his friend. "That's what I wanted to tell you, Craig. I'm leaving."

"Leaving? What, permanently?"

Ray nodded. "People are already gossiping, waggling their fingers, telling us we had to have known, all of that. I'm sorry, Craig."

Stunned, Craig didn't know what to say. His friend, the only true friend he'd ever known, was moving away? "What am I going to do without you?"

"You've got Samantha, you'll be fine." He stood up, looking towards the view of Spraggs' Farm in the distance. They had played there many times. "I'm going to miss this place."

"You'll come and visit us, won't you Raymond?"

Ray turned to Eric and did not answer. Shifting

his gaze to Craig, he forced a tiny smile. "I'll write, Craig. I promise."

Craig went to stand up, but Uncle Eric's arm left the back of the seat and pressed down on his knee, preventing him from rising. "Take care, Raymond," he said. "We'll just sit here for a while and chat."

Ray walked away, choosing the far exit to the quarry and not the steps that would lead him to Breck Road.

"I wanted to talk to him some more," said Craig, eyes clamped on where Uncle Eric's hand remained on his knee, squeezing.

"Well, you can't." His voice changed in tone, more harsh. "He's gone and that's for the best." He stared at Craig and sighed. "You've caused me a lot of pain and heartache, Craig. Your mother too."

"*I've caused you*? What are you talking about?"

"You know full well. I warned you to keep out of it, didn't I? Because of your constant meddling, many people have lost their lives. That, my dear little Craig, is down to you." The venom in his uncle's voice made Craig realise the danger he was in. He snapped his head around, looking for an escape route. It was hopeless. As soon as he made even the slightest movement his uncle would stop him.

"So it was you."

A single arched eyebrow. "What was?"

"You came into my room, didn't you? Sneaked in to warn me off? Threatened me, my own uncle."

"You're bright, Craig. You have a knack for working things out, intuitively. You should be like your friend when you leave school – Inspector Fallon."

He stopped whilst a young woman in a dark blue raincoat strolled by, dog straining at its leash. It was a large dog. She paused whilst the dog relieved itself in the tall grass. "Baxter's dog. What will happen to it?"

"We've taken Skipper in."

"That's kind. Always was kind, your mother." He slipped into thought for a moment before he turned, the grip on Craig's knee becoming stronger. "His letters, Craig? His journal. That's what I really wanted to talk to you about."

A man appeared at the top of the stairs, breathing hard with his exertions. He spotted the young woman and waved. They went up to one another and embraced.

"Billy's letters are safe. The ones he received from his former army friend, the one who was dying."

"Ah yes. Billy used those, did he? To tell his version of the story?"

"I've given them to the police. All of them, including the journal."

"Really?"

There was something in his tone that made Craig think his uncle didn't believe him but he pushed on regardless. "You and Billy knew each other in the War, didn't you? Bob Bewdsley too. All three of you, in that church tower." His uncle's expression changed, hardening, those once warm, convivial eyes suddenly so very cold. "It was you, all along. It was you who shot Billy in the leg after you'd murdered that other soldier."

"That was an accident, nothing more."

"An accident? You murdered that soldier and then you covered it up. You've been covering it up ever since, haven't you Uncle Eric."

"That's an interesting theory, Craig."

"It's more than that. I have proof."

Folding his arms, Eric studied his nephew closely. "Really? And what sort of proof have you got?"

Craig rubbed his knee, thankful that at last those fingers weren't digging into his flesh. "Remember those model soldiers, the ones I wanted so badly? You wrote out an order for me, with a letter attached, telling them who you were, that you didn't want a repeat of the previous order, the one they hadn't posted. You told them to honour my original order, you remember that, don't you Uncle Eric?"

Clearing his throat, Eric's smile looked strained. "Of course, but I don't see how—"

"You wrote it out on your company's letter-headed paper. Your company whose offices burned down."

Frowning, Eric grew anxious, shifting his position on the bench. His expression looked pained. "That still doesn't prove I—"

"The handwriting matches those of Billy's army friend from the Army. Those letters were written by you, Uncle Eric."

"That's what you think is it?"

"It's what I *know*. The handwriting is identical. I'm sure an expert could confirm it."

"Well, that's never going to happen. I think you've still got those letters, Craig, and I want you to give me them, together with the journal before this all gets out of hand. There's no truth in these silly accusations you've made if you must know. None at all."

"I think there is. You're due to come up for selection as your Party's prospective parliamentary candidate."

"My, my, you really are the little detective aren't you?"

"You used Bob Bewdsley to kill those people. Janet Stowe, Fender, Stan Prentis, how many others? You knew Bewdsley was unstable and you used him to do your dirty work in order to keep your reputation untarnished. You were probably the one who advised him to change his name. That was the clever bit. It kept me in the dark, being he was the dad of my best friend."

"You should write fiction, Craig, you'd sell a million."

"So, you deny all of it?"

"Of course I do."

"You came into my bedroom and threatened me. If news of that alone got out, serious questions would be asked about you, Uncle Eric. Then they'd probe deeper, investigate more closely the fire at your company's headquarters. A policeman was burned to death in there, but of course, you know that as well, don't you? You know because you did it."

"I think you've said enough." He dusted away some imaginary dirt from his trousers and stood up. "I'll call around after tea and you can give me those letters. Then you can return to your stupid, infantile little world of playing soldiers and dreaming of your dad."

"Fuck off."

Eric's face grew white. He leaned forward, lips drawn back in a snarl. "You ever repeat any of this to anyone, I'll break your scrawny little neck, understand."

"It's true, though, isn't it? Every word."

"Like I said, you're bright. You worked it all out on your own. What I did back then, in those mad moments, I've lived with every day. Yes, Bob helped after I'd shot that soldier. He had to. He took that girl home, didn't he? Married her. If he'd ever said it was me who'd murdered that soldier, I'd take him down with me. He knew that."

"So you got him to murder Janet Stowe."

"Fender made a bloody mess of everything, trying to blackmail them all. And poor old David Howarth. It was his father I killed, but he never knew that, thank God. Nobody knew any of it, except for Bob, Billy, and me."

"I hate you."

"Ooh, so hurtful." He scoffed then stood upright. "This is over now, Craig. All of it. I'll see you later."

"I won't give them to you."

"Oh yes, you will."

"No, I won't. Do you know why?" Craig saw that tiny crack appearing in his uncle's show of vicious contempt. "Because what I told you is the truth – I have already given them to Inspector Fallon, together with an explanation. I reckon even now he's got an expert matching up the handwriting."

"You're lying. You've still got them."

"No." Craig smiled. "I've given them to Inspector Fallon."

"You've done *what*? You little shit!"

Like a cobra striking at its prey, Eric's hands shot out and grabbed Craig around the throat. Craig wriggled desperately, but Eric held on, applying more pressure until Craig's head went into a spin, a strange, throbbing whine revolving around inside his skull.

The young man and the woman rushed forward, bustling Eric to the ground, the dog going wild, barking as if possessed. The man had his knee in Eric's back whilst the woman tried desperately to snap on the handcuffs.

"Be careful," screamed Craig, rubbing his throat as he leapt to his feet.

His warning came too late, and as he watched, he knew it.

Using his superior strength and training, Eric wriggled free and rolled over. He went into a stance. Moving with the grace of a ballet dancer, bobbing and weaving, he slipped the man's right hook and hit him with a series of lightning-fast moves. A three-finger strike to the midriff folded him like a penknife, a back-fisted blow snapped the man's head back and a final solid straight punch dumped him unconscious to the ground.

The young woman did her best and struck hard with her baton. But Eric, not even out of breath, easily parried it, moved in close, and locked her arm. She squealed, Eric rammed his elbow into her jaw and she went limp in his hold, the baton clattering to the ground.

Craig saw it all and had no response to any of it. Even the idea of running did not break through the fog of inertia that seized his thinking, as well as his limbs. Then, in a frenzy of snarling, snapping jaws, the dog attacked. Craig instantly came out of his petrified state and took his chance. He swept up the woman's fallen baton and swung it in a wide arc. Eric, struggling desperately with the dog, its jaws clamped around his forearm, had no chance to react. The baton made a horrible cracking sound as it connected with the side of his head. He dropped like a stone.

It all went still, apart from the groans coming from the two fallen police officers. "I think I've killed him," Craig mumbled to himself and dropped the baton. He stared in disbelief at his uncle's inert body, the dog sniffing and prodding frantically.

"I don't think so, Craig," said Fallon, out of breath, appearing over the top of the steps. A whole army of police officers were moving in from every direction. "Are you all right?"

Holding his throat, Craig slumped onto the bench, waiting until the wooziness eased off. "You took your time, Inspector."

"We had to be sure. You got everything?"

"I think so," said Craig, unbuttoning his denim jacket. He pressed the button on the small rectangular device he had fastened to his waistband. Carefully he unhooked the large pendant around his neck, which concealed a microphone and was connected by a wire to the recorder. He looked at it for a moment and handed everything over to Fallon.

"It's not admissible in court on its own," explained Fallon, "but together with those letters, the journal, and your testimony, your uncle will be spending the rest of his life behind bars."

Craig looked over to where police officers were taking Uncle Eric away whilst others tended to their gradually recovering colleagues. If there was any relief or rejoicing at everything being over at long last, he didn't show it. Instead, he sat and allowed the dog to nuzzle up to him. Smiling, he stroked its head and thought of home.

A MEETING OF BEAUTIES

THE NEXT DAY, in an attempt to return his life to something akin to normality, Craig visited his favourite book shop, to do what he loved best – browsing through the shelves, daydreaming about which title he'd like to read next. If he had the money. He'd found a slim volume on calligraphy. He'd always wanted to write well, and the book offered the chance to learn. He delved into his pockets and he had just enough. Mum had given him a pound, perhaps as a form of truce. With his head buried in the pages, he moved towards the counter.

"Hello, Craig."

He pulled up short and gasped in surprise.

It was Melanie. For a moment he couldn't speak. He had hardly given her a thought since the altercation with Danny, believing she would never acknowledge him again, and yet here she was smiling.

"How have you been?"

A shake of his head, and a shrug. "Not so bad. What about you?"

The smile broadened. "Okay, thanks." She stared. He stared back. "I'm okay, I promise."

The assistant coughed and Craig, taking the hint, hurriedly returned the book, now forgotten, to its shelf. Ignoring the assistant's blast of annoyance, he nodded to the door. "Let's talk outside."

It was mid afternoon, and the town buzzed with traffic and shoppers preparing for the weekend. They stood together on the pavement, awkward, a little embarrassed, before Melanie suggested they go for a coffee at the cafe around the corner.

After they ordered, they sat and drank.

"They never sacked me," she said at last.

His mouth dropped. "They never... But that woman, she said—"

"She changed her mind. Isn't that wonderful? God, my dad would have killed me. When I went to take back my uniform, my supervisor smiled, told me it was nothing to worry about, that I was a good worker, a 'pleasant girl' and that if I wanted it, the job was still mine."

"That's great news." A darkness fell. "And Danny?"

Her smile disappeared in that instant and, for something to do, she watched a passing bus through the window. "I've finished with him."

"Oh."

"Is that all you can say?"

"I'm not sure what to say...Are you happy?"

"Relieved, I suppose. Dad hated him, Mum too. They never wanted him in the house, hated him even calling for me. They said he was a bad influence and, I suppose after what happened, that's exactly what he was. So ..."

"So ... you've finished."

"Yes. Done and dusted." Her smile returned. "You still play tennis? I seem to remember you were pretty bad at it."

"Thanks. And no, I haven't played, not since...not since that day. Things have got, well, complicated."

She had a look of expectation about her, as if she wanted him to continue, to elaborate. For his part, Craig didn't want to. She was nice, kind, thoughtful in many ways, but, as he had said, life had become complicated. Samantha, and how he felt about her, changed everything.

Now, as Melanie sat opposite him at the tiny table, Craig noticed a change coming over her. Gone was the expectation, replaced by something more serious. This time when she spoke, her eyes no longer held his. "Craig, I'm not sure how to say this..." She bit her lip. "You're nice, I don't want you to think I'm..."

Her words fell away, but he knew. There was no need for any further explanation. His hand brushed across hers. "It's all right, Melanie, I understand."

She arched an eyebrow. "You do? What is it you understand, Craig?"

"That you don't want us to be anything more than friends."

Her mouth opened, but no sound followed. "How old are you? Thirty?" She laughed. "How come you're so perceptive?"

"Life, I guess. So much has happened. I've changed – grown up. I've realised a lot of things, but mainly how fragile life can be. Here one second, gone the next. I don't regret anything that happened between us, Melanie, except the bad things, of course. Maybe, we met at the wrong time, but I'm glad we can still be friends."

"Me too," she said softly.

As Melanie went to stand up, Craig saw Samantha standing on the far side of the street, waiting to cross. Melanie, noticing his gaze, said, "Who is that?"

Samantha came through the door. For a moment, time stopped as the two girls measured one another, like gunfighters playing out a scene from one of the many films he'd seen at the cinema. Only this was real, and Craig was stuck in the middle of it.

They all waited.

"Well, I'd better go," said Melanie at last. She smiled, lifted her hand in a tiny gesture of farewell and that was it. She walked away.

"Who was that?"

Craig heard the tone, the little crackle around the edges of Samantha's voice. Could that be jealousy? "A friend."

"Nice friend." Icicles formed on her lips and the chill crossed the space between them and settled around his heart. He could see the conflict playing out behind her lovely eyes, a struggle between anger and uncertainty. Girls were a mystery to him, so much unspoken, one moment full of sparkle, the next blazing rage. He doubted he would ever understand them.

"Her boyfriend attacked me," he said quickly, hopeful that this explanation would be enough.

Of course, it wasn't. Her words came like finely aimed darts. "Why would he do that, because you fancied her?"

What reply should he give – the truth was yes, he did like Melanie and he could never fully understand the reasons why she approached him that first day up at the tennis courts. Those reasons were as much a conundrum as girls. His mum always told him that he was an 'angel', his dad that he would 'break many hearts', but he had never known what either remark truly meant.

"I don't fancy her," he said at last. "Her boyfriend thought I did, but…" He shrugged, took her hand and motioned for her to sit. She seemed so fragile this close up. Her clothes were different now. Gone the tight jeans and shirt, replaced by a flowery dress, which hugged her trim waist, accentuated her hips. He couldn't help but smile. "Sam, you mustn't worry. I told you, I'm with you now."

The look in her eye revealed a tiny glint of relief. He picked up her hand in both of his and kissed her fingertips. Her mouth opened slightly, lips full. "I know what I did was wrong," she said, "and I'm not asking you to forgive me, but…"

"Sam, that's over now. You have to forget about it and stop torturing yourself with this … guilt."

"Yes, but…There are things about me you don't know, and maybe…" She brushed away a rolling tear with the back of her hand.

"Maybe I'd like to find out," he said, and he smiled again, holding her gaze.

"You would? Wow, Craig, you're…You're so grown up."

He gave a little laugh. Hadn't Melanie said exactly the same thing only moments before? "Only in some ways."

"The important ones, that's for sure." Her breath shuddered as she took a breath. "Do you really, truly forgive me?"

"Of course."

"And that girl? She's so pretty. I just need to know...You're not...You know, you're not going out with her?"

He did a double-take. "*Going out with her?* No, of course not." He took her hand again and drew her close, voice dropping to a conspiratorial whisper. "You're pretty too."

He felt her stiffen, but only for a moment. Her head came up. "You think so?"

Stupid question, he thought. Had she ever studied herself in the mirror, the shaggy hair, button nose sprinkled with freckles, those massive crystal clear blue eyes? And that mouth. How he longed to taste her lips.

Without another word, or thought, he did just that. He kissed her. Long and hard. Right there, in the café, with everyone stopping and staring and he didn't care, not for a moment.

A REVELATION

IT WAS DECISION TIME.

He had tried his utmost not to think about it, not since the day it had happened. One minute Dad was there, the next he was not. His life flittered away as easily as a bird's feather on the breeze, and Craig hadn't said a word about it. How could he? His Mum was devastated, Nan beyond consoling. How much worse would they have been if the truth was known? Even an inkling would have set everyone against Craig forever.

The night was drawing in, his soldiers needed to be stored away and there was nothing else to look forward to. He felt very lonely all of a sudden and his room an unkind, unforgiving place. Skipper lay on the bed, oblivious. Oh, to be like him, Craig thought. No worries, no concerns, only at how empty his belly was.

Listening to Sam on the phone helped a little. Her dad answered, and he seemed pleasant enough, asked no questions, and as they talked, the subject of Craig's calling around came up, once again and they agreed he would call at the weekend. He would stay for tea and later, her dad would drive them to the cinema. A night together, alone. Their first of many. His heart buzzed with the thought.

The following weekend seemed like a lifetime away, however. So much could happen in the meantime. Look at the past week, he mused. Killers behind bars, or dead. Billy, fighting for his life. Mum had relented, allowed him to visit, but there never seemed to be any change. He lay there, like a stone slab, the machines doing all his breathing for him. Not the Billy he knew. Would he ever be again?

He held up one of his soldiers and studied it as if for the first time. It was a model of an English Civil War 'roundhead', in the act of thrusting with a non-existent sword. He'd 'lost' it many years ago, how Craig could not recall, but it was his favourite, and he'd christened him 'Captain', always chose him as the leader, and never killed in battle. Thoughts turned to those hoplites again. Why hadn't they come? Apart from Sam, everything continued to keep going so wrong, from the smallest of things, like those hoplites, to the biggest; Billy.

He squeezed his eyes shut. Billy had shown him how destructive bottling things up could be. How guilt eats away at one's very soul. Billy had lived with his guilt for over twenty years and had given up on his life, smoking and drinking himself to almost an early grave. Aged before his time. A little like Queequeg, the mysterious South Sea Island harpooner from Moby Dick, Craig suddenly thought. Then he shook his head. No, not like him. Queequeg, believing himself to be dying, arranged for his coffin to be made, then had roused himself. Not so Billy. Billy had not thought about dying, just gone through the motions of being alive. Now, having unburdened himself of all that guilt, he had suffered a massive heart attack. Relief brought it on, perhaps, made him more perceptible to an attack as every muscle in his worn-out body relaxed. Not a suicide. He was too proud for that. Just a desire to dwindle away, not to help himself but to accelerate his demise by not...

Craig clamped his hand over his mouth at the shock of his thought.

It made perfect sense. Of course, it did.

Billy *had* done it deliberately – he had stopped taking his medication.

Quietly, lest he was heard, Craig wept for a life that seemed to be out of his control, full of misery, loneliness, and despair and for a friend who could face it no longer and had sought the only real method of escape – death.

ON A CLIFF EDGE

THE FOLLOWING morning didn't help his mood. Dull, overcast, the sky a heavy lead colour. He stood at his window and looked out across the rooftops, staring into the distance. The plan was for him to go up to the hospital as soon as he could, but first he wanted to see what the postman brought. He daren't think about it too much, believing that if he kept his mind clear, neutral, he might be rewarded. Always think the opposite, then what you wished for would come true, that was his adage. It tended to work, with a sickening regulatory.

But not that morning. The post slipped through the letterbox and fell on the hall carpet. No package. The postman would have knocked if there had been. Spirits low, he stamped into the kitchen and made himself a piece of toast. It was

Wednesday and his Mum was home. She came up behind him, sifting through the post. She sighed and dropped the letters onto the kitchen table. "Liverpool today, Craig," she declared, her mood becoming buoyant.

"I can't, Mum. I've got to go and see Billy."

As a further reminder of how Billy's sickness had changed everyone's lives, Skipper came bobbing in and rubbed himself up against Mum, just as a cat would do. She laughed and bent down to tickle the dog's head. "He's a funny little fella," she said. She straightened up and frowned as Craig nibbled at his toast. "You seem a bit tense today. I'm sure everything will be all right. Billy is the sort of person who seems to shrug off most of what life throws at him."

Craig swallowed down his toast. "I hope so. I have a suspicion he might have brought all this on himself."

"Why do you say that?"

"I don't know." He brushed crumbs onto his plate. "Just a feeling. And I'm sick of waiting for my soldiers – it's been weeks."

She nodded, always so in tune with his mood, able to accept that what he wanted, or needed, was more important than anything else. "Uncle Eric's letter hasn't worked then." The mention of his uncle threw them both into a black hole of depression.

"Perhaps I can give them a ring." He looked at her and she turned away before he could see her tears.

Later at the hospital, his pessimism received a good kick in the teeth. Grinning, the nurse told him he could go and sit with Billy.

However, any hopeful feelings were short-lived. Billy was nothing like he expected. He was worse. The shock of seeing him this close, festooned with tubes, skin stretched thin like rice paper, cheekbones protruding like a living skull, was almost too much for Craig to bear. He slumped down on the small chair next to the bed and watched the rise and fall of his friend's chest as he struggled for air.

A hand fell on Craig's shoulder and he looked up to see the nurse, eyes serious. "He's very ill," she said needlessly. "He very nearly didn't make it."

Craig knew the reason, but he asked anyway, "But, I thought …Why does he look so awful?"

She said the words he dreaded to hear, despite having already considered them. "His medication. He hasn't been taking it. He's very lucky to be alive."

"Lucky?" Craig shook his head, "Look at him. I knew he'd not been taking his pills, I *knew it!*"

"You mustn't blame yourself. He's such a proud man, perhaps he knew his life was fading away and didn't want to prolong it anymore."

"He already looks like death."

She patted his shoulder. "I know you were desperate to see him, but try not to be too long. It was his wish to see you; he said so when he woke up before. He said you were his friend, his *best* friend." She smiled. "If he comes round, don't let him get too tired. Press the bell if you need anything."

She left and Craig reached out and took Billy's hand. The old man's eyes flickered open and a thin smile crossed his face. He spoke in little more than a croaking whisper. "Craig...thanks for coming...I knew you would...I've been worried...About Skipper."

Craig smiled. Typical of him to think of his little dog first. "He's safe. I've taken him home."

Billy closed his eyes. "Thank God. That makes me feel so much better." He coughed once and for a moment, Craig tensed, ready to reach out for the alarm button. Billy's throat sounded hoarse, breath rattling with every word. "I'm all right," he said and raised his hand slightly and waggled a finger. "It's just a tickle."

"You mustn't tire yourself; the nurse said so."

"Well, they fuss a lot. It's their job." He winked. "I wasn't sure if you'd come. After my stories. What I'd done. Keeping it all so secret. That wasn't right."

"I told you I wouldn't judge you."

"I know, and I'm grateful. Not many could listen

to what I said and still come and see me. The truth is, I *am* going to be judged…very soon."

"Billy," Craig squeezed the man's hand, "you've got to stop thinking like this. Stop punishing yourself. It's killing you."

"I've been punishing myself every day since it happened. I thought – I *hoped* – that falling in love would somehowtake it all away…but when she reacted the way she did, it was a confirmation. A confirmation of everything I'd always suspected." Now it was Billy's turn to squeeze Craig's hand, with surprising strength. "Craig. I wish things had been different. I wish…" A sudden cough and he yanked his head away, his breathing coarse as rubble.

"You've got to rest now, take it easy. I'll go and get the nurse."

Billy squeezed Craig's hand tighter still, the look in Billy's eyes, full of panic, a hint of terror. "No! No, I need you to listen to me…*please*. I have something to tell you. Not a story, a wish. I haven't got a son, Craig. I always wanted one, but…if I had a son, I would want him to be like you."

Craig reeled as if from a blow, hardly daring to believe what his friend said. The tears welled up, despite all of Craig's best efforts to force them down. He hung his head, unable to find anything of any significance to say, just a simple, "Thanks."

"You showed me that through kindness and acceptance, someone as gnarled and as bitter as me can change. The tragedy is, it's too late, but it's not too late for you."

Craig's heart almost stopped. Frowning, he looked up. "For me? What do you mean?"

"Break the mould, Craig. Don't do to yourself what I have done and allow mistakes and regrets to eat away at your soul. Find yourself someone to love, stay with them, grow old with them, and have a *son,* Craig. A son you can teach to have the same values as you."

"But Billy," the first tear fell. He did not attempt to stop it, "I'm not like that. I'm not as good as you think I am. I have a secret too, a secret that is so bad, Billy, so bad that…" He pressed a finger and thumb into the corners of his eyes and squeezed them tight. "I've never told anyone about any of it, not even Mum."

The suspense clung to the very walls, the only sound the rattle in Billy's chest. He patted Craig's hand and smiled. "Tell me, then."

Craig looked at his friend. A friend who may not be around for very much longer. He'd struggled so long with the thought of what to do for the best. Somehow, meeting Billy, hearing his story, put everything into focus. He needed a release, to unburden himself of the guilt, the shame, the self-loathing. The decision he had been putting off ever since that dreadful day when Dad died. It had to be made, here and now. To tell it all. The decision to reveal the truth of his own fallen past.

"We were on holiday," Craig began, his voice at first tremulous as the memories returned. "We had such a lovely time, the sun shone every day, so hot, and we would go down to the beach and swim in the sea. We were in Dorset, not far from a place called Lyme Regis, which is world-famous for fossils. I'd never seen a fossil, except in books. Dad said we should go and have a look. So the next day, that's what we did. Just us, whilst Mum and Auntie Ida went into town to do some shopping.

"I remember we took some things from the hotel. A bit naughty that was, I suppose. A knife and fork, imagine that. The two great fossil hunters, armed with a bunch of cutlery." He couldn't help grinning, looking back at Dad surreptitiously slipping the 'tools' into his pocket after breakfast. "We found some cliffs that seemed to promise a find or two, and there were caves close to the top. It proved a difficult climb. The cliff face was hard, in parts as sharp and as jagged as broken glass, so sharp it could so easily slice through your hands, make a real mess if you didn't pick your spot. We managed it, despite it being so treacherous. I remember there was a sign telling people to be careful of crumbling rocks but I didn't think anything of it. I wish I had."

He paused and clamped his two hands together as if he were praying. "It was me, you see. My fault. I scrambled down and found this piece of shale and I tugged it and it came away and there...there was this fossil. I couldn't believe it. It wasn't anything incredible, like a Stegosaurus or anything, just a simple ammonite, the sort anyone could find anywhere. But to me, it was wonderful, the most exciting thing I had ever found. Like an idiot, I stood up without thinking, holding it high, waving it around like it was some huge trophy...and that's when it happened..." He placed his fingers against his lips. "I tipped backwards and fell down the cliff. All I can recall is this horrible feeling of being totally out of control, my feet in mid-air, nothing to stop me as I pitched over. Before I knew it, I landed. I was lucky because I lay on a ledge about eight feet below. All I remember was looking up to the top of the cliff, winded, but alive and Dad yelling at me to stay still, that he was going to get help. If I'd tried, I could probably have reached out my hand and touched him. He must have thought so too, but when he took a step I heard it, a terrible creaking, groaning sound, like that of an old sailing ship, timbers giving way in the swell. I watched Dad. He stopped, turned to look at me, and his eyes bulged, his face becoming deathly white.

"The thing was, you see, the ledge that I was lying on was splitting. That was the sound I heard. It was going to give way, and beneath me, there was a sixty-foot drop, straight to the beach and almost certain death.

"Dad didn't hesitate. He climbed down, slowly at first, but as more pieces of the ledge crumbled beneath me and fell away, he speeded up. I wanted to help, but as I sat up, two things happened. One, more of the ledge crumbled, and then a sudden jolt of pain ran through my back as if it was on fire. I must have hit a rock or something, and when I tried to move I realised I'd caused serious damage to myself. I had to lie there and wait.

"Dad seemed to be thinking the same, and he descended with more speed. As he got closer, he took hold of a piece of shrubbery that was growing out of the side of the cliff and reached out his other hand towards me. I bit down on my lip, sucked in the pain, and grabbed it. He hauled me up, the pain burning like a red-hot poker, but the relief of being safe overcame everything. I threw my arms around him and held him so tightly. He still had hold of the bush, but with one hand he managed to swing me up onto the cliff face above us. I found a decent footing, then another. I bit through the pain in my back and climbed, inching my way upward, keeping my breathing even. I paused and glanced down at Dad, who grinned like an ape. My Dad, my hero, and I knew that later, over tea, when Mum asked what had happened, he'd change the story, to prevent all hell being let loose. He must have read my thoughts because he shook his head and said, 'You're a silly little...' That was all he managed because then..." The tears sprang unchecked, cascading down his face in a flood. The pictures he'd kept so well hidden of those final moments for so long reared up, so real, so vivid. "Dad fell...the bush just came out of the rock...and he fell...and I couldn't help him...My limbs, they were frozen. I looked into his eyes and for a single moment, it was as if he was suspended in mid-air by an invisible string, and what passed between us, in that single glance, I can't say. Love, companionship, both. All I know is he was my dad, and if I hadn't been so stupid, hadn't been so selfish, I wouldn't have gone down to that ledge and found that fossil and he...He fell, all the way to the bottom and I just stood there and watched him, not knowing what to do. He bounced off..." He squeezed his fingers into his eyes, tried to fight back the pain, the anguish, but nothing could help now, the memory so raw, conjured up after being suppressed for so very long, it would not now remain quiet. "When he hit the ground, I didn't know what to do, whether to cry out or what, but I could see he was… gone. The way his body was, his legs twisted under him. I couldn't move, not for a long time. All I remember was staring down this long tunnel towards him. Nothing else existed. No sight, sounds, nothing. Just him, lying there all broken on the beach.

"I don't know how long I stood there, but at some point, I must have scrambled back to the top and ran to the first person I saw and I tried to tell them, but they didn't understand. I found myself in a nightmare world, nobody listening, flitting around like ghosts. My sense of direction had completely disappeared and I must have looked like some mad thing, arms flapping around, yelling and screaming, trying to force someone to stop, and help. No one did, they just stared at me as if I was a leper, someone they shouldn't approach. So I ran, all the way into the town to the post office. I made them understand and then I saw Mum and Auntie Ida…"

He wept. Billy placed a hand on his head. The seconds ticked by into minutes.

Through eyes that burned with too many tears, Craig saw the blurred outline of Billy, his face so concerned. "The ambulance men finally got to him. It was awful, Billy. Took hours. I sat on the top of the cliff and watched them, with Auntie Ida holding me. Mum was like a mad thing, screaming and pounding a policeman's chest as if it were his fault.

Kept on asking him why they hadn't put fences up to stop people climbing down. The policeman had asked me, you see. He'd asked me what had happened. And me...I...I'd lied, Billy. I didn't tell them that it was me, you see, that it was me that Dad had tried to rescue. I told them it was Dad who had found the fossil, that he was the one who climbed down to the ledge and had slipped and fallen. Nothing about me being stupid and thoughtless and Dad trying to save me! I lied. It was all my fault that Dad was dead, all of it."

"But Craig, it was an accident."

"No, it wasn't, Billy! *It was my fault*. Dad would be here now if it wasn't for me, it's as simple as that. You can dress it up in as many ways as you like, but the truth will never change. If it wasn't for me, he'd still be here, and life would be as it should be, but it's not, and it's because of me, and I've never told anyone the truth of it. No one, not until now."

"Is it what happened that has made you feel so guilty, or that you haven't told your mum?"

"Tell Mum? My God, she'd hate me if she knew the truth. Disown me, never speak to me again."

He caught the shift in Billy's gaze, and became aware of someone else in the room a moment before the voice spoke, "I would never do any of those things, Craig."

In that frozen moment, Craig felt all his fears

loom up like some enormous, terrible creature ready to consume him. He whirled round and saw his mum and Auntie Ida, standing in the doorway, looking. How long had they been there, how much of his confession had they heard? His life, he knew, was about to enter a new phase, one full of resentment, anger, and blame.

He went to get up, but sat down almost at once, legs like rubber. He shook his head over and over. "I didn't mean it, Mum," he blurted out. "He climbed down to help me, Mum. It was cracking, you see, the ledge, it was going to fall. If Dad…"

Mum held up her hand and she came forward, a smile on her face. "Craig. Hush. It's all right. I've always known Craig. I've always known the truth."

Something like a huge mechanical device squeezed his ribs like a clamp. Hardly able to breathe, he gaped at her. "What? You've always known? But how…when…"

"The police told me. They had to make investigations, Craig. They found the remains of the bush, traced it back to where it grew, inspected the ledge, saw how it cracked under somebody's weight. Your weight. At the inquest, the coroner gave his verdict, *death by misadventure*. That's all we need to know, Craig, and that's the truth of it." She stepped forward and put her arms around him, holding him close. He breathed in her perfume, felt her love, and he let the tears come as all the pain seeped out of him.

"I miss him so much, Mum."

"I know you do, and so do I. But we have each other and that's all that matters."

No one else spoke for a long time, but when Craig finally found the strength and the courage to lean away, Billy took his hand, smiled and said, "You must move on now, Craig. Begin a new chapter, one without anger, resentment, or blame, but one filled with something that will wipe everything away forever. Love."

A VERY SPECIAL PRESENT

HE STOOD outside the little chapel and looked at the birds in the trees. Their lives, so untroubled, so carefree and uncomplicated by emotion. He wondered if they ever woke up on any given morning and said to themselves, 'Today, I'm going to do something different'? But they couldn't; they were slaves to nature, to instinct. He, however, was not. He had choices, and those choices were now made. He was no longer going to allow dark thoughts to dominate his life. Today, the old chapter would be closed and a new one begun.

Samantha stepped up and he smiled at her. She looked so lovely, dressed in a simple black skirt and white blouse. Her makeup was subtle, showing off the fresh loveliness of her face. He put his arm around her waist and held her close, so happy that she had accepted his invitation to come, to share these last moments, these last farewells.

He watched the last few people drift by, heads down, their steps heavy, and he saw a small woman approaching. When she got close, she offered him her outstretched hand. "You must be Craig?" she asked.

Frowning slightly, Craig took her hand. "Yes. I'm sorry, but I don't..."

"My name is Mary. I'm Billy's ex-wife."

They travelled back to Billy's house in the funeral car, no one speaking. All in all, it had been a miserable affair, a few old men from the allotments, Craig and Samantha, and Mary of course. And a younger woman, with a man Craig recognised as Taylor, the policeman. He didn't say anything, merely giving Craig a nod. The woman stepped forward and held his hand. "I'm Millie," she said quietly. "Billy was my dad. What you did for him, I'll never forget." She leaned forward and kissed him lightly before she drifted away.

Those few mourners, looking so awkward, out of place, embarrassed to be there perhaps, the sum total of a lifetime of friendships. Craig recalled Dad's funeral, the church packed, so many people the overspill had to wait outside in the pouring rain.

Mum said there were nearly two hundred there. *Two hundred*. How could a man, an ordinary man, be so well thought of, so loved? He hoped he would discover the answer one day.

The car pulled up outside Billy's old house. They waited in silence, each lost in their own thoughts for a moment before they went inside. It was cold and empty and Mary busied herself with making tea whilst Craig and Samantha sat in that same, worn-out old room where Billy had shown the photographs and told his story. Not so very long ago. Not so very long ago at all.

"So many things in here," said Samantha, her voice very low, full of hushed reverence. "Such a shame such a lovely man has gone."

Craig nodded. Yes, and a shame that he had been alone for so long, shunned, trapped by his own inability to share the truth, to make peace. But Craig liked to think that maybe, in the final few moments of his life, Billy had made a true friend and found someone who cared.

Mary came in with the tea, settled the tray down on the table, and filled the cups. "I'm not sure about the milk, it's been in the fridge, but..." She took a tentative sip. "Yes, it's fine. I bought it a couple of days ago when I first came down." She sat, crossed her legs and smiled, hands wrapped around the teacup as she took more sips. Craig stirred Samantha's cup and passed it to her. She smiled, and Craig wondered why Mary had brought them here. He didn't have to wait long to find his answer.

"Well, Craig," said Mary, putting the cup down. "I think I've got to say 'thank you', for what you did. Helping Billy in his last few days."

Craig shrugged. "I didn't do very much."

"Oh but you did," she turned, opened her bag, and delved inside. She brought out a well-folded manila envelope and tugged free the letter inside. A large letter, more than three pages. She studied each page. "He wrote to me and told me all about it. He wasn't much of a one for letting his thoughts out, but you seemed to have stirred up his creative juices. It's all here, how you'd helped him 'find peace' as he says. His words. You'd helped him 'find peace' with what had happened. I couldn't do that, you see. I couldn't help him, no matter how much he begged and pleaded. I felt it was so awful what he'd done. That he'd married me, knowing that he carried that around with him..."

"I know. He told me." Craig pushed his teacup away, not wanting it. He glanced across to Samantha, saw the questions burning in her eyes, and he knew that he would have to explain it all to her one day. He turned again to Mary. "He told me how every day he regretted it, how he had to live with the guilt of what he'd done, what he'd said. The story he told you, the lie that in one, mad moment he had become a monster, and I know that if he had had the power, he would have changed it, made it all so different, told you the truth. But like he told me, war is monstrous, Mary, and it makes ordinary men do terrible things. He'd honoured the debt he owed Bob Bewdsley and my uncle, but he knew that was wrong. He knew that truth should always be the thing we should honour the most. That's what Billy taught *me*."

"Yes. He said as much in his letter." She scanned Billy's words, trying to find the passage she needed. "Yes, here it is. Everything. His final confession. If he'd told me the truth, about Bewdsley, I would never have left him and Millie, well Millie would have had a father. It was unforgivable what he did, Craig. In a way, it was as bad as what Bewdsley did." She looked down at the paper in her hand. "He says you like soldiers."

"I do, but not because I like war."

"No, he says that too. You're like him, you see. He collected them for their uniforms, spent a fortune on books and paints, spending hours in here, surrounded by his 'little men'. Strange contradiction isn't it, how soldiers can dress so beautifully yet do the most dreadful things."

Craig gawped at her. He'd heard the words, but

they didn't make any real sense. "He *collects* soldiers?"

"*Collected,* yes. Didn't he tell you? No, well he liked to keep things to himself, as we all know. You see, my regret is that he didn't tell me about what had happened *before.* It was almost as if he felt that, once we were married, he could tell me because he knew he had me, I was his, like a possession. I don't think he thought for a single moment I would leave him."

"I think he didn't tell you because he was afraid. Afraid of what you would do once you knew the truth. Or, his version of the truth."

"Yes, and that's what I mean. Before being married, I could have just simply gone, left him, and Millie would never have had to suffer the way she has."

"But you left him anyway."

"Yes, but I don't think he believed I would have the strength to do that. I suppose he hoped that in time I would accept what had happened and see him as the man I thought he was. Strong and brave and in love."

"But you couldn't."

"No. Which was why…Oh, never mind. That's all done with now." She put the letter back inside its envelope. "Yes, he collected model soldiers, and he had done for years." She stood up and went over to the wall and took down the photograph of Billy's tank crew. She looked at it, then thrust it towards him. "He wanted you to have this."

Craig took it from her, held it, and gazed at the faces of men he had never met but felt as if he knew. He nodded. "I'll treasure it."

"I'm sure, but..." she waved the envelope, "I think you'll find what he's given you upstairs is actually a far more valuable treasure."

He frowned. "I...don't understand."

"You will. I don't want you to worry about any of it, because everything is all right, Craig. My solicitor has made it all legal, and I'm not going to object. It was his last wish, after all." She motioned towards the door. "Upstairs. You can't miss it."

Still blank, Craig looked at Samantha, who smiled and gave his forearm a reassuring squeeze. He gently laid the photograph down on the sofa and stood up. At the foot of the stairs, he looked up for a moment before he slowly began to climb.

There was only one room with its door open, so he went down the landing, taking his time, not knowing what to expect. At the threshold, he paused, took a breath, and went inside. He almost yelped.

It was a room the like of which he had never seen before, dominated by a large table, covered with green baize. Behind this, all along the far wall were glass-fronted cabinets, with glass shelves, brightly lit by strip lights. On each shelf stood row after row of the most exquisite, beautifully painted model soldiers. He gazed at them, not able to fully take in the sheer joy of what he saw. A world of wonder, a world of dreams, all of them come true.

Billy had left Craig his entire collection of model soldiers, accumulated over the years, all hand-painted, all ready to do battle. Men from the Seven Years War, infantry, cavalry, canons. Hundreds, no *thousands* of them, pristine, perfect.

He managed to tear his eyes from the cabinets and turned to the table, bare except for a small regiment of models, obviously placed there for a very special reason.

Craig knew what the reason was and what the soldiers were without having to move any closer and he smiled, despite the tears which streamed down his cheeks.

They were Greek hoplites.

The End.

ACKNOWLEDGMENTS

A huge thank you to Gemma Clarke for offering such brilliant suggestions and advice about this novel, a novel which has been in the making for many years. I 'found' Gemma by sheer chance; I wanted a beta reader and Gemma became so much more than that. We have now worked on two of my books and I would not hesitate to recommend her to any fellow writers out there who are struggling with getting their book ready for publication. Thank you, Gemma, from the bottom of my heart.

ABOUT THE AUTHOR

Born on the Wirral, I live in Spain for the present, but my dream is to retire (Hah, what is that? Retire?) and live on a narrowboat along one of the many waterways around the Welsh border. I work as a teacher, a profession I've been in for almost 25 years, but writing is my first love.

To learn more about Stuart G. Yates and discover more Next Chapter authors, visit our website at www.nextchapter.pub.

Fallen Past
ISBN: 978-4-82419-912-6
Large Print

Published by
Next Chapter
2-5-6 SANNO
SANNO BRIDGE
143-0023 Ota-Ku, Tokyo
+818035793528

16th October 2024